Map of Bones

Montana Mysteries #1

S. C. Zipp and J. J. Wolf

Wolf Publishing

Copyright © 2021 by S. C. Zipp and J. J. Wolf

All rights reserved.

No portion of this book may be reproduced in any form without written permission from the publisher or author, except as permitted by U.S. copyright law.

Ebook ISBN: 979-8-9854200-0-5
Paperback ISBN: 979-8-9854200-1-2
Hardcover ISBN: 979-8-9854200-2-9

Cover photo by Katie Felde © 2021

This book is dedicated to Rick (Fred) Barthule, former Broadwater County Sheriff in Montana. At a time when women law enforcement officers were unheard of in Montana, he hired me as a deputy and gave me the most challenging and satisfying opportunity of my lifetime.

I have lived a very exciting life and accomplished many things. Graduating from the Montana Law Enforcement Academy at the age of 45 and serving as a deputy are the achievements I value most. NOW THIS: At age 84 this book would not exist were it not for Rick's influence on my life. THANK YOU RICK, WITHOUT YOU I WOULD HAVE HAD NOTHING TO WRITE THIS BOOK ABOUT. —S. C. Zipp

To Sabrina for her courage and grit and because she knew immediately we'd make a great pair. —J. J. Wolf

Chapter One

JORDAN GIBBONS LOOKED OVER the corner box that was to be her office. It could kindly be described as spartan—two tiny windows, a steel gray file cabinet, wood desk, an uncomfortable black leather chair, and an old coat tree to hang her jacket on. The computer was massive and ancient; she'd have to upgrade that for a laptop. Not that she planned on spending much time in this office anyway. The file cabinet took up an uncomfortably large piece of real estate in the small room. It probably held a file on every single person who had ever lived in Keystone County. Even with that, Jordan guessed the bottom two drawers were completely empty.

Keystone County was geographically the third largest county in Montana. It was also the most sparsely populated, surrounded by some of the most rugged mountains in western Montana. Lombard was nestled in the only area that could possibly be called a valley. Keystone's populace was spread out among farms and ranches around the town with few people living closer in.

The former sheriff had been born less than ten miles down the road. He'd died less than three. At least two of the hometown deputies had been waiting in line for his job. The sheriff's death was the reason Jordan was here. The little Montana town of Lombard had been a quiet place until two months ago when its longtime sheriff was found resting peacefully in his favorite armchair, a worn copy of Louis L'Amour's *No Traveller Returns* by his side, and a gunshot wound to the back of his head. The fatal shot had been fired from his own county-issued revolver.

The sparse office Jordan was moving into had belonged to the deceased sheriff. For whatever reason, Sheriff Blodgett had chosen it over the larger designated sheriff's office that was near the front of the building. She pushed aside the ancient keyboard to make room for the small box that contained everything she would be contributing to her new office: a Starbucks coffee mug, a small potted plant, a box of new perfect-tipped Sharpies, and her favorite stapler. She was about to set the box on top of the desk when a scrap of paper that had been tucked under the keyboard caught her eye. She picked it up and read the only message left by the office's previous occupant.

If anything happens to me, call Shelly.

Except for the message, there was nothing unusual about it. It was a corner torn from a legal pad. But who was Shelly? Jordan had gone through Sheriff Blodgett's file before she got here. She didn't remember any Shelly listed among his family members or close associates. His wife's name was Angela. Hopefully this Shelly wasn't some long-concealed mistress. Those kinds of situations tended to rear their ugly heads when Jordan investigated murders involving "family man" and "pillar of the community" types like Sheriff Blodgett. Revelations like that only served to make the whole business messier for everyone involved.

Jordan opened the bottom file drawer. As she suspected, it was mostly empty, but there was a nearly new box of manila folders. She pulled one out, wrote Brady Blodgett on the top with one of the Sharpies she'd brought with her, and put the little piece of paper inside. She hadn't looked, but she assumed the late sheriff didn't already have a file on himself. She put the file on top of the cabinet and went back to unpacking.

Her coffee mug took its place to the left of her keyboard, in immediate arm's reach. She wished it would magically fill itself with a double mocha Frappuccino topped with whipped cream and a few slivers of dark chocolate sprinkled across the top. She guessed the local cafe served two types of coffee; straight black or watered down with cream and flavored with sugar. Good coffee was one of many sacrifices she'd made when she left civilization in favor of a job with a more prestigious title and a salary that was just barely above what she made as a first-year cadet.

The stapler was next. It had to be perfectly flush with the top of the desk. The plant, the only living thing that she kept close without managing to kill it, took its place on the left corner. She leaned back. That was it. If the dinosaur of a computer was out of the way in favor of a slim black laptop, and the surface of the desk was steel instead of scarred oak, her immediate workspace would be almost exactly as it had been in Seattle. Jordan stood to hang up her jacket. A timid knock came to the door. "Come in, Becca," she called to the secretary who had shown her the office.

Becca reminded Jordan of a particularly skittish bird. From the back she was bone-thin, but as soon as she turned sideways, a pronounced bulge announced her about-to-burst pregnancy. "The commissioners are here to see you, Detective," Becca said. Even with the bulge, her scant frame did little to block out the three men behind her. Becca smoothly sidestepped the men in a motion that would have even impressed Jordan's former ballet instructor.

Jordan stood up straight and squared her shoulders. She was expecting this visit. Maybe not quite so soon, but under the circumstances, it was inevitable. Becca placed three chairs in front of Jordan's desk, making her tiny office very crowded. As the men removed their jackets before being seated, Jordan had the opportunity to look them over. The youngest of the trio was about thirty years old. He appeared to be a rancher, a cowboy type. He took the chair on her right. The next commissioner was older, tall and slender with a shock of gray hair, well-dressed, and wore an eye patch. He had the air of a professional or businessman and settled into the middle chair. The third man remained standing. He was over six feet tall and beefy. If he had ever been muscular, his muscles had all turned to flab. His western-style, blue button-down shirt stretched over his generous belly. He wore a large silver belt buckle. What little hair he had was also silver, but he stared at Jordan from beneath dark eyebrows.

Jordan could feel all three men evaluating her. She didn't know if they had taken the time to look through her file and count the cold cases she'd solved, or if they were judging her solely on her appearance. She knew her age, not quite twenty-seven, was a mark against her. It probably didn't help her case that she was built more like a ballerina than a bullfighter; with a slender build, bright hazel eyes, and long dark hair that she always kept up in a bun. She extended her hand, bracing herself for that first handshake. The one that men like these always made more firm than necessary.

The largest man ignored her outstretched hand and instead stared at her dumbfounded. "You're Jordan Gibbons?"

"Yes, sir," she said directly. His obvious displeasure rattled her, but she couldn't show it. On the other hand, he appeared unable to hide the fact he was stunned and could not equate her with what he had expected.

His face bunched up, like he was trying to get a better look at her without moving closer. "You're the one that put a lid on the Stillaguamish Stalker case after twenty-five years?" His struggle to pronounce Stillaguamish gave her a twinge of satisfaction.

She looked him directly in the eye. "With the help of a good team, yes."

He glanced back at the men behind him as if to confirm that they were seeing the same thing he was. Two of the three looked surprised at the woman in front of them, and Jordan guessed that the woman part of that equation was the hardest for them to take in. It probably didn't matter to them that she had four certificates of commendation from her short career as a detective in Seattle or that she had a master's degree in criminal justice and a third-degree black belt in Krav Maga—not that any of them would know what that was anyway. Nor would they care. It was obvious she did not meet up to the expectations of the older two. She did not look like Montana material to them.

The heavy-set commissioner began to speak to Jordan as if he were lecturing an inexperienced cadet. "Well, we don't have the kind of resources you'd have in Seattle. Our deputies do their own leg work instead of relying on other people to gather evidence for them," he said. "You'll be expected to actually go out and—"

The second man cut off the first man and moved to shake the hand Jordan hadn't quite had the presence of mind to withdraw. "I'm Carl Heyward. How do you like our neck of the woods?"

Jordan gripped his hand. "Nice to meet you, Mr. Heyward. I really haven't had much time to look around, but the flight in was beautiful."

"Prettiest country around," Carl said.

"Big Sky and all, right?" Jordan wanted to bite her tongue. What a stupid, cliché thing to say.

"The biggest," Carl answered. He pointed to the man who had come in first. "That's Dane Judd and this is Whit."

Jordan reached for Dane's hand again. This time he reached out and smothered her slender hand in his meaty one. As expected, he gripped too tight and held on too long. Jordan was struck with an unfamiliar, immediate reaction of her own. She was certain she was not going to like him.

"And Whit?" She waited for the third member of the group to supply his last name. Until now he had been effectively blocked out by Mr. Judd, so she hadn't had a chance to get a good look at him. He was just under six feet tall with reddish brown hair and the kind of chiseled face that would have worked equally well on an REI poster or an upscale cologne ad. He was remarkably handsome in a rugged way, but it was his startling gray eyes that set him apart from others—they were the first thing she noticed about him.

"Palmer, but Whit's enough." His grip was just as firm as the others, but also warm and rough.

Something about him reminded Jordan of her Spokane grandpa who'd been a farmer.

Mr. Judd shoved her plant aside and rather ceremoniously parked his ample right butt cheek comfortably and casually on the right front edge of Jordan's desk, as if to establish he was in command of the meeting. The deliberate way he did it made it seem like he intended it to be an affront to Jordan. If that was his intent, he hit the mark.

Judd's next move was equally unappreciated. "Now that we've got introductions out of the way, how do you plan to go about this investigation? I'm going to warn you that the people around here aren't going to take kindly to an outsider butting into their business, so you'll need to—"

"No need to scare her right out of the gate, Dane." Carl abruptly broke in. He looked at Jordan with an almost kind, fatherly expression. "People around here are like most people you'll run into—willing to help if you're willing to ask. Don't make the mistake of thinking you have to do everything on your own."

"But don't expect the resources or 'team' you're used to." Judd said the word team like it was a foul word. "How exactly are you planning to conduct this investigation? Have you been out to the house yet? That's what you need to do very first thing."

Jordan wasn't used to having her every move questioned, or the course of her investigation laid out for her. Especially not by some backwoods county commissioners. She'd just arrived. As the person in charge, she had no obligation to share her intentions with them and they had no right to ask or even offer their advice.

Miffed, Jordan lifted her eyebrows a bit, but she responded to his inappropriate inquiry. "I read over some preliminary reports on the flight over.

Heading out to the house is my next order of business, after I set up my office."

"Office looks set to me. Unless you plan on hanging curtains or something." Mr. Judd smirked toward the two men on the other side of the room.

Jordan forced herself to let his comment go. "Actually, I could use a decent laptop. The computer sitting on my desk is a dinosaur."

"It was good enough for Sheriff Blodgett. You are going to have to accept the fact that Keystone County is not Seattle and manage to make do." If possible, his piggish eyes narrowed even more. "I want you to know I take this case personally. The late sheriff was my oldest stepsister's boy."

"Sorry for your loss," Jordan said, although he didn't sound any more broken up by the sheriff's death than she sounded sympathetic.

He waved his red hand like he was brushing off a fly. "No use wallowing in the tragedy of it. As I was saying, you were brought here because we thought you could deliver results, not so you could spend taxpayer money on extraneous purchases. We just spent a load of money on new sidearms for the entire department."

Jordan bristled at his suggestion she was asking for something extravagant. "I appreciate the firepower, commissioner, but this isn't the Old West, and not every confrontation comes down to who can draw the fastest. A computer is a basic tool of law enforcement, not something extra."

Whit spoke up. "We know that. Every deputy in the county has a laptop that docks with their vehicle. Becca probably just hasn't issued you yours yet." He sounded annoyed, whether at her or Mr. Judd, Jordan wasn't sure. Maybe both. "If the one you're issued isn't sufficient—"

"It had better be," Judd grumbled.

Whit faced Judd. "With the taxpayer money the state is putting up to bring her here, we might as well give her the tools she needs to do the job." He turned back to Jordan. "Let Becca know whatever you need. If she can't get it for you, contact me and I'll work it out."

"Thank you." Jordan appreciated Whit's voice of reason after Judd's display of animosity.

Judd began to speak again. "Not that we are going to give you free rein to—"

Whit stood and firmly cut off Mr. Judd's remark. "We will be on our way and let you get settled in so you can start doing what you were recruited to do."

Judd and Whit exchanged a withering look that made Jordan think the conflict between them was longstanding. Whit turned to the door; Mr. Heyward followed his lead.

Not quite done, Mr. Judd reluctantly stood. His parting shot was pompous, officious, and irritating. "Results, Miss Gibbons. That's what we'll be waiting for."

Chapter Two

JORDAN WAITED UNTIL SHE was sure all three of them had left the building. "This is important, Becca. For the next thirty minutes I do not want to see or talk to anyone. Not one is to even approach my door. Understood?"

"Yes, Detective. I can do that."

Jordan shut her door firmly and was grateful it had a lock on it. She savagely twisted the knob, strode across her office, and threw herself into the chair behind her desk.

After taking an enormous, deep breath she lowered her head between her knees and grabbed her head with both hands as if she was in pain. The sound she made was somewhere between an elongated pitiful groan and an angry grunt. What in the hell was she doing here?

The confrontation with the commissioners had completely demoralized her. In Seattle she had earned, received, and deserved the respect and admiration of not only her law enforcement peers, but all of King County. Here, barely halfway through her first day, she had been subjected to doubt about her investigative ability, ridiculed and made fun of because she was a woman. Curtains in her office, really?

The Attorney General of the State of Montana, Adam Bentley, had sought her and her expertise out in distant Seattle and made her the chief and only detective in the Keystone County Sheriff's Department. Bentley was under pressure to find the murderer of the man who had been the most well-liked and respected sheriff in the state of Montana and had sought Jordan out personally. Yet Judd treated her as an underling and insulted her authority. He had the temerity to plop his ample butt down on her desk and lecture her as if she was a wayward child. His inquiry about how she was going to investigate the sheriff's murder was highly irregular, as was his telling her what she needed to do first.

Having mentally reviewed all her grievances, she sat up in her chair and regained her composure. She had not gained such notoriety and acclaim before she hit thirty by letting others make decisions for her. Judd was on her radar. She vowed to give him a run for his money. She hadn't sacrificed so much to be put down by a redneck pig like him.

Jordan wouldn't admit, even to herself, that she lived in constant terror of failure. Her mother had groomed her to be a "Belle of the Ball," seek the good things in life, and hobnob with the yacht and country club crowd. When Jordan chose what they considered to be a lowly law enforcement path, her parents were outraged. An only child, she had once been close to her parents, but her career choice had led to now near-total estrangement.

Jordan's job relocation to Montana, a state her parents believed was buried in the past and populated by Neanderthals, was unacceptable to them. She had her own reservations about Montana. Her first meeting with the commissioners had cemented her view about the close-minded rednecks who inhabited the state and the town of Lombard in particular.

Her meteoric success as a cold-case detective was due to hard work and dedication to duty. She was a classic workaholic. When she was in the middle of a case, nothing else mattered. That's how she had to treat this situation. She could block out Judd and the others and just get the job done. The attorney general had hinted at a more prestigious position if she solved this one. She had no intention of staying in Montana, but maybe a win here would mean a job in a less backwoods state like Colorado or even a triumphant return to Seattle. This assignment was not on the career path she had mapped out for herself—it was a minor detour. A place to clear her head and get out of a bad situation.

Jordan stood, pushing aside the doubt and feelings of inadequacy Judd had dredged up in her. She was ready to do battle, get the job done that she'd been recruited for, and shove it back in the giant redneck's face.

"Becca, I'm heading out," Jordan called, shoving her arms back into the jacket that she hadn't gotten to hang up. It was late May. Spring was still chasing away a harsh Montana winter and there was still a bite to the air.

"Where should I tell people you've gone?" Becca asked.

"Scene of the crime." Jordan pulled the office door shut behind her.

"What?" Becca braced herself on the back of the chair as she stood up, a feat that made Jordan feel guilty because she was the cause of it.

"Out to Sheriff Blodgett's place." Jordan wasn't used to people keeping track of where she was. On the cold-case unit, she was free to come and go as needed. Here, she assumed everyone in the office would want to know where she was and what she was doing all the time.

"When do you think you'll be back?"

"I don't know. Maybe an hour? If someone needs me, you can get me on the radio or my cell phone."

"Wait." Becca waddled over. "I have something for you." She handed Jordan a file stuffed with paperwork and crime scene photos.

"What are these?" Jordan knew she sounded impatient, and Becca didn't deserve that.

"Printouts of everything associated with the sheriff's murder," Becca said.

"Printouts?" Jordan looked at her, dumbfounded.

For the first time, Becca looked unsure of herself. "Blodgett always had me print everything out from the previous day's calls or whatever he was working on to have it ready for him to peruse over his morning cup of coffee."

Jordan took the file, a little in shock at the stack of hard copy photos and various reports, but mostly from the office's backward methods.

"Becca, great way to show how old-fashioned this office is," a male voice boomed from the hallway.

"Sorry, Brend ... I mean, sorry, Sheriff," Becca answered.

A tall man with flashing blue eyes and a thick head of dark hair came through the door. "Sorry I wasn't here to greet you in person, Detective Gibbons. I was out on a call." He extended his hand. "I'm Brendan Carlyle, the interim sheriff here. I can take that pile of paperwork off your hands and set you up with a secure file transfer of everything associated with the case."

Jordan shuffled the paperwork to shake his hand. "Thanks. I'd appreciate that."

He reached for the file. "Might take a couple of days. I've been working to bring this office out of the dark ages."

"In that case, I'll hang onto this so I can get up to speed," she responded, pulling the file back.

"Where're you heading?" Sheriff Carlyle asked.

"Out to Sheriff Blodgett's house. I want to get a feel for the place."

"Not much left there, but if you'd like, I could come show you around and we could talk about what happened for a bit."

"That would be—"

"Sheriff, sorry to interrupt, but you're supposed to be meeting with the Lady Lions in about twenty minutes," Becca said.

"Right." Sheriff Carlyle gave Becca a look that made Jordan think he didn't appreciate being reminded of the appointment. "Sorry, I forget being a sheriff is as much about being a politician as it is about being a cop. We'll have to talk later."

"Sounds good," Jordan said. She headed for the door.

"Detective." Becca stopped her again.

"What now?" Jordan said, her impatience coming out.

"You'll probably need these." She held out a set of keys. "You've been issued the Expedition while you're here."

"Thanks." Jordan backtracked sheepishly and retrieved the keys.

The vehicle they'd issued her spoke volumes about where this town put their trust and their money. It was a Ford XLT Expedition, fully loaded. As Whit promised, it had a laptop, scanner, and radio in it, all state of the art. It was a high-tech mobile office.

All the tools commonly contained in patrol units—rubber gloves, blankets, plastic sacks, a shotgun, even a cuddly teddy bear to calm a traumatized child—were neatly and compactly arranged in a storage unit located in the rear of the vehicle. This was the first thing that Jordan really liked about her new position. This vehicle felt like a fortress and more like a place to hide out and think than her boxy office. She wondered how Mr. Judd would feel about her hanging curtains here.

As Jordan pulled out of the police station, she reflected on the events of her first morning in Lombard. She liked Becca and appreciated her efforts to help her get settled in. One encounter with Judd had been one too many. As for the other two commissioners, the jury was still out. Heyward seemed friendly enough, but quiet. Whit was rugged and good-looking, the kind of "face of Montana" cowboy another woman might dream of meeting in Big Sky country. A younger, more naïve version of herself probably would have found him attractive. He was nice, but while part of her appreciated Whit standing up to Judd in her behalf, a larger part of her hated that he felt she needed the rescue.

She had to question why the commissioners had selected Carlyle as the interim sheriff. He had breezed into the office and berated Becca for giving her the printed information. He impressed her as being overly friendly yet not quite sincere. She appreciated that he might hold some animosity toward her. The sheriff's office, still reeling from their sheriff's death, probably took umbrage at an outsider being assigned this case. His treatment of Becca concerned her. She wondered if he was that overbearing to everyone all the time. Her first impressions of her new assignment left a lot to be desired.

Chapter Three

IT TOOK LESS THAN five minutes to pass through the entire town. It consisted of a bank, post office, elementary school, two bars, and a grocery store. There was also a general store she was sure was stocked with outdoor gear, denim pants, western shirts, and a large inventory of boots—the kind of thing she'd seen everyone in town wearing. The last building at the edge of town was a hardware and farm supply store which it seemed every remote small town needed. There wasn't much delineating town from country. The houses just gained more and more acreage until they turned into farms and ranches.

As she turned down the long lane that led to the deceased sheriff's house, Jordan internally prepared herself for her first view of the house. She was used to visiting crime scenes long after most people forgot they were crime scenes. It helped her get the perspectives of both the victim and the killer. They'd come together in that place and whether they liked it or not, both had left something behind that said a lot about who they were. The sheriff's property, a couple of miles outside of town, consisted of a farmhouse, a barn, a big garden area, and a fenced-in pasture. The garden spot was bare, the ground untilled, but the flower bed in front of the house had daffodils and tulips coming up, along with a crop of bright green weeds poking through tufts of brown quack grass.

The property was unoccupied. Fearing her life might also be in danger, the sheriff's wife had left town shortly after the murder for an extended stay with her sister over an hour's drive away in Missoula. Jordan was surprised at the old Ford Maverick in the yard. She parked next to it and put her hand on the hood. The engine was still warm. It wasn't likely the vehicle belonged to the late sheriff. A noise led her to the open barn door. A slim, sandy-haired teenager was crouching in the entrance of an empty stall.

"Hello?" Jordan called out.

The boy stood quickly, cracking his head on a bucket hung on a nail next to the stall. He said a few choice words and then turned. "What the hell, Jerry! I thought ..." He turned, recognizing that she wasn't Jerry. He stared at Jordan.

"Sorry, I didn't mean to scare you," she said.

"You, you're the wom ... the new woman ... the new detective," he finally spat out.

Jordan wondered how quickly the news of her arrival had spread. "Yes. Detective Gibbons, and who are you?"

"Peyton." He didn't volunteer a last name. He looked barely seventeen. He shoved his hands in his pockets, didn't look her in the eye, and he kept shifting his weight like he didn't know how to stay still. He also had the distinct odor of weed radiating from him. He was underage for the marijuana, but this kid probably wasn't worth the effort of taking him in over a couple puffs on a joint.

"Well, Peyton, do you mind telling me why you're here? I was told the family had left this place pretty much deserted."

"I came to feed the cats. We took all the other animals back to our place, but the barn cats aren't exactly tame. Aunt Angie would never forgive us if we didn't come by and feed them. I was checking on this one who just had kittens." He stepped aside to reveal a stretched-out yellow cat with a litter of tiny blind kittens nursing beside her.

"How often do you come to take care of the cats?" From the way he kept glancing at the straw stack in the corner of the barn, Jordan guessed his stash was hidden somewhere close by. He probably offered to take care of the cats so he could come for some alone time, or maybe not quite so alone time. And just who was Jerry? Jordan wondered if this Jerry might be the small-town dealer. Again, probably not worth her time, but something to be added to her mental file.

"I dunno. Three or four times a week?"

"Ever go in the house?" she asked.

"No. The cat food's out here. I don't really like the idea of hanging out where the sheriff bit it."

"Did you know him very well?" Jordan had automatically slipped into interrogation mode even though she doubted this kid had any information worth her time.

Peyton looked at her like she was an idiot. "I mean, everyone knew him. He was the sheriff."

It bothered Jordan that even a seventeen-year-old seemed to assume she didn't know anything. She thought of something else. "Do you know if the house is unlocked?"

"There's a key in the birdhouse on the back porch," he said, pointing.

Jordan had picked up a key to the house with the other things in the sheriff's file, but she was curious who might have had access to the house the night the sheriff died. "Was it always there?"

"I guess. It was here a few years ago when they were on vacation and they had me water the plants."

"So, it was probably here the night he was murdered?"

"Probably. But the killer probably didn't need to use it. No one locks their doors around here."

"Right." She'd forgotten: small town—small enough that even the sheriff felt safe enough to leave his doors unlocked at night. Locked doors were something she'd have taken for granted in Seattle, but here, there were a lot of differences she'd have to consider.

"So do you want me to show you where the key is or what?" Petyton asked.

"Sure." She followed him to the back porch. He slid the key from under the birdhouse and handed it to her.

She turned the key over in her hand. It was shiny and silver, not like a key that had been hidden under a birdhouse for years. "How long ago did you say you watered the plants?"

"I dunno, three maybe four years ago. I was still in junior high."

"Is this the same key?" She held it up for him.

"Nah, that other one had an American flag on it."

Interesting. The key she picked up at the office looked new too. She'd thought the sheriff's office had made a duplicate for the file. Her suspicions were confirmed when she got to the back door. The lock was brand new. Something had caused the sheriff enough concern that he changed his door locks. But why would he do that and leave a new key in the birdhouse? She fit the key into the lock and turned the handle.

Peyton got more fidgety. "You need me to hang around or ..." He backed away from the half-opened door like he was expecting Sheriff Blodgett's body to still be splayed across the floor in a pool of blood. That wasn't how he was found, but it still seemed like an odd reaction for a teenage kid. Maybe he had a weak stomach, or maybe he had another reason for not wanting to stay. Was he still expecting Jerry, whoever that was?

She nodded. "You can go."

He hurried down the stairs, grabbing his cell phone out of his back pocket as he rounded the corner.

Jordan pushed the door open and stepped inside the house. There was a heaviness about it. Every other murder house she'd been in had the same feeling about it, like the walls had sucked in the dark act that had happened there. It didn't matter that there was a hand-painted wooden sign that said "Blodgett" hung in the entryway or a handmade quilt laid across the back of the couch. What was once inviting about the house was overshadowed by the last uninvited guest who had taken one life and altered every other life that one had touched.

Or maybe the murderer had been invited.

Jordan closed the door behind her, hating to shut out the sunlight, but also not wanting to attract any extra attention. The room was about what she'd expected. The decor was dated, with a big stone fireplace and wood paneled walls. The kitchen was more updated, but with a definite "cowboy" vibe to it—rough oak cabinets, dark stone countertop, even horseshoes trimmed with artificial ivy on the wall behind the little eat-in bar. A big window behind the bar showed off the Flint Creek mountain range and the sun just starting to go red around the edges. Jordan stopped for a minute to appreciate the view the sheriff probably enjoyed with his morning coffee and while eating supper.

There was a rugged wildness about the cut of the mountains and the expanse of space all around. The mountains here weren't like Mount Rainier, standing solitary against the sky any time the weather was clear enough to see it. She supposed the mountains and even the valley were beautiful, but she missed the city skyline and the waterfront. She missed the hustle of the people around her, the ocean smell of the Puget Sound, even the constant damp of the air. She hadn't even been here twenty-four hours and her hands already felt papery, and her lips had turned a couple of shades redder from the dry air.

Jordan would have never imagined herself here six months ago or even six weeks ago. She'd been doing well with the Seattle PD. She had a small office to herself where she pored over cold-case files and spent hours on end doing research. She lived in a tiny, overpriced apartment in nearby Bothell in a bad neighborhood with a horrible commute, but she had good coffee, the respect of her superiors, friends for the weekends, and Brock.

Except she never really had Brock.

Going into the living room, she took a few minutes to get a feel for the people who had lived here. The bookcase was full—westerns, true crime novels, war stories, and what looked like cowboy poetry. The television was old and set into a bulky cabinet that had one door closed. This was a couple who was more likely to read than binge watch TV. A shelf of games stood in the corner, but only the cards looked well used.

Details. She'd learned to read a room to get to know the people who'd lived in it. More than that, she'd learned to read a room to find out about the people who'd died in it. That was the next stop: the sheriff's study where he'd been shot.

It was the third door on the right down the hall. The doors were all shut, so she had to open all three of them. The killer had been bold enough to come all the way into the house and down the hall, like they knew the layout of the house. He or she knew that the sheriff's wife wouldn't be home, or had come prepared to kill them both, and the sheriff's wife just got lucky.

The sheriff's study had wood panels, like the main room. There was a big wooden desk and another well-stocked bookcase. This one held more true crime stories, law books, and lots of western novels. One wall was covered with certificates, commendations, and family pictures. She leaned closer to study a picture of a much younger sheriff holding up a silver belt buckle that rivaled the one Judd had been wearing. Underneath it read, "Champion Steer Wrestler 1988." It didn't get any more Montana than that. Next to the picture, she touched a bare spot on the wall. There was a nail hole and a big enough space for something to have been hanging here. What was missing from the wall?

Behind the desk was a big window with the same view as the one from the kitchen. There was an empty space on the floor facing the window. It was obvious the sheriff's chair had sat next to the bookcase and toward the view, with his back to the door. Either he felt safer with his back to an interior door than the window, he didn't want to miss the view, or he just felt secure in his own home.

Behind the desk, Jordan noticed a sheepskin cushion on one side of the room. She knelt beside it and plucked a piece of dog hair from the worn surface. The cushion was big enough to accommodate a large dog. So where was the dog when the sheriff got shot?

She finished her preliminary walk around the house, comparing the crime scene photos Becca had given her with different rooms in the house. A small closet behind the Sheriff's chair was most likely where the killer had hidden until the fatal shot was taken. Jordan had a hard time believing that anyone trained in law enforcement would have been so unaware of his surroundings that someone could have snuck up on him. There had only been one shot, at close range and through the back of the head.

Then there was the matter of the murder weapon. The sheriff's wife said it had been kept in a locked drawer in the desk. Jordan inspected the desk. There were scars in the wood around the locked drawer that showed it had been pried open. A pocketknife found at the scene appeared to be the tool the killer had used to get into the drawer.

The marks around the drawer bothered Jordan. The gun would have had to have been taken before the sheriff came into his study. The broken drawer wasn't something that would've been immediately apparent from the door, but would a sheriff who had recently changed his locks really sit down to read a book without surveying his surroundings? Everything she had read about Blodgett showed him to be vigilant. What could have distracted him so much that night that he missed what was going on around him?

She needed to know what Sheriff Blodgett had been working on before he died.

Chapter Four

THE OLD MAVERICK WAS gone when Jordan left the sheriff's house. She'd stayed longer than she'd intended to. As she pulled out, she realized she was starving, and there was no food in the house she'd rented just outside of town. She'd dropped off her luggage and then gone straight to the sheriff's office. Somewhere in the back of her mind she'd thought about making a grocery run on the way home to pick up some essentials and getting takeout for dinner. Then she remembered where she was. The only grocery store in town was already closed. There were no little take-out places except possibly in Anaconda and she didn't have the energy to drive that far.

Back in town, a sign proclaimed BEST RIBS AROUND at a combination diner, casino, and bar called the Silver Horseshoe. She shuddered at the thought of a loud, greasy bar, but it was probably her only choice.

Once inside, she sat herself at a table in the corner and opened her briefcase to look over the files Becca had given her. She pulled out the crime scene photos, forgetting about food as she compared the pictures from the night of the murder to what she'd seen in the house today.

The waitress's "What can I get for you?" startled Jordan out of her work-induced trance. Jordan closed the file, aware of a curvy, platinum blonde woman looking over her shoulder. "I didn't get a menu yet."

The woman pointed at a plastic-coated menu stuck between the salt and pepper shakers. "Right there."

"Right. Sorry." Jordan raised her voice to be heard above the twangy country music, the sound of pool balls clacking together, and the buzz of conversation. "What do you recommend?"

"The ribs are the best around."

"I've heard. Do you have anything lighter, maybe a salad?"

The waitress looked at her with an expression that made Jordan think that greens were something that the food on the menu here ate, not something that was prepared for the customers. "The ribs come with coleslaw, and we have a couple of side salads, nothing very filling. The French Dip's my personal favorite."

Jordan picked up the menu. It had been ages since she'd allowed herself to eat what was featured in colorful photos, but she hadn't eaten anything besides a mini quiche in a coffee shop at the airport before she left Seattle. That had been almost ten hours ago. "French Dip with a side salad instead of fries," she finally said.

"Good choice." The waitress wrote it down but didn't leave. She tucked her little notebook in her belt and said, "I'm Chris, by the way. Christine Peters."

"Jordan Gibbons."

"Thought so. You're that detective the AG brought in from Seattle to figure out who murdered the sheriff, right?"

"That's me." It unnerved Jordan that along with everyone else, this woman already knew who she was.

"So ... any leads?" Chris asked, indicating the files in front of Jordan.

Again, Jordan felt like her competence was being judged, this time by a woman not much older than she, who worked in a cheap diner and wore lipstick that was at least two shades too pink. "Nothing I can discuss right now."

"Right." Chris stepped back. "Well, welcome. I hope you catch the bastards who did it. Everyone liked Sheriff Blodgett."

"I guess not everyone," Jordan said.

Chris stared at her for a second. "Yeah. Guess not."

She left, and Jordan went back to studying the files. She was aware of furtive glances coming from the other tables. She wished she'd asked Chris if she could get her meal to go. She wasn't used to so many people paying attention to her. It was a lot easier to be anonymous in Seattle. She'd done some of her best work in a little coffee place on Beacon Hill. With the absence of digital pictures on a laptop to scroll through, she spread the photos and documents out across the table in front of her. A small piece of paper fell out and fluttered to the floor. As she leaned over to pick it up, a boot landed next to the paper. Jordan sat up, face to belt buckle with the biggest cowboy she'd ever seen in person.

"Hey," he said, "you drop something important?"

Jordan stared at him, sizing him up. "Just a piece of paper."

As she picked it up, he slid into the other side of the booth, barely fitting under the table. "Looks like you have a lot of pretty important pieces of paper here."

Jordan hastily gathered up the pictures she had spread out on the table and tucked them back into the folder. "Can I help you with something?" She kept both hands on the file, even though her fingers itched to touch the gun at her hip.

"Just wanted to meet the new cop in town." He glanced over his shoulder and smirked at the three men at the bar who'd probably pushed him to come over to her table. They looked like they were all at least ten years older than her, but they reminded Jordan of guys she'd known in high school. He stretched his hand across the table. "Grant. Grant Robbins."

She locked eyes with him but didn't reach to shake his hand. "Nice to meet you, but I'm a little busy right now, if you don't mind."

His face spread in a lazy grin. "You know, if you're looking for someone to question, like in private, I'm available."

She didn't blink. "If your name comes up in my investigation, I'll let you know."

He leaned forward. "Actually, I have some dirt on Blodgett's replacement you might be interested in."

"Sheriff Carlyle?" Jordan said. She leaned closer to the man, even though she found him repugnant.

"He's a thief," the man said in a low, dramatic voice.

"A thief?" Jordan asked.

He leaned so close Jordan could smell the beer on his breath. "Saw him myself, stole a knife from this very restaurant."

"Really?" she asked in her flattest voice. She was positive this man was playing with her.

He reached for the file. "They said Blodgett was shot in the back of the head. What's that look like?"

Jordan snatched it from him and stood up. This time she couldn't control the urge to put her hand on her gun.

He got up too, his girth pushing the table forward as he stood. He laughed. "You gonna shoot me for being friendly?"

"You'd better back away, Grant. Gun or not, Detective Gibbons could take you apart. She has a black belt in Krav Maga." The voice behind her startled Jordan, but she didn't flinch.

"Krav whata?" Grant's face wrinkled in confusion.

"It's a martial arts practice the Israeli army uses. She can probably kill you with that spoon."

Jordan didn't turn, but the man behind her walked forward enough for her to see his profile. It was one of the county commissioners, the young one named Whit. Perfect.

"Better off to just have a beer with me and let Detective Gibbons do her work."

The man grunted something like "whatever," then left the booth. Whit nodded at her as he walked by. Jordan didn't know if he was expecting thanks, but he wasn't going to get it. She didn't need him to rescue her again.

Just when she thought he wasn't going to say anything directly to her, he leaned over. "Probably best to do your work at the office. People around here are too curious for their own good." He followed the bigger man to the bar. Jordan was left fuming, feeling once again chastised and belittled.

Chris came back with Jordan's sandwich. "Can I get that wrapped up to go?" Jordan asked.

"Don't let them get to you. They're just messing around. Grant and all of them are pretty harmless. I wouldn't worry—"

"I'm not worried. I can take care of myself."

The waitress set the food down. "Of course you can. What is that kava manga stuff Whit was talking about, anyway?"

"Krav Maga. It's a mix of martial arts."

"Maybe you could teach it to the rest of us sometime. Probably a good thing for any woman to —"

"—to go. Can I get this to go?" Jordan picked up the plate and thrust it toward the waitress. She wasn't in the mood for chitchat.

"Right. Of course." Chris took the plate from her and headed back into the kitchen. Jordan knew she'd offended her, but she was too tired to care.

She gathered up the files and tucked everything back into her case. She had to walk past the bar. She didn't look, but she was sure all the men's gazes followed her to the register. Jordan added a big tip to alleviate her guilt at being rude to the waitress.

Chris handed her the bag and then lowered her voice. "Whit's right about one thing. The people around here are too curious for their own good. It's most likely what got the sheriff killed."

Chapter Five

IT WAS DARK BY the time Jordan pulled onto the long lane that led to the little house she was renting. It felt odd to have so much space. Apartments were few and far between in this area. The house seemed like the best option. She'd taken it, sight unseen, after a few phone calls and photos on the internet. It was surrounded by close to an acre of wild grass and overgrown hedges, and there was a stand of trees near the turnoff to the road. The closest neighbor was at the far end of the lane. The house was cold and dark and quiet, with an empty mustiness that greeted her when she flipped on the light.

She cringed again as she was greeted by the powder-blue couch, heavy dark wood end tables and huge entertainment center and bookcase. The house had come decorated according to the elderly owner's tastes. Jordan had left most of her things in storage in Seattle, only bringing the essentials— some clothes, bedding, books, dishes. The woman who lived here had gone to live in a retirement home closer to her daughter. Jordan guessed they couldn't sell the house right away, so renting seemed like the best option.

It felt like she was staying in someone else's home. She sat down at the table, reheated the sandwich, and set the thick stack of files in front of her. She'd decided to go back through all the cases the sheriff had worked on in the last few years. What the waitress said about Sheriff Blodgett getting killed because he was curious led her to go back to the office and gather up a bunch of his files.

It was like trying to follow one thread of an elaborate tapestry. Every case was interconnected with every other one. Every person here was somehow interconnected with everyone else. To an outsider like her, it was hard to sort through.

She nibbled at her sandwich while reading reports on domestic dispute calls, drunk and disorderly conduct arrests, a couple of minor drug charges (Peyton's name was surprisingly absent from those), and one charge of auto theft that turned out to be just a bunch of teenagers joyriding around town. Nothing that should have led to the sheriff's murder.

She wrapped up what was left of her cold sandwich and moved to throw it away. A knock on the door stopped her. Her heart raced. Brock used to show up around this time of night unannounced. It would be just like him to follow her from Seattle, to ask for her to take him back. To expect her to take him back. She'd begun to rehearse exactly what she'd say to him when she saw the bent female figure through the thin curtains. She opened the door to a whiff of fresh baked banana bread.

"Hello." Jordan did her best to sound friendly instead of exhausted and impatient.

"Oh." The little white-haired woman clutched the banana bread to her chest when she saw Jordan, like she wanted to hide it. "I was expecting Sarah. I saw the light in the window and assumed she'd come back to finish clearing out her mother's things."

"No. Sorry. I'm renting the house from Sarah."

Without being invited, the woman made her way across the threshold. "Oh. Well, I'm glad it's getting some use since Molly had to move. I guess that means we're next-door neighbors. I'm Rachel McKee."

"Jordan Gibbons." Jordan reached out her hand and the woman shuffled the loaf of banana bread to shake it.

"Welcome, Jordan. Are you here by yourself, or is your husband around?" Rachel took another step inside, glancing around the room behind Jordan, as if she was looking for a nonexistent man.

"No husband," Jordan said firmly.

"Oh." Rachel's eyes widened. "It's not a good idea for a woman to be out here alone."

Jordan had to suppress a laugh, thinking about the safety of this little house compared to the apartment she'd occupied in Seattle. "It seems pretty safe to me."

The woman clutched at the pink crocheted sweater draped across her shoulders. "I suppose it is, but I haven't felt really safe since that thing with Bonnie Golden."

"Bonnie Golden?" Jordan tried to think if there'd been anything in the files about a woman named Bonnie. The name didn't sound familiar.

"It's been almost fifteen years now, but it still gives me the creeps to think about. They only found a couple of pieces of her, and no one was ever put away for her murder. If you're going to live alone, you should get yourself a dog, even a little one. My Bunny may be small, but she makes a whole lot of noise when someone comes around. 'Course, that didn't help Bonnie out too much. Poor old Sampson. They say the killer got to him too. He was kind of a brute, but—"

"Sampson?" Jordan asked.

"Yeah, you know, like in the Bible. Sampson and Delilah." She eyed Jordan suspiciously, and Jordan wondered if the next question would be whether she had ever read the Bible.

"Right." That wasn't what Jordan was asking, but she didn't have the energy to have Rachel backtrack the conversation to try and figure out who Sampson was.

Rachel seemed to reconsider the banana bread in her hand. "Take this as a welcome to the neighborhood." She gave it to Jordan like it was a consolation prize for Jordan not having a husband or a dog to keep her safe.

Jordan accepted the gift, still taken back by her chatty neighbor. "Thanks."

"No problem. If you need anything don't hesitate to come over." She looked Jordan over and nodded. "I have a great-nephew you should meet—tall, decent looking, fairly quiet. Really, that's the best kind of man for you. My late husband barely said a word." Rachel laughed. "Of course, he wasn't always that way. When we were dating ..."

Jordan's mind wandered as her neighbor continued chatting. She decided that the woman's husband probably realized early on in their marriage that it was pointless to try to get a word in with his wife and gone completely mute.

"You work at the sheriff's office?" Rachel said.

Jordan was embarrassed when she realized how far her thoughts had drifted. "Yes."

"I put in a complaint there, more than once. Maybe you could follow up on it for me?" Rachel asked.

"A complaint? About what?" Jordan asked.

"The noise, crop dusters, out at all odd hours. Odd times of the year too. I'm used to it going on in June and even July, but I've heard at least three so far this year and it's not even the end of May. I put in a complaint with Rebecca at the desk, but I don't know if she ever passed it on. Could you make sure that happens?"

"I could look into it." Jordan said without conviction.

"I'd appreciate it." Rachel smiled. "I might just enjoy having an in with the sheriff's department. They're usually quick to brush off an old woman's complaints and concerns."

Jordan guessed this particular old woman had put in her share of complaints to the sheriff's office. She regretted telling Rachel she'd look into it. Her new neighbor seemed like the type of woman to nag about that sort of thing.

Rachel's phone buzzed from a pocket of her sweater. She pulled it out and looked at it. "Sorry, I have to take this." She put the phone to her ear, waved goodbye and launched into a conversation with whoever was foolish enough to call her.

Jordan shut the door with relief. She stared at the loaf of bread in her hands. She wasn't sure how to take her neighbor. In Seattle, she'd lived in the same apartment for three years and hadn't once had a conversation that extended beyond the weather with anyone who lived there. Jordan set the bread on the table and went back to the files, fighting back a yawn. It had been a long day. If every time she sat down to work someone came to interrupt her, she might as well go to bed.

As she stacked the files, she noticed a bulge in a thick yellow envelope. She opened it up and a worn red leather dog collar fell out. On the back was a long-faded name stamped into the leather.

Sampson.

Chapter Six

THE SMELL OF COFFEE—ACTUAL, good coffee—greeted Jordan when she walked into her tiny office the next day. She opened the door to find one of the deputies standing by her desk with a steaming paper cup. She remembered him briefly from her tour of the building yesterday. There was something about his dark wiry mustache that made her think of a rat.

"Hey, Detective. Thought you might be missing the good stuff." He handed her the cup.

She breathed in deeply. It had been a rough night in her little rental house. She didn't sleep well, missing the noise of the city street below her apartment and racked with questions about the case. All she'd had for breakfast were a couple of pieces of banana bread—another one of those foods she hadn't allowed herself to eat in a long time. It was heavenly, but not very filling.

He nodded at the cup. "I guessed, but you look like someone who would appreciate a double shot of mocha."

"This is perfect. Thank you ..." She paused, not able to remember his name.

"Ray. I think you got a pretty poor welcome into our little town yesterday and I wanted to make it up to you."

Ray Harding. Now she remembered. He was one of the men who was vying for the sheriff's job. He'd run against Sheriff Blodgett in the last election. How badly had he wanted the job? How bad did he feel about losing the interim position to the current sheriff?

Jordan took a sip. She hated to admit that it was almost as good as anything she'd had in Seattle.

"Where did you find this?"

"A little coffee hut on the way in. I'll take you there sometime after work."

Jordan took another sip so she didn't have to say anything to that. She set her stack of files down on the desk. "Actually, maybe you could help me with a couple of things. The pocketknife that was used to pry open the drawer in the sheriff's study. Any leads on where it came from?"

"We know it wasn't Blodgett's, but everyone around here carries a pocketknife. This one was pretty generic."

"You dusted it for prints?" Jordan asked.

"Of course." Ray sounded offended. "I got a couple of good prints off of it, but no matches."

Jordan took another sip of coffee, thinking. "I've been going through Sheriff Blodgett's files. I can't figure out exactly what he was working on."

Ray leaned against her desk. "Yeah, that's Brady for you. He wasn't very organized. Kind of ran things his own way. Didn't keep good records and would rather be out shooting the bull with whoever from the Silver Horseshoe than—"

"Don't you have a call you need to take care of, Ray?" The woman at the door was older, brown hair with a bit of gray at the roots.

"Just Cora griping about some stray dog lying in her pasture. She thinks it might be sick or injured,"

Ray said.

"The call came in almost ten minutes ago. Better get on it." The woman pushed her ample figure through the doorway.

"I wouldn't want to keep you from doing your job." Jordan stepped out of Ray's path to the door. "Think about what I asked, and we can talk later."

"You bet." Ray stood up and headed out. As he passed the other woman, he gave her the kind of look you'd expect from a kid who'd just been reminded he has chores to do. The exchange between them amused Jordan.

The woman smiled a toothy red lipstick smile, but it felt genuine. "Hi, you must be Detective Gibbons. I didn't get a chance to meet you yesterday, but I'm Beatrice Baker, the senior dispatcher. Everyone just calls me Beats."

It confirmed what little Jordan knew about the odd symbiotic relationships that developed between dispatchers and their officers. Dispatchers worth their salt often felt a deep and abiding responsibility for the safety of their officers. Officers were keenly aware that the dispatchers were their lifeline. Consequently, they tended to take turns ordering each other around, making it difficult to determine who's in charge of who.

"Nice to meet you, Beats," Jordan said.

Beats looked at Jordan's coffee cup. "Wow, Ray sprang for the good stuff. I guess he's currently between wives. Well, almost."

Jordan didn't like what she was implying, not that she hadn't already guessed there was probably more than just a warm welcome behind the cup of coffee.

"I couldn't help but overhear what you were saying to Ray. He's wrong about Sheriff Blodgett, but he's been pretty bitter toward Brady ever since he lost the election."

"How bitter?" Jordan questioned.

Beats laughed. "Not that bitter. Ray's a weasel and a kiss-up sometimes, a decent deputy most of the time, but a murderer? Not likely."

"Do you know where else the sheriff might have kept his files? I couldn't find much on what he was currently working on. Did he have a laptop or—"

"No. Brady was old school. He kept most of what he was working on in that file cabinet or in his head. He was smart and personable. He knew how to get close to people and make them spill their guts before they realized what they were doing. Made a lot of friends that way, made a lot of arrests that way. Some enemies too."

Jordan looked at the files spread in front of her. "Like who? Anyone who might want to see him dead?"

Beats shook her head at the question. "Anyone who's been in law enforcement as long as Brady has people who'd probably want them dead. It's just a matter of finding out who."

"I guess so."

"Hey, I gotta get back in case a call comes in. If you want to get a decent cup of coffee without Ray, let me know." Beats turned to leave the room.

"Thanks." Jordan went back to the files.

After a few seconds, Beats stuck her head through in the door. "Hey, if you really want to know what the sheriff was into just before he died, you should check in with Shelly."

Shelly Curtis. A former Keystone County deputy. She was Sheriff Blodgett's mentor. Even after she retired, they played cards together every Thursday to discuss whatever was going on law enforcement–wise. Beats, once she got talking, was a wealth of information, including the former deputy's phone number. Jordan left the office for the privacy of her vehicle to make the call.

"Hey all." A strong female voice came through. "I'm off the grid for a few days moving the ninety and nine up to Rattlesnake. Don't bother leaving a message unless someone's dead or dying. If it's important now, it'll still be important when I get back."

Jordan didn't know what to think when she hung up the phone. Beats told her that Shelly was "somewhere in her sixties, sharp as a tack, a bit crusty on the outside, but inside gentle as a baby lamb." Jordan didn't know where Rattlesnake was, or who or what the ninety and nine were. It looked like Jordan was going to have to wait to talk to Shelly. Never mind that it was pretty much the only lead she had in this case.

A tap on the window made Jordan jump. It was Deputy Ray Harding, the one who brought the coffee. She sat up and opened the door.

"I think you're going to want to see this."

Chapter Seven

JORDAN DROVE BEHIND RAY'S patrol car to an open field just outside of town. At one end there was a large black dog that looked like a cross between a Lab and some kind of shepherd. It was huge and crouched down like it was protecting something.

Ray explained on the way across the field. "It started out as a feral dog call, but then I saw what he had. Unfortunately, I don't think he'll let anyone get close enough to touch it."

He took out his cell phone and snapped a couple of photos of the dog, then he tried to get close enough to get a picture of what the dog was sitting on. A low rumble came from deep in the dog's throat.

"What are you doing?" Jordan asked.

"I always take pictures when I come upon what might be a crime scene," Ray said.

"You don't wait for forensics to do that?"

Ray laughed. "Forensics for us usually means sending someone in from the Montana Bureau of Investigation in Helena. If we wait that long, there's too much chance the evidence has been moved around or messed with somehow. Before you came around, I was the closest this department had to a detective." He snapped another photo and the dog growled again.

"Maybe now isn't the best time for photos. Your subject seems a little camera shy. I think you're making him more nervous."

Jordan slowly closed the gap between herself and the dog. When she got closer, she realized he was tied to a lone fence pole with a worn rope. The rest of the fence had long since fallen down or rotted away. There was a bone under its front paws that looked suspiciously human. A low growl came from deep in the dog's throat. Jordan moved closer. "It's okay, we're not going to hurt you." She extended her hand.

"I wouldn't do that. He nearly took my hand off," Ray said. His hand rested on his gun. "I've called animal control."

Jordan got down low, her hand still out. "You look scared, boy. It's okay." The dog had a collar that looked almost new, but no tags that Jordan could see. Inch by inch she got close enough for him to sniff her fingers. He growled again, but it ended in more of a whimper. The dog was thin and dirty, there was a spot on his hindquarters that looked like a bullet wound and dried blood. She put her hand on his scruffy head and tried to reach for the bone. He showed her his teeth but didn't growl or move to bite her.

This close, the bone appeared to be a human femur, and there was something underneath it. It looked like a shirt, blue and yellow plaid. It was stained and dirty and looked like it might have been buried at some point, but not long enough to have been worn by the person whose bone the dog was guarding. His eyes and nose were dry. Jordan guessed he'd been tied in that spot long enough that he was dehydrated.

"Do you have any water?" she said to Ray without looking away from the dog.

"Yeah. Hold on." He came back with a bottle of water and Jordan poured some in her hand, careful to keep it from dripping on the shirt or the bone. The dog lapped it out of her cupped hand. She kept pouring and letting him drink until the bottle was empty. She reached for the shirt again. He growled. She tried the bone, but he wasn't going to let go of it, either.

An animal control officer arrived with a long loop on a stick and a muzzle. He looped the dog around the neck and Jordan helped him put the muzzle on. Only after he was muzzled did they cut the rope that held the dog. The animal control officer tugged on the leash. The dog stood with a sharp yelp and revealed a maggot-infested wound on his hindquarters. The officer leaned down to inspect the wound. "It looks pretty bad. We might want to just put him down."

"No!" Jordan said emphatically. "I need you to take care of him. He might be an important witness."

The animal control officer looked at her like she was crazy, but he nodded. "I have something in the truck that will help him relax enough to get him inside. Can you hold onto him, Ray?"

"I got him," Ray took control of the leash.

Jordan stayed at the dog's side, wincing as she looked at the dog's leg and breathed in what smelled like rotting flesh. She held his head as the officer stuck a needle behind his shoulder. As the dog's eyes closed, he gave Jordan a look of pure betrayal.

After the dog was loaded in the truck she turned to Ray. "We need to rope off this whole area and process it as a crime scene."

He knelt beside her in the dirt and indicated the bone. "You think it's human?"

"Yeah," Jordan said. She looked at the departing vehicle. "Any chance you know who that dog belongs to?"

"No. Pretty much everyone around here has a dog."

"Did Sheriff Blodgett have a dog?" Jordan asked, remembering the dog bed in his office.

"Used to, but that's not the sheriff's dog. It ran off the day before the sheriff was killed." Ray said.

"Are you sure it ran off?" Jordan asked.

A kind of realization dawned across his face. "Maybe not."

Jordan pulled a pair of gloves from her truck. She gingerly picked up the piece of filthy plaid fabric. It looked like it came from a shirt. When she turned it over, there was a rust-brown spot that she'd bet was blood.

This wasn't the case she'd signed up for, but she had a feeling this was the case she was going to get.

Chapter Eight

JORDAN FOCUSED HER MAGNIFYING glass on the ripped fabric they'd found wrapped around the bone. They'd trimmed away the bloodied pieces and sent them to the lab in Missoula to try to get a DNA match, but there were splotches of purple dye she hadn't been able to identify.

"We got a hit on the shirt. Maybe the dog, too," Sheriff Carlyle said as he walked into Jordan's office. He held up a printed photo of a pretty, golden-blonde-haired young woman with a heart-shaped face and wide blue eyes. "Her name is Sadie Larsen. She rolled into town about four months ago. She was working as a waitress at the Silver Horseshoe until she stopped coming in about a week ago. She lived in the Blakes's basement apartment. Her landlady saw the news report on TV and recognized the scrap of fabric as one of Sadie's shirts. They said she was feeding a stray, but they told her she couldn't keep it at the apartment."

Beats paused on her way down the hall with a cup of coffee. "I know that girl. The dog too."

"You do?" Jordan asked.

"She came in a while ago. She wanted to file a missing person's report, except on a dog." Beats said.

"When was this?" Jordan asked.

"About a week ago. Becca has a record of it somewhere." Beats held the coffee cup in both hands and blew on it. "She said she needed the dog for protection, and that someone had taken it."

"Did anyone follow up on it?" Jordan asked.

Sheriff Carlyle looked at Beats and Beats looked back at Jordan. Beats shrugged. "She's a pretty blonde, right? If anyone followed up on it, it would have been Ray. Again, I'm sure Becca has it somewhere in her files."

Jordan tried to keep down her frustration at the lack of professionalism she felt in this office. "Do you remember if she said why she didn't feel safe?"

"Nope, only that she was pretty upset about the dog being gone. An urgent call came in while she was here, so I didn't hear the whole story." Beats took a drink of her coffee and then headed back to the dispatch office.

"We generally don't make a big deal out of missing dogs." Carlyle laid the picture on the corner of Jordan's desk.

She picked it up and studied the woman's bright smile. "Any idea why no one reported the woman missing?"

Carlyle rested his hand on the gun at his hip. "She was kind of a stray herself. No one really knew her and when she stopped coming to work, they just assumed she'd moved on. Waitresses are in and out of the Horseshoe all the time."

"I think it's pretty clear that didn't happen this time," Jordan said.

"I agree. I was just about to start organizing a search. It's possible the girl this shirt belongs to is still alive."

"Hold on there." Commissioner Judd walked into Jordan's office. "What you're asking for is a lot of time and resources. No one has said Ms. Larsen is actually missing. More than likely she just got bored in Lombard and ran off. The lab hasn't processed the shirt yet. The blood could belong to the dog."

Jordan felt like her judgment was being questioned, again. She waited for the sheriff to back her up, instead he nodded. "You're right. We probably shouldn't make that call until we hear from the lab."

Jordan looked between them in disbelief. "Really? We're not even going to try to find her?"

Carlyle shrugged. "We can put her photo out to the neighboring counties."

Jordan worked to keep her frustration in check, reminding herself that she was new here. "Can we at least have the lab results expedited?"

Judd looked down at her condescendingly. "You're going to have to learn patience, little lady. We don't have the resources you had in the city."

Jordan bit her tongue against the reply that automatically came up with the "little lady" comment. "Put out the dispatch now. I'm going to go check out her apartment, and I'd like to talk to her landlady. Then I'll set up some interviews with the people she worked with at the Silver Horseshoe. And what about the bone? How long before forensics gives us any idea about it?"

"It could be a couple of weeks, but I think most of us here can guess where it came from," Carlyle said.

"You want to enlighten me?" Jordan said.

He took in a breath, like he wasn't sure he wanted to explain. "About fifteen years ago there was a woman who went missing. She was kind of a drifter, a lot like Ms. Larsen. She disappeared the second time she drifted into town, but no one thought much about it. Then part of her was found out by the creek."

"Part of her?" Jordan asked.

Carlyle continued. "During hunting season, some hunters found pieces of her remains. Not enough to positively identify her but enough to indicate she hadn't just moved on. It was the biggest case this county's ever seen, and it was never solved. It caused a big stir through the whole state."

"You mean the Bonnie Golden case," Jordan said.

The two men exchanged a glance, like they didn't expect her to do any research.

"Yes," Judd finally said. "But that was years ago."

"So ... a similar case, one where the killer was never put away, and now we have another woman missing?" She turned on Judd. "And you don't think we should try to find her?"

Judd narrowed his eyes on her. "Aren't you supposed to be focusing on what happened with the sheriff?"

Jordan's temper flared and she turned on the two men. "Commissioner Judd—can you not see that I am working on the sheriff's murder? I've done some research on the Bonnie Golden case. When Bonnie Golden was murdered, her dog disappeared too. Sheriff Blodgett's dog went missing two days before he was killed. Sadie Larsen's dog was found four days after she went missing. He had a bullet wound in his hip and was guarding a femur bone which now is believed to be Bonnie Golden's. The bone was wrapped in a piece of fabric which has been identified as being from one of Sadie's shirts. The blood on it was fresh, opening the possibility that Sadie could still be alive. Consequently, I believe we should set up a county-wide search for her, immediately. All three cases are undeniably similar, which leads me to believe that they are related. In other words, I am working on the case that I've been assigned. Now how soon can we get a search party together?"

Judd shook his head. "It's just as likely that the woman got tired of Lombard and moved on; she left the dog tied up in the field because she knew she couldn't keep it. The dog got hungry and dug up a bone that may or may not be human. Maybe left her shirt behind because she felt guilty or something."

Jordan stared at him in disbelief. "And reported the dog missing?"

Judd rolled his dark eyes into the folds of his forehead. "Maybe she was looking for attention. Who knows what goes on in the head of a woman like her."

Jordan turned to Carlyle for help. "Sheriff, you can't possibly—"

Judd cut her off. "If you haven't noticed, Keystone is a pretty damn big county, full of back roads and mountains and places where you could hide one of your bright yellow Seattle taxis and no one would ever find it. I'm not about to authorize the funds it would take to comb the mountainside looking for a woman who probably just took off until you have a positive ID on that bloody shirt and some idea of where we should start looking." He turned to the sheriff. "Brendan, I believe we have a meeting."

As he walked out the door, Jordan knew why she'd felt she wasn't going to like Judd the first time they met.

Chapter Nine

"HOW'S HE DOING?" JORDAN stretched her hand out to the pitiful, still scroungy dog splayed across the veterinarian's table. He whimpered and licked her hand.

"He's a fighter. He'll be okay," said the vet, Dr. Green. "But he won't be up and around much for a while, and he'll probably always walk with a limp. He had a bullet lodged pretty good in his hip."

"Were you able to recover the bullet?" Jordan asked. She was afraid Dr. Green would say they had to leave it in for the good of the dog. She didn't want to have to order a surgery that might hurt this poor animal further, but the bullet was vital to her case.

"Yeah, Ray picked it up earlier today and took it directly to the crime lab in Missoula."

"How long ago do you think the dog was shot?"

"Less than a week. If I had to guess, I'd say about four days. The infection was in the advanced stages. He wouldn't have made it another 24 hours. It was lucky that you found him when you did."

"It would've been luckier if we'd found the girl he belongs to."

"Agreed," Dr. Green said. "Any leads?"

"Not much. But maybe the bullet will help." She scratched the dog's head. "If anything else comes up, let me know." She started to walk away. The dog raised its head and whimpered after her.

"Actually, there is one thing," Dr. Green said. "Judd made it clear that the taxpayers wouldn't be paying for any care for this animal beyond removing that bullet as evidence. He suggested I put it out of its misery."

Jordan turned around, her blood boiling. "This dog is a witness in a murder investigation. Whatever you do, do not put it down. I'll talk to the other commissioners, and I'll personally guarantee that the bill will get paid."

"Glad to hear it. Now, if this dog had any kind of owner to speak of, I'd say we'd keep him another couple of days for observation and then turn him back over to them for care. Since he doesn't, I can look into the shelter or see if I can find someone to take him in."

Jordan looked into the dog's sad, hopeful eyes. She thought for a second about the lonely little house she had to go home to and her neighbor's suggestion to get a dog. She also considered what might happen to the dog if a foster family wasn't found and Judd had anything to say about his upkeep. "Call me when he's ready to be released. I'll take care of him myself."

Dr. Green nodded. "You're a good person, Detective. I think you and this dog will be good for each other."

On the road from the vet's office, Jordan contemplated what she'd just done. What was she going to do with an injured dog? She'd never had so much as a goldfish before. She was never home, and it wasn't like she was going to be here forever. It would be impossible to find an apartment in Seattle that was dog friendly, especially a dog as big as that one. She'd been so mad at the thought of Judd having the dog put down that she'd spoken before she thought. It seemed to be an ongoing problem in her life.

Sadie had been missing for over twenty-four hours and Jordan still hadn't made contact with the elusive Shelly. She was on her way to meet with Sadie's landlady and do a search of the apartment. The woman met her at the basement apartment in a pair of ratty jeans, and an unlit cigarette stuck between her teeth. The house was close to town. It had a small yard and was within walking distance of the school and the Silver Horseshoe.

"When was the last time you saw Sadie?" Jordan asked.

The woman chewed on her cigarette as if in thought. "I don't know. She came by and paid her rent on time. Other than that, Sadie kept pretty much to herself. We barely saw her."

"Was this her dog?" Jordan handed her a photo.

She took it and shook her head. "It's the dog she wanted to be hers. Gave him a name and everything, Brownie, I think it was. I caught her heading downstairs with him one evening. She said he was a stray she'd found. I told her there was no way we were letting her keep a dog that size in that little apartment. We just put in new carpeting, and we couldn't have him running around the yard, digging stuff up and leaving messes everywhere. I've spent a lot of time on this lawn. We've got the nicest yard in town." She waited, like she was expecting Jordan to compliment the yard.

"What was her reaction?" Jordan asked.

"She got really upset. She said she needed the dog for protection. I told her that she lived in the smallest, safest town in the world. Course, that was before Blodgett got shot. Found out anything about that?"

Jordan ignored the question; she didn't feel like she had to explain herself to this woman. "Did she say specifically who or what she needed protection from?"

"No. I told her she had twenty-four hours to get rid of the dog." The woman reached in her pocket, like she was looking for a lighter, but she still didn't light the cigarette. "I never saw the dog again, so I assumed she'd taken care of it."

"But you aren't sure when Sadie went missing?"

"No. Her rent wasn't due for another week. I wouldn't have thought anything was off if I hadn't seen that bit of fabric on the news. Sadie wore that plaid shirt all the time."

"What about her car?"

"She didn't have one. Some guy dropped her off the first day she came. He didn't get out of the car, so I didn't get a good look at him. She didn't have much with her when she moved in. A couple of suitcases, a couple of cardboard boxes. The apartment came furnished. My son used to sleep down there. When he joined the army, we—"

"Thank you. I'll make sure I get the keys back to you when I'm done," Jordan said, even though she was frustrated again at the lack of notice people seemed to pay in Lombard.

Sadie's basement apartment was barely more than a hallway that had been turned into a kitchen and a tiny sitting area. It led to a larger bedroom and a bathroom. Jordan had somehow expected it to be a mess. She'd already prejudged the woman in the picture as flighty, disorganized, and not very smart. As soon as Jordan walked into Sadie's apartment, she knew she was wrong.

There wasn't much in the apartment, but what was there was clean and organized. Jordan's attention went immediately to a little glass-topped desk in the corner. There was a computer mouse and mouse pad, but no laptop. The top shelf of a salvaged bookcase was full of true crime books. The second shelf held color-coded cardboard file holders, the kind teachers used. They were all labeled. As she read through them, Jordan recognized the names of prominent cold cases across the country.

Jordan put on a pair of gloves and thumbed through the files until she saw one labeled "Steilacoom Strangler." She pulled the file. It had the word "CLOSED" printed in all caps across the front. Jordan opened it. On top of a stack of papers was a copy of the front page of the *Seattle Times* featuring Jordan's photo under the headline "Rookie Detective Solves 30-Year-Old Murder." The picture of herself startled Jordan. She looked through the rest of the file to see if there was anything else about her or the case, but compared to the files, this one was sparse. She went back to the picture, noting the dark-haired man in the background. His features were out of focus, but she knew it was Brock. She shut the file and put it back on the shelf. Her biggest triumph was colored with too many bad memories.

She went back to the desk. Besides the mouse pad, there was a blue notebook with a line of pineapples along the bottom. There were a handful of pages missing. She picked it up and could just read the outline of three phone numbers that were pressed through from the pages above.

The first one went to a number with a Texas prefix. When she tried it, she got a message that the number had been disconnected. The next two started with 406, the sole area code for the state of Montana. The last two numbers weren't clear in the second phone number. The third phone number rang three times before Jordan heard the familiar message:

"Hey all. I'm off the grid for a few days moving the ninety and nine up to Rattlesnake."

Chapter Ten

THE NEXT MORNING, JORDAN parked her vehicle at the end of a long dirt road. Ahead and up the mountain there was only a shoestring trail that she didn't think even the Expedition could handle it. The directions she'd been given were sketchy at best. This was the nearest anyone could guess to where she would find Shelly, moving cattle up to her summer pasture.

"They probably set up camp at the base of Rattlesnake Ridge. If you wait there long enough, someone is bound to come down," Beats had said.

It looked like someone had indeed set up camp here. There was a horse trailer and a camp trailer, two pickups, and a makeshift corral. Jordan leaned against the truck. The emptiness of the space made her nervous. Her phone didn't have any connection here. She had the radio, but she was far from anyone who could provide back up if she needed it.

She didn't want to admit that the discovery of the dog and the shirt and the missing girl had rattled her. She was used to working cold cases, cases where the killer had long since gone into hiding or moved on. She knew she'd be dealing with a different kind of killer here. Deep down she'd hoped it would be easy, something the local authorities had overlooked or a small-town dispute that had gotten out of hand. Now it seemed like she might be trying to solve a cold case and maybe more than one fresh one.

Forensics hadn't come back on the blood or the bone yet. The dog collar wasn't definitive proof that the sheriff's murder, Sadie's disappearance, and the fifteen-year-old cold case were connected, but Jordan's intuition told her they were. If she could talk to Shelly, if she knew what the sheriff was working on before he was killed, then maybe she could dismiss or solidify the connection.

Footsteps, or actually hoofbeats, caught her attention. She watched the trail until a cowboy hat-clad man on a black and white horse came over the hill and into view. She moved to the bottom of the trail to meet him.

"Ho!" He pulled the horse up short and looked down at her in surprise. The gray eyes under the tan cowboy hat gave him away. "Hello, Detective, what brings you out here?" Whit Palmer, again. Why was he everywhere?

Jordan stepped back from the horse. "I'm looking for Shelly Curtis. Is she around?"

"Up top." Whit nodded in the general direction of the trail. "What do you want to talk to her about?"

"It's not really something I'm at liberty to discuss with anyone else."

"Something about the woman that's gone missing, Sadie Larsen?" Whit guessed.

"Do you know her?" Jordan asked.

"I know of her. She was a waitress at the Horseshoe, right?"

"Yes." Jordan automatically measured Whit's tone to see if he knew more about the missing girl than he let on.

"And you think her running off has something to do with the sheriff's murder?"

"Maybe." It annoyed her that like everyone else, Whit just assumed Sadie had run off.

"You don't sound very sure." The smirk was in his voice, even if it wasn't on his face. Or maybe Jordan was just imagining it. He climbed off the horse and led it back to the trailer.

Jordan unconsciously touched the scar on her shoulder and gave the big animal a wide berth as it passed. "When will Shelly be coming back down?"

"We're really just getting started for the day. No one will be coming back down until late. I only came down to get the meds Shelly takes with lunch. She left them in the trailer this morning." Whit threw the reins over the back of the pickup without tying the horse up. "You could wait here or come back later."

Jordan glanced at her watch. "When you say late, how—"

"Give me a sec." Whit disappeared into the trailer. He emerged with a bottle and resumed the conversation. "Shelly won't stay on the mountain past sundown. She sleeps in the trailer. I'm on watch tonight, so I won't be coming down again."

Jordan didn't want to go all the way back into town only to turn around and come back. She measured the steep trail with her eyes. "Is it a long hike up? I did a lot of hiking in the Cascades in Washington."

"You don't look like you're dressed for a hike," Whit said. Jordan didn't want to admit that he was right. She hadn't considered the area she was heading into this morning. She was wearing tall leather dress boots, a pair of slacks, a white blouse and a professionally tailored blazer.

"I'll manage." Jordan said.

"If you hike it, by the time you get up there, Shelly will be on her way back down. Quickest way up is on a horse. Might be easiest on your feet too." He nodded at her boots. "Those boots don't look like they were made for walking." He chuckled at his own joke, but Jordan felt like he was laughing at her.

"There's only one horse," Jordan pointed out. She didn't tell him that she was grateful for that. Just being this close to the horse he rode down on filled her with terror.

"Scout can take us both up, he's strong enough. You're what, maybe 120 pounds? 130?" He looked down at her, his lips forming not quite a half smile.

"I guess I'm not supposed to ask that."

Jordan looked from the wiry horse to the cowboy. She lifted her chin. "I've never ridden before." It was a lie. She had ridden before, but it wasn't an experience she wanted to repeat.

He looked at her as if she'd said she'd never been in a car before. "Really?"

"Really."

She watched what little respect he had for her drain out of his face. "Doesn't matter. I'll be the one in control. All you really have to do is hang on."

Jordan stared back at him, thinking how inappropriate it would be to ride up the side of the hill, clinging to a man who was as close as she had to a boss in this place. It was kind of what had gotten her into trouble in Seattle. Brock hadn't exactly been her commanding office—he worked in a different department—but he outranked her enough to make dating him a bad idea—frowned on if not technically forbidden. Maybe that was what had attracted a younger, more naive version of herself to him. She wasn't young enough to make that mistake again.

Jordan squared her shoulders toward the trail. "If you point me in the right direction, I'll go ahead and hike up on my own."

Whit shook his head. "I'm not going to go up the ridge and leave you on the trail to fend for yourself."

"I can—"

"I know. You can take care of yourself. But this area isn't called Rattlesnake Ridge for nothing. I doubt a rattler is going to care how many ways you know how to kill a man with your bare hands."

Jordan felt the heat rising in her face. "That's not what Krav Maga is."

"Well, unless it's an ancient form of snake charming, or for that matter bear charming, I'm not leaving you alone on the trail."

"You came down alone," Jordan pointed out.

"Not exactly alone." He patted his horse on the rump and then secured the bottle of medicine in a leather bag attached to the saddle. "And I know my way around here. Look, if I ever go to Seattle, I'll let you show me around on the subway or something."

"Seattle doesn't have a subway. It's a monorail, and not exactly—"

"Whatever. I need to get back up there. You can either ride with me or wait in your vehicle until Shelly comes down." He tightened the cinch on the saddle and climbed up. "Your call. You're in Montana, you might as well learn how to ride." He moved one foot out of the stirrup and reached his hand to her.

She folded her arms across her chest and took a step back. "No. Thank you. I'll wait."

"Suit yourself. I'll let Shelly know you're waiting for her." He tipped his hat and then turned the horse toward the trail.

Jordan followed as soon as he was around a bend. There was no way she was waiting at the bottom of this hill. Less than ten minutes up the steep incline in she was rethinking her decision. Her gun banged against her hip with every step and her feet hurt. She'd taken her jacket off and left it in her vehicle before starting the climb. She wished for her hiking boots, a comfortable bra, and a pair of spandex leggings. She was mad at herself for the choice of outfit she'd made. Her mom would have considered it to be inappropriately casual, but a few days in Lombard had taught her that no one dressed the way she did. The locals spent their days in plaid shirts, Wranglers, or overalls. She'd aimed to come off as professional but had only emphasized her place as an outsider.

She made it up to the first ridge and paused to catch her breath. She wasn't used to the altitude or the dry air. She couldn't help but admire the view. She could see a good piece of the valley from here; it was dotted with tiny buildings and circled farmland, a strip of blue river bisecting the land, and mountains that rose on almost all sides. A cool breeze tickled the back of her neck. She leaned against a boulder at the side of the trail and yanked off her boot. Somehow, she'd managed to get a rock in it.

"Don't move!"

Jordan froze and looked up to see Whit pointing a pistol in her direction.

Chapter Eleven

JORDAN PUT HER HAND on her gun, estimating how quickly she'd be able to draw and fire.

"I'm not going to shoot you, Detective, but I need you to go to your left, slowly." He gestured to her with his gun.

"Wha—"

Whit pressed his finger to his lips. A telltale rattle sounded close, too close, behind her. A trickle of sweat rolled down her back. Slowly, one small step at a time, Jordan sidestepped away from the rock. She didn't dare look behind her. Whit kept his gun trained on the same spot. Once she was clear of the boulder, he squeezed the trigger. A shot rang out, pinging off the rock. The horse didn't even flinch.

"And that's why we call it Rattlesnake Ridge," Whit said. He holstered his gun. "Still want to take your chances hiking up?"

Jordan took a shaky breath and turned to look at what was left of a good-sized rattlesnake. Whit was a good shot. She felt like an idiot. She was sure that was the opinion he held of her as well.

"Thanks."

Whit rested his hand on the front of his saddle. "The offer to ride up double still stands, or you can walk beside the horse, or you can ride, and I'll walk. Whatever you choose, we're sticking together."

She looked over the spotted horse. It was huge and powerful. For now, the horse stood still as a statue, waiting for Whit to tell him what to do, but at any minute it could decide to charge down the hill with her clinging on his back helplessly. It could buck or he could rear over and crush her under its massive weight. Jordan considered her options. Was she more afraid of the horse, or more afraid of another snake?

"So do you want to walk in front of or behind Scout?" Whit's smile looked genuine, but behind it she could imagine him mocking her. She wondered what he would say to the men at the Silver Horseshoe when he got back to town.

That's what it came down to. She was more afraid of being laughed at and humiliated than she was of either the horse or the snakes. "I'll ride."

"Good choice." Whit moved his foot out of the stirrup and extended his hand a second time.

Jordan took a breath and reached for his hand. She swung up in a smooth motion, barely looking at the horse. She gripped the back of the saddle tightly, trying to keep from trembling or at least to keep from letting Whit know she was afraid.

"You okay?" Whit asked, his face showing genuine concern.

Jordan took two long calming breaths before she could answer. "Yeah."

She was immediately grateful for all the hours she'd spent doing barre workouts. If she ever needed leg strength, balance, and flexibility, it was riding uphill, behind the saddle, on a horse with large, muscular hindquarters, while doing everything possible to keep from touching the man riding in front of her and trying to keep from having a full-on panic attack in the process.

"You can't tell me why you want to talk to Shelly? You haven't found a smoking gun or got a signed confession yet?" Whit sounded like he was joking, but Jordan was too tense to be in the mood for teasing.

"Just something to do with the case," she answered shortly.

"Something important, because if it isn't important, you shouldn't be out here wasting your time. Shelly's not—-"

"You read my resume, right?" Jordan cut him off, frustrated that he was questioning her judgment, like everyone else. "I mean, you'd have to have read it. You knew about the Krav Maga thing."

"Of course I read your resume," Whit said. "I wasn't going to sign off on bringing you here if I didn't think you were competent."

"Then treat me like I'm competent. I'm following up on a lead and I think Shelly's the only one who can answer certain questions for me. That's all you need to know."

"Yes, ma'am." He touched his hat. There was an edge to Whit's voice that bordered between sarcasm and annoyance.

They rode in awkward silence for several minutes. The only sound was the clopping of the horse's feet on the trail. Jordan was trying to relax, concentrating on the scenery around her, when the horse slid on a bit of loose gravel. Whit pulled up hard to keep them all from going down. Jordan gasped, making a quick decision between grabbing Whit's waist and being dumped sideways down the steep slope of the trail. She gripped his waist hard.

Jordan knew he could feel her body shaking against his, but for a few seconds she couldn't force herself to let go. He probably felt, if not heard, the pounding of her heart. He held the horse steady and looked over his shoulder at her. "You okay?"

"Yeah. How much ..." She breathed in, moving her death grip back to the saddle. "How much farther?"

"Another twenty minutes up the trail. Are you sure you're okay? I can let you ride in the saddle for a while."

"No," Jordan said. She was terrified of being the one in control, even if she wasn't sure her inner thighs would hold on that long.

"Sorry to scare you. Scout's usually a lot more sure-footed than that, but he is getting older."

"I wasn't—" But Jordan couldn't deny she'd been afraid. She took a breath. Maybe talking would get her mind off her fear for the next twenty minutes. "He seems like a good horse. Have you had him long?"

Whit patted the horse's neck. "He is a good horse, the best actually, and a good friend. I've had him for his whole life and a good chunk of mine."

"I never had a pet growing up," Jordan said.

Whit let out a sound that was somewhere between a laugh and an offended snort. "Scout's not a pet. More like a partner. We trust each other. I was there when he was born some twenty years ago. I'd been waiting for him to arrive because my grandpa had promised me the next colt that was born, but that day I got home from school late. I went into the barn to find Scout's mom in labor. She was weak and struggling. For a while it didn't look like either of them would make it. I was the only one home, so I did what I could to help.

"By the time he finally made it into the world, his mom was too weak to stand. I covered her up with a blanket and then I carried him into the house and set him by the fire to dry off and warm up while I made him a bottle. You should have seen the look on my grandma's face when she came home to find a newborn colt in the middle of her kitchen, sucking down a bottle of milk. It was the first of many bottles I gave him."

"His mom didn't make it?" Jordan was caught up in the story in spite of her fear.

"She pulled through but never quite had enough milk to keep him going, so I fed him a couple of bottles a day. Eventually he got to where he'd follow me around everywhere I went. Even while I did chores."

"I guess that explains why he seems to trust you so much."

"In a lot of ways, we saved each other. I was a pretty lonely kid in those days. My dad took off when I was eight years old, and my mom retreated into her own world that didn't have any space for me. I needed someone to talk to and Scout here is a pretty good listener."

Jordan had noticed the horse moving his ears back and forth while Whit spoke. "He looks like he really understands what you're saying."

"Of course, he does. God and Mother Nature conspired to create horses to be the best listeners in the animal world. Horses have been partners to man since the beginning. They listen and understand what you need them to be. This one knew I needed a friend."

"That's a great story." Jordan said. She hoped she sounded sincere because she was sincere. But his story made her realize that Whit would never respect her if she told him she was terrified of this creature that meant so much to him.

"Scout is fast, strong and smart. One of the best rodeo ponies around."

"Rodeo?"

"Rodeo. You know, that sport where a bunch of cowboys and cowgirls get together and—"

"I know what a rodeo is. But I've never met anyone who actually competed in a rodeo before."

"Well, be prepared to meet more than a few of us. It's more than just a sport around here or something to pass the time on the weekends. It's a part of who we are, an entire way of life. Rodeo kind of saved my life too. It gave me friends and goals and something to work toward."

Jordan sniffed. "Are you one of those guys who has to prove their manhood by getting on a wild bull? That always seemed pretty crazy to me."

Whit looked over his shoulder, shaking his head at her. "I tried it a couple of times when I was younger. I busted up my ankle pretty good. Now I do roping. Mostly single, but sometimes I do team roping with a partner. Of course, my best partner is right here." He reached up and stroked Scout's neck. "There's a rodeo the end of next week you should check out. This is the preseason so it's more of an exhibition and not as long. It'd be a good introduction for you."

The last thing Jordan wanted to do was attend a rodeo, but she didn't want to show Whit her disdain for the sport. "I'm pretty busy with the case right now, but I'll think about it."

"You do that." Whit seemed disappointed in her lack of enthusiasm.

The silence stretched between them again. The only thing Jordan could think about was the pain in her inner thighs coupled with an uncomfortable gritty wetness down her legs and across her behind. The horse had sweated profusely on the way up. So much so that horse sweat had run down her legs and into her expensive boots. She was sure her pants were ruined and maybe the boots too. It would probably look like she'd had a fear-induced accident when she got off. If this ride ever ended.

Finally, they rounded a bend. To her relief, a group of horses and black cows and calves stood in an open meadow in front of them. Whit directed the horse off the trail. He stopped in front of a woman with short white hair, a slim build, and a straight back. She was talking to a tall cowboy but turned as soon as she saw Whit's horse. "Whit, we were about to send out a search party. What the hell?" The woman stopped as Jordan dismounted, doing her best not to fall when she landed on her wobbly legs, and ignoring Whit's hand to help steady her.

"Shelly Curtis?" Jordan said.

The woman walked closer. "That's what it says on my driver's license."

"I'm Jordan Gibbons, the detective working on Sheriff Blodgett's murder." Jordan held her hand out.

Shelly gripped her hand firmly. "I know who you are. What I don't know is why on earth Whit brought you all the way up here."

Jordan met the woman's earthy brown eyes. "Your message said to come get you if someone died."

Chapter Twelve

"I GUESS THAT QUALIFIES as important," Shelly said. Whit looked from Jordan to Shelly, waiting for an explanation. "We were about to have some lunch. Would you like to join us?"

"I don't nee—"

"Around here when someone invites you to eat with them, the proper response is, 'thank you,'" Shelly said. "Don't tell me you aren't hungry."

"Thank you, but I'd like to—"

"Just thank you is enough for now," Shelly said brusquely.

Jordan opened her mouth to say something else, but she caught a subtle shake of Whit's head. She closed her mouth and followed Shelly to a circle of logs around a long-dead fire. This woman, more than twice her age, was as commanding and intimidating as her first police sergeant. It was clear how Shelly survived her years as a woman in law enforcement, even in a place as rough as this. It was the kind of thing Jordan could respect, even if she felt dressed down by her.

Jordan was impatient to get Shelly alone and talking, but Shelly directed her to wash her hands and help make sandwiches. "We have a hungry crew to feed. Out here everyone pitches in."

Whit obeyed Shelly without hesitation, moving toward a tub full of water hauled from the nearby creek. After a couple of minutes, Jordan did the same, although she felt like Shelly was treating her like a hired hand instead of a competent police detective. She and Whit pulled sliced meat and cheese from a cooler and laid it out on a folding metal table. Jordan didn't know how they got either up the mountain. She didn't think even Whit's horse could have carried everything up.

"Who's dead?" Shelly finally asked as she pulled out a plastic container of cookies. Whit paused as he sliced a tomato.

Jordan glanced at him. "Can we talk someplace a little more private?"

"If privacy is what you're after, then you're going to have to wait. This place is about to get a whole lot less private," Shelly said.

One by one, five other cowboys, ranging in age from early teens to over fifty, came to retrieve sandwiches. Some sat on the logs to eat. A couple grabbed a sandwich and headed back to the herd of fat cattle. The only other woman was a twenty-something beauty with red hair the same color as her horse.

"My granddaughter, Tawny," Shelly said as the cowgirl sat down on a log next to Whit. She gestured to Jordan. "This is Detective Gibbons."

The young woman seemed to size Jordan up, finding her seriously lacking. Tawny smiled condescendingly and pulled off a pair of leather gloves, stained purple, before reaching to shake Jordan's hand.

Jordan didn't reach to shake the woman's hand. "Can I see your gloves?"

Tawny gave Shelly a questioning look but handed her the gloves.

Jordan turned the gloves over in her hands. "Can you tell me where these stains came from?"

Tawny looked at the gloves, then down at her jeans. There was a matching purple handprint on her left leg. "Dammit Whit, if these jeans are ruined, I'm going to kill you."

Whit grinned back at her. "If you came up here in jeans you were worried about getting ruined, then you've become more of a diva than I'd thought."

Tawny threw a grape from the cooler at him. He caught it in between his teeth. "Show off," she said, but her face lit up with admiration.

"The stains," Jordan reminded her. "What are they from?"

Tawny rolled her eyes and Jordan got the idea the cowgirl thought she was an idiot. "Whit sprayed the thistles up the ridge. It keeps them from taking over the whole meadow. The spray has a purple dye in it, so you know where you've sprayed." She looked pointedly at Whit. "If you're careful, it doesn't get all over everything."

Whit held out his hands to show they were clean. "Careful? I was the one who was spraying, and I managed to keep it off me."

Shelly's eyes bored into Jordan's. "Why do you ask?"

"Just curious." The wheels in Jordan's head were spinning. It looked like the same purple she'd seen on Sadie's shirt, but she wasn't ready to talk about that in front of Whit and Tawny.

The meal seemed to take forever. Finally, the cowboys started to disperse. Whit finished off his third cookie and then mounted Scout. He turned to Tawny. "Coming, princess?"

"That's 'queen' to you, thank you very much," Tawny said, making a point of wiping her hands on her jeans as she stood.

"Yeah. You're a royal something," Whit replied as Tawny climbed back on her horse.

She circled the horse to follow Whit. When she was a few feet away Jordan heard her say, "Least I know enough not to wear dress boots up a mountain." Jordan watched them go, her stomach twisting with something she didn't want to acknowledge.

Shelly stretched out on a folding chair and gestured for Jordan to sit. "What's so important you can't discuss it in front of Whit? Who died and what does it have to do with me?"

Jordan leaned forward. "I'm not actually sure the person is dead, but I have the feeling she's in trouble." She told Shelly about the mangy dog with a bullet wound in his thigh that was guarding a bone and a strip of bloodied and torn fabric. Shelly nodded a few times but didn't say much. Jordan concluded with, "Can you tell me what the sheriff was working on just before he got killed?"

"Sounds like you already have a guess," Shelly said.

"There was a leather dog collar in an envelope among his files. I think it belonged to a woman who was murdered years ago, Bonnie Golden."

"Technically it belonged to the dog, but you're right."

"There weren't any notes in his files about it. Do you know where the sheriff got it?"

"Yep." Shelly rubbed her hand across her cheek. She suddenly looked tired and older than she had before.

"Where was it found?"

Shelly stood and started packing the food away in the cooler. "In my flower bed. A month ago, I was putting in a new bare root rosebush and I dug it up."

Jordan moved to help her. "You think the killer buried it there fifteen years ago?"

"No. I think it was buried there fairly recently. Did you see the collar? There's no way leather would look like that if it was put in the ground over a Montana winter, much less fifteen Montana winters."

"Oh." Jordan let that sink in for a few minutes. "Do you know what happened to Bonnie's dog?"

"Not any more than we know exactly what happened to Bonnie herself, except dog bones turning up don't cause as much of a stir as people bones."

"And you're sure the collar belonged to Bonnie's dog?"

"No. But if it wasn't the same collar, I'm pretty sure someone wanted me to think it was." The cooler packed, Shelly closed the lid and sat on top of it. Again, Jordan got the impression that the conversation was difficult for the older woman.

Jordan sat on a log beside her. "Was anything else found in your flower bed? I didn't find a report on it."

"Nothing else was found and there wasn't a report," Shelly said.

"Why not? I know the Keystone County's Sheriff's Department is a little lax, but—"

Shelly stood. "The Sheriff's department isn't lax. There wasn't a report because they didn't search the flower bed. I did. I sifted through it myself."

"You didn't bring the police in to search at all?"

"I told Brady everything. We agreed it was best to keep it between us."

Jordan stared at her for a minute in disbelief. "But it was a pretty obvious clue to an unsolved murder. It could have been a message that the murderer was back."

Shelly pursed her lips. Obviously, she wasn't used to being chastised by someone younger than her. "That's exactly the message he wanted to send and exactly the message that Brady and I didn't want to get out. He feeds on attention, on sensation."

"He? You mean the person who killed Bonnie Golden? Do you know who he is?"

Shelly met Jordan's eyes, her voice low and serious. "No, but I've dealt with him long enough to know what he's like."

"But now he's possibly killed again. Why didn't you bring this information to me or really anyone involved with the case sooner? Especially after the sheriff was murdered?" Jordan's voice had risen so much that the nearest cowboy turned around and raised his eyebrows at her. "It can't be a coincidence that the ripped shirt was found with a human bone. If that bone turns out to be from Bonnie Golden and the shirt from Sadie Larsen, the killer has all but announced that he's back in town."

"Exactly," Shelly said.

"And you didn't think it was important to get that message out sooner?" Jordan said.

"I didn't think it was prudent."

"I want to search your flower bed. The rest of your property as well. I'll get a search warrant if I have to. And I need you to tell me everything you know about the other case. Now, before someone else dies."

Shelly narrowed her eyes at Jordan, a movement she found rather threatening. "If you don't let me get involved, if you make this into another big, sensational case, I can guarantee you that someone else will die."

Chapter Thirteen

"I NEED TO GET the detective off the mountain," Shelly said to the nearest cowboy. "Go get the mule for me."

Jordan was ready to protest. Riding down the mountain on a mule didn't sound any better than riding up on a horse. She'd rather hike down, snakes and all. Then the man pulled up in the mule—an all-terrain vehicle with two seats and just enough space in the back for the cooler. Two cowboys hoisted it into the back of the mule and strapped it down.

"We'll take the back way down. It's a little longer, but not as steep as the trail you came up on. We can talk as we go." Shelly climbed into the driver's side of the mule.

They headed down the trail, going the opposite way Whit had brought her up on Scout. He was still sitting on the black and white paint. He swung the rope, catching an errant black calf in a motion that appeared effortless. He tipped his hat as they passed by on the way down.

There were so many questions swirling in Jordan's head that had to do with the case, but for some reason what came out was, "How do you know Whit? Is he related to you?"

"Not by blood, but I consider him kin as much as any of my own. I've known Whit since he was a baby. His grandma Helen and I were best friends in school. The Palmers are good stock, with one exception. Whit's dad ran off with another woman when Whit was about eight years old. His mom never quite recovered from it, got into some bad stuff and died young. Whit was raised mostly by Helen. I'd like to think I had a part in his upbringing too. Since Helen passed, I'm all the family he has. He's a good kid. Good man now, I guess."

"I guess." Jordan resisted the urge to glance back. She was thinking of a young Whit with sad gray eyes, left alone by both his parents with only a horse for a companion. She shook the image off and got back to business. "What can you tell me about the Bonnie Golden case?"

Shelly tightened her grip on the steering wheel. "I'm going on the assumption that you've read all the reports that were filed in the case?"

"Pretend I haven't." Jordan said. She'd poured over every shred of anything she could find that mentioned the case, but she wanted to hear the whole story from Shelly, someone who'd actually lived through it. Her experience in cold cases was that even years later, the people who were involved in what happened were better sources of information than anything that had been written down.

Shelly let out a long breath, like she was preparing to tell a story that she'd told too many times before. "Bonnie was fleeing a failed relationship the first time she drifted into town. She learned her paramour was married. She waitressed at the Silver Horseshoe. She wreaked havoc on the local scene and made a lot of enemies. When she and Whit's father hooked up and left town, the natives were relieved and never expected to see her again."

"Bonnie and Whit's dad? I didn't see that in the file." A million implications and questions were attached to that one statement.

Shelly waved her hand like it wasn't important and continued on. "Nine years later, she returned. She brought three things with her—a bad reputation, a lot of enemies, and a stalker. She seemed to be a changed woman, though. Seemed like she just wanted to be left alone. She rented a cabin located in a deep ravine fifteen miles west of town. It was remote, isolated—nearly inaccessible. She lived the life of a recluse and made rare trips to town for supplies, but she always stopped at the sheriff's office to seek his help. She said a man was stalking her and wanted to kill her. The sheriff was skeptical and offered little help. He advised her to get a guard dog and she did. Sampson was huge, ferocious, and well trained, but that didn't stop things. I had my own issues with Bonnie Golden, but I felt for her. Men don't understand what it is to be a woman living alone and to be afraid like that. The Sheriff didn't take her seriously, right up to the point where she disappeared.

"I was working as a deputy at the time and realized Bonnie had not been in to pester the sheriff for quite a while. I asked around town, but no one had seen Bonnie recently. I had some words with the sheriff about it, but he was convinced she'd just left town. I disagreed so I went to her cabin to check on her. Bonnie, her vehicle, and her dog were gone. The cabin looked as if she had just stepped out the door. With all her belongings there, most people assumed she would just come back eventually.

"When hunting season began a couple of months later, a hunter brought in some bones that looked human. There were three ribs and part of a backbone. About ten days later, another hunter found what looked like half of a hand. These remains were found high in the mountains in areas only accessible by foot. The bones were small, indicating they belonged to a woman. With only Bonnie missing in the area, we returned to her cabin. Nothing had changed since our first visit. I called in some favors with a friend who worked in the FBI Office in Butte. Me and two men from his forensic unit unofficially inspected the cabin. It was meticulously clean. We couldn't find so much as a fingerprint. Eventually we found a minute spot of blood on the bathroom floor, nearly under the trim alongside the tub. Then we discovered a tiny amount of what looked like fine sawdust on the hinge side under the linen closet door. Tested, it proved to be human bone. On that basis, an extensive official investigation ensued. The eventual conclusion was that Bonnie's stalker had killed her and her dog and dismembered them into small pieces in the bathtub with knives and a saw. He had scattered the remains in the mountains likely by plane, then returned to the cabin to remove all evidence using vinegar, hydrogen peroxide and ..."

Startled by that information, Jordan stared at Shelly. "What a gruesome story!"

Shelly nodded grimly. "Worst thing I'd ever heard of one human doing to another. The preponderance of evidence convinced even the most avid skeptics that Bonnie was dead.

"It was the biggest case this town had ever seen and became national news. It was sickening the way the sheriff jumped on the bandwagon and milked the situation for all it was worth, especially after it was he who'd left her vulnerable like that."

Jordan shook her head; she'd already seen some terrible things in her career, but this was more than she expected from this sleepy little town. "I'm kind of in the same situation. Sadie Larsen is missing. I'm going to bet the blood on the shirt turns out to be hers, but I can't seem to get anyone to take the situation seriously."

"Sadie Larsen? Can't say as I've heard of her," Shelly said.

Jordan watched Shelly's reaction as she said, "She knew you. At least she had your phone number."

Shelly wrinkled her forehead in concentration. "I don't recall ever speaking to her if she did have my number."

"She's new to town, waitressed for a while at the Horseshoe," Jordan said.

"Oh, her," Shelly said. "Pretty blonde thing? The kind who looks like an angel, but causes all sorts of hell wherever she goes?"

"I don't know about that."

"I knew who she was, but I never spoke to her. If she had my number, I'm not sure where she got it." Shelly looked thoughtful. "Any idea how long she's been missing?"

"Not exactly. She hasn't been back to work in the last week and we have her dog with four days' worth of rot attached to a bullet wound in his hip."

"Sounds like you should be back in town organizing some kind of search," Shelly said.

"That's what I said, but Judd wants to wait for more proof before he loosens the county purse strings."

"Judd." Shelly hmphed. "He was criminally incompetent then, and he's doing everything he can to prove he still is."

"He wants me to tell him exactly where to look before he'll give the go ahead for the search. That's why I was asking about the purple dye. The shirt we found had some purple spots on it. They looked a lot like what your granddaughter had on her jeans."

"Lots of people spray for weeds in the high pastures this time of year, but it'd be worth it to find out who all uses that kind of spray and where they've been spraying. There's no good reason a woman like Sadie Larsen would be out in the thistles. You might check in with Whit on that."

"Whit?"

"He went to school for that kind of thing. He has a master's degree in agronomy. He advises farmers and ranchers from here to Texas." There was a distinct pride in Shelly's voice as she said it.

"I'll ask him. But we need more than just a vague idea of where to look for Sadie. What kind of leads did you follow up before?"

"There wasn't a lot to go on. Bonnie had never named her stalker. I doubt she even knew who he was."

"Do you think he was local to Lombard? Or did he follow her here?"

"I know she left behind that bad relationship in Missoula."

To Jordan, that statement was like a rub against an old wound. She pushed it away. "Any chance it was him, or maybe a jealous wife?"

"Both were fully investigated with ironclad alibis, as were a lot of the usual suspects around town. The pieces just never came together. Sheriff was sure it was someone Bonnie knew and had made an enemy of somehow."

"What happened after the case went unsolved? Where are all the players in it now?" Jordan asked.

"I quit the sheriff's office over it and became a private detective. Couldn't stomach the way things were handled. I put everything I had behind

Blodgett to take Judd's place. He's never quite forgiven me for that defeat."

Something struck Jordan, something that she hadn't realized when she had gone through the files. "Did you say Judd?"

"Yeah, Dane Judd was the sheriff at the time. You may have met him already. He goes by Commissioner Judd now."

The inside of Jordan's mouth suddenly tasted sour. "We've met."

Chapter Fourteen

JORDAN ARRIVED AT THE sheriff's office early to prepare for the meeting with Angie Blodgett. Beats met her at the door and handed her a slip of paper. "Shelly came by early this morning and left this for you. She thought it might be helpful."

Jordan walked into her office, sat down, and began to read. It was a copy of the sheriff's obituary. It read:

> My name is Shelly Curtis. Brady Blodgett and I have been close friends since early childhood. We have always lived within a few miles of each other; we worked together for years as rancher neighbors and partnered as deputies locally from the time my husband died until Brady was elected sheriff. As such and as so often happens, we developed an unusually strong bond. His wife Angela, extremely distraught over his violent and untimely death, invited me to write and deliver his

eulogy. I felt extremely honored to be asked to do so; with some degree of difficulty, I herewith comply with her request.

Brady Blaine Blodgett was born on the Fourth of July 1953, in this very same Lombard community. His parents were Edna Blaine and Clarence David Blodgett. Brady, their only child, was joyfully welcomed into their home nearly fifteen years into their marriage. He was ranch raised and learned how to work, and work hard, very early on. He did very well in school, excelled at team sports, and was well liked by teachers and students alike. He completed two years of college, somewhat unusual back in those days, but came home to help his ailing father run their ranch. Brady's remarkable life was tragically ended by the hands of a coward and a murderer when he was but 67 years of age.

Brady entertained a lot of interests and picked up a myriad of varied skills as a young adult. Brady and Angela met on a Christmas hayride in 1973 and married on his birthday that next summer. They were not blessed with children but sought out ways to touch the lives and influence many of the area youth.

Ideally suited for one another, Brady and Angela worked closely together on whatever Brady was doing at the time. For instance, when he first became interested in law enforcement, she immediately became a dispatcher so they could work side by side. When he was elected sheriff, Brady really came into his own. Many unusual situations crossed his path; he had a special God-given gift of discernment that enabled him to accomplish many amazing feats of daring as a peace officer. His personality was such that his colleagues throughout the state learned to know and respect him for his often unorthodox but unarguably successful methods and odd exploits. He frequently traveled to other departments to be of assistance whenever needed.

His loss will be felt statewide. Gone but not forgotten; tales will still be being told of Brady Blaine Blodgett for many years yet to come.

"Sheriff's wife here's to see you," Beats said through the open door.

"Thanks." Jordan put down the paper and braced herself for what was sure to be an emotional meeting. She stepped into the hallway. She couldn't hold the interview in her office since that had been Sheriff Blodgett's office. She'd rather have met with Angela Blodgett in a more neutral and comfortable location, like her sister's home, but since the late sheriff's wife was already on her way back into town when Jordan called her, here was the logical spot.

The woman was standing in the little lobby area, twisting the strap to her purse. Beats had her hand on Mrs. Blodgett's shoulder.

"Mrs. Blodgett?" Jordan said.

The woman turned around. "Oh. You are young."

Jordan brushed the comment aside as best she could and extended her hand. "Detective Gibbons. Thank you for meeting with me. I'm so sorry for your loss. Would you like to go next door and get a coffee, or ...?"

"Call me Angie, and here is fine. I just asked Brendan to clear out for a bit so we could talk." The interim sheriff nodded his assent as he walked out the front door. The late sheriff's wife taking charge of this interview was the last thing Jordan expected. Angela Blodgett wasn't exactly the broken weeping widow she'd expected her to be.

She led Jordan into the sheriff's office and sat down in a chair opposite the desk. Jordan closed the door and instead of sitting in the chair behind the desk, pulled up another one next to the woman.

Angela looked around the office. "I see Brendan hasn't changed much or made himself at home yet. Probably just as well. If Dane Judd has anything to say about it, he won't ever get the chance to call this office his for real."

There was a slew of questions in that one statement but trying to figure out small-town politics and whatever animosity was between the commissioner and the interim sheriff wasn't why Jordan was here. She took a breath and turned to the woman who was looking around the office with controlled sorrow. "I'm sorry to have to bring you in here. I just need to ask a few questions about the night your husband was shot."

"Don't be sorry for doing your job. You're here to figure out who killed Brady. I'll do what I can to help you," Angie said.

"The report said you were at your book club the night the sheriff was killed, and that was a regular thing?"

A small smile played around Angie's lips. "Twice a month, although there was usually a lot more gossiping and wine consumption than book reviewing, but it was a good group. We'd been together for several years."

"And how many people knew you'd be at your book club?" Jordan asked.

"Like I said, we'd been at this for years. Any man who had a wife in the group would know it was going on, friends and relatives probably too. Our book club time was sacred."

"Right." Jordan looked down at her notes, but the only question that stood out was near the bottom, so she moved to that. "You had a dog; do you have any idea what happened to it?"

"Grunion was Brady's dog. I'm more of a cat person. He was a big mastiff mix mutt, loved Brady, tolerated my cats and me."

"And when did Grunion disappear?"

"Two days before Brady died. I came home from the store and the dog was gone."

"Any idea what might have happened to him?" Jordan asked.

Angie peered at her over square-rimmed glasses. "I think whoever killed Brady killed the dog first. Isn't that what you think?"

"Yeah." Jordan felt stupid for even asking, of course that was obvious. "He was a big dog though, right? Any idea how someone got him off your property?"

"Grunion was a big friendly teddy bear, but he knew people. The only way someone bent on doing Brady harm could have gotten him off the property would have been if he was dead."

"Did you ask around after the dog disappeared? Did any of your neighbors see or hear anything?"

"Brady did a complete investigation. As far as I know he didn't turn up anything. No one lives very close."

Jordan was silently cursing the wide countryside and the entire layout of Montana for making this so hard. Neighbors were spread out. Everyone had a truck. Everyone had a gun and lots of space to dispose of a body, dog or human.

"What did your husband do after the dog disappeared?" Jordan asked.

"He went out and bought new locks for all the doors. He told me I should go visit my sister in Missoula. I didn't because like I said, book club is sacred. I didn't think enough of what it meant that the dog was gone, but Brady did."

"He changed the locks, but he still left a key in the birdhouse?" Jordan asked.

"You know about that key?" For the first time Angie looked rattled, like the mention of the hidden key brought something up she hadn't considered before.

"Your nephew Peyton showed it to me."

"No." Angie shook her head. "I was the one who put the new key in the birdhouse. I wasn't accustomed to locking the doors, but Brady insisted I keep them locked. I wanted to make sure I had a way to get back in if I lost the key."

"Did anyone else know about the hidden key?" Jordan asked.

Angie sat for a second, thinking. "My neighbor Rosemarie and as you said, Peyton. He'd fed the animals for us a couple of times when we went on vacation."

"Did you ask him to take care of the cats?"

"I guess he could have taken it on himself, but, no, that didn't come from me."

Jordan made a couple of notes, making a point to investigate Peyton's background.

"Do you know where your husband kept his police issue sidearm when he was home?"

"You mean the gun he was shot with?" Angie's voice was surprisingly strong. "He locked it in the desk drawer."

"The one that was forced open?" Jordan said.

"Yes. I heard that it was broken into, but what I don't understand is how someone got past Brady, forced open that drawer and then shot him without ending up with a gut full of lead. Brady kept a little pistol in the side pocket of his chair."

"Maybe it was taken when he was in another room —maybe the bathroom?" Jordan provided.

"Not likely. Brady was very vigilant, very observant." She shook her head. "He noticed little things. He was good at making people think he was a stupid backwoods redneck, but he was always observing."

Angie's face got far away. "Even when he wasn't on duty, he was always paying attention to what was going on around us. Drove me crazy sometimes. He made a drug bust that way once, one he never got credit for because it was out of his jurisdiction. He was driving home from hunting and saw some lights out in the middle of a field out past Butte. He said he honestly thought for a bit it was a UFO. When he got closer, he realized it was a small plane sitting on what could barely be called an airstrip.

"There were a bunch of men unloading something from the back of the plane. Brady was dressed for hunting, and he was good at not appearing threatening. He walked right up to them and started making conversation. At first, they all clammed up, but after a bit of talking with him they told him straight up that they were running some kind of drugs out of Mexico: marijuana or crack or heroin or something like that. He said they acted like it was a legitimate business; even asked him if he'd like to get in on the action, 'like a damned multilevel marketing scheme' was how he put it. They said they were always looking to open up new sales areas and that he could make some good cash on the side."

"He asked them why they were flying into the middle of a field, and they said they had to keep moving their drops around to stay one step ahead of the moronic, red-necked lawmen that inhabited Montana."

"He chuckled along with them, said he'd think about it, but that he had to get on his way. He laughed all the way to the state patrol office in Butte. He gave the cops there the location of the drop and headed home. He pointed the story out to me in the paper a day or two later. It was just a blip in his life. He was always stumbling onto those kinds of things. He was a good man, a good cop."

Jordan could see the facade of strength that Angie had when she walked in melting before her eyes. She stood and extended her hand to help the woman up.

"I think that's enough for now. I have the notes from the interviews you did already. If there is anything else you can think of that might be helpful ..."

"I know the drill. I worked in this office myself for a few years as a dispatcher after Brady and I got married." Angie took Jordan's extended hand and stood, but she didn't let go. "I heard those words a hundred times, probably more. I never dreamed I'd be on this end." She shook her head. "No. That's not true. I dreamed more than I care to remember of being on this side, of being the one who was mourning and answering hard questions and trying to think of something, anything I could have done differently to have prevented what happened to him." She steeled herself, recovering some of her strength. "Do you have a husband?"

"No," Jordan said.

"Parents?" Angie shook her head. "Of course you do. I'll let you in on a little secret. No matter how proud they appeared to be when you put on that first uniform, they were terrified. And every time they saw you in that uniform thereafter, they were terrified again; terrified that someday all the bad you fought to take out of the world would come back to claim you. For me, the bad walked through my front door and there wasn't anything I could do to stop it." Her dark eyes reached for something in Jordan's soul. "Your job is to stop it from happening again."

Chapter Fifteen

"GOOD MORNING." RAY WAS waiting outside Jordan's office when she came in. "I have good news and bad news. We got the ballistics report from the bullet that was removed from the dog."

She could smell coffee and saw a cup in his hand, the good stuff again. She assumed the bad news outweighed the good. Jordan took the coffee first, guessing she'd need it, then reached for the report. She skimmed it. "You're telling me the bullet that hit the dog was fired from another one of the sheriff's guns?"

"Yeah. I had a hunch, so I took one of the bullets we'd tested in the sheriff's .45 down to Missoula myself. The guys there confirmed both bullets were fired from the same gun."

"Good work, except, weren't all the sheriff's guns taken in as evidence after he died? The dog was shot less than a week ago. How did that—"

"That's the bad news. We don't have the gun. It's gone from the evidence locker."

"Gone?" Jordan looked at Ray incredulously. "Was it returned to the sheriff's wife, or ..."

"It disappeared, probably stolen."

"From the evidence locker?"

"That's what it looks like," Ray said.

"Who has access to that room?" Jordan's frustration was rising.

"Everyone in the office. It's only locked when no one is here," Ray said.

Jordan mentally reviewed what she knew had been collected from the crime scene. "Are you sure it was there? I went over that catalog of evidence. I don't remember seeing a .45 on the list."

"It might not have been processed correctly," Ray admitted. "That was a crazy night. I was the first one on the scene. I remember seeing that gun in particular. Blodgett kept it in a case behind his desk. I assumed it was picked up with the rest of the weapons."

"You weren't the one who processed it?"

"No, ma'am."

"What kind of lax operation is this? One of you didn't take it out for target practice and leave it somewhere, did you?" Jordan said.

"No," Ray said shortly.

"The murder weapon, the sheriff's revolver, that hasn't disappeared too, has it?"

She could see there was more he wanted to say, but all he said was "No," again. Ray appeared to be better at holding his tongue than she was.

She took a breath, processing what her next step needed to be. "If the gun was never taken in as evidence, how did you do ballistics testing on it?"

"Every gun owned by a member of the sheriff's department undergoes ballistics testing. We keep a database and a catalog of bullets. That's the first place we check when a crime is committed with a gun. Doesn't matter if it's poaching, petty vandalism, or murder. Blodgett wanted to make sure our department was above board on everything."

Jordan sighed and took a long drink of her coffee. From the lobby she heard a familiar voice. "Hey, Becca, I need to have a few words with our little detective woman." The voice belonged to Commissioner Judd.

Jordan swore under her breath. "I have to get to Anaconda. I'm meeting with the missing woman's former roommate. I don't have time to deal with him."

"Go out the back door. I'll take care of Judd," Ray said.

"Thanks." It was an unexpected and welcome save. Jordan almost regretted what she'd said to Ray before, even if he'd probably lost the one solid piece of evidence they had in this case.

"Detective Gibbons stepped out for an interview," Ray said as she closed the door behind her. Jordan breathed a sigh of relief as soon as she was back in her truck. It was stupid and childish for her to avoid Judd and let Ray take the heat from him, but she didn't have it in her to try to play nice with him today.

Crystal Vix lived in a seedy apartment in a town called Anaconda. In Jordan's opinion it was a completely ridiculous name for a little Montana town where there had never been anything like a giant snake. Whatever the reason for the name, Crystal had lived there with Sadie Larsen for almost six months before she moved to Lombard.

"You found her yet?" was the first thing Crystal said when she opened the door to let Jordan in.

"Not yet." Jordan sat on a faded and stained floral couch and Crystal sat opposite her. The contrast between this place and Sadie's perfectly kept apartment was glaring. She wondered how the two women had managed to live together for so long. "If there's anything you can tell me that might help find her, I'd appreciate it."

Crystal nodded. Her hair was colored so bright a red that it was nearly purple. Her low-cut black T-shirt barely contained her ample breasts. Her bloodshot eyes were rimmed with dark eyeliner that looked freshly applied, and her hands were twitchy. It was hard to tell whether she was nervous and had been crying or if she was high on something.

"Did Sadie tell you why she decided to move to Lombard?"

Crystal nodded enthusiastically. "Yeah. She needed a fresh start."

"Fresh start? What was she leaving behind her?" Jordan said.

"She broke up with her boyfriend."

"What was the boyfriend's name?"

Crystal picked at a loose thread on one of the couch cushions. "I don't know. I never met him. They hadn't been dating long. I heard him here one night, just before she left. They were screaming at each other."

"Was he threatening her?"

"I guess so." Crystal didn't sound sure.

"You guess so? Did he say anything that could have been construed as a concrete threat?"

"The only thing I remember him saying was, 'Stay away from him,'" Crystal said. "Everything else was kind of muddled. They were out here, and I was in my bedroom. I don't like getting in the middle when people are fighting."

"Do you know who Sadie's boyfriend might have been talking about? Who did he want Sadie to stay away from?"

"I bet it was another guy." Crystal said it earnestly, like it was an important piece of information.

Jordan forced herself to stay patient. "Do you have anything else on Sadie's boyfriend? A phone number? An address? Where he works?"

Crystal shook her head with each question. "It was a short fling. Sadie's usually were. Anyway, she'd already found someone else, somebody from Lombard. I think that might have been the guy they were fighting about. The one Sadie's boyfriend told her to stay away from."

Jordan felt like she was finally getting something useful. "Someone who lives in Lombard? Did Sadie tell you what his name was?"

The woman pressed her index fingers to her temples. "Willie? Walter? I'm pretty sure it started with a W."

Jordan was getting frustrated with the lack of attention Crystal appeared to pay to anything. "Did she give you a description of him?"

"She said he was gorgeous, that he had the prettiest gray eyes. She met him at a bar here in town."

A cold feeling settled in the pit of Jordan's stomach. "Could his name have been Whit?"

"Maybe?" Crystal didn't seem sure of anything.

Jordan let out a breath. "How long ago did she meet this guy?"

"Couple of months." The woman thought for a minute. "Yeah, at least three months ago. She said he invited her to move over to Lombard. That it would be easier for her to work on her case."

"Her case?" Jordan asked, even though she could guess what Crystal was talking about.

"Yeah, Sadie liked to play detective. She had all these cold cases she was looking into. She's really smart."

"Do you know what particular case she'd been working on?"

"No."

"But it had to do with Lombard?"

"I think so," Crystal said.

"Maybe the Bonnie Golden case?"

"Maybe?" Crystal's eyes went wide.

Definitely on something, Jordan thought. She stood up, trying not to show how frustrated she was. "Did she talk about this new guy like they were in a relationship, or was it just something hopeful on her part?"

"Sounded like a relationship, but like I said, her relationships never lasted very long. She was pretty enough to attract a lot of attention from guys, but not good at holding onto them. I think it's the type of guy she went after. They were never good for her. Like Mike."

"Mike?"

The girl covered her mouth, like she'd just remembered something. "Oh. Mike."

"Who is Mike?"

Crystal was suddenly animated. "That was the name of her boyfriend. I heard her yell his name. She said, 'I'll do this on my own if I have to, Mike.'"

"Do what?" Jordan asked.

"She didn't say. The next thing I heard was the door slamming shut." She screwed up her face like it took a lot of effort to remember anything. "But there was another guy named Mike. This guy in prison she was writing to. Sadie was kind of obsessed with true crime stuff. She even talked about taking classes in criminal justice. And she wrote to prisoners, said she could get them to talk to her. She wanted to be someone like ... well, someone like you. Maybe that's where it came from. Anyway, I remember there was a Mike who was in jail. She wrote to him a lot."

"Any idea if they were the same Mike?" Jordan asked, even though the question seemed obvious.

"Maybe?" Crystal looked at Jordan as if she could supply a definitive answer.

"Do you have a last name on this guy? Or do you remember what jail he was in?" Jordan asked without much hope.

"No. But she left the letters here. They were under the bed in her room when my new roommate moved in. I meant to give them back to Sadie, but I didn't get the chance." Crystal untangled herself from the couch and moved to the back bedroom.

Jordan wondered why the letters weren't the first thing Crystal had thought of, but then again, Crystal appeared to have the attention span of a goldfish.

"Here they are. I don't know if this is all of them." Crystal handed her a file box full of letters. Like everything in Sadie's basement apartment, the letters were in an organized file.

"Was Sadie still writing to this guy when she moved out?"

"I don't think so."

"Maybe because he got out of jail, and she was seeing him in person?" Jordan asked, hoping to trigger another burst of memory from Crystal.

"Maybe?" Crystal said.

Frustrated, Jordan stood. "If you think of anything that might help me find either the new boyfriend or the old boyfriend, please let me know." She reached for her business card, then realized she didn't have any here with her current information. "Do you have something I could write my phone number down on?"

"Sure." Crystal stood up and opened a drawer in the kitchen. After rummaging through it for a few minutes she brought back a crumpled piece of paper that had been torn from the same pad of paper that was in Sadie's new apartment. The one with a line of pineapples at the bottom of each page.

Jordan took the paper, but before she wrote her name, she saw a rough sketch on the back, wavy lines and what looked like mountains. "Did you draw this or did Sadie?"

Crystal looked down at the piece of paper. "Had to be Sadie. She had a thing for pineapples."

"Can I take it with me?"

"Sure." Crystal said. "Sadie had bunches of drawings like that."

"Do you know where the rest of them are?"

"I might have thrown them away." Crystal looked around the apartment, but from the looks of it, she had never thrown anything away.

"Do you know what she was trying to draw?"

Crystal shook her head. "Sadie didn't tell me much about what she was doing."

Jordan wrote her number on another piece of paper—one she was sure Crystal would lose immediately. Then she bagged up the letters and the piece of paper. She wasn't sure if either of them would lead to anything, but with so little to go on, she had to start with something.

Chapter Sixteen

JORDAN SCANNED ANOTHER ONE of Sadie's letters from a man named Greg. The Mike Sadie's roommate had mentioned wasn't the only convict whose correspondence filled Sadie's file box. Greg was talking about someone he'd shared a cell with. Someone who'd showed him a map of gold somewhere in Montana. He was bragging that he could replicate the map and that he would send it to her.

Jordan had gained an odd respect for Sadie through reading the one-sided conversations that came from the men who were in a jail somewhere. The letters were all printed out emails, but for the most part, Sadie had only printed the body of the email. Few showed any indication of where the convicts were being held or contained more than a first name. The answers that came from the convicts showed that Sadie had mastered the art of getting hardened men to open up and deceitful men to tell the truth.

Jordan had read through all the letters from Mike last night. Those qualified as love letters more than any of the other ones. Almost every man had asked Sadie to send photos, and there were even a few "after I get out" proposals, but Mike, whoever he was, seemed sincere. He was the only one who sounded like he really cared about Sadie. His last letter was handwritten and ended with, "I can't wait to see you in person. Two more weeks."

"Looks like you're up to your neck in it again."

Jordan looked up from the pile of Sadie's correspondence to see Chris, the waitress who had served her before, standing beside the table.

"Sheldon said to bring you this on the house, and to apologize for making you wait." Chris set a cup of coffee and a blueberry muffin on the table in front of her.

Jordan had made an appointment with the Silver Horseshoe's owner, Sheldon Miles, to ask him about Sadie and question any of the staff who had worked with her. She'd made the appointment early in the morning, hoping not to see anyone else from town. Unfortunately, the restaurant was full of early risers.

"Thanks."

"That looks like Sadie's handwriting." Chris gestured to the word "Private" written on the top of the file box.

"It is." Jordan looked up at the waitress. "Did you work with her a lot?"

"Not much. Sheldon likes to put the pretty waitresses on at night, since they bring in a lot of business. I work mostly days."

"You're pretty," Jordan said. It was true. Chris had a friendly smile, pretty eyes, and gorgeous blonde hair.

Chris waved her away. "Thanks for saying it, but I'm old news. The guys around here are more interested in the endless revolving door of pretty girls Sheldon brings in. He has this whole system. He keeps track of who sits at what table, who the waitress is, how long the guy lingers, what they order, how much they tip. He pays a bonus based on what we bring in. He calls it a 'commission.' He actively scouts for waitresses. We're a small-town bar, but we get our share of out-of-towners."

"That's incredibly sexist and basically terrible."

Chris shrugged, like it was no big deal. "It must work for him. He's driving a new truck and heading out of town every other weekend. Days work out better for me anyway. I can be at work when my kid is at school."

"You have a kid?" Jordan asked. Chris was about the same age as Jordan. For her to have a child, especially one who was old enough to be in school, was a little surprising.

"Yep. A little boy. His name is Trey." Chris pulled her phone out of her apron pocket and showed Jordan a towheaded little boy who was missing one of his front teeth.

"He's cute. He has your eyes." Jordan said. She gestured to the other side of the booth. "Can you sit for a minute?"

"Is this an official interrogation?" Chris asked warily, already sitting down.

"Something like that." Jordan swept the papers into the box and put the lid back on. "How long had Sadie worked here?"

"A couple of months. She came from Anaconda."

"Do you know why she left there?"

"She said something about a bad relationship and that she wanted to make a new start. Honestly, the same thing we get from most of the waitresses who come from out of town. None of them seem to stay long."

"Did you ever see her with any guy in particular?" Jordan asked.

Chris bit her front lip, hesitating for a minute. "Besides the crowd who monopolize the pool table in the back? No, not really."

Jordan thought she was avoiding the question. She thought her next question through carefully. "She didn't mention coming here to meet someone?"

"She said—"

"Chris, the tables are stacking up." Sheldon, the owner of the restaurant stood at Chris' shoulder. "You can talk to the detective on your own time."

Chris slipped from the booth, blushing, and ducking her head, but there was also an expression of relief on her face. "Sorry."

Jordan extended her hand. "Mr. Miles, thank you for meeting with me."

"Call me Sheldon." He smiled and shook her hand, but there was the same wariness about him that Jordan had sensed from a lot of the locals. "Let's go talk in the back." He nodded to the blueberry muffin. "You can bring that if you'd like."

"No, thanks. I appreciate the gesture, but I don't need that much sugar this early in the morning."

"Good girl. A lot of women don't know how to pass up things that aren't good for them." He glanced at Chris when he said it.

Jordan followed him into the office, steamed at what he'd just implied. She reminded herself for what felt like the millionth time here that she needed to act like a professional.

"How long did Sadie worked here?" she asked, after settling into a chair in his backroom office.

"A couple of months."

"What did you know about her when she came?" Jordan asked.

Sheldon leaned back in his chair. "Not a lot. She'd waitressed before and had okay references. She told me she was coming to Lombard to make a clean start. She was friendly and pretty easy on the eyes, the kind of girl who would bring in business and make guys linger over their drinks."

Again, Jordan had to remind herself to be professional. "Do you remember any particular guys lingering over their drinks? Anyone she talked to or spent more time with than normal?"

Sheldon looked toward the ceiling as if he were thinking or maybe avoiding her gaze. "I'm sure there were a lot—it always happens with a pretty new girl—but I don't know specifics. I don't get into any kind of personal business with the girls who work for me. You'd have to ask the other waitresses."

Jordan leaned closer, trying to get him to meet her eyes. "Really? I heard a rumor that you kept pretty close tabs on who waited on who and how much your customers spend, based on the waitresses' appearance."

He smiled and leaned against the desk like he was proud of himself. "That's just good business."

"So who lingered over Sadie's table?" Jordan said.

"Pretty much every man who walked through that door. She was pretty, sure, but she was also a sweet talker, brought in a lot of business. It was a damn shame when she disappeared."

"That must have been hard for you." Jordan fought to keep the sarcasm out of her voice. "When did you first notice she was gone?"

"The second or third day she didn't show up for a shift. I was out of town the first couple of days, and I think Chris covered for her, wanted to keep her out of trouble."

"Did you call the police or file a missing person's report?"

"No. Didn't even think about it. I figured she'd drifted in, and she'd drifted out. I wasn't happy about it, but I didn't think there was anything to it."

"Did she ever give any indication that she didn't feel safe?" Jordan asked.

Sheldon paused like he was thinking. "I know she didn't like walking home by herself. A lot of times she'd get a ride from one of the other girls. A couple of times some guy picked her up."

"Can you describe him, or describe his car?"

"It was a Ford F150, but that doesn't narrow it down much. He wore a cowboy hat, again not something that narrows things down much. He looked kind of tallish." Sheldon shrugged helplessly. "Again, you might get more from one of my other girls."

"Is there anyone else you saw her with?"

"Lots of different guys, like I said. Sadie was pretty and friendly. I was sad to see her go."

One of the other waitresses leaned into the office. "Sheldon, the supplier is here. He needs your signature."

"Sure thing." Sheldon nodded to Jordan. "Give me a minute."

As soon as he was gone, Jordan noticed a black binder on the side of his desk. It had to be the book Chris had told her about. Jordan glanced around and then flipped through it quickly. She found Sadie's name, along with the days she'd worked and a notation of who she'd served and how much they'd spent. The whole thing was distasteful, but Jordan had to give Sheldon credit for how thorough he was. He even had a notation alongside some of the customers' names that said, "Coffee. Black."

Jordan hadn't been here that long, but it seemed like a lot of the names didn't sound like family names native to Lombard. If that was right, there were quite a few people coming to the Horseshoe from out of town. Whit's name on the page caused Jordan to pause. In the margin next to his name Sheldon had written 'lingered' and then 'drove her home?'"

Sheldon's heavy footsteps caused Jordan to flip the book closed, grateful everyone here wore boots. "Sorry about that," he said.

"No problem."

"Now, where were we?" Instead of taking his seat behind the desk, Sheldon perched on the edge, leaning over Jordan.

She wanted to stand and face him, but she stayed in her seat. "You were telling me who lingered over drinks when Sadie was waitressing."

He smiled. "I already told you, sweetheart. Lots of men. I couldn't narrow it down."

Again, Jordan got the idea that he was hiding something, maybe what she'd just read in his ledger. She wished she'd been able to get a longer look at it. She stood. "If you think of anything, call me."

"I will. And if you ever get tired of detective work, give me a call. You're the kind of woman who would make men linger over their drinks too." He smiled like he was giving her a compliment.

Jordan tightened her hand into a fist and pretended she didn't see his outstretched hand. "Thank you for your time, Mr. Miles." She stepped out the door before she did something stupid.

She had almost made it all the way out of the restaurant when Chris intercepted her. Jordan hoped she was planning to finish whatever thought she'd started earlier. Instead, she said. "Hey, there's a rodeo this weekend. My mom already agreed to babysit, but I don't want to go alone."

Jordan looked over her shoulder at Sheldon coming out of his office. She thought about what Chris had to put up with, being a single mom and working with a man like him. Chris probably didn't get the chance to go out much. As much as Jordan disliked the idea of a rodeo, it might be a good way to get Chris to open up more. "Sounds like fun."

"Great. Give me your number and I'll text you with the details." Chris sounded genuinely excited. She wrote Jordan's number on an order pad. "See you Friday!"

"Yeah, see you." Jordan couldn't believe she'd just agreed to go to a rodeo.

Chapter Seventeen

"MICHAEL HUBBARD." Ray set a page of notes on Jordan's desk. He'd been scouring databases of criminals in search of the elusive Mike.

"Who is this guy?" Jordan asked.

"One of the men Sadie was writing to. He was initially convicted of armed robbery and assault with a deadly weapon three years ago. He was suspected of a lot more, but not convicted of anything beyond the robbery until six months ago."

"Any connection to Lombard? The name sounds familiar," Jordan said.

"It should. But not because of Lombard. You helped put him on trial."

"What?" Jordan picked up the file. "I haven't had that many cases. I wouldn't have forgotten."

"You weren't directly involved with his case, but you helped uncover evidence from another case that led to his conviction."

"What was he convicted of?" Jordan asked.

"Murdering an old girlfriend. It's a guess, but it's a good one."

"In a twisted way, that makes sense. Her roommate said Sadie wanted to be some kind of detective," Jordan said.

"You think she got mixed up with a convict she shouldn't have?" Ray asked.

"Could be, but not this one." Jordan scanned the papers he'd handed her. "I don't think this is our Mike. He's still behind bars. It has to be someone who's already gotten out. If what I read last night was any indication, Sadie wasn't good at keeping any kind of distance between herself and the guys she was writing to. He talked about them getting together after he got out. He said in a couple of weeks."

"So how do we figure out who that might be?" Ray asked.

"It's going to take some combing."

"Sounds like a project we could work on over super at the Horseshoe, my treat," Ray suggested.

Jordan looked up from the papers. She had the distinct impression Ray had just asked her out. "Not a good idea. It will entail a lot of phone calls and as I've discovered, there isn't much in the way of privacy at the Horseshoe."

"I could go pick up something and we could work here. I don't mind staying late." Ray looked up at her hopefully.

She raised her eyes to meet his, deciding that subtlety wasn't a language Ray understood. "Also not a good idea. I make it a point not to get involved with people I work with."

"That must be a new thing." Sheriff Carlyle walked into Jordan's office. "I need a minute with the detective."

"Sure," Ray said, but he stood up grudgingly and glowered at Carlyle on his way out. Jordan hadn't missed the lack of love between those two. It made sense, given that they would both be competing for the open position of sheriff in a few months when the election rolled around.

"What can I help you with?" Jordan asked as Carlyle closed the door.

"First, the results came back on the blood. It does belong to Sadie Larsen. I'm calling for a full-fledged search, something we should have done the minute we found the dog."

"Finally." Jordan stood. "What do we need to do to make this happen?"

"Sit down for a second." He looked down on her with a piercing gaze and she sat. "I talked to a friend I went to school with who works as a deputy for Snohomish County."

Jordan sucked in a breath. Snohomish was a bordering county to King County, where Seattle was. "Someone I might know?" she said casually.

"Not sure. But he had heard your name in relation to a little bit of a scandal in the Seattle Police Department."

Jordan forced herself to meet his gaze. "And?"

"I'm not asking you to confirm or deny it. I just want you to know that that won't fly around here."

"Fly?" Jordan could feel her face going red, more with fury at his accusation than with embarrassment.

"The last thing this sheriff's department needs is a romantic scandal. Ray isn't even all the way divorced yet."

"Really? You think I would ever ... with Ray?" Jordan tried to bite her tongue against everything she wanted to say to him. It didn't work. There had been too many things in the last few days that made her want to strike back.

She stood. "There's a woman out there who's been missing for over a week, and we finally got the go-ahead to start looking for her, but instead of getting the ball rolling on a search party, you decide to warn me about how I behave around the men in this office? I've been busting my butt since I got here, trying to find some kind of lead, and you've been spending your time digging into something that isn't relevant and frankly is none of your business."

"Jordan." Carlyle's voice had a warning note in it.

"That's Detective Gibbons, and I have work to do." She pushed back her chair and stormed out of her own office, too furious to think about where she was going.

She walked to the front of the station. She needed to get to work, to prove that she could solve this thing, but she had no idea what it took to organize a search party in this county. Beats would know. Jordan was positive Beats knew more about what happened in this office than any of them.

"Detective Gibbons, there's—" Jordan ignored Becca's greeting as she continued to the dispatcher's office.

The door was open and the radio was silent. Beats turned to face Jordan. "What's got you so—"

Unable to hold it in any longer, Jordan blurted out, "Why are all the men in this town such—"

"Hello, Commissioner." Beats cut Jordan off with a wide smile for whoever was standing behind her.

Jordan froze. The last person she wanted to see was Judd. It seemed he was constantly looking over her shoulder.

"Detective." It was Whit's voice behind her. "Sorry to interrupt, but Shelly told me you were interested in all the places that had been recently sprayed for thistles."

She turned to face him, forcing her expression back to something more neutral.

"I put together a map of the most likely locations, based on when they were sprayed in relation to when Sadie Larsen disappeared. I think our best bet is to head back up to Rattlesnake and start the search there."

Chapter Eighteen

Whit's truck was at the trailhead of Rattlesnake Ridge, joining the gathering group who'd come to search. He was standing next to the same black and white horse they'd ridden up before: Scout, Jordan remembered. This time there was a smaller horse next to his, a palomino like the one that used to live across the fence from her grandpa's house. Both horses were saddled and ready to go.

"Detective." Whit tipped his hat as Jordan approached. "Shelly asked me to bring an extra horse. Goldie's for you. She's really gentle. Just stay close to me, and you'll be fine."

Jordan backed away. "No. Thank you. I have one of the department's ATVs."

"Are you sure? There are places up here that an ATV can't get to, and I assume a horse would do a lot less damage when it comes to preserving any kind of evidence we might find."

"I'm sure." Even as she said it, Jordan knew Whit was right. She surveyed the growing crowd. There were too many people and too many ATVs and horses traipsing all over the mountain. Not to mention the cattle that had been grazing up here for the past week. If there was evidence to be found, it would almost certainly be destroyed. Of course, the most important thing was finding Sadie, if by some miracle she was still alive. If she wasn't alive, the sooner they found her body the sooner this could be turned into a murder investigation.

Sheriff Carlyle climbed in the back of a pickup to give directions to the searchers "Deputy Harding is passing out search grids. Please stay within your designated search areas. If you come upon anything that looks suspicious, don't touch it. Radio one of us and we'll come take a look."

"What are we looking for?" someone from the gathered crowd yelled. "The woman, a body, or a murderer?"

Jordan jumped in to answer. "An article of clothing, a torn piece of cloth, shell casings, anything. Please tread as lightly as possible. This whole area could be a crime scene."

"I thought this was a search and rescue operation?" another man from the crowd yelled.

"It is." Sheriff Carlyle gave Jordan a dark look. He didn't seem to like her jumping in on his turf. "We have to go with the assumption that we're looking for a woman who might be in trouble. Finding her is paramount."

Jordan walked back to where the ATVs were parked, passing Whit on the way. He was tightening the cinch on Scout's saddle. "Any chance we'll find her alive?" he asked.

"It would have been better if we'd started immediately, but there's always a chance." Jordan said. "But if it was the same person who did this before ..."

"Yeah. Let's hope it's not." Whit swung up on Scout and followed the rest of the searchers toward the top of the hill.

Jordan turned back to the place where the county vehicles had been parked, but all the four wheelers had been claimed and were halfway up the mountain. She stood for a second, dumbfounded that she'd been left behind. She picked up her radio to yell at someone; she just wasn't sure who.

Shelly drove up in her mule. "Need a lift, Detective?"

Jordan was more than a little put out that she had to find her own ride, but she didn't have any other options. "Thanks." She climbed in the mule. "And thanks for asking Whit to help figure out where to search."

"No problem. I figured you were pretty busy chasing down leads." Shelly put the mule into gear, moving away from the crowd, toward the path they'd taken before.

"I was. I am," Jordan said. "Any way you could go up the other path? I feel like if we go this way, everyone will beat us to the top."

"This is a search, not a race. We're just as likely to find something down here as we are at the top." Even as she said it, Shelly pushed the mule to move faster. "How's it going? Have you found out anything yet?"

Jordan hesitated, but she needed a sounding board. "That the sheriff's department is pretty lax on evidence preservation."

"Sounds like there's a story behind that one."

"The gun that shot the dog was Blodgett's."

"So the cases are connected?"

"Maybe. It was Blodgett's gun, but it was likely taken from our own evidence room, some time between the sheriff's murder and the dog getting shot. No one knows anything about how that might have happened. I can't prove much without a weapon."

"That is a problem. What else have you found out?"

"There are a whole lot of people in this town who aren't very observant. No one I've talked to seems to know anything about anything."

Shelly smirked. "Maybe you aren't asking the right questions, or at least not asking them in the right way."

Jordan wasn't in the mood to be lectured. "I'm doing everything I can, but people aren't very forthcoming with information. And the men in this town ..." Jordan shook her head. "Maybe if I dressed like a guy." She was hoping for sympathy from the former officer. Shelly had to have encountered this kind of thing in her career.

"It seems to me that the men in this town are more likely to open up to a pretty young woman."

"That's exactly the problem. They don't take me seriously," Jordan said.

"Are you taking them seriously?"

"What's that supposed to mean?" Jordan asked.

Shelly concentrated on the trail ahead for a minute. "If you come off as arrogant, like you already know everything before you ask, people are going to be less forthcoming."

"Arrogant? Because I know my job?"

"You're a smart woman, good at looking at evidence and figuring things out, but when it comes to talking to people, at least the people around here, maybe you come off as too smart."

Jordan stared at her, incredulous, "You want me to play the dumb broad and bat my eyes to get guys to open up to me?"

Shelly pulled the mule to a stop and turned to look at Jordan. "No. I want you to play the respectful detective looking for information. You're off your territory here. Admit you don't have all the answers and you need help. The men in this town, the women too, know their business. Most of them have had to grow up hard, one way or another. They're not going to be impressed with your brand of intelligence. When you question someone, they're the expert, not you. You need to acknowledge that." Shelly put the mule in gear and headed back up the path.

Jordan sat in silence. Shelly's words stung. She'd been doing the best she could, asking the right questions, being professional. Arrogant? Could she help it if she was smarter than most of the people here?

After a few minutes of silence Shelly spoke again. "What have you found out about the missing girl?"

Jordan shook off the hurt. "She was some kind of amateur detective, interested in cold cases. She has all these files in her apartment, probably twenty or more cases, and she's dug up a ton of information. I went through all of them. She didn't have one on the Bonnie Golden case, or if she did, someone took it."

Shelly suddenly swerved off the path. Jordan gripped the edge of the mule to keep from falling out. "Where are we going?"

"Short cut. I've been running cattle up here since I was a little girl. I know all the side paths to the top." The path they'd moved onto was not much of a path. It was rockier and steeper, and Jordan had to hold on to the side roll bars on the mule to keep from bouncing off her seat. She was starting to think it would have been safer to ride up on Whit's horse. "You did say you were in a hurry to get to the top, didn't you?"

"Yeah. But I was kind of hoping to make it in one piece."

"Haven't lost anyone yet. Just hang on." Shelly shifted again as the trail got steeper. "You think she might have been getting close? That maybe she got too close, and someone came after her?"

Jordan gripped the edge of her seat. "That's the going theory."

"And Blodgett too?" Shelly asked.

"Yeah," Jordan said.

"Who do you think did it?"

"I don't know," Jordan admitted. "Sadie was writing to a bunch of convicts. Maybe it was one of them."

"You think she stumbled on someone who had something to do with the Golden case before?"

"If she did, I haven't found out who it was yet, but I only have half the conversation and I'm missing a lot of information."

"What's your next step?"

"Combing through about a million prison records. Trying to figure out who all she was writing to."

"That doesn't sound like a lot of fun."

"And digging through your garden."

"That sounds worse," Shelly said. She stopped the mule.

"What are we doing here?" Jordan said.

"Waiting for the rest of them to catch up. This is where Whit started his project." Shelly climbed out and turned toward the valley. "Sure is a beautiful view."

Jordan got out, but she looked at the ground. This part of the ridge was covered with dead and dying purple-colored thistles, and in the middle of it were a bunch of footprints. There were three sets of prints. Two were cowboy boots, one large and one small, and the third set of prints were sneakers. Jordan got out to photograph them.

"Those are probably Whit's." Shelly pointed to the large set of boot prints. "See how he stands back and stays out of the dye. He knows not to get too close."

"The smaller boot prints might be Tawny's, but she had it on her hands, so I'd bet she picked it up when she was working on the fence, over on the other side." Shelly gestured to a shaded area. "Also, the dye was still wet. This up here is in the sun. It would have dried by the time we brought the cows up."

"Right. If any of them are Sadie's prints, they're probably the sneakers. I didn't get the idea she was much of a cowgirl," Jordan said. She scanned the area until she found purple markings on a big boulder. "Someone got the dye all over themselves and then went this way." She took more photos and then climbed over the rock, following the trail.

A figure in a plaid shirt crouched on the other side of the rock.

Jordan froze, her hand on her gun. "Sadie?"

The face that turned toward Jordan's was that of a teenage boy. For some reason, he looked familiar.

Shelly finished crawling over the rock behind Jordan. "Peyton, what the hell are you doing all the way up here?"

Jordan recognized the boy from Blodgett's barn. "I came to help with the search. I went on ahead, hoping I could find something. I came back behind the rock because I needed to pee, but I found this." His chalk-white face made it clear that even though he said he'd wanted to find something, actually finding it had shaken him.

Jordan moved closer to what the boy was looking at. It was another scrap of fabric, soaked in blood and wrapped around another bone.

"Peyton, why don't you join the other searchers," Shelly said gently.

The boy nodded and headed down the trail.

Jordan slid on a pair of gloves and got down on one knee to examine the bone. It was the other femur to match the first one. The fabric this time was denim. She touched the blood gingerly with a gloved finger.

Jordan looked at the stream of horses coming up over the ridge. She keyed her radio. "Hold everyone back there. We need to keep this area contained."

"Did you find something?" Sheriff Carlyle's voice came through the radio.

"Yes," Jordan answered.

"Is it the girl?"

"No."

"Hold there. I'll be up in a minute."

Shelly stepped closer. "This blood is too fresh to have come from someone who died a week ago. This has been out here less than a day. Either she's being kept alive somewhere, was killed recently, or we have another victim."

Jordan looked at Shelly. She keyed the radio again. "Tell everyone to stay back, but to keep searching. There's a possibility she's alive."

Sheriff Carlyle reached them as Jordan bagged up the cloth. "How soon can we find out if this is Sadie's blood?" she asked.

"Couple of days, if we ask for a rush and pay to have someone fly it directly to Missoula," he said.

"Do it," Jordan answered. "I don't care what Judd says about that cost. Take the bone too. Not as big of a rush—we know that victim is dead." She stood, looking over the searchers on horseback knocking through the brush on the other side of the trail. She couldn't shake the feeling that Judd's delay had cost Sadie her life.

Chapter Nineteen

WHIT LAZILY HALF-SAT, HALF-LAY on the bank of the main irrigation ditch, whittling a whistle from a switch off the willow he was resting under. Its shade provided welcome respite from the sun. The weather was hot for this time of year. Having volunteered to irrigate his friend and neighbor's hay and grain crops so he could spend three days visiting his son and family, Whit waited for his latest dam set of water to soak to the bottom of the field.

Whit found irrigating to be a pleasant, quiet time and ideal for just thinking things over and sorting things out. Uppermost on his mind were the changes he'd undergone since Jordan's appearance in Keystone County. He was only beginning to realize what a profound and puzzling affect the feisty Seattle-based, big-city detective had wrought on his whole way of thinking. Jordan arrived in Montana carrying a heavy load of disdain for all things Montana. That preconceived negative mindset made her difficult to work with and was hindering her investigation of the sheriff's murder. She was frustrated, but so were the locals.

Whit passionately loved everything about his home state and could not even imagine ever living anywhere else. Montana was high, wide, and handsome—so diverse—and it had something and some place for everyone. Rolling hills, plains as flat as a platter, high mountains; grasslands, dense forest, farmland, and prime grazing for livestock and wildlife of every kind—even badlands comparable to those of North and South Dakota. With all of that in Montana's favor, he couldn't fathom why she seemed to dislike his marvelous state, the people, and the ways of life of Montana. But he supposed he might feel the same way about Seattle if he were suddenly transplanted there. What her presence had done for him was to greatly enhance his appreciation for the very same things she found so distasteful. The other thing that gave him pause to wonder at was why did it even matter to him what she thought, either one way or another?

He got up, shouldering his shovel and moving back to check the dams, trying to keep busy so his mind would stop wandering. It didn't work. Jordan Gibbons was beautiful; any man in town could see that. Every man in town had seen that. Even though she'd more than proven she could take care of herself, Whit still felt protective of her. He'd felt that on the trail up to Rattlesnake and at the Silver Horseshoe when Grant was hitting on her. Not that Grant was that much of a threat, even if he looked it.

But there was someone in this town who was a threat, and Whit was at least partially responsible for putting Jordan on the trail of a ruthless killer—and possibly responsible for putting that killer on her trail. He had to admit she was doing a credible job of investigating a case that kept taking unexpected twists and turns and expanding in scope by distressing leaps and bounds. One murder had likely escalated into two, and more murders seemed not only possible, but very probable.

He closed his eyes, remembering his unexpected trip the month before and the disruption to his quiet life caused by one phone call and the revelations from the past it contained. He couldn't shake the feeling that it was all related. Now not just his own life, but his peaceful little town was embroiled in turmoil. Fear increased every day that went by without answers. Would others become future victims of the rampage? And who? The very way of life of their small community was being compromised.

When and where would it all end?

A nagging voice wondered how much of this was his fault.

He should have told Shelly the truth from the beginning. Maybe if he explained everything now ... He sank his shovel into the soft earth on the ditch bank, then tossed a shovelful behind him. He couldn't ask her to help him now. It was too late. What was done was done. He only hoped the past would stay buried.

The task before him finished, Whit jerked his shovel up and slung it against his shoulder. His stint irrigating had given him too much time for thinking. Ordinarily he was comfortable with his own thoughts but now he longed for the company of others and getting back to more normal activities. He needed some distraction with less stressful issues.

Rodeo season was about to commence, and he was looking forward to that diversion—even more so than he did every year. Maybe that would give him some relief. The thought put him in a better mood. He even whistled a bit as he strode back to his truck. He didn't notice the figure standing at the edge of the field until the painfully familiar voice said, "Hey."

Whit stopped mid-whistle and stared for a few minutes before he found the voice to address the man in front of him. "I thought I'd never see you again."

"I'm afraid it's not going to be as easy as you thought to get rid of me."

Chapter Twenty

IT HAD BEEN A long week. The search on Rattlesnake hadn't turned up anything else. Ray's combing through files of convicts hadn't either. Jordan still had plenty of work to do, but when Chris called, she decided to go ahead with their plan to go to the rodeo. She thought about what Shelly said about her not knowing anything about the people around here. Maybe attending the rodeo would give her a better idea of what Montanans were like.

"I can't believe you've never been to a rodeo," Chris said for about the tenth time as they walked through the gate to the dusty fairgrounds.

"They have them in Washington but not really in Seattle, and honestly, I never really saw the point," Jordan said.

"You're in for it." Beats had joined them at the grandstand. "A rodeo is not like any sporting event you've ever seen before."

"I know the gist of it," Jordan said, feeling like she needed to defend her lack of rodeo acumen. "I've seen clips of it on TV—bull riding and that kind of thing, right?"

"Yeah, but there is so much more to the rodeo than bull riding," Beats said. "Although that's usually the most exciting event."

"My favorite event is cowboy watching. Unofficial, of course," Chris added with a toss of her high ponytail.

Jordan followed them up the stairs to the stands that flanked a wide arena. The air was warm, the first hints of real summer coming through. It smelled like greasy hamburgers, dust and manure. "Did it already start?" Jordan asked as they took their seats. Something was being announced over the loudspeaker.

"Nah, just the mutton busting," Beats said. "They pad a kid up, put a helmet on him and set him on a wild sheep."

"Speaking of cowboy watching." Chris nodded to the edge of the arena. A muscular cowboy leaned over the next "mutton busting" contestant. He was strapping a helmet to the kid's head. The man had his back to them, but when he led the boy or girl (it was hard to tell with so much padding) to the chute, Jordan recognized Whit's familiar limp. She wondered if it was from the ankle he broke during his short bull riding career.

"Gorgeous, tough—good with kids and horses, what more could you ask for in a man?" Chris asked.

"Interest," Beats said.

"Hey." Chris shot back a hurt look.

"It's not just you. Whit doesn't seem to want to be roped by anyone," Beats said.

Whit set the kid on a fat wooly sheep. The kid lowered his hand, the chute opened, and the sheep took off. The miniature cowpoke clung like a tick to the back of the sheep until it stopped suddenly at the far end. The sheep's passenger flew off and landed on his or her rump. Whit ran across the arena to help the young contestant up.

"Mind if I join you ladies?" Jordan turned to see Shelly climbing up beside them. She moved with surprising agility for her age.

"Hey, Grizz," Beats said.

"Grizz?" Jordan asked.

"An old nickname." Shelly said.

"There has to be a story behind that," Jordan said.

Shelly shook her head but Beats grinned. "Back when Shelly worked as a deputy, she was either the sweetest, easiest person to work with, or the meanest cuss in the office—teddy bear or grizzly bear—depended on what you were in for. Animal abuse or criminal stupidity got you the grizzly, lost kid or bad end of a domestic and you got the teddy bear."

Instead of commenting, Shelly kept her eyes on the cowboy they'd all been watching. "Looks like Whit got roped into doing the mutton busting again, pun intended. That man needs to learn to say no." Her face lit up as she watched Whit help the next contestant get ready to ride.

"Seems to me he's an expert in saying no." Chris's remark had a touch of bitterness to it.

"Is he competing tonight?" Jordan asked, trying not to sound too curious.

"Calf roping," Shelly said. "It'll be a bit. The kids are about done, so they'll be setting up for the main events soon."

"Tawny riding tonight?" Beats asked.

Jordan turned, curious at the mention of Shelly's granddaughter.

"Tawny's in Colorado. She has bigger circuits to ride these days," Shelly answered.

"You should see Shelly's granddaughter," Chris broke in. "She's the best barrel racer in the state, beautiful to watch."

"We've met," Jordan said simply.

She turned her gaze to the activity that surrounded her. She was fascinated by it all, taking special note of the crowd. There certainly weren't any Seattle types in the gathering. There were a lot of peculiar, strangely dressed people—wearing mostly cowboy hats, jeans, and shirts with snaps, but there were also a lot of T-shirts, camo, and baseball caps. These were the kind of people her friends in Seattle would have made fun of over a good cup of coffee.

The kids especially got to her. They wore miniatures of the clothing their parents were wearing—smaller cowboy hats, plaid shirts and belt buckles, even tiny cowboy boots. She assumed they all wanted to grow up to be cowboys and cowgirls. It was a different world.

Jordan considered rodeo to be more of a spectacle than a sport. The intensity of the crowd and the participants who were getting ready to compete gave her the impression that it was much more than that. As she watched the barrel racing and steer wrestling, she found herself caught up in the excitement, standing when the rest of the crowd stood. At the same time, the thought crossed her mind that anybody who would participate in a rodeo had to be somewhat crazy. Still, she knew those competitors were serious about what they were doing. They had come to participate, and they had come to win, and they had worked hard to get there.

A voice boomed over the loudspeaker, announcing the saddle bronc competition.

"Ready, ladies?" Chris held out a quarter.

"What's that for?" Jordan asked.

"During the rough stock events—saddle bronc, bareback, and bull riding—we all guess the scores. The one who's the furthest off holds the quarter until someone else loses," Beats explained.

"At the end of the event, whoever is holding the quarter buys the first round of drinks," Chris added.

Jordan looked down at the arena. The first cowboy climbed into a chute and onto the back of a wild-eyed horse. "I'm not sure that's fair. I have no idea how the events are scored."

"Cowboy has to stay on for at least eight seconds to get a score. He has to keep his feet in the stirrups and 'mark out' by touching the horse's shoulders on the first jump. His ride is scored by how rhythmically he rides the bucks. He can earn up to fifty points for the ride and the horse can earn up to fifty points. The points are combined for the total score," Shelly said.

Jordan's head was spinning. She was positive she'd never catch on. "I don't think—"

"Watch for a while and ask questions when you have them. You're a smart woman. You'll figure it out." Jordan got the idea that Shelly was offhand lecturing her again. She took it as a challenge.

She watched the first few rides closely, asking a lot of questions while the other ladies filled her in. By the fourth one she thought she'd figured it out. She and Chris had been passing the quarter between them. Chris always scored too high. Jordan too low. The last ride came up and Jordan was sure she could call it. Beats and Shelly each called a score that Jordan guessed would be close. Chris was way off again. Jordan thought she could win this one—at least beat Chris. Then she remembered the picture of the little boy Chris had shown her. As a waitress in a small-town bar, Jordan guessed that Chris's budget was tight. She threw out a number she knew would be wildly off. Jordan caught Shelly's eye as Chris handed her back the quarter.

"Looks like you're getting the hang of it," Shelly said.

"What are you talking about?" Beats said. "That guess was terrible."

"Looks like I owe everyone drinks." Jordan stood. "What are we drinking?"

Shelly put her hand on Jordan's arm, pulling her back into her seat. "Stay for a minute. You're not going to want to miss this one."

Jordan looked up to see cowboys lining up for the calf-roping competition. She sat back down. She was curious to see Whit compete in the sport he'd seemed so serious about. He was the last one to back in alongside the calf. He seemed like a completely different person. He was intensely focused on the calf in front of him. Scout, the horse who had been so calm in the face of a gunshot, was dancing nervously, keyed up and ready to spring. Jordan found herself holding her breath in anticipation. The gate swung open. The calf took off. Whit was right behind it, swinging his loop. He caught the calf, piled off the horse, and tied it up so fast she hardly realized the event was over. The grandstand erupted. Jordan stood with everyone else, even though she wasn't sure what had just happened.

"He won!" Chris shouted in her ear. "By like two seconds."

"Is that good?" Jordan asked.

"In rodeo, two seconds is an eternity. Most of the timed events are determined by tenths or hundredths of seconds." Shelly explained. Jordan felt something like pride swelling up in her chest as she realized how good Whit was. She had a sense of how hard he'd worked to attain that much skill.

The announcer's voice boomed, "Your winner and hometown cowboy, ladies and gentlemen—Whitmore Palmer!"

The crowd roared as Whit took his victory lap. Jordan stood with the rest of the crowd as he circled the arena in a slow lope. Her heart thudded in her chest with Scout's hoofbeats as he got closer. She couldn't stop staring. Whit caught her eye as he rode past. He smiled and put a finger to the brim of his hat, tipping it in her direction.

"Did you see that?" Chris grabbed her arm.

"Drinks," Jordan said. She slipped into an exaggerated Southern accent, trying to hide her embarrassment. "What are all ya'll having?"

Chapter Twenty-One

THE LINE TO THE concession stand was shorter than it had been the last time Jordan had stood in it. Although she'd learned a lot, she was buying her second round following the bronc riding. Through the rails she could see the setup for the final event, bull riding. She knew that one could be counted on to be dramatic, dangerous, even thrilling. She imagined that was why the line was so short this time.

"Can I buy you a drink?" Jordan turned, looked up, and recognized Grant, the giant who had annoyed her at the Silver Horseshoe her first night in Lombard.

"No, thanks," Jordan said, pretending to be enthralled by the rodeo clowns warming up the crowd. There were two of them, doing tricks with some of the kids who'd come down out of the stands. One was Clint. Shelly told her he was a good friend of Whit's, and a local dog breeder. The second one had his back to her, doing a coin trick with a little girl in a pink cowboy hat.

Grant watched with her for a minute, but instead of leaving, he moved closer. Jordan took a step back and ran into the person waiting in front of her. She apologized and then faced Grant. Before she could tell him to give her some space he leaned down, talking low. "I have some information that might be important. Maybe you could meet me after the rodeo? We could talk at my place."

Jordan met his eye. She highly doubted that he had anything important to tell her. More likely this was his idea of a pickup line. Whatever it was, she had no desire to be alone with this hulk of a man. "I'm afraid I can't do that. If you need to talk to me, it will have to be at the sheriff's office."

She turned back to the arena, hoping he'd get the hint and leave. Clint's dogs were in on the act, pretending to fall dramatically when he pulled out a toy gun. The other clown turned around. There was something familiar about him, but Jordan couldn't quite decide what that was.

Grant leaned down, shaking his head. "Sheriff's office won't work. It has to be somewhere"—he looked around like he was expecting someone to be listening—"private."

Jordan forced her expression into a polite smile but stepped away again. She didn't like the way he'd said the word private. "Sorry. I have to conduct all of my interviews at the sheriff's office. Tomorrow afternoon work for you?"

He shook his head. "I can't do that. I'm on a long-haul starting tomorrow morning."

"Maybe we can catch up after you get back. Call me and we can set up an appointment." It was Jordan's turn at the counter, so she turned her back on him to order the drinks.

Grant was still waiting after Jordan had collected the drinks. He handed her a napkin from the dispenser on the condiments table. It had his name, address, and phone number on it. "I'm back by Wednesday after next. Stop by any time after that.

No need to call first." He leaned close again. "It has to do with what I told you before."

Jordan gave a noncommittal nod and the man backed away. She considered throwing the napkin away, but since he was watching she folded it up and put it in her pocket instead.

On the way back to the grandstand, Jordan heard a familiar voice. She stopped. It sounded like Whit, but at the same time it didn't. She'd never heard anything like anger in Whit's voice, but this person sounded furious about something.

She turned to see the rodeo clown who had seemed so familiar a few hundred yards away, off to the side of the grandstand. It was Whit; he'd been part of the act. He hadn't told her about that part of his rodeo career. Despite the painted-on smile, Whit's face was serious. He was talking with a man wearing a long duster that hid his form and a half-crushed cowboy hat that covered his face. Whit handed him something and the man slipped it into his jacket.

Jordan moved slowly closer, so neither of them would notice her. Whit's voice was low and harsh. "This is the best I can do. You can't keep coming to me for more. You can either accept my offer or ..."

But Jordan didn't hear the rest. The speakers erupted with the drumbeat of heavy metal music and the stands above her rocked with the stomping of a thousand pairs of cowboy boots. The bull riding event had begun. The noise was so loud and sudden, Jordan almost dropped the drink carrier. When she looked again, Whit and the man he was with had parted ways.

Jordan had a funny feeling about the guy Whit had been talking to. She sidled along the fence, her hands full of the drinks, following him toward the chutes where the first bull rider was getting ready.

"It's time for another local boy, Lonnie Mahan!" The announcer's voice echoed as the crowd yelled. "Ya'll recall Lonnie made a pretty decent showing last year. That man sticks to a bull like a burr on a long-haired dog, but tonight he's drawn the toughest bull out there—Raging Thunder!" The crowd roared even louder. Apparently, the bull had his own following. Jordan could see the beast through the fence. He was big and rangy and the color of old-fashioned oatmeal that had been cooked too long.

The man Jordan was tailing paused by the fence, slipping a hand into his pocket underneath the coat. When he moved there was a visible bulge in the coat. Jordan reached for her own gun and then reminded herself she was in Montana. Half the crowd probably carried a concealed sidearm. Other than her gut, Jordan didn't have any reason to suspect this man of anything.

The announcer continued his spiel about the monster raging in the chute. "Yes sir, this bull is as mean as a rattlesnake when disturbed from his daily sun bath. Don't let his advanced years fool you. He's had years of experience at this rodeo game and he's tricky and unpredictable."

Lonnie, the young bull rider was hovering on the fence above the chute. His expression was grim but determined. Despite the cool evening, sweat glistened on his face. The air was heavy with anticipation. Jordan glanced up and saw the man she was following lean against the fence, as enthralled as the rest of the crowd with the event that was about to take place. He tipped his hat back, and for a second Jordan thought she was looking at Whit. She stepped closer, but the man turned away.

Lonnie lowered himself into the chute and onto Thunder's broad back. Jordan's gaze was drawn to the arena as the young man nodded. The chute opened and the raging bull shot out into the open. The bull was in fine form and giving it all he had. Jordan didn't know much about bull riding, but it appeared Lonnie was making what was probably the best ride of his young life. She was sure he'd make the full eight seconds. At the very last second before the buzzer rang he was soundly ejected from the bull's back, dead center in the arena. He landed unsteadily on his feet, but the distance he had been thrown and the force of his landing momentarily delayed his scramble for safety.

The clowns were there, and the pickup men, but the bull chose to ignore them with utter disregard and pursue the hapless cowboy. By then Lonnie had decided which fence to run for and was desperately hightailing it to safety at breakneck speed—directly toward Jordan.

The bull, panting heavily and angrily tossing gobs of saliva every direction, was close behind him and gaining. Jordan took a couple of steps back, gripping the drinks so hard that they sloshed over her wrists. She made eye contact with the desperate cowboy as Lonnie grabbed the fence, planning to leap atop the rail out of harm's way. The bull bunted him in the butt and launched him over the fence. Fortunately, Lonnie had gained a firm handhold on the top rail and so was able to limit his flight and land on his feet on the other side of the fence. Unfortunately, he landed so close to Jordan that she fell backward, spilling the drinks all over herself.

The crowd had risen to their feet when he was thrown and were wildly cheering his escape. Lonnie gallantly tipped his hat to the crowd and raised both his hands high above his head. Only then did he notice Jordan sprawled out at his feet. She could tell he was in pain, but he bent down and offered her his hand. She took it. As he pulled her to her feet the crowd roared again. Laughter and cheers rang in her ears as she looked around, trying to figure out exactly what had just happened.

"Sorry about that," the young cowboy said, as if he had just bumped into her in the grocery store. He turned and limped away. The bull stood quietly, intently watching Lonnie's departure. He snorted in Jordan's direction before he executed a slow turn and lazily trotted toward the exit gate of the arena to join his friends.

Jordan stood, still in shock, her clothes covered in the remains of the drinks she'd been holding. She looked around, trying to decide what to do next. The bull rider had walked away to nurse his injured pride and backside. The man she'd been following had disappeared. The crowd had already moved on to the next spectacle. She was cold, wet, and stunned.

"You okay, Detective?" It was Whit, his voice much softer and concerned than it had been a few minutes ago. He was still wearing his clown makeup.

"Fine." Jordan reached down and picked up the wasted drinks and dumped them in the nearest trash can.

"I'm glad to see you made it. It looks like you got an up close and personal look at what a rodeo is like."

"Yeah." It was all she could get out. She was pale and shaky and the liquid that had permeated her shirt was sticky and cold.

"C'mon. I probably have something you could change into in my trailer," Whit said.

Chapter Twenty-Two

JORDAN FOLLOWED WHIT TOWARD the area where the stock trailers were lined up. The competitors were loading up horses and trading stories about the rodeo as if it had already entered the hallowed halls of legend. Jordan got more than a few curious looks as they passed. Whit got congratulations on his ride. His truck was hitched to the same three-horse trailer he'd used at the search. Scout wasn't around and Jordan was grateful for that. She guessed he was in one of the corrals or stalls on the other side of the grounds.

Whit disappeared into the front of the trailer. When he came out, the makeup had been rubbed off. He held up a shirt with the word "Queen" emblazoned across it in silver letters.

Jordan raised her eyebrows. "Cute," she said sarcastically.

"I think this is Tawny's." He put the shirt to his nose. "Yeah, it reeks of her perfume."

Jordan tried to keep her face neutral as he tossed her the shirt, but he read something in her gaze that made him hurry to explain. "She left it up at the camp on Rattlesnake. I picked it up to return to her. Tawny has never been good at cleaning up after herself."

"Thanks," Jordan said, but she found herself wishing Whit had offered one of his shirts. "Where can I change?"

"There's a sleeping area on the other side." He gestured around the trailer.

Jordan stepped inside the little compartment. It was more of a standing area with a loft bed than a camper. She took a quick inventory of the room. It was neat, but the bed looked like it had been slept in. The smell of leather and horse sweat permeated every corner. There was a little closet on one side. Jordan pulled it open with a twinge of guilt for snooping when Whit was being nice to her.

A couple of clean shirts and an extra pair of Wranglers hung on a rack. Underneath there was a worn pair of work boots, stained purple. She looked closer, but there was no way to tell when the boots had gotten stained. In the back of the room there was a balled-up jacket. She pulled it out to look closer. It looked about Whit's size, but it smelled of cigarette smoke, something she'd never smelled on Whit. She checked both pockets, coming up with a handful of 50-dollar bills.

A rap came at the door. "Doing all right, Detective?"

"Yeah. Give me a minute." She replaced the money and pushed the jacket back to the corner.

She held up the shirt Whit had given her. It smelled sweet and spicy—cinnamon, vanilla, and maybe sandalwood, scents Whit apparently wasn't very fond of. Jordan couldn't help but wonder why Tawny felt it necessary to wear perfume on a cattle drive. There was nothing she could do about her beer and Diet Coke-soaked bra and jeans so she just pulled the shirt over it. The shirt was tight, the word "Queen" stretched in a way that overemphasized her breasts. She had a feeling it was meant to fit that way.

Jordan opened the door and stepped out. "Thanks, I—"

She screamed, stepping back into the open door as she came face to nose with a dark horse with a wide white blaze across his face. He threw his head back and snorted. One eye was shiny, white, and ghostlike. The rest of him was dark, almost black, and he was huge and powerful.

"Detective, are you okay?" Whit came around the side of the trailer, carrying a saddle.

Jordan braced herself against the door, trying to get as far away from the huge animal as she could. She sensed this horse was a force to be reckoned with. He was a veritable bundle of nerves. She watched as he impatiently pawed the ground with his left front hoof. He would reach forward, solidly plant it, and drag it and dirt back toward him.

"Stand!" Whit commanded. The horse blew out a breath but stopped pawing the ground.

Shelly came around the trailer and nodded to Jordan. "Thought I might find you here. Chris had to go relieve her mother, so I told her I'd give you a ride home." She grasped the horse's halter, said, "Back" and pushed him a few steps away from Jordan. As soon as Jordan had room to breathe she shut the trailer door and put some distance between herself and the horse.

Shelly nodded at the horse. "How's he coming along?"

"Good. Popeye's on the high end of the hot scale, but he's learning."

Shelly stepped back, admiring the horse. "Strong back legs and hindquarters. Looks like he's built for quick starts, speed, and endurance. All desirable traits in a rodeo horse."

"Hot scale?" Jordan asked, watching the horse from a safe distance. Although he dutifully remained in the spot where Shelly had left him, he was jumpy and alert to every sound. His ears flicked individually and together in every direction toward any noise or movement; his eyes moved incessantly. Both eyes were dark now. Jordan wondered if she'd imagined the milky white one.

Whit pulled a horse blanket and saddle from the side of the trailer and moved to saddle the horse. "A good friend of mine, Lyle, taught me that. He was a cavalry officer in World War II and broke and trained horses all his life," was Whit's reply. "He told me there are basically only two kinds of horses, hot ones and cold ones. Popeye is hot. The mare I brought up to Rattlesnake, Goldie, is cold. "Lyle would never start working with a new horse until he knew which it was. The two must be trained entirely differently. He wrote a book titled *How to Break and Train Your Own Horse, and Why You Should*. Lyle could tell their temperature just by observing them, but he devised a simple test that even a novice can use to determine which their horse is."

"What was that?" Jordan was curious. She'd always been fascinated with the personality differences in people but hadn't considered it in horses.

"Ride up to a small stream or ditch with water in it. It's a good idea to have someone cross it ahead of you. Do not force your horse to cross; wait to see what they will do. A hot horse will jump it, a cold horse wades through it."

"Does that really work?" Jordan asked.

"Yep." Whit tightened the cinch and then paused. "Of course, there are varying degrees of both hot and cold. Lyle was adamant that horses like Popeye, on the high end of hot, absolutely must be broken to word command. Otherwise, they're unsafe. Popeye responds to 'stand,' 'trot,' 'lope,' and 'go.' 'Go' puts him in high gear. More importantly, no matter how dire the situation if I holler, 'Stand!' he freezes in place until I signal it is safe for him to move. That command has saved my bacon several times. I highly recommend it."

"Lyle worked magic with horses. Especially with the gifted but difficult ones," Shelly recalled, running her hand down the horse's neck. "I imagine this one is like that."

"I'm curious," Jordan asked. "Why Popeye?"

Whit grinned. "I named him Popeye because of his right eye. When he's calm and relaxed his eyes look alike. If anything startles or upsets him, he snorts, squarely plants all four feet, and that eye becomes almost completely shiny white. He 'pops' his eye."

Jordan laughed at herself. "That's what he did when I got out of the trailer. I thought he was a demon horse. Coming face to face like that scared both of us. Why does that happen?"

"Might be genetic," Shelly broke in. "It's most apt to occur in Appaloosas. The sclera is the tough fibrous white membrane that covers and encircles all the eye, except for the colored cornea, and extends all the way round to the optic nerve located back of the eye. It is the white of the eye and serves to protect the eye. I know of no concrete explanation why Popeye's sclera covers his cornea when he is alarmed, but it does. His eye almost seems to turn inside out and all you see is the sclera. He probably doesn't see much out of that eye when it gets turned like that.

"And there you have it. Popeye pops his eye," Whit said.

"He doesn't look like an Appaloosa." Jordan was happy that for once she knew something. "Don't they usually have spots on their rear end?"

Whit slid a bridle over Popeye's head, straightening the bit of mane in the front. "You're right, but he is an Appy. He has the striated hooves that are so tough they often don't require shoes, a thin mane and tail, and the distinctive rather blocky body type. The other colts from the stable I bought him from were all spotted except for Popeye and his brother. I bought both of them because I liked the way they moved—they seemed to almost glide. Over time, Popeye seemed the more promising of the two, so I sold Baldy a couple of years ago."

"Promising?" Jordan asked.

"For my next roping horse. Scout's getting old. I hate to do it, but it might be time to retire him. That's why I'm training this one. Speaking of which ..." Whit untied the horse, backed him a couple of steps and swung up into the saddle. "If you ladies will excuse me, I'm going to take some time to work Popeye over in the arena."

Jordan glanced at the empty arena. "This late?"

"I haven't had much time to work with him. They said they'd leave the lights for me to turn off." He tipped his hat. "Goodnight, Shelly, Detective."

Jordan watched him ride away. The horse and cowboy silhouetted in the lights from the grandstand made something of a poetic view. As Whit got closer to the arena, Jordan swore she saw someone step out of the shadows and meet him by the stands.

She turned to Shelly. "Did you—"

"Come on, Detective," Shelly said, setting her hand on Jordan's shoulder. "You've learned enough about rodeoing for one night."

"Right," Jordan said, but she couldn't help but wonder who Whit might be meeting with on the deserted fairground.

Chapter Twenty-Three

BECCA STARED OUT AT the curtain of gray outside the office window. Although the opening of rodeo season usually forecasted summer, the day after the rodeo was just plumb mean and a completely miserable day in Lombard. It had been pouring rain most of the night and there was no letup in sight. Anyone who had been out in it, even briefly, had soggy shoes and soaked jackets, and most were wet through to the skin.

Everybody's disposition matched the weather to a T. Grumpy was the mood of the day. The sheriff's office was no exception. Pretty much everyone had left. Even Jordan, who had worked almost nonstop since she'd arrived, was doing research at home. Of the three deputies on duty, only Ray was still around. The other two had been called to the far northwest part of the county.

Becca's pregnancy was of general interest with all her coworkers. Probably because she was so skinny. Her slight build and burgeoning belly size seemed fascinating to all of them. They'd started placing bets on when the baby would come. Everyone but Ray. Ever since she had started to show, Ray had acted like he was scared to death of her and avoided her like the plague. Ray's experience being around pregnant women was sorely limited. Although he had been married twice, neither union had produced any offspring. His peculiar behavior toward her was a continual source of amusement among the rest of the crew.

Ray had been sitting on the other side of the office from her all morning. His only comment to her was to yell across the room to ask if she could possibly have any fingernails left. She'd taken offense to his statement. She hadn't been filing that long, just long enough to get rid of a little rough spot. Besides what she did shouldn't have been any concern of his. It wasn't like he was doing anything useful. He'd spent the better part of the past three hours drying his boots, scraping mud off them, and pretending to be reading some work-related material. Whatever it was couldn't have actually been work-related because he was enjoying it too much.

Becca decided to be the bigger person and get some work done. Brendan had been nagging her to finish transferring all her notes and ledgers into the new computer that was sitting on her desk. He'd rudely informed her that she should burn the paper notes she'd meticulously kept as soon as she got everything in the computer. He'd even gone so far as to take her big ledger out of her desk and put it in his own. She wasn't going to let Ray accuse her of slacking or let Carlyle yell at her because he had to do her job.

She laboriously pulled herself into an upright position. She could tell that watching her struggle was distressing to Ray, but he didn't offer to help. After standing a few moments while her back took on the load she glanced at Ray and pointed to Carlyle's office. He nodded, indicating he would man the radio and phone, and went back to his reading.

Becca took the extra set of keys and went into Carlyle's office. She looked around but couldn't find her ledger anywhere. Finally, she got down on her knees to look in the bottom desk drawer. There it was. She blew out a long breath, contemplating whether to ask Ray to help her get the heavy book out of the drawer. Deciding she didn't want to see the pained look on his face again, she got herself into position and then hoisted the ledger up onto the sheriff's desk. A sharp stab in her lower back told her immediately that it was a bad move. She breathed through the pain until it subsided. Then she carried the ledger back to the dispatch office. Ray barely raised an eyebrow as she waddled past him. He most definitely didn't offer to help.

She sat the heavy book down on her desk and slid carefully into her chair. She rubbed at a new ache in her back as she opened her computer to the right database. She flipped back to the page where she'd left off before the sheriff took the ledger. It was a listing of all the new equipment that had been purchased for the sheriff's department—the new computers Whit had wrangled and Beats' new radio. Becca admired the neat rows of her own handwriting. She'd worked hard to make it so precise and beautiful. Blodgett had often commented about how easy it was to read her notes. She missed the former sheriff. He had been so much nicer to her than Carlyle.

Becca breathed through another pain in her back. Maybe she should call Beats to relieve her and take the rest of the day off. But they needed the money. She flipped to the next page where she had recorded the serial numbers of all the new firearms. She ran her finger down the numbers. The last one stopped her. Something about the way the last number was formed wasn't right. In high school one of her friends had shown her the European way of making a seven, with a line through the base. Since then she'd always written them that way. The last digit on one of the serial numbers had been changed from a seven with the neat line through it to a nine. She took a pencil off the desk and circled the number in question. She leaned over her computer, scrolling down to see what number had been entered in Sheriff Carlyle's database.

A sharp pain in her back took her breath away. It felt like her insides were being torn apart. She leaned forward, trying to breathe through the pain, but it didn't stop this time. She gripped the edge of the desk, knocking the ledger into the open drawer. Another wave of pain hit and she couldn't hold back anymore. She let out a terrifying, elongated screech.

Ray stood up. He found himself standing frozen in place, spraddle-legged, wondering, "What in thunder was that?"

It was no secret that many people, maybe most, engaged in law enforcement play in a game they called "What if" in their leisure time. While driving —watching an oncoming car—what if that car veers into my line of traffic? What would I do? What if that guy on his roof down the street trips and falls off it? Officer on night patrol: What if I see two or three guys come out the back door of that business? While sitting in a restaurant: What if the next person to come in here has a gun and starts shooting?

While he had played that game many times, Ray had never played "What if a very pregnant woman and I are alone in a building, and she lets out the most bloodcurdling scream I have ever heard?"

Although trained and accustomed to responding to unexpected emergencies, Ray found his feet were glued to the floor precisely where they landed when he was ejected from his chair. Finally coming to his senses, as he rushed toward the front desk, he shouted, "Becca, are you okay?" Under the circumstances that was a rather dumb question.

She didn't seem to be at her desk, so he started toward Carlyle's office. He'd almost passed by her when he managed to hear her weak answer. "No Ray, I am not okay! I need help!"

He stepped timidly to the other side of the desk. She was lying flat on the floor, unable to get up.

He moved toward the dispatch office, but Becca yelled, "There's no time for that!"

Coming to his senses, Ray realized she was right. The other deputies were miles away, there wasn't time for the volunteers manning the ambulance to go and get it. He bent over, picked her slight frame up and ran as fast as he could out the main door into the pouring rain—now at deluge stage. He put her in the back of his patrol vehicle and wrapped her in the obligatory blankets always on board. He jumped into the driver's seat and floorboarded it toward their tiny but usually efficient medical facility, located three quarters of a mile out of town. As he negotiated the left turn at the end of Main Street, he hydroplaned, lost control, and slid into a ditch.

After the initial shock of the accident wore off, Ray turned to the backseat and asked sheepishly, "Are you okay?"

Becca had been crying and moaning from the backseat, but now she let out another bloodcurdling scream, quickly followed by, "No! I'm having a baby!"

Ray contacted the hospital on his radio. After listening for a minute, he glanced at Becca in the rearview mirror. "We're good, they're only about ten minutes out."

"Ten minutes?" Becca shrieked. "The baby is coming now!"

"Can't you just cross your legs or—"

"Get back here NOW!" Becca's demand crescendoed into another scream of pain.

Finally grasping the gravity of the situation, Ray climbed in the back with her. Somehow in the rush of blood and screaming, Ray found the calm to do what needed to be done. When the medics from the hospital showed up, Ray—for the first time in his entire life, was holding a neatly bundled newborn baby boy in his arms, and soothing Becca the best he could. Despite the trauma of the moment, she seemed to be doing well.

Chapter Twenty-Four

"I HEARD YOU'RE THE new county midwife," Jordan said as Ray stopped digging and leaned against his shovel. It had taken two days for the ground to dry up enough to begin the search in Shelly's garden. Becca and the new baby were doing well, but Ray still looked like a deer caught in the headlights whenever anyone mentioned the birth in the back of his patrol car.

"Never, ever, ever again," he said. "I had no idea babies coming into the world made such a mess. My vehicle will never be the same."

"You might change your mind when it's your own," Shelly said.

"Not likely. Even in the improbable event that I ever do have one of my own." Ray shook his head and went back to digging.

"So has anything been accomplished here besides digging up my favorite peony bush?" Shelly looked at the yard with a sense of resignation. "Does the name Mike Hubbard mean anything to you?"

"He was one of the men Sadie was writing to. I checked him out, but he's still in jail."

"But he was tied in with a case you solved the beginning of last year," Shelly said.

Jordan stared at Shelly in disbelief. After going back through her own files, Jordan had just backtracked enough to find the link that Ray had pointed out to her. "How did you—"

"I'm retired. My kids are grown. I have time to do research, and I pay attention. The question is, what is the link between our Sadie, our killer, and you?"

"Me?"

"It could be just a coincidence that a man you helped put behind bars happened to be corresponding with a woman who ends up disappearing right after you're brought in to investigate a murder in the same town. But I'm not big on coincidences, more on connections. We're all a bunch of dominoes: one push in the right direction and we fall, taking out the next one, and then the next one in line. Sometimes that push leads to love, sometimes that push leads to murder, once in a while, both. Sometimes it leads to a garden completely torn up because some jackass decided to bury a message in the middle of my roses." She looked at her partially exhumed flower bed and sighed. "Come in. I'll show you what I've been working on."

Jordan followed Shelly into her house. It was a two-story ranch house with a wide rock porch and a great view of the same mountain Sheriff Blodgett most likely died looking at. Shelly took her into a little office in the back. She'd set up a whiteboard with different colored markers. On the board, she'd listed the three victims and how they related to each other.

A picture on the wall beside the whiteboard caught Jordan's attention. A young, handsome man in a Montana state patrol uniform stared out from the frame. He looked solemn, but his eyes twinkled. Judging by the hairstyle and uniform, Jordan would guess the photo was about thirty years old. She could just make out the name Curtis on the man's badge.

"Your husband?" she asked.

Shelly looked away from the whiteboard. "Yes."

"Where is—"

"Gone. Killed in the line of duty. Thirty years ago."

Jordan sucked in a breath, not sure how to respond to Shelly's revelations. "I'm sorry to hear that."

Shelly nodded. "Losing him was what inspired me to become a deputy. I had three small kids, food to put on the table, and a need to do something noble to make sure he was never forgotten."

"You have three kids?" Jordan asked. She could never understand how anyone in law enforcement had kids. It added a layer of risk to everything they did. Jordan had a policy of not letting anyone get too close. Less collateral damage that way.

"Yep. Two boys and a girl. All grown with kids of their own. Not one of them are on this board," Shelly said.

"Right." Jordan turned back to Shelly's notes. "We have Blodgett, who had just started investigating a cold case. Then we have Sadie, who was so obsessed with real-life mysteries that she was writing to convicts. Last, we have Bonnie Golden, who was the center of the biggest case this area has ever seen."

Jordan nodded as Shelly moved to other names written around the board. Some she recognized— Michael Hubbard and Sadie's roommate, Crystal. Jordan's name was even there. She read off some unfamiliar names. "Who are these guys?"

"All men Bonnie had some sort of fling with."

"Judd too?"

"No. They weren't involved with each other, at least not that I know of."

"Then why is he on the board?"

"I pretty much add him whenever there's something to be solved. I've been waiting for nearly thirty years to catch him in something dirty," Shelly replied. "That, and Chris saw him talking to our victim about a week before she went missing."

"How did you find that out?" Jordan asked.

"I ask a lot of questions."

"I questioned Chris at the Horseshoe. She didn't say anything about seeing Judd and Sadie." Jordan picked up one of the markers and twirled it between her fingers.

"I'd imagine not. Judd carries a lot of weight in this town and not just the kind that he wears above his belt. He's not a man to cross."

Jordan stopped twirling the marker and pointed it at Shelly. "But she told you."

"I like to think I carry some weight in this town too. And maybe I'm not a person to cross either."

"I don't like the idea of you going around questioning people. That kind of thing should be left to me and the deputies. Did you forget there's a killer out there who's already shown he or she doesn't like being investigated? Look what happened to the sheriff."

"I know how to talk to the people around here. Besides, I can hold my own."

Jordan looked at the wiry, no-nonsense woman. She didn't doubt that Shelly was right. "I can't have regular citizens out doing my job. It's not safe and the sheriff's office could be liable—"

"The sheriff's office has never been held liable in this town for something a nosy old woman did. I doubt that's going to change any time soon. You asked for my help in this investigation and I'm providing it. Now, about our list."

Jordan swallowed the words she wanted to say. Instead, she studied the board. "We should add Whit."

"Whit?" Shelly looked at her like she'd suggested they add Mother Teresa to the chart.

"Sadie's old roommate said Sadie had come to Lombard because of a new boyfriend. Someone with pretty gray eyes."

Shelly stood her ground. "While I agree Whit has striking gray eyes, that's hardly definitive proof that he had anything to do with our victim."

"I thought this was more of a relationship board, not a proof board."

Shelly shook her head. "Whit doesn't belong on this board. He's the last person who would be mixed up in anything amiss."

Jordan pointed to her own name. "You put me on the board and I just got here."

Shelly tented her fingers below her chin. "There's a connection between you and the killer somehow. I feel it. I'm just not sure what it is. What can you tell me about the case that involved Michael Hubbard?"

"He was a small-time drug lord in a little town called Maple Valley. Everyone knew what he was doing, but they couldn't pin anything on him. Then a connection to him came up in a cold case. Turns out there was an old girlfriend of his who went missing when he was in his early twenties."

"So, Hubbard has a history of killing young women," Shelly said.

"But he's still in jail," Jordan said.

"Yeah, but that's the thing with those small-time drug lords. They generally build a web that runs through the whole town."

"I'm more concerned about a connection to the Bonnie Golden case than one that involves me. For some reason Sadie decided to concentrate on that case. I think it has to do with the Mike she was writing to, or the guy she was coming here to meet. Any Mikes in town who might have been connected with Bonnie and have been in prison?"

"Not that I know of," Shelly said.

Jordan stared at the web of names in front of her. It seemed impossible to sort out. What if the cases weren't even related? She glanced out the window as a bit of commotion started outside. She looked at Shelly and they both headed to the front door.

One of the searchers was speaking to Sheriff Carlyle. He'd arrived sometime after Jordan went into the house. The sheriff nodded at him as he accepted a plastic evidence bag. He walked right past Jordan and presented the object to Shelly. It was a silver belt buckle, tarnished so badly that it looked blue. Jordan could barely make out the image of a cowboy throwing a rope over the neck of a calf.

"You recognize this belt buckle?" Carlyle asked.

Shelly leaned closer, without touching the buckle. "Yes."

"It belongs to Whit Palmer, doesn't it?" the sheriff said.

"No," Shelly said. Jordan watched to see if it looked like she was lying. She didn't know if Shelly would go so far as to lie to protect Whit.

"Whose is it, then?" Jordan asked.

"It belonged to Whit's dad."

"Whit's dad?" Jordan asked.

Shelly turned to face her. "Yes. Charlie Palmer was a champion roper."

Jordan's mind went back to the list of names from Shelly's board. She realized Whit's dad hadn't been listed with the men Bonnie Golden had been involved with. "Do you know where he is now?"

Shelly shook her head. "By all accounts, he died in an accident soon after Whit graduated from high school, but I never saw a body or attended a funeral, so I can't say whether that's true or not. Whit's mom was long gone, and no one bothered to inform Whit officially if his dad had actually died."

"You'd think they would have looked into that when the ranch passed to Whit," the sheriff added.

Shelly shook her head. "Not necessarily. If Charlie was written out of the will, it wouldn't matter if he was dead or alive. Whit would get the whole spread."

"Do you know that for sure?" Sheriff Carlyle asked. It seemed like an odd question for him to ask.

"No. Whit's a grown man now, and I don't get involved in his financial affairs," Shelly answered.

"Do you know who had this belt buckle last?" Jordan asked. She saw something in Shelly's gaze that made her suspicious.

Shelly looked from the sheriff to Jordan and finally let out a breath. "Charlie sent it to Whit as a graduation present."

Jordan could tell it took effort for Shelly to admit that Whit might have any connection to the case. "Any idea how it ended up in your garden?"

"No." Shelly hesitated. "But I may have an idea as to why it's here."

Jordan looked in Shelly's eyes. For the first time, she saw fear there. "Why is that?"

"It's a message from the killer. He wants to make sure we know he's back."

Chapter Twenty-Five

JORDAN WAS IN THE middle of a phone interview with *The Missoulian* newspaper when her cell phone rang. She wasn't enjoying the interview—the reporter seemed more interested in Jordan's life in Seattle than in any developments in the case. On the fifth ring, on impulse, Jordan told the reporter she had an important call coming through and picked up the phone. It was Dr. Green.

"Brownie is ready to leave the clinic. In fact, it's urgent that you get here as soon as possible," he said.

Jordan hesitated. She hadn't done anything to prepare her house for a dog. "Now isn't the best time. Maybe after—"

"Judd just drove up. I'll keep Brownie hidden until you get here. Use the back entrance." The man sounded nervous. Jordan remembered what Shelly had said about Judd not being a man to cross. Was he so intimidating that the old vet couldn't stand up to him?

Jordan made a quick decision. "I'll be right there." As she got into her vehicle, she scrolled through her contacts, looking for the number she'd vowed never to call, but she was desperate. She had no idea how to take care of a dog.

Judd was driving away from the front of the office as Jordan surreptitiously slithered in the garage door in back. She felt like a fugitive as she met up with the staid, almost elderly vet. They exchanged a brief, if furtive, celebratory smirk. Although the whole thing seemed a little childish, Jordan decided to take it as a win that she had circumvented the Honorable Dane Judd, the self-important County Commissioner of Keystone County.

Brownie was celebrating too. He began twisting and turning with pure delight the moment Jordan entered the room where he'd been hidden. When she leashed him and started toward the garage and her vehicle with him in tow, his tail almost wagged off his body and he came dangerously close to turning inside out. The vet gave something to calm him so he wouldn't hurt himself, carried him to the garage, and deposited him on the front seat of Jordan's Expedition atop the soft blanket she'd pulled from the emergency kit.

Jordan was surprised at how exhilarated she felt. She was anxious to show him his new home and start spoiling him. She'd always wanted a dog. He had been through so much. He deserved some good in his life and she intended to see that he got it. He was so grateful and appreciative of any kindnesses she had shown him. She was surprised at how happy he made her. The ride home went quickly enough. Brownie was somewhat calmer when they got there but still excited.

Rachel and her little dog Bunny were waiting in the driveway when they got there. "I'm glad to see you took my advice." Rachel acted like the whole thing was her idea. "Although I might have started you out with something less huge and less injured." She gestured to the pile of things she'd put on the front porch—food, a dog dish, even a bright red squeaky ball. "This should be enough to hold you over until you can get your own things."

"Thanks," Jordan said.

Rachel waved her hand, "That's what neighbors do."

Jordan watched Brownie as he spent a minute or two sniffing unfamiliar smells. She couldn't help but wonder what her mother would say to all of this. Absolutely nothing good, Jordan was sure. That thought filled her with more satisfaction than it should have. She helped Brownie up the steps and into her home. Brownie, finally worn out, made himself comfortable on the living room rug. Promptly curled up and went to sleep.

Jordan sighed. Maybe she could do this.

Chapter Twenty-Six

"DETECTIVE?" WHIT STOOD JUST inside a rough but well-kept barn. "How can I help you?"

Jordan stepped out of her vehicle, the silver buckle in the evidence bag gripped in her hand. "I needed to ask you about this." She held out the buckle, watching his expression carefully.

A line tightened around his jaw. "Where did you find that?"

"Shelly's garden."

He let his breath out slowly. "She sure is growing some strange things in her flower beds this year."

"You heard about the collar too?" Jordan asked.

"Yeah. It's a small town." Whit hung the bucket he'd been carrying on a hook on the wall of the barn. He pulled the doors closed, wiped his hands on his jeans and then reached for the belt buckle. "Can I?" Jordan handed it to him. He turned the buckle over in his hands, running his thumb across the imprint of the man throwing the rope. "Honestly, never thought I'd see this again."

"When was the last time you saw it?" Jordan asked.

"About fourteen years ago. The day Charlie, my dad, sent it to me. His idea of a high school graduation present."

"And you what, lost it immediately?"

He looked up at Jordan, his gray eyes hard. "I threw it. Went out to the far end of the property and I threw it as hard as I could."

Jordan held her breath for a few heartbeats. She wasn't used to the anger rolling off Whit. He sounded like he had at the rodeo when he was talking to the man under the stands. "I can understand why you didn't want it. Shelly told me about your dad and Bonnie Golden."

The line on his jaw grew harder. "I need to finish up my chores."

"Okay if I come?" Jordan said. In response to his raised eyebrows, she clarified. "I have a few more questions, but I'd hate to keep you from your work."

"Sure." But Whit didn't sound sure.

Jordan followed the long-legged cowboy to the end of the corral. She had a hard time keeping up with his strides, but she wasn't about to let him see her trot after him like an obedient puppy. Whit's pickup was parked at the end of a big haystack. He climbed up the stack and started throwing bales into the truck bed.

Jordan climbed to the top of a fence nest to the haystack to be out of the way, but close enough for him to hear her. "I take it you have no idea how the belt buckle ended up in Shelly's flower bed."

"No, ma'am."

"And you can't think of anyone who might want to use it to send a message?" Jordan asked.

He threw another bale of hay into the back of the truck. "Nope."

"Where is your dad now?"

Whit paused, his back to her, his gloved hands wrapped around the wires of another bale of hay. Through his T-shirt, Jordan could see the muscles in his back tense. "Dead." He turned and threw the bale in the back of the truck with more force than was probably necessary.

Jordan waited for him to reach for the next bale before asking, "Are you sure about that?"

He paused again and it took a minute for him to meet her gaze. "That's what they tell me."

"You haven't seen him lately?"

"I don't make a habit of talking to ghosts." Whit's voice had an edge to it. Jordan couldn't tell if his defenses were up because his dad was a sensitive subject, or if he had something to hide.

"I saw you talking to someone at the rodeo, a man in a long coat. It looked like you gave him something. Could you tell me who that was?"

Whit paused again, a wariness flashing in his gray eyes. "Tom Pitkin, an old cowboy that used to ride with me on the circuit awhile back. He's had some hard times lately. I was just helping him out."

"Do you know where he is now? Could he verify your story?"

Whit turned to face her. His eyes snapped with irritation. "I have no idea where Tom went after that night. I'm not sure what me giving an old friend a little help has to do with my dad's belt buckle."

"Shelly mentioned that she wasn't exactly sure if your dad had really passed or—"

"He's dead enough to me," Whit bit back.

"I take it your relationship with him wasn't exactly ..."

"He was never much of a dad." Whit put the last bale in the truck and climbed down from the stack.

Jordan jumped off the fence, taking in the sheen of sweat on Whit's face. His shirt clung to him, where just a few minutes earlier it had been dry. She didn't know if the perspiration was from the exertion or if it was a sign he was lying. "If he did come back to Lombard, do you think he'd look you up?"

Whit pulled his gloves off and threw them into the open window of the truck. "Dead or alive, I'm not sure why he'd come back. He was in a hell of a hurry to leave the first time. Didn't matter that he was leaving his wife or his kid."

"Leaving them for a woman who ended up murdered, eight years later? You were what, fifteen when Bonnie disappeared?"

Whit turned to face Jordan again. "Seventeen. But Bonnie Golden had long since moved on from him too."

Jordan was starting to feel like she was interrogating a hostile witness. "Do you know where your dad was at the time Bonnie disappeared?"

Whit snorted. "I didn't know where he was most of his life."

"But now?" Jordan probed; she hadn't missed that Whit's answer wasn't direct.

"No. I haven't seen him. And I have no idea how the belt buckle got from the far end of my property to Shelly's garden." Whit slammed the end gate to his truck shut. "Sorry I can't be more help, Detective, but if that's all, I've got cattle to feed." His defensiveness was a new side to him, and Jordan didn't like it. She tried to think of something she could ask that wouldn't be off-putting. She felt like there was something more behind the relationship between Whit's dad and the murdered woman.

Whit whistled. A couple of half-grown puppies came bounding from somewhere behind the house. Instead of going to Whit, the dogs stopped in front of Jordan, wagging their tails.

"Hey, guys." Jordan held out her hand. One of the pups sniffed her palm and then dropped to the ground, his head resting on her foot. Jordan reached to scratch the dog's head. "You're a sweetheart." The other puppy clamored up her arm for attention.

Whit's face softened. "Their names are Owl and Duke. Duke is the one with different colored eyes."

"They're adorable," Jordan said. The dogs rolled over and she knelt to scratch both bellies.

"They're good friends to each other and me too." Whit watched Jordan and the dogs for a long moment. "They like you. Funny, I always thought dogs were a good judge of character." Jordan looked up from the dogs, inexplicably wounded by Whit's dig. His face split into a smile. "I was joking, Detective."

"How long have you had them?" Jordan asked.

"A couple of months. My friend Clint sold them to me."

"The rodeo clown?"

"Yeah. He breeds Blue Heeler and Australian Shepherd puppies. Most of the time he makes better money doing that than rodeoing. His dogs are bred to be smart and trained to be cow dogs—except for the ones in his rodeo acts. He's good with dogs."

"Maybe you should give me his number. You've probably heard I recently acquired a dog," Jordan said.

Whit leaned down and scratched Owl's head. "The missing girl's dog, right? The one who was guarding the bone?"

Jordan stood. "Yeah."

"It was good of you to take him in. I heard you saved him from Judd's frugality."

"I had to. He's an important witness in a murder investigation. I'm not sure money is the only reason Commissioner Judd wanted him euthanized. He seems to want to hamper every part of this investigation and then come after me when I don't make any progress." As soon as the complaint was out of her mouth, Jordan regretted it. Judd was Whit's fellow commissioner, so maybe Whit was in on the tight purse strings too. She just had a hard time putting Whit and Judd in the same category.

Whit chuckled as Owl playfully chewed on the bottom of his jeans. "How is he doing?"

"Commissioner Judd?"

Whit laughed. "No, the dog."

"Okay, I guess. Dr. Green says he'll heal. He's not eating much and he gets really anxious when I leave him. I'm constantly scared he's going to hurt himself worse. Believe it or not, he slept on my bed last night and I slept on the couch. I was worried I'd accidentally kick him in my sleep, so I snuck out of the bed after he fell asleep. Unfortunately, I know nothing about dogs." Jordan looked at Whit, sure that would be another strike against her. "My parents were firmly against any kind of pet. "

"Your parents weren't dog people, huh?" Whit said.

"Not a chance. Pet hair would have messed up their perfect carpet and perfect furniture and perfect world. Not that I didn't do enough of that myself without any canine assistance."

Whit's gray eyes went wide in mock-horror. "You shed all over your parent's furniture?"

Jordan laughed. "No. Mostly I just messed up their ideal world. They weren't big on me becoming a cop." She stepped back. The conversation shifting to her made her uncomfortable. "Speaking of animals, I should let you get back to your cows."

Whit smiled, his expression more open. "Are you still on the clock?"

"On the clock?" Jordan asked.

"I mean, is this conversation costing the people of Montana anything?"

"When I'm in the middle of an investigation, I'm never really off. But you know as well as I do, besides expenses, my price was set. This conversation isn't costing the state of Montana anything more than what they're already paying me."

"In that case, would you be willing to help me get this hay out to the cattle?"

Jordan looked at him incredulously. "You want me to help you ... feed your cows?"

"I was thinking you could help me finish up, and then I could give you Clint's dog food recipe."

"Dog food recipe?"

"Guaranteed to help any dog get his appetite back. He makes it for his mama dogs after the pups are born. I don't want Judd to think I'm using a taxpayer-funded hired hand, but this job is easier with two. The kid who usually helps me around here is on a trip with his family."

Jordan looked at him warily. "What would I have to do?"

Whit smiled and his eyes sparkled. "Do you know how to drive a stick?"

Chapter Twenty-Seven

"JUST KEEP IT AT a steady speed. I'll divide up the bales and toss them out," Whit said as they drove to the far field. Jordan was driving, the dogs between them, with one's head resting on her leg. The other was on Whit's lap, his head hanging out the window.

"You do this every day?" Jordan asked.

"In the winter, yes. But not for much longer now. The grass will be grown up enough for these ladies to take care of themselves pretty soon." Whit jumped out to open the gate. As soon as Jordan drove through, a herd of black cattle surrounded the pickup.

"You good up there?" Whit asked.

"Just like driving in Seattle traffic," Jordan answered.

He climbed in the back of the truck. "Not too fast. I don't want to go flying out the back and I don't want you to take out any of my herd."

"Got it, boss," Jordan called back.

She drove in a straight line while Whit threw the hay out the back. Fewer and fewer cows followed the truck as they got to the end of the field. Whit rapped on the cab of the truck, signaling her to stop. "That's it."

He jumped out of the truck, walked around to the driver's side, and opened the door. "My turn to drive."

"Did I do something wrong?" Jordan asked.

"No, but I need to drive if I'm going to show you where I threw that buckle. It gets a little rocky in a couple of areas and I don't want to blow out a tire."

"Sounds like you don't trust me," Jordan said, but she slid across the bench seat, ending up mostly in the middle, next to Whit. Both dogs clamored for space at the window, barking at the disappearing cattle. As they drove, she looked out across the ranch, at the new grass showing green through winter's brown and the expanse of rolling hills that led to the mountains. "This really is beautiful country. How much property do you have?"

"Just over thirty-two hundred acres." Whit pointed through the windshield. "From the bend in the river up to the base of that ridge over there."

"All yours?"

"Yep. For the last five years since my grandma died."

"No other heirs to fight over the land?" Jordan was thinking of what Sheriff Carlyle had asked about Whit's dad.

Whit stared out at his land. "None that I know of."

Jordan reached for the seat as the road got bumpier.

"Hold on," Whit said, shifting into four-wheel drive.

"To what?" Jordan said.

He grinned. "Whatever you can find. The road only gets worse from here."

She considered how to bring the conversation back to Whit's family, but she could only think of hers. "I have a confession to make: this isn't the first time I've done farm chores like this."

"Oh?" Whit looked mildly curious and amused. "Did you do a class trip to a farm?"

"My grandpa who lived in eastern Washington had a little farm. He grew wheat and had a few cows and some other farm animals. When I'd go visit in the summer, he'd take me out to feed the calves and the chickens. He used to call me Jo Jo." Jordan looked out over the field. She hadn't thought of her Grandpa Brown in ages, but now she felt a twinge of sadness as she remembered his rough but gentle hands showing her how to hold the bottle so a calf wouldn't pull it away.

"I knew you had a bit of country girl in you somewhere." Whit's eyes glowed with the setting sun. "Your mom's dad or your dad's dad?"

"Mom's. She couldn't get away from that little farm fast enough. My grandma died before I was born, so we hardly visited Grandpa Brown. He was a good man though. You remind me of him."

"I'm not sure how to take that," Whit said. "No woman has ever told me I remind her of her grandpa before."

"It's a compliment. Trust me," Jordan said. "What about your family?"

"One set of grandparents raised me, but I barely knew my other set. My mom's parents were businesspeople in Missoula, gone now, but I only met them a couple of times. Mom's parents didn't want her to marry my dad, even though she was already pregnant. That didn't make it any easier for us to go see them, especially since most of those visits were about us needing money. I think they blamed him for ruining my mom's life." He shook his head. "They were probably right. They thought she was going to go to college and make something more of herself than the wife of a crop duster and a washed-out rodeo cowboy."

"Your dad was a crop duster?" Jordan hadn't heard this part of Charlie Palmer's background. "That's a pretty high-risk occupation. How'd he get into that?"

"It was my grandpa's idea. He'd been a crop duster when he was younger and he had his own plane. I think he figured it was a way for my dad to earn an honest living. Maybe a way for him to get his adrenaline fix too. Grandpa paid for the training, fixing up the plane and the runway, but like most things Dad tried—it didn't last long."

"Where's your grandpa's plane now?" Jordan asked.

"Believe it or not, at the far end of my property there's a small runway, a hangar, and an old plane. Grandma never had the heart to sell it. I guess I haven't either. Grandpa was a pilot in Vietnam. After he got home, he mortgaged the ranch to build the runway and the hangar." Whit looked far away. "The ranch has never made much profit. Grandpa thought the crop-dusting business would bring in enough money to keep it going."

"I'd love to see it sometime."

"Grandpa's plane?" Whit's face closed down again. He shook his head. "The road to get there is tougher than this. It's been washed out, so you'd have to go by horseback. He built the runway out there because it was the only level place on the ranch."

Jordan thought back to what Shelly had told her about the theory that Bonnie Golden's murderer had used a plane to scatter her remains all over the county. "Do you know how to fly?"

Whit looked at her strangely, like he wasn't sure if he should answer that question. "Grandpa took me up a few times, and taught me the basics, but the plane was old and fuel was too expensive to just go joy riding."

She could tell there was something about the plane bothered Whit. Jordan didn't know how to push that one either. "How long were your parents together?"

Whit turned back to the road ahead. "Too long, not long enough. I was eight when he got involved with Bonnie. I don't think she was the first, but she was the one who convinced him to take off."

Jordan studied Whit's profile, noting the line in his jaw. He was obviously angry with his dad and Bonnie too. But how angry was he now, and how angry was he back then? Jordan didn't know the right questions to ask to find out. Finally, she asked, "What about your mom?"

The line in his jaw softened. "She died when I was pretty young. Drug overdose. My dad leaving broke something in her that never got fixed."

"I'm sorry." It was a lame thing to say, but it was all she had.

"I had Grandma and Shelly, and the people in Lombard were all kind of family. We take care of our own here."

"I've noticed," Jordan said, trying not to sound bitter. She was thinking about how much more information Shelly was able to get than she was.

The truck lurched sideways as they went into a dip in the gravel road. Something banged against the glove compartment and it fell open. It was a black gun case.

Jordan picked it up. "May I?"

Whit shrugged. "Sure."

Jordan opened the case to reveal a silver-plated pistol. "This is a pretty gun, Commissioner. I assume you have a permit for this?"

Whit laughed. "I don't need a permit for that in Montana. Better check your firearm laws, Detective. Besides, it won't hit much unless you're at pretty close range. It was my grandpa's. He gave it to me when I graduated from high school."

"And you carry it around in your truck?" She acknowledged the rifle racked in the back window. "Because in Montana, one gun isn't enough?"

"I was planning to take it to Heyward to be restored. I put it in there so I wouldn't forget it the next time I went into town. Apparently, that didn't work."

"Apparently." Jordan examined the gun for a minute and then put it back in the case. "Belt buckles and guns are appropriate graduation presents in Montana?"

Whit laughed. "Yeah. What did you get for graduation?"

Jordan hesitated. "A trip to Europe and a car."

Whit whistled. "Your parents must have been pretty proud that you graduated."

Jordan shrugged, "That was before I told them I was planning to be a cop."

"I'm guessing that conversation didn't go over well."

Jordan looked out the window. She didn't like that the questioning had gotten back to her, but maybe Whit would be more open if she was open with him. "For a while I did the whole scene: private school, ballet lessons, country club. It didn't take long to figure out that it wasn't for me, but I didn't know how to be my own person. Then I took a self-defense class after school when I was a junior in high school. It was taught by a female cop. I liked her approach, so I quit ballet and signed up for her Krav Maga class without telling my parents. I spent a lot of time after class talking to the officer who taught the class. She was the first person I'd ever met who seemed to get me. She inspired me to find my own path. I became a cop right out of high school. Up until that point it was the only teenage rebellion my parents had ever experienced from me."

"Becoming a cop was rebelling?" Whit asked.

"According to them, becoming a cop was throwing years of good breeding, civility, and education out the window."

"But you did go to school. A master's in criminal justice, if I remember right."

"Yeah. I took classes online or at night whenever I could while I was working. My parents had money to pay for school, but it wasn't the kind of education they wanted for me, so I did it on my own."

"You seem to be good at it," Whit added.

"I'm very good at it." Jordan didn't say it like she was bragging, just stating a fact. "Not that they'd notice."

"You don't talk to your parents?"

"Barely. But never about work. I think they're still waiting for me to grow out of this phase. Don't get me wrong, my parents have the 'deepest respect' for law enforcement." She put "deepest respect" in air quotes. "They're both businesspeople. Dad made a bunch of money in a start-up tech and then went out on his own. Mom is a designer of sorts. She has a very high-end dress shop in Seattle. They're both into the Seattle socialite scene. To them, police officers are more like hired help, there to clean up other people's messes."

"What about when you solved that big case in Seattle?" Whit asked.

"Crickets from them. They were a bit more vocal about me coming here though."

"Not big on small-town Montana?"

"Just another example of how I'm throwing my life away."

"Why did you come out here? It looked like your career in Seattle was going pretty well."

Jordan stared out the window at the mountains growing closer. She thought of all the reasons she'd left Seattle, reasons she never wanted to tell Whit or anyone else about. How stupidly cliché of her to lose the career she'd worked so hard for over a man. How against everything she thought she stood for. "I needed some space, and the case intrigued me."

Whit raised his eyebrows. "We definitely have space, but I'd think the last thing you'd be interested in was the murder of a small-town sheriff. When Heyward suggested your name to the AG—"

"Heyward was the one who wanted me here?"

"Yeah, surprised me too."

Now Jordan had something else to occupy her thoughts. Heyward was the quietest of the three commissioners, the one she knew the least. Why would he have sought her out?

"Here we are." Whit stopped the truck at the edge of a ravine. "Just at the right time, too."

Jordan looked across to the mountains. The sun was just starting to set, painting the mountains fiery red, rose, and gold. Whit got out of the truck and held the driver's side door for her. For a second Jordan got the feeling that Whit had brought her here just to show off the sunset. It was spectacular. "Wow."

"Gorgeous, isn't it?" he said, smiling.

"Breathtaking. Sunsets are hard to see in Seattle unless you get out in the open or near the water. There are too many trees, and in downtown, buildings that block your view. I mean, nothing beats the sun coming up over Mount Rainier with the Puget Sound in the foreground, but I'd say this is a close second." She stepped back, aware that she was standing closer than a professional distance from Whit.

He moved toward the edge of the ravine. "This is the place. I stood on the edge and threw it as far as I could."

Jordan looked at the depth of the ravine and the rugged country around it. It wasn't likely anyone recovered the belt buckle from here. Either Whit was lying, or the buckle, like the dog collar, was a fake. She pulled it out and held it up in the light.

"Any chance this isn't your dad's buckle?"

Whit took it from her and turned it over again. "If it's not, someone put a lot of time into making it look like his."

"Is there anyone who might want to tie you to the Golden case?" Jordan asked.

"Are you asking me if I have any enemies?" Whit looked mildly amused at the idea. "None that I can think of."

"Shelly thought the belt buckle was a message from the killer."

"A message to who?" Whit asked.

"Not sure. You, or her, maybe both." Another thought came to her. "Do you have any idea where someone would get a belt buckle like this made?"

"There's a shop in Anaconda, Montana Silver. They do custom belt buckles like this for all the rodeos around here, have done them for years." He looked back at the buckle. "Might have even made the one my dad wore. I'd start there."

"Thanks," Jordan said. She looked at the sunset. She wasn't sure how to tell Whit she'd seen what she wanted to see and asked what she wanted to ask, and she should be heading back. Worse than that, she wasn't sure she wanted to head back.

As she turned that thought over, something a few feet down the ravine caught her eye. "What is that?" She pointed to an oddly shaped white rock, resting on an outcropping of boulders a few feet down the ravine. She stepped closer to the edge to try to get a better look.

"What's going on? Detective, watch it!" Whit grabbed her wrist as her feet slid on some loose rocks.

"Thanks," Jordan said, catching her breath and her footing before pulling away from him. She got down on her knees and peered over the edge. "Do you see what I see?"

Whit got down beside her, his hand on her back. Jordan couldn't tell if he was trying to steady himself or keep her from slipping again. He followed her gaze to the whitish-brown object. He let out a low whistle. "Is that what I think it is?"

"Give me a hand and we'll find out." Jordan turned around on her stomach and reached her hands to Whit so he could lower her over the edge to the outcrop of rocks where the object sat.

"Are you sure about this?" Whit asked. "Could be a mountain goat skull, or just a strange rock."

She looked up at him, realizing how out of character it was for her to trust someone this completely, especially since she came here on a suspicion that he might be involved in a murder. But she was too curious about what was on the ledge to back out now. "Unless you don't think you can hold me."

"I can hold you alright. I just ... okay." He took her wrists in his big rough hands. "Be careful. It's a long way down, and the ledge might not be as sturdy as you think."

"Just don't let go."

With Whit hanging on, Jordan inched over the edge. She looked up, catching Whit's gaze of concentration, concern, and something like terror. She dangled in thin air for a minute. "A little lower." Her feet touched the ground. She tested the sturdiness of the ledge. It seemed secure. "I'm good," she said.

"You sure?"

"Yeah."

Whit let go. He leaned back so his face didn't show anymore. Jordan could hear him breathing as she picked her way along the ridge. She bent close to the rock without touching it. This close she could see it was half a skull. More than that, there was a scrap of blood-soaked fabric beneath the bone.

"Well?" Whit called from above.

"It's human."

Chapter Twenty-Eight

"DETECTIVE, CAN I TALK to you a minute?" Sheriff Carlyle said as the forensics team that had come down from Helena continued their work by the ridge. It was now completely dark, the only light coming from floodlights rigged on the edge of the ravine, and those set up by the news crews that had come from as far away as Missoula. Jordan walked with him past Whit's truck, empty except for his two dogs sleeping on the seat. Whit had locked them in after everyone started to arrive. Jordan wasn't sure where he was now, probably not far. He'd stayed for the entire investigation.

When they'd reached the perimeter of activity, Carlyle started in on her. "I was just wondering how you ended up out here, alone with Whit Palmer."

Jordan gave him a look that she hoped portrayed at least a fraction of her annoyance. "I came to question him about the belt buckle. Shelly said he was the last person known to have it."

"That doesn't explain how you ended up all the way out here," Carlyle said, his eyes snapping with suspicion.

"Commissioner Palmer told me he threw the buckle into the ravine, so I came with him to see where that was."

"In his vehicle or yours?"

"I really don't know what this has to do with my investigation," Jordan replied.

"It has to do with what we talked about before. If you need to question someone, that shouldn't include a romantic drive into the sunset."

Jordan's face flamed with anger. "My 'romantic drive' as you put it, netted us an important clue and I—"

"Detective." Ray's voice cut through the night. "Oh, there you are." He held out a paper cup. "Thought you might like a cup of coffee. It's not the good stuff, but it'll warm you up."

Jordan accepted the cup, fully aware of Sheriff Carlyle's dark gaze resting on her. "Thanks, Ray."

"Some lucky break, right?" Ray asked. "You go out driving with Whit and you find—"

"I was following up on a lead," Jordan said, squeezing the paper cup until it burned through the cover and the heat seeped into her fingertips. "There was no luck involved. I'm going to have a word with the ME."

"We're not done here," Sheriff Carlyle said.

"We can talk later." Jordan walked away, knowing she'd regret anything she said now. She was too tired and too angry at his implications to have this conversation. It didn't help that part of her agreed with him. She had let things get too friendly with Whit today.

When she stepped back into the light she found Shelly there, talking to a female Medical Examiner. "You believe the skull has been moved?" Shelly was saying.

"Definitely. If it had really been here since Bonnie was killed, there would have been more plant life growing around it," the ME said.

"And it wasn't moved by an animal?" Shelly asked.

"No. There is evidence it was buried at some point. It looks like it was actually cleaned off, made whiter, more visible."

"We were meant to find it," Shelly said. "Dammit. That's two for Whit."

"Two for Whit?" Jordan asked.

"Hello, Detective," Shelly said.

"Doing my job again?" Jordan asked.

Shelly ignored the question. "How long do you think it's been down there?"

"Impossible to tell exactly, but not long."

"Any chance it was dropped from a plane?" Shelly asked.

"Not likely. It would have been more damaged on impact," the medical examiner said. "The other bones maybe, but not this one."

"That blows my original theory out of the water, especially since you said it was buried," Shelly said.

The other woman nodded. "I'd agree with that. If it had been dropped out of a plane and not buried, some animal would have dragged it off a long time ago."

Shelly looked thoughtful. "I guess that means access to a plane is no longer a determining factor for Bonnie's killer."

"And the blood on the shirt?" Jordan asked.

"Same as before. I would guess less than twelve hours old."

"But it didn't attract any wild animals," Shelly said. "Couldn't have been there that long."

"That's a good point. I guess that goes for all the blood we've found," Jordan conceded. "So she's definitely still alive?"

"If this turns out to match the other two samples you sent in, then I'd say the woman was alive sometime this morning. Beyond that I couldn't say."

"He couldn't just be keeping her blood?" Shelly asked.

"It would have coagulated too quickly," the ME replied.

"This didn't happen before, this kind of taunting. Bonnie just disappeared. We might have never found any part of her if it hadn't been for …" Shelly turned to Jordan, her eyes suddenly wide. "Was there anything missing from the sheriff's house?"

"Nothing was noted in the report," Jordan said. "There was a gun that went missing later, but—"

"Not a gun. We need to go to Blodgett's house. Can you meet me there tomorrow, evening, like six o'clock? I have an appointment in Butte I can't miss."

"Yeah, of course. What are we looking for?" Jordan asked.

"I'll know it when I see it," Shelly said. "What led you and Whit to—"

"This is a restricted area. Law enforcement personnel only." Sheriff Carlyle joined them from the dark edges of the scene, interrupting the question Shelly was about to ask. He smiled, but beyond the smile was irritation.

"Evening, Sheriff," Shelly said. Her voice had changed. She sounded casual, like she was meeting the interim sheriff at the Silver Horseshoe instead of on the edge of a crime scene.

"Evening, Shelly," he said. "What do you make of all of this?"

Shelly looked around. "Hell of a circus."

"That it is," Carlyle said. He cleared his throat. "With all due respect, ma'am … this is an open investigation, and you aren't exactly—"

"I know. Not my circus, not my monkeys," Shelly said. "Whit. You ready to head back?"

Jordan hadn't seen Whit walk over. He looked exhausted and worried. Without thinking, she handed him the coffee Ray had given her. "You look like you need this more than I do."

He accepted the cup. "Thanks. Do you need a ride back to your Expedition?"

"When she's finished here, we'll get Detective Gibbons back to her vehicle." The sheriff looked from Jordan to Whit, his eyes alive with suspicion.

"Right," Whit said. "Don't forget to stop by for that recipe before you head out, Detective."

"Right," Jordan said, but she wished Whit hadn't brought it up.

After Shelly and Whit were out of earshot, Sheriff Carlyle glowered at her. "So now you're swapping recipes with Commissioner Palmer?"

"When I'm off duty, I don't think it's any of your business what I swap with Commissioner Palmer." Jordan knew immediately it was the wrong thing to say, but she stared back at the sheriff without flinching anyway.

His expression hardened, but instead of the dressing down she expected, he turned to Ray. "We're pretty much wrapped up here and Detective Gibbons has had a long day. Could you get her back to her vehicle ASAP?"

"I'm fine, Sheriff," Jordan broke in. "This might not be wrapped up for—"

"As I keep reminding you, this is not the case you were hired for. We've got things here. Go home, Detective. That's not a request."

Jordan wanted to argue, but a subtle shake of Ray's head stopped her. He was probably right. There wasn't much left at this scene besides packing up. She was tired and pushing things with the sheriff might be a bad idea now. She'd have to fight this battle another time.

"What'd you do to piss off Brendan?" Ray asked as soon as she got in his vehicle. "Not that he's not easily piss-off-able right now."

"I'm encroaching on his territory. He believes the whole idea of me being here undermines his authority," Jordan said. She had no desire to tell Ray the real reason the sheriff was on her case. "He thinks I should be focusing my efforts on finding the sheriff's killer, but he's an idiot if he doesn't see how these two cases are related."

"Yeah, well, he's under a lot of pressure to put both cases in the bag. People really liked Blodgett, so Brendan is trying to fill some big boots. That, and he's got Judd breathing down his neck all the time."

"Judd?" Jordan asked.

"Yeah. He was in the sheriff's office for a good hour this afternoon. I'm not sure what it was about, but neither of them looked very happy when they came out. I guess I'm saying you should go a little easy on him."

"I thought you didn't like the Carlyle. I was told you were upset that you didn't get the interim sheriff's position," Jordan said.

"I was, I am, and I don't like him. I fully plan on beating Brendan's ass when election time comes around. It doesn't mean I don't want to see this case get solved. There's still a woman out there, maybe still alive, who needs our help."

"Yeah." Jordan leaned back against the headrest, feeling as exhausted as Whit looked. Ray was right. She couldn't lose sight of what she was trying to do. This wasn't just about figuring out what happened to the sheriff or even Bonnie Golden; it was about keeping the same thing from happening again.

Chapter Twenty-Nine

MONTANA SILVER AND AWARDS was a small shop with plenty of Montana bling. The interior had dark wood paneling; there were racks of earrings, bracelets, and necklaces, as well as a huge glass display case in the front. It was filled with silver and turquoise rings and other jewelry, a few small silver statues, but mostly belt buckles. The walls were covered with pictures of cowboys and cowgirls from various rodeos wearing more belt buckles.

The man behind the counter was young, early thirties and built short and thick—not fat, just thick. An oval belt buckle circled his Wranglers. He smiled widely when Jordan walked toward him. "Good morning, ma'am. How can I help you?"

"Do you make custom belt buckles?" Jordan asked, knowing it was a stupid question considering everything she was surrounded by.

"Yes ma'am. You looking for something for yourself or your husband?"

"Neither." His smile faded as she pulled out her badge. "I'm Detective Gibbons from the Keystone County Sheriff's Department." She laid the belt buckle on the glass counter in front of him. "I was hoping you could tell me if this was made in your shop?"

He picked it up, running his finger over the smooth metal. "I'm not sure. It says 1989, but I don't think it's that old." He turned it over. "Probably not real silver, either. It's got a bluish tint, rather than the black patina you'd expect from real silver."

"So it wasn't made here?" Jordan said.

"Could have been. Not everything we make is silver, but my dad does the metal work, and it's not likely he'd do a replica of an award like this without a good reason. Too many guys walking around pretending to be rodeo champions who never sat a horse." As he said it, the man hooked his thumb through his belt loop, angling his hand so Jordan couldn't miss the depiction of a steer wrestler on his own buckle surrounded by the words "Sheridan, Wyoming Bulldogging Champion."

Jordan ignored the man's preening. "Is your dad here? I'd like to speak to him."

"Yeah. He's in the back. Give me a second."

"Thanks."

While she waited, Jordan looked at the pictures above the counter. She'd assumed the people in the pictures were models, but as she looked closer, she could see that most of them were pictures taken after a rodeo, the winners holding up their belt buckle proudly. Smack dab in the middle of the wall, in all her glory was Tawny, a silver buckle at her waist, a rhinestone tiara perched on her red hair.

Jordan turned away from the photo. She pushed through a rack of silver necklaces, picking out a silver butterfly with turquoise wings. She turned it over, admiring the details. It struck her that this was a distinctly western piece, something she wouldn't have looked twice at in Seattle.

"That would look very nice on that pretty neck." A shorter, gray-haired version of the man she'd just spoken with walked toward Jordan. She put the necklace back as he held out his hand. "Dawson McBride."

She gripped his hand. "Jordan Gibbons. Your work is beautiful." She said it sincerely, not sure when she'd gained an appreciation for cowboy art.

"Thank you, ma'am. My son says you have a belt buckle you're wondering if I made?"

"Yes." She handed him the buckle from the counter.

"I make a lot of belt buckles, so normally I'd say we need to go back to the inventory book, but I remember this one, because like my son told you, I don't usually remake awards like this."

"What made you do this one, then?"

"A dark-haired young woman came in a couple of months ago. She said her boyfriend was upset because he'd lost his dad's belt buckle and she wanted to surprise him by replacing it. Said her boyfriend's dad had passed and it would mean a lot if he had the buckle back. She had a picture of the dad wearing the buckle with the kid on his lap. The dad had even signed the picture, something like 'Here's to more great memories.'"

"Did you make a copy of the picture, so you could use it to duplicate the buckle?"

"I did."

"Can I see it?"

Mr. McBride directed his son to get the picture. When the younger man came back, he had two versions of it. One was a photocopy of a man who looked a lot like Whit, except with a more pronounced nose and heavier eyebrows. The boy on his lap was in an embroidered cowboy shirt, with a small black cowboy hat and a bolo tie. He looked about five years old. Whit was just as cute a kid as Jordan would have expected. The second picture was zoomed in to see the details of the belt buckle.

Jordan picked them both up. "Can I have a copy of these?"

"Take those. I don't have any use for them," Mr. McBride said.

"Thanks. Do you have the name of the woman who brought it in, a credit card receipt or anything like that?"

"She paid cash on the spot. The only name she gave was Golden."

Jordan shook her head. "Do you remember anything else about the young woman? If I showed you a picture, would you be able to pick her out?" She pulled out the picture she'd brought of Sadie.

He shook his head slowly. "Maybe, but she wore dark glasses both times she was in here. Her hair was darker and shorter, but it could have been a wig."

"Did you ever see the boyfriend?" Jordan asked.

She could tell the question made the man uncomfortable. "Once, briefly. He didn't come into the shop, but he was standing right outside that window." The man nodded toward the big picture window in the front of the shop.

"What did he look like?"

"Tall, square jaw, black cowboy hat. But I didn't really see him that well."

Jordan tried to keep her face neutral. "Do you know who he was?"

The man hesitated. "I know who the dad in the picture was, so I guess maybe …" Jordan held her breath as he continued. "The dad was Charlie Palmer, so the kid was most likely Whit. But I'm not positive it was him."

"Did it look like him?" Jordan pressed.

"Maybe," Mr. McBride said without commitment.

"Maybe? Could you be more specific?"

"The guy might have looked like Whit, but he didn't act like Whit."

"I thought you only saw him through the window."

He let out a long breath. "I felt bad for the woman. She seemed so excited to give him the buckle, but he didn't look very happy to see it. Kind of shoved it back at her and climbed in his truck. Whit wouldn't have treated her like that."

Jordan thought of how quick Whit's demeanor changed when she brought up his dad. If Sadie had tried to impress him with the buckle, he might have gotten mad about it and acted out of character.

"Look, the guy could have been lying to impress her. He probably told her some story about his dad being a rodeo champion, found the picture of Whit and his dad somewhere, and then told her some sob story about his dad being dead."

"That might almost be a plausible explanation if the buckle hadn't been found in Shelly Curtis's flower bed." Jordan waited for a minute for that to sink in. Then she asked, "Are you willing to give me a positive identification on either the woman who bought the buckle or the man who she was with?

"No," Mr. McBride said.

"You've been a lot of help," Jordan said, even though she was frustrated. She took the pictures. "If you think of anything else—"

"It wasn't Whit's truck."

"What?" Jordan turned to face Mr. McBride's son, who had been watching quietly from behind the counter. "Are you sure?"

The man stepped closer. "Positive. The truck they got into was an older Ford. Texas plates."

On the way out of Anaconda, Jordan called Ray. "Are you still working on the convicts Sadie was writing to?"

"As we speak," he said.

"Do me a favor, see if you can trace any of those emails back to Texas."

"You got something?" Ray asked.

"Maybe. Let me know what you find." Jordan hung up and focused on the drive ahead of her. She didn't want to think about the direction this investigation was taking.

Chapter Thirty

WHEN JORDAN RETURNED, THE sheriff's office was a maze of confusion. Jordan had no idea what had transpired in her absence, but she knew right away Beats was furious, not at all her usual self. She took her aside and asked what was wrong. Beats, still spitting out fire and brimstone, was more than happy to tell Jordan all about it.

"Have you met that new deputy—Duncan Fanshaw? The one from Bozeman?" Beats demanded. "I swear he's dumber than an old rusty fence post. And—relative stranger that he is—he is entirely too familiar. When I was dispatching today, he sauntered over to my desk and leaned solidly against my shoulder like we were dear old friends. He said, Beats, I want to show you my new gun, and he had the audacity—and stupidity—to position it no more than two or three inches from the end of my nose.

"The gun went off—nearly deafening me; he clutched his chest, lost his balance, fell back a step or two, and started yelling. When he moved his hand away from his chest a few seconds later his shirt was already thoroughly soaked with blood. His hand was not only covered with blood, it was dripping more blood with every movement. My first thought was that he had a chest wound—but it turned out he had only shot himself through the hand. I am ashamed of what I did next, but what is done is done."

Jordan fought to kept her face neutral; she had a feeling Beats wasn't ready for find humor in the story. "What did you do?"

"My anger knew no bounds. In all my many long years I do not remember ever being quite that mad. I abruptly stood up with such force that my chair went careening halfway across the room and nearly knocked him over. I stuck my face close to his and then I let it rip.

"At the top of my lungs I shouted, Duncan, you crazy, idiotic, damn fool! What the hell were you thinking? How could you possibly do something that stupid? That dangerous? I became as crazed as I thought he was. My tongue lashed out at him with every single swear word I have ever used, read about, or heard anyone else utter, and I applied them all to him. I questioned his intelligence, and even cursed his relatives. I was sorely tempted to grab some object or other, anything solid, and pound the crap out of him. I thought better of that, told another deputy to take over the desk, hurriedly wrapped his hand in a towel, shoved him out the door, into my car, and headed for the hospital. I burned his stupid ears with expletives all the way there. All the time the doctor was working on him I raged on, telling the doctor what I thought of his patient.

"When I finally calmed down enough to realize the gunshot had frightened me out of my mind—and I was behaving like a stark raving mad banshee—I sat down, shut up, took deep breaths, and tried to find that level-headed, reasonable person inside me that I was accustomed to dealing with.

"Jordan, I usually do not get involved in such matters, but if Dumber-Than-Dumb-Duncan has not been fired by quitting time tonight I guarantee you I am going to raise all Billy hell until he does get his walking papers and is safely out of town. He is a hazard, and I want him gone."

Jordan shook her head. "Beats, if someone that careless and irresponsible stuck a gun that close to my face and it went off, I probably would've turned the gun on him and finished the job, or at the very least let him bleed to death on the floor. That man has no business with a gun, much less a badge."

Beats sat down; her story and her experience obviously had exhausted her. "And now I have to file a damn report on the whole thing. Could you get the ledger out of Becca's desk for me? I need the serial number from Duncan's gun."

"Ledger? Isn't it on the computer?" Jordan asked, gesturing to the one on Beats' desk.

"Not likely. Becca usually records things in the ledger first, and then she or Carlyle enter them in the database. With her on maternity leave and Carlyle overstrung as he is, there's no one to enter it. Duncan hasn't been here that long." She gestured toward Becca's desk. "Bottom drawer on the left."

Jordan went to Becca's vacant desk and recovered the black ledger from the bottom drawer. Before taking it to Beats she flipped through a couple of pages. She remembered what Judd had said about new firearms. She found the page where they'd all been recorded, including Blodgett's gun, the one he'd been shot with. The serial number was written next to his signature. The last digit of the serial number was nine, the same as the murder weapon, but the last number had been circled and next to it was a neat curlicue question mark that could have only been made by Becca.

Chapter Thirty-One

GRIEF AND REGRET WERE written across Shelly's face as she looked around the sheriff's house. Her eyes trailed over the worn set of cards, the shelf of books, and the empty dog bed.

"You haven't been back here since the sheriff was shot?" Jordan said.

"No," Shelly answered simply. She trailed her fingers along the dark wainscoting that lined the hallway as she headed toward the sheriff's office.

"Do you know what you're looking for?" Jordan said.

"Maybe. I'd think Angie would have noticed and said something but ..." Shelly stopped at the doorway to the sheriff's office. She stopped at the place where the chair once stood. She studied the walls, covered with awards and pictures. "It's what I thought."

"What?"

"The picture's gone." Shelly walked to the space above the bookcase where Jordan had noticed the nail hole before.

"What picture?"

Shelly shook her head. "At the beginning of the Bonnie Golden case, I received a gift from the murderer. It was left on my desk at the sheriff's office in a plain brown envelope. It was an aerial photograph, showed a good chunk of our county. The only thing unusual was a red symbol next to the river—the exact location where the hunters had found what was left of Bonnie. Later I deciphered another symbol. This one led to part of her arm clear up by the old mines. That's why I assumed her body had been scattered by airplane."

"It was a map of sorts."

"Yeah. A map without a key. I spent hours poring over that damned thing. I was convinced the killer had kept track of all the places he'd discarded Bonnie Golden's remains, but he'd only marked that one."

"A map of gold," Jordan said, remembering the letter she'd recovered from the box in Sadie's old apartment.

"More like a map of bones," Shelly said. "It looks like someone has that map and the key. And now they have us running all over the county, putting the pieces back together, gift-wrapping them in Sadie's torn up clothes soaked in her blood."

"If the photo was given to you, why did the sheriff have it?" Jordan asked.

"I gave it to him just before I left the sheriff's office. We couldn't find out what happened to Bonnie. All our leads had gone cold. Blodgett had handily beaten Judd in the election and I was tired and ready to be done. I handed the whole thing over to Brady, retired from the department and became a private detective. He hung the picture above his bookcase. He wasn't ever going to let that case go." Shelly turned back to Jordan. "Maybe he should have."

Jordan paused a minute to let Shelly collect herself, but the woman was already moving on. "You said the dog was shot with the sheriff's gun. Do you know which one it was?"

"The .45."

Shelly nodded. "It would have been an easy one to grab. He kept that one in the case behind his desk." She walked over to the empty rack. "Except you said it was stolen from evidence."

"I'm not exactly sure about that. Ray said he saw the gun, but I couldn't find it in the catalog of evidence taken from the scene."

"It was here, but then it wasn't. And then it was used to shoot that dog? Interesting." Shelly walked to the desk and picked up an obsidian paperweight, carved into the shape of a wolf.

Jordan watched Shelly, knowing the question she needed to ask would probably make the other woman mad. "Do you know where Whit was the night the sheriff was shot?"

"Whit?" Shelly put the paperweight down. "What does he have to do with this?"

"I checked out the belt buckle at the shop in Anaconda. A woman who looks similar to Sadie asked them to replicate Charlie Palmer's belt buckle as a present for his son."

Shelly looked at Jordan with that penetrating gaze she had. "And that present ended up buried in my yard. Sounds like that was how it was supposed to be delivered."

"Except the shop owner saw someone with the woman who bought the buckle. Someone who looked like Whit."

"Whit was in Texas the night the sheriff was murdered," Shelly said.

"Texas?" Jordan asked, her interest piqued.

"At a rancher's conference. Hundreds of people probably saw him. That's about as ironclad as an alibi gets, don't you think? Now about that map—"

Her thought was interrupted by a loud bang from the barn outside.

Jordan drew her gun.

Chapter Thirty-Two

SHELLY PUT HER HAND over Jordan's. "Probably just a car backfiring." Shelly walked to the living room and peered between the curtains. An old black car was parked in the space behind the barn.

"Looks like Peyton is at it again." She let the curtain drop. "He must have moved his stash closer to town since the sheriff is gone."

Jordan watched the young man get out of his car. "He can see my vehicle, right? My Expedition? How stupid is he?" Peyton looked around the yard, glancing at the police car before he slipped into the barn. "He was here when I came before. He said he's been feeding the cats."

"He may be, but I guarantee that's not all he's doing," Shelly said.

"I'm going to check it out," Jordan said.

"You sure about that?" Shelly asked. "This is a small town. You've got to pick your battles."

Even though it was almost the same rationale Jordan used the last time she encountered Peyton, Shelly's suggestion rubbed Jordan the wrong way. Maybe it was because she'd spent the morning in Carlyle's office as he re-explained her role here in Lombard, the limits of her authority, and the chain of command. He hadn't brought up her past affair or asked what was going on with Whit, but even those unsaid words hung between them.

Making a small-potatoes drug arrest right now when she was supposed to be concentrating on a murder investigation more than likely would further annoy the illustrious sheriff, but it also felt like a good way to do some actual police work.

"Of course I'm sure." Jordan slipped out of the house and walked around to the back of the barn.

Shelly followed her. Peyton was in one corner, peering under an old stairway. "Jerry, is that you?" he called. He didn't turn around to see that neither of them were Jerry until Jordan was right next to him.

"Can I help you find something?" Jordan asked.

Peyton stepped back, tripping on the bottom step. He recovered without falling, but still dusted himself off like he had. "I was just trying to find Aunt Angie's cat." His eyes trailed to the corner of the barn and the pile of hay he'd been looking at before.

It seemed bigger to Jordan this time. She moved toward the stack, watching Peyton's reaction as she got closer.

"Which one is missing?" Shelly said.

"The black one with the white mustache," Peyton said. "He doesn't like to hide in the haystack though."

"Is there something in the haystack you want to show us?" Shelly said.

"No ma'am," Peyton said. "I'm just looking for the cat."

"Then you won't mind if I take a look?" Jordan asked.

"I already looked in the haystack," Peyton said.

Jordan crossed the barn. "If the cat doesn't like to hide in the haystack, why did you look there?"

Peyton looked around, like he was looking for an escape. At the same time he seemed frozen in place. "I need to go home."

"Let me look around a little first." Jordan picked up the first couple of bales on the fringes of the stack.

"I hope you know what you're doing," Shelly said.

"I have an idea." Jordan went through the bales methodically, until she'd nearly torn apart half the stack. Her hands were burning and a line of sweat trickled down her neck. She was just about to give up when she uncovered a wooden crate, the same size as the bales, but hidden in the middle of the stack.

She met Shelly's gaze. "What do you think you've found?" the older woman asked.

"I'm not sure yet." Jordan scanned the shelves of the barn until she saw a small crowbar.

"I don't think you should do that," Peyton said.

Jordan ignored him, jamming the crowbar under the lid of the box and prying it off with a loud screech of wood on wood. Inside were several hard black bricks wrapped in plastic.

"What the hell is that?" Shelly walked over and knelt beside Jordan as she sliced into one of the packages.

Jordan pressed her finger into the brick. "It's been awhile since I saw this, but I'm going to guess it's black tar heroin."

The door banged as Peyton pushed against it. Jordan hurdled one of the bales, unholstering her gun as she got closer. "Freeze!" she yelled. "Down on the ground."

Peyton dropped, throwing his hands in the air. "It isn't mine! It isn't mine!"

Shelly stood over the frightened teenager protectively as Jordan put her gun away, twisted

Peyton's hands behind his back, and pulled a pair of handcuffs off her belt.

"Maybe we should take the time to hear him out, if he says the drugs aren't his—"

"What about this?" Jordan pulled a plastic bag of marijuana from his jacket pocket. "If he has something to say, he can say it when I book him at the sheriff's office."

Shelly put her hand on Jordan's wrist to stop her from putting the cuffs on Peyton. "He might be more willing to talk here, and without those things—"

Peyton jumped up, his head knocking into Jordan's chin. She fell backward, stunned by the blow, and dropped the handcuffs. Peyton took off, bursting through the barn doors.

Jordan reached for the radio on her belt as she jumped up. "I need backup!" she yelled into the radio. "I'm at Blodgett's place and I have a suspect on the run."

She clipped the radio back onto her belt as Beats' voice crackled from her holster. "Did you hear that, Ray? How far out are you?"

"At least ten minutes."

"Anyone closer?" Beats asked.

Jordan heard enough of the exchange as she ran to gather that Ray was the closest to her position. Ten minutes might as well be forever. She was on her own. She kept her eye on Peyton. His initial burst of speed had put him far ahead of her, but she sensed he didn't do much running and she could probably outdistance him. There weren't a lot of places for him to hide. He cut left, ducking through a gap in the fence. He was headed for an open field with little cover. Jordan reached the same gap as her own Expedition passed by her on the road.

"I'll head him off on the far side of the field," Shelly yelled as she sped by.

"Do you have a description of the suspect?" Beats asked.

Jordan keyed her radio as she squeezed through the gap and sprinted across the field. She didn't have enough oxygen to get out a full description, so she just said. "Probably sixteen or seventeen years old, tall with blond hair. Says his name's Peyton. I'm still in pursuit."

"Peyton ...? Come again?" Beats sounded less like she misheard Jordan than that she disbelieved what she was hearing.

Jordan didn't have time to answer. She'd reached the far end of the fence. Peyton was just standing up from slipping between two rails. Jordan scrambled up the fence and launched herself up and over and straight at Peyton's back. He went down with a giant huff of exhaled breath. His face slammed into the packed dirt road.

She put one knee into Peyton's back, drew her gun, and pushed his face into the dust. "Don't move. I mean it!" She commanded. This time Peyton stayed still. She reached for her handcuffs and realized she'd dropped them when she started the pursuit.

Shelly pulled up next to them. "The extra set of cuffs," Jordan yelled. "In the—"

"I know where they are."

It seemed to Jordan that Shelly took her sweet time, even though she obviously knew where everything in the vehicle was kept. She came out with the cuffs and a medical kit. She held the cuffs out to Jordan and then knelt beside Peyton.

"You okay?" Shelly said. Jordan knew she wasn't talking to her. A puddle of blood streamed from Peyton's nose. "Give him some room to breathe."

Peyton coughed and a spatter of blood dotted Jordan's uniform.

Jordan finished cuffing him and rolled him to the side as Shelly pressed a packet of gauze against his nose. Jordan leaned back on her heels to catch her breath. Her jacket was covered in dust, her pants were torn, her hands were bleeding, and long pieces of hair had escaped from her bun.

"I'm telling you this is a mistake." Shelly handed Jordan another piece of gauze for her hands. "But since you just broadcast who you were arresting to anyone in the county with a police scanner, the damage is already done."

"No mistake. I bet once we tear that stack apart we'll find a whole lot more heroin. Our friend Peyton is in a lot of trouble. I'm not entirely sure it was a coincidence that he found the bone up at Rattlesnake."

"It's not mine!" Peyton insisted from behind the gauze Shelly still held to his nose.

Jordan read him his rights. Her reading was interspersed with Peyton saying again and again. "It's not mine."

"You're going about things the wrong way," Shelly said when Jordan had finished.

Jordan pulled Peyton to his feet. "No. I'm going about things according to the law."

"Which in this case might be the wrong thing to do. If you hadn't scared the poor kid to death, he might not have run. He might have actually given us something useful, but now—"

"With all due respect, it's been a long time since you were a cop." Jordan blew a piece of hair out of her face and tightened her grip on Peyton's arm. "And if you don't mind, I have a suspect to take in, book, and interrogate."

"I need to talk to my dad," Peyton said as Jordan directed him to her Expedition.

"You can call Daddy from the station," Jordan said, pushing him into the backseat.

"That might not be necessary." Shelly nodded down the road. An oversized green pickup followed by an impressive rooster tail of dust turned down the lane and sped toward them.

Jordan leaned back into the Expedition and asked Peyton, "What did you say your last name was?"

"Judd," Shelly supplied.

Chapter Thirty-Three

JUDD WAS OUT OF his pickup before it came to a complete stop. "Detective Gibbons!" he roared. "Why is my son in the back of your vehicle?"

He came toe to toe with Jordan, so close that his girth was inches from touching her, so close that spittle from his lips flecked her face. He towered over her, but she refused to back down.

"I found your son in the Blodgett's barn."

"He was feeding the cats!"

"Really? Was he feeding them heroin?"

Judd stopped for a minute, his expression twisting in confusion. "Heroin?"

"I found a crate of black tar heroin, hidden in the middle of the haystack in Blodgett's barn, and your son standing guard."

Judd sucked in a breath. "And I suppose you had a search warrant when you found the alleged heroin."

"It was a crime scene I—" Jordan realized her mistake immediately.

"As I recall the house was the crime scene, and the sheriff's department has already cleared the scene for the owner to reoccupy the entire property. So in essence, you and your civilian friend over there were trespassing. In fact, you were trespassing on a property I recently acquired."

Jordan tried not to let the weight of that revelation show on her face. "I thought I heard a gunshot. I had probable cause to investigate."

"You're telling me you don't know the difference between a backfiring car and a gunshot?" Judd laughed, but his face stayed the same shade of angry violet. "And what probable cause did you have to assault my son?"

"He ran and I pursued him."

"Before or after you accused him of being a drug lord? Before or after you pulled your weapon? Before or after your illegal search?"

Ray's vehicle pulled up, followed closely by the sheriff himself. Judd turned his attention from Jordan and strode over to the sheriff's car as he got out. Ray wisely stayed in his vehicle, pretending to take a call on the radio. Jordan turned to follow Judd.

"Better to stay put," Shelly advised. "Let them battle it out for now."

Jordan gritted her teeth, but she was in enough trouble. After a quick but heated discussion, Sheriff Carlyle released Peyton from the back seat of the patrol vehicle. He uncuffed the teenager and remanded him into his father's custody.

"This is not over, Ms. Gibbons!" Judd yelled.

"We need to secure the barn," Jordan said to Sheriff Carlyle after Judd had left. "And put a call in to the DEA. I know what I saw."

Carlyle shook his head. "I'll put in a call to the judge and see if we can get a proper search warrant, which at this point I don't think is likely. Hopefully, Judd will cool down enough to not press assault charges. Again, not likely."

Jordan was surprised he wasn't yelling at her again. He only seemed tired, resigned. She worked to keep her tone even. "If we get ahold of the DEA. I could —"

"I'll handle it." His voice was calm, but sharp. "Frankly, Detective, I'm tired of telling you the same thing repeatedly. I'm tired of cleaning up your messes because you think you're smarter than everyone else around here. Go back to the office and fill out the appropriate paperwork on this one. Make sure every i is dotted and every t is crossed. After that, go home. Take a long hot bath and get it through your head that you aren't the only competent person in our little sheriff's office. Think about what it is to work as a team. Think about falling in line and following the chain of command once in a while. Think about what it's going to mean to your illustrious career if you get thrown out of a tiny operation like ours for insubordination and questionable investigative techniques."

Jordan started to say something, but she knew there was only one thing she could say at this point. "I'm sorry, sir."

Chapter Thirty-Four

"DID YOU PUT SOME kind of deposit on this place?" Jordan's neighbor, Mrs. McKee, was waiting in Jordan's living room when she got back home. "'Cause I don't think you'll be getting it back."

"What happened?" Jordan surveyed the damage to her house—torn up pillows, shredded paperwork from the sheriff's files, broken dishes she'd left on the coffee table.

"My guess is Brownie here doesn't like staying alone all day," Mrs. McKee said.

For an injured dog, Brownie had laid a path of destruction that rivaled a midwestern hurricane. "How did you get in my house?" Jordan asked her neighbor. Mrs. McKee was sitting on the couch, sipping what looked like coffee from the pot Jordan had set to be ready when she came home.

"We heard him barking, so we came over to see what was wrong," Mrs. McKee said. "Brownie was going crazy when we got here. He was so upset we were afraid he'd hurt himself, so Bunny and I decided to stay. She has a calming effect on other dogs." The usually yappy little dog was quietly curled up with Brownie. Brownie whimpered when he saw Jordan. She wasn't sure if it was an apology or if he was chastising her for being gone so long.

"I tried to call, but you didn't answer. You should really keep your phone with you all the time, in case of an emergency."

"But how did you get into my house?" Jordan asked.

"Oh, Molly gave me a key, years ago." Mrs. McKee said it like it was no big deal, but to Jordan it felt like her friendly neighbor had crossed a line. "No need to thank me. That's just what neighbors do. Which reminds me. Have you looked into the noise complaint I put in yet? I heard that damned crop duster again, just shy of a week ago. Too late in the day to be spraying."

Jordan let out a long breath to keep from saying something she'd probably regret. She'd already done enough of that today. "How did Brownie get in here? I left him shut up in the garage."

"You really shouldn't leave him out there alone for so long. He's obviously suffered a traumatic experience. But maybe you aren't very familiar with dogs. I've had dogs my whole life, big dogs, little dogs, cow dogs, lap dogs. They can have the same quirks and fears that we do. Why, once we had this blue heeler who was afraid of our rooster. The bull he could handle, but that little red rooster, you should have seen the way he tucked in his tail and—"

She hadn't said it, but Jordan suspected Mrs. McKee had come and let Brownie out of the garage. The garage was insulated, with a dog door to the fenced back yard. Jordan obviously wasn't the first person to keep a dog there, but she didn't have the energy to try to justify her actions again today. "Mrs. McKee, I've had a very long day. I'd appreciate it if you would—"

"I'm sorry to hear that. I know all about bad days. This morning my stomach started acting up again, I don't know if it's the dairy thing. Dr. Hamblin said I should lay off the cheese, but I love it so much. Anyway, then the Thompson's cows were in my garden again and if you think getting those animals out of my yard is a picnic, well, just be glad you don't have anything in this yard that's worth eating. Molly used to keep this place up so nice. It's a shame to see it let go."

Jordan tried to say something, but her neighbor wasn't done yet. "I was just sitting down to watch the news and we heard poor old Brownie making such a fuss, so of course I got out of the chair and came right over."

"Again, thank you, but I—"

"—a dog psychologist or maybe it's a psychiatrist. I read about them somewhere. Probably not one in Lombard, but maybe Missoula or Billings. I'm not sure I buy into that sort of thing, but if there were ever a dog that had been traumatized, well—"

"—Mrs. McKee." Jordan's head was pounding. Her nerves were shot. "I'm really tired and I need you to leave."

"I don't under—"

Jordan moved to hold the door open. "You need to leave. Now."

Mrs. McKee stood for a long moment, her mouth gaping like a fresh caught trout. The shock faded to hurt, then to indignation. "Come on, Bunny, we're obviously not wanted here." The old woman gathered up her dog and headed for the door. "You're not in Seattle anymore, Detective. Here we treat each other with civility and we're grateful when our neighbors go out of their way to do us a favor."

Jordan didn't have the words or the energy to either apologize or to try to refute the woman's statement. Mrs. McKee walked through the door with a hurt sniff. Jordan was just about to close it and lock the door behind her neighbor when she heard Mrs. McKee say, "Big shot detective isn't receiving visitors right now, although I imagine she'll make an exception for you."

Jordan shut the door. She didn't care who else was out there. She wasn't letting anyone else in. She walked away from the door, moving a shredded pillow out of the way and slumping into a chair as a pair of boots ascended her front steps. The doorbell rang once and then again. Then there was a knock. Finally, Whit's voice came through the door. "Detective?" Jordan sighed with resignation, walked over, and opened the door.

He waited on her porch, a couple of bowls balanced in his arms. Jordan stood up straight, trying to look more professional than haggard. "Hello, Commissioner."

"I realized I forgot to give you that recipe, so I made you a batch."

Jordan caught a whiff of chicken coming from the bowls. She was starving. "Recipe?"

"For Brownie. To get him to eat."

"Right." She wanted to cry when she realized the food he was carrying was for the dog.

"Not sure he deserves it tonight." Jordan moved out of the way to let Whit inside. "But he's probably hungry from all the destruction he caused."

"I take it your place doesn't usually look like this?" Whit's eyes sparkled, but she wasn't in the mood to be teased.

"I usually try to keep the level of destruction to a minimum," Jordan said.

Whit sat the bowls down, took his hat off, and put it on the table. He walked over to the dog in the corner and knelt beside him. "How's it going, boy?" Brownie licked Whit's hand. He nodded to the bowls on the counter. "One of those is for you if you're hungry."

"You made me dog food?" Jordan asked.

Whit laughed. "No, soup, and I didn't make it. You'll be grateful for that, although I do make a pretty good chili. Shelly made the soup. There are potato rolls too."

Jordan opened the two bowls. They both smelled so appetizing that she couldn't decide which was for the dog. Whit seemed to understand her confusion. "Human food on the left."

Jordan reached into the cupboard for a bowl and then paused. "Did you eat?"

"A while ago, but I'm always up for Shelly's soup, if you're willing to share."

Jordan pulled out two bowls and ladled soup into one. Whit took the other bowl, dished up some dog food for Brownie, and took it to the corner. He didn't bother to ask if it was a bowl that was okay for the dog to use. It wasn't. The bowl was part of a set her mom had given her after complaining that Jordan didn't have anything nice in her apartment. With no respect for Japanese porcelain and an obviously renewed appetite, Brownie started wolfing down whatever it was Whit had made.

Whit watched the dog with satisfaction. "What was Mrs. McKee doing here?"

"She heard Brownie barking, so she let herself in to check things out."

"That was nice of her."

"Yeah." Jordan tried to say it without irony, but she knew it came through anyway. Across the room, Brownie was already done with his meal, the bowl slipping across the floor as he licked it clean. Jordan watched the dog for a few minutes. "I'm not sure I can keep him."

"Why not?" Whit asked.

"I'm never here. This case has me working all hours of the day and night, and clearly Brownie can't be left on his own." The dog looked up, his clear brown eyes staring at her, like he understood she was talking about him. His expression held no apology, only curiosity.

"I wouldn't think he'd be able to do something like this." Whit gently touched the dog's shaved hip. "He's still not getting around very well."

"Apparently he gets around better than I thought he could. I left him locked in the garage." Without waiting for Whit, she sat down at the table, tore a piece off one of the rolls and dipped it in the soup.

"What would you do with him?"

"No idea." Jordan took a bite and closed her eyes. It was amazing: creamy, hearty, just the right amount of chicken and spice. Jordan had never learned to cook much beyond the basics, so most of what she ate was takeout. She appreciated the soup, but it made her feel guilty about what had happened between her and Shelly earlier that day. "I'm guessing Shelly doesn't know you were bringing her soup to me."

Whit stood in the middle of the room, looking distracted. "Something happen between you two? She didn't mention anything."

"Yeah. I guess you could call it 'creative differences.'"

"What kind of creative differences?"

"I made an arrest today that she didn't agree with." Jordan said. She was thinking that Whit must have spent today under a rock if he hadn't heard about what had happened in town.

"You made an arrest? In which case?"

"Neither."

"Neither?"

"Shelly wanted to go to Blodgett's house, she had a hunch something was missing, and she was right. While we were there, we ran into Peyton Judd. He was acting suspicious. I followed him into the barn and discovered a stash of drugs."

Whit's eyes got wide. "You arrested Judd's son?"

Jordan took another bite of the roll, chewed and swallowed it before she answered. "Yeah. No one bothered to explain to me that he's above the law."

"He's not. He only thinks he is. But he's always been kind of small potatoes, not worth the effort."

"It didn't look small to me. More like big potatoes —with big chunks of black tar heroin inside."

"Heroin?" Whit whistled. "That kid's moving up in the world. Or I guess, down."

"He said it wasn't his. He said he had no idea where it came from."

Whit moved to the coffee table beside the couch. He seemed to be studying the broken plates without touching them. "But you took him in? Booked him and everything?"

"We didn't exactly get that far."

Whit looked at her. "What's that supposed to mean?"

"He ran. I tackled him. Then I cuffed him and put him in my vehicle. Daddy came to get him and now I think I'm facing assault charges for doing my job."

"You tackled Peyton Judd? That might explain this."

"Explain what?"

Whit picked up a piece of torn paper from the floor. "Have you looked at this mess?"

Jordan swallowed the last bite of soup, eyeing what was left in the big bowl and regretting her offer to share it with Whit. "It's not hard to see."

"No. I mean, have you really looked around yet?"

Jordan walked over to Whit. "What are you talking about?"

He handed her one of the scraps of paper. "I don't think Brownie did this."

Jordan examined the paper. It had been shredded, but with more precision than if it had been done by a dog. She moved around the room, picking up one of the couch pillows next. The cuts in it were clean, like they'd been made by a knife.

Whit took the pillow from her. "Jordan, someone broke in and trashed your house."

In that moment, Jordan realized two things; one, this was the first time Whit had used her name instead of just "Detective" and two, he was right, the dog hadn't made this mess. Someone besides just her nosy neighbor had been in her house while she was gone.

Chapter Thirty-Five

"YOU SHOULD CALL THE police," Whit said. Jordan laughed, but it was a tired, bitter laugh. "I am the police."

"You know what I mean. You need to file a report, collect evidence, dust for fingerprints, figure out who did this, maybe get some protection."

"Not worth it." Jordan reached for a garbage can and picked up a few scraps of paper. "I have backups of all of these on my computer, and nothing that was damaged is worth much. At least I know it wasn't Brownie on an anxiety-fueled, destructive rampage."

"Jordan, someone broke into your house," Whit repeated.

"I think 'breaking in' is a bit harsh, don't you? When I came home, my neighbor was sitting in my living room drinking a fresh pot of my coffee. She has a key, and she didn't understand why that would bother me. Apparently in this town keys are given out like Halloween candy. Sheriff Blodgett kept his key in a birdhouse. Clearly, calling the police would be overreacting. This"—she held up a piece of her favorite coffee mug—"was just one of my neighbors expressing their concern."

"At least call the station. Brendan ... Sheriff Carlyle would want to know about this."

Jordan stood and faced him. "I think Sheriff Carlyle would take this as another sign that I can't do my job. Judd and the rest of them too. I don't need to give them another excuse to get rid of me."

"Jordan. No one is trying to get rid of you."

"Really? That's not what it sounded like when the sheriff found out I'd arrested Judd's son today."

"Peyton has always been on the edge of what's acceptable as far as the law goes. The sheriff's department has given him a lot of leeway because, frankly, he's not the smartest kid around and yeah, he's Judd's son. I know there's no way you could have known that. We just do things a little differently here in Lombard."

"You think?" Jordan laughed again. "Do the people around here even know what the rest of the world is like? I'm tired of wading through the nuances of small-town politics and layers of community drama. I just want to cut to the chase and find out what's going on around here, without everyone deciding I'm the enemy just because my mother's mother's mother wasn't born here."

"Maybe you need to give us a chance," Whit said.

Jordan snorted. "How about giving me a chance? It feels like I'm swimming upstream in a river no one wants me in."

Whit stepped closer. "There are a lot of people who want you here." For a long minute Jordan thought he was going to put his hands on her shoulders, maybe even wrap his arms around her. "If you would just—"

She stepped out of his reach. "Commissioner, I appreciate your concern and the dinner. I really do, but it's been a hell of a day. I'm exhausted and as you pointed out, I have a mess to clean up, photograph and tag. Beyond that, I believe I've earned the rest of the evening off." She walked to the door and held it open for the second time that evening. "If you don't mind."

"Not at all, ma'am." Whit picked up his hat from the table and nodded at her with the formality he hadn't used since the first time they met. As he passed through the door he said, "Shelly knows about the soup. She asked me to bring it to you, said you'd had a rough day."

Jordan closed the door behind him, leaned against it, and took in a big sigh. More than anything she wanted to take a long hot shower and get in bed, but that would have to wait. She moved around the room examining what had been destroyed, taking pictures, and trying to decide if anything was missing. Dusting for fingerprints would probably be futile. Rachel McKee had likely touched every surface in the house, maybe even rifled through her drawers—just being a concerned neighbor. Jordan couldn't stop arguing in her head with Whit, with Shelly, with Carlyle, with all of them. Rehashing why they were all wrong kept her guilt at bay.

She went into the garage. The door was covered in scratch marks from Brownie's claws, especially around the edge of the door handles. The handle into the house was a lever, the kind someone installed when they had trouble opening a round door handle, someone with arthritis like the former owner. Brownie must have knocked it open and gotten into the house. Instead of causing the mess, Brownie had probably chased away whoever had made it.

She followed the trail of destruction to the closed door to her bedroom. There were scratch marks on this door too. A breeze hit her as Jordan walked in. The window was open. As injured as he was, Brownie must have chased whoever did this into the bedroom. They shut the door behind them and climbed through the window to escape. Jordan walked over and looked out the window. A pair of boot tracks led from the overgrown flower bed. She took a couple of pictures. As she turned around, something caught her attention.

At the foot of her bed there was a scrap of shredded cloth. She reached for it but stopped when she saw the rust-colored stains. She knelt, examining the scrap more carefully. She startled when she recognized it.

It wasn't a piece of clothing from the missing girl. This time the bloodied fabric was torn from one of her favorite shirts.

The blood was still wet.

Chapter Thirty-Six

JORDAN TOOK MORE PICTURES and then bagged the bloody cloth in one of the evidence bags she had with her. She filled out the tag and left the rest of the mess. She closed and locked the window. Then she checked her closet for the shirt that the piece of fabric came from. It was missing, but there was no way to know when it was taken. She locked both doors and made sure the other windows were all closed and locked, not that it would do any good. If Rachel McKee could get into her house, she could only guess how many other people the former owner had given a key to. She'd get a new lock for the house tomorrow. She'd take the bagged evidence into the sheriff's office and fill out the reports tomorrow. Tonight, she was too tired and too overwhelmed to make anything like a coherent decision.

She dressed in sweats, leaving her shoes by the side of the bed just in case, helped Brownie into the bed, and curled up beside him. She left her revolver on the nightstand before she lay down for what she knew would be another sleepless night.

A low growl from beside her woke Jordan after what seemed like only a few minutes. She touched the dog's neck. His fur stood on end. "What is it, boy?"

She listened. Outside Bunny was yapping a warning. Jordan was up in a heartbeat, her gun gripped in her fist. She slipped her shoes on and tiptoed across the floor. She stood to the side of the window and peered out. A pickup was parked at the end of the lane, partially hidden under the trees. She was sure it hadn't been there when she went to bed. Outside, she heard her neighbor shushing the dog. Rachel's door opened and shut. Bunny was still barking, but it was muffled.

Jordan moved to the back window, listening. Quiet footsteps circled the side yard. She waited until they faded toward the front before she slipped out the back door. She followed the footsteps for a few minutes in the dark. In the light of Mrs. McKee's porch, a man's shape emerged from beside the house.

"Don't move!" Jordan commanded. "Down on the ground!"

The figure froze. "Jordan, it's me."

She kept her gun leveled at his back even as he turned. "Whit? What the hell are you doing sneaking around my house?"

He rubbed his hand across a patch of auburn stubble on his chin. "I was worried about you."

She lowered her revolver. "Worried? About me? You know I have a gun, right? That I'm a trained police officer? You should be more worried about yourself. I almost shot you."

"Sorry. You weren't taking the break-in seriously. Whoever trashed your house could have come back while you were sleeping."

"I'm a light sleeper, obviously. And as you so aptly put it, I can kill a man with my bare hands, black belt in Krav Maga, remember?"

Whit leaned against the side of the house, trying to catch his breath. "I started thinking about everything that's been going on. Something doesn't feel right. The things that ended up in Shelly's flower bed and then someone breaks into your house. It feels personal."

"If you're so worried, maybe you should go prowl around Shelly's house instead," Jordan suggested.

Whit looked at her in genuine horror. "Hells no. She keeps a revolver on her nightstand, and she's known to shoot first and ask questions later."

"I'm not sure it makes me feel better that I'm less terrifying than a sixty something-year-old woman." Jordan ran her fingers through her hair, ratty and tousled from her brief sleep.

Whit looked at her for a long moment. "I don't think I've ever seen you with your hair down. I didn't know it was so long. I like it."

Jordan laughed incredulously. "You're seriously complimenting me on my hair right now?"

He grinned. "Would you rather I told you, you looked like—"

"Shh!" Jordan held up her hand.

Another set of footsteps trod up the gravel driveway. In one quick motion, she raised her gun and pushed Whit against the wall of the house, so they were both hidden in the shadows.

The footsteps grew closer. A flashlight beam shined hot in her eyes. "Freeze! Drop your weapon!" Ray shouted.

Jordan lowered her gun. "It's me."

"What are you doing out here?" Ray asked.

"I live here," Jordan said.

"Your neighbor called in a report of a possible break-in. She said she saw someone prowling around your house."

"It was me." Whit emerged from the shadows.

"Whit? Why were you sneaking around outside the detective's house?" Ray's eyes got big with perceived understanding. "Oh."

"It's not what you think, Ray." Jordan raised her hand to her eyes. "Put the flashlight away. I can't see."

Ray clicked off the flashlight. Jordan noticed the light on in her neighbor's window and Mrs. McKee and Bunny's silhouette standing there. She was sure her neighbor had been watching the whole time.

"Actually, there was a break-in," Whit said. "Someone went through the detective's things, destroyed some of her files."

"Is that true?" Ray asked.

"Yeah," Jordan said reluctantly. So much for a decent night's sleep. "I was hoping it could wait until morning, but I guess I'd better show you what they left for me."

"What they ... Jordan, was there something in the house I didn't see?" Whit said.

Jordan glowered at him as Ray's expression went back into a smirk. "Another piece of bloody fabric, only this time it was torn from my clothes."

"And you didn't think you should report that?" Whit said.

"To who? This is my investigation. I'm the one that's going to be bagging evidence and filing out a report," Jordan said, pushing through her back door.

"Brendan is not going to like this, any of this. After he sent you home, he had a long visit with Judd. Neither of them looked or sounded very happy when he left." Ray followed Jordan into the house. He whistled when she turned the light on, revealing the mess. "Someone's got a bone to pick with you."

"Pretty much the entire town, right? The bigger problem is narrowing down which of my new enemies did this." Jordan walked over to the table where she'd left the bagged cloth before she went to bed.

It was gone.

Chapter Thirty-Seven

STILL KEYED UP FROM her crazy night, Jordan answered the phone on the first ring.

"They're gone!" Shelly was uncharacteristically incoherent and upset.

"Shelly? What ... Who's gone?" Jordan glanced at her clock, already getting out of bed.

"My dogs," Shelly said. "All three of them."

The implication in that sentence hit Jordan immediately. "I'm on my way." She haphazardly dressed, she and her vehicle out of her driveway in mere minutes.

When she arrived at Shelly's, Shelly was pacing back and forth on the porch in obvious distress. Her appearance rattled Jordan. She'd never seen Shelly anything but composed and calm. "When was the last time you saw them?"

"Ask questions on the way. We don't have time to waste," Shelly said, already moving for Jordan's Expedition.

"On the way where?"

"Newspaper office." Shelly climbed in the passenger side.

"Why would we ...?" The destination didn't make any sense to Jordan.

"Just drive," Shelly said, slamming her door.

After a few minutes of listening to Shelly try to contact the neighboring ranchers on her phone, Jordan asked again, "When did you last see them?"

"Last night when I put them out. The weather was nice enough I let them sleep on the porch. I usually let the dogs in the house and fed them about 5:30 and have my own breakfast over with by six. I couldn't sleep so I got up a bit before five and opened the kitchen door. Usually they'd be waiting to burst through the door. When they didn't come, I stepped out on the porch and called to them. Again, nothing. That had never happened before. Shelly hung her head in her hands. "I shouldn't have left them outside. I know something is terribly wrong."

Jordan fishtailed around the corner and through Shelly's gate to the main road. "Did you hear anything last night? Anything at all?"

"No. Not so much as a yip out of any of them. My bet is he drugged them. That's the only way he would have gotten them off the property without them making some kind of racket."

"Any idea who might have—"

"We both have an idea!" Shelly snapped. "But neither of us know who he is or how to stop him."

"My house was broken into yesterday," Jordan said after a few minutes of quietly debating whether to bring it up.

Shelly looked at her through bloodshot eyes. "Your dog?"

"Fine. I think he chased off whoever it was. Maybe they didn't realize I had a dog."

"Maybe. No. Newspaper," Shelly directed as Jordan automatically turned toward the sheriff's office.

"Newspaper? Are you sure about this?" Jordan said as they pulled into the little building that housed Lombard's twice-weekly local paper, the *Ledger*. "Wouldn't it be better to—"

Instead of answering, Shelly jumped out of the vehicle before it was fully stopped, rushed to the *Ledger*'s door and frantically pounded on it. The editor cautiously cracked open the door, saw who it was, and ushered Shelly and Jordan inside.

"I need you to splash the news of my dog's disappearance in this morning's paper," Shelly said before he'd closed the door.

"Paper's already printed, Grizz. You know that," the editor said calmly.

Shelly stepped toward him. "What I know is that you owe me for the time I saved your behind and your paper during that embezzlement scandal twenty years ago." Jordan raised her eyebrows, but no one offered an explanation. Shelly continued, her voice raising a notch. "What I know is that this town is not going to be safe until we figure out who did this, and the first step to finding our murderer is finding my dogs!"

The man looked helplessly at Jordan, but Jordan wasn't about to go against what Shelly was saying. It was her first real look at the Grizz Beats had told her about. "I think you'd better do what she says," Jordan said.

The man threw up his hands. "What do you want it to say?"

Jordan's phone rang as Shelly hashed out the wording with Lombard's editor. It was Whit. He sounded a little sheepish. "Sorry to call so early. I just wanted to check that everything is okay this morning."

"It's not. Shelly's dogs have gone missing," Jordan said. "We're at the newspaper office."

"I'll be right there." Whit hung up before Jordan could say anything else.

Chapter Thirty-Eight

IF JORDAN WERE TO write the headline for that day, she would have titled it, "Lombard on a Thursday, A Day of Infamy."

She had doubted the sagacity of putting a notice in the paper until she saw the people gathered at the general store, waiting. "Is this normal?" she asked Whit as he laid a heavy stack of newspapers on the counter. He'd volunteered to help deliver papers because they were going to be so late.

"Special edition today. Make sure the word gets out," Whit said to the store owner before heading back outside with Jordan to deliver the next set to the Silver Horseshoe. "People living in Lombard are of one mind when it comes to being set in their ways. Living so far from what you would call civilization, our activity choices are limited. You can usually tell what day of the week it is by what's going on down on Main Street. The *Lombard Ledger* is published and delivered on Thursdays."

"Hasn't Lombard ever heard of the internet?" Jordan asked.

Whit shook his head at her, but he didn't sound annoyed. "Of course. The *Ledger* is delivered electronically as well as in print, but sitting down to coffee and talking about what's in the paper is still a public affair. Thursday is my 'Breakfast at the Horseshoe' day."

"Don't you work on Thursday?" Jordan asked.

Whit stopped. "You still don't get it. Breakfast at the Horseshoe on Thursdays is good business. It gives me a chance to make connections, see who might need some advice running their property. You might consider it. Sheriff Blodgett used to spend Thursday mornings at the Horseshoe."

Jordan surveyed the overall-clad men who were sipping coffee in the cafe. "Somehow I don't think I'd be very welcome."

"You should give us a chance," Whit said. He greeted the men getting up from their chairs as he put another stack of papers on the counter.

"Are you the paperboy now, Whit? Your ranch doing that badly?" Chris approached with a wide smile.

Whit nodded to her. "No, ma'am. I'm here on important business."

"What's going on?" Chris picked up the paper and read the insert printed in bright red ink.

> Sometime during the night, Shelly Curtis's three best friends—Whiskey, Oscar, and Freckles, were taken from her yard.
>
> They did not come to breakfast this morning.
>
> Considering recent similar tragic events in our area it is hoped this matter will immediately mobilize our

community.

They MUST be found before any harm comes to them or more precious lives are lost.

Remember Bonnie Golden and Sampson; Sheriff Blodgett and Grunion; Sadie Larsen and Brownie.

WRITTEN TODAY

Chris put the paper down, her face serious. "Is this for real?"

"I'm afraid so," Whit answered.

Chris pursed her lips. "Poor Shelly. Any idea if Mac knows yet?"

"Mac?" Jordan asked.

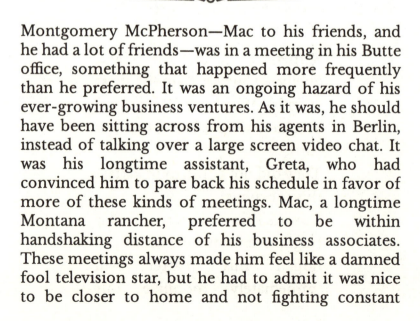

Montgomery McPherson—Mac to his friends, and he had a lot of friends—was in a meeting in his Butte office, something that happened more frequently than he preferred. It was an ongoing hazard of his ever-growing business ventures. As it was, he should have been sitting across from his agents in Berlin, instead of talking over a large screen video chat. It was his longtime assistant, Greta, who had convinced him to pare back his schedule in favor of more of these kinds of meetings. Mac, a longtime Montana rancher, preferred to be within handshaking distance of his business associates. These meetings always made him feel like a damned fool television star, but he had to admit it was nice to be closer to home and not fighting constant jetlag. As Greta liked to remind him, he wasn't getting any younger.

He leaned back in his chair. His mind wandered from the meeting to his family ranch in Keystone County. He hadn't been there in months. He'd need to get out there, and soon. Bernie, his ranch manager, was more than competent, but Mac missed the open spaces and freedom of his ranch. The ranch was one thing, but there was something he missed even more that resided in Keystone County that he missed even more. He glanced at his calendar, thinking of what excuse he could use to send her flowers or some small gift. Maybe he could invent a reason to stop by. Not that he should need an excuse. He and Shelly had been close since they were teenagers. Still, there'd been a wall between them for the past thirty years. A wall most likely constructed when she decided to marry someone else.

She'd continued to keep that wall up, even though Mac had done everything he could for her when her husband had been killed in the line of duty. He'd stood by patiently at first when she became a Keystone County deputy, and then proudly when she'd earned a reputation as a detective and later a private investigator. He'd watched her manage three kids, her police work, and her family ranch after her parents died. He'd offered help where he could, but Shelly was fiercely independent. To him, her independence was alternately supremely attractive and maddening.

It was the general rule that he was not to be disturbed when he was in a meeting of this caliber. Greta knew that more than anyone, so he was surprised when she walked in. Without a word she slipped to the front. She leaned over and whispered three words in his ear.

"Shelly's in trouble."

He stood immediately and left the room. Greta would make some excuse or another for him. His latest multimillion-dollar deal was forgotten in the wake of more important matters. After he skimmed the message Greta had handed him, his first call was to the Butte airstrip where he kept his private plane. When he'd been assured it would be ready to go when he got there, he called Bernie at the ranch.

"I need you to get the trailer and as many horses as you and the boys can get ready. I'll be there in less than an hour."

"Already on it, boss," Bernie replied. "The truck will be waiting for you at the airstrip when you arrive."

"I appreciate it. I'll see you soon." Mac pocketed his phone with satisfaction as he headed to the parking lot. Bernie and Greta were two peas in a pod, always anticipating his needs and standing by. That thought made him retrieve his phone for one more call—this one to his favorite waitress, Chris, at the Horseshoe. His employees weren't the only ones who had learned to anticipate needs. He hated that Shelly was in distress, but maybe this time he'd find the right combination of events to unlock that stubborn woman's heart.

Chapter Thirty-Nine

JORDAN WATCHED THE CROWD gathering outside the Silver Horseshoe. She guessed that under normal circumstances, three missing dogs probably wouldn't constitute a community crisis and initiate so much public fear. As it was, Lombard's residents were already unnerved by the determination that Sadie Larsen had most likely been kidnapped. They knew her dog Brownie was found barely alive after being shot. There were people here who remembered the Bonnie Golden case and remembered that her dog had disappeared as well. Everyone knew that Grunion, Sheriff Blodgett's dog, had mysteriously disappeared a day or two before Blodgett was found shot to death in his own home.

"You want to explain all of this, Detective?" Carlyle said, approaching Jordan from the direction of the sheriff's office. "I gave you the morning to sort out what happened at your place last night. I wasn't expecting you to call out the cavalry."

"Shelly's dogs went missing this morning."

"I know that. The whole damn county knows that," Carlyle said. "I wish you had come to me before you went to the paper. The last thing we need is panic in the streets."

"Shelly insisted," Jordan answered.

"Of course," Carlyle spat out. "What Shelly wants, Shelly gets."

"She's done a lot for this community," Jordan said. She'd seen that as she watched the people read the insert and the way they'd interacted with Shelly as they gathered, but she had to admit she was stunned by the community's reaction. "People keep coming out of the woodwork to help her."

It looked like every person in the county was present and accounted for. Anyone not already there was on their way. Jordan knew Carlyle was right about one thing—the disappearance of Shelly's dog had already fostered panic and fear.

Carlyle shook his head at the gathering crowd. "All of this undermines our sheriff's department. She hasn't come in to file a report and she hasn't asked for our help in the search."

Jordan turned to him calmly. "Would you have given her the help if she asked, or do you need to give Judd a blood sample first?"

She could tell her words stung him. His mouth tightened at the corners. "Detective, you don't understand how things work around here. We don't have the money or manpower you had in Seattle to chase down every little lead."

"Seems to me you have plenty of manpower. It looks like people here care a whole lot more about what's going on than you give them credit for," Jordan shot back.

As if to prove her right, the town fire siren sounded. People cheered and clapped when an ancient Lombard resident—a man Jordan had heard rarely ventured outside his home—came down the street in a long retired Civil Defense truck, loudspeakers blaring the news.

Carlyle swore under his breath.

"Is there a problem, Sheriff?" Jordan was trying not to sound smug, but there was something vindicating about this whole situation.

"This." Carlyle spread his arms wide. "This is a circus and has the makings of a PR nightmare."

"I'm not going to disagree with you there," Jordan said.

He turned to look at her, his face dark. "I suppose you plan on joining the search."

Jordan shrugged. "Seems like the next logical step in my investigation. Especially since missing dogs appear to follow a pattern that was established before."

"I suppose you think I should call out the reserves and get the sheriff's office involved?" Carlyle said.

"That's the last thing we want." Shelly's voice coming from the crowd stopped Carlyle. He turned around to face the full wrath of the older woman. "You and the sheriff's office have been criminally negligent in this whole thing from the beginning. We don't want your help. We don't need your help. You've stymied Ms. Gibbons' investigation from the start and I'm not about to let you botch this one up." Her opinion fully expressed, Shelly turned and marched back to the gathering crowd.

Carlyle stood for a moment, his mouth agape. Jordan was both impressed and a little frightened by the fire she saw in Shelly. Even Carlyle seemed to be afraid of her. After a long moment he shook his head, as if to gain back some of his composure. "I'll expect you to make a full report." He headed the other direction down the street.

Despite the seriousness of the mood and the obvious frustration of the sheriff, Jordan had the sudden urge to laugh out loud.

"This is crazy, Beats," Jordan said to the off-duty dispatcher as she joined her on the street. "A girl goes missing and I can't drag details out of anyone. Three dogs go missing and the whole town shuts down to help."

"You have to understand, Jordan, the missing dogs aren't just any old dogs. They're Shelly Curtis's dogs. Everyone in the county knows them. Shelly never goes anywhere without them. And a good chunk of this town owes Shelly in one way or another." Beats observed the crowd for a minute. "Besides, this is the next escalation. People are scared. You need to figure this one out. "

"I know." Jordan said it more to herself than to Beats. She could feel the pressure mounting by the minute. Just when she thought she'd seen everything, a bigger-than-life sky blue four door, four-wheel drive truck threaded its way toward her through the mass of vehicles parked in the street. The truck was pulling a gigantic horse trailer—the biggest Jordan had ever seen. The trailer was full of saddled horses. The rig came to a stop near her.

The man on the passenger side climbed out and seemed to be looking for something or someone. He was tall, well over six feet, well-dressed with a full head of thick dark brown hair. There was an air of importance about him. The driver bounded out of his side of the truck, scurried to the rear of the trailer, and started leading horses out. He handed the reins to whoever was handy to take them and went back after the others until the trailer was empty.

People stood back in a sort of friendly respect as the man walked through the crowd until he found the person he was looking for. He extended his arms in front of him. Shelly burst out of the crowd and fled into his open arms, then physically collapsed against his chest. He held her gently but firmly as she burst into uncontrollable sobs.

Jordan didn't know what to think. No one else seemed surprised at what had just transpired. The man helped Shelly to his truck, placed her on the second seat, made her comfortable with a pillow and warm blanket, and then climbed in beside her and shut the door.

Jordan realized she'd been staring ever since Shelly disappeared inside the big truck. She turned to Beats. "Who is that?"

Beats kept her eyes on the blue pickup. "Montgomery McPherson—Mac to pretty much everyone. He's a local rancher who pastures his cattle near Shelly's on Rattlesnake. He is also an international businessman and as rich as all get out. And he's been in love with Shelly since high school."

"Shelly has a boyfriend?" Jordan was fascinated and somewhat scandalized at the idea.

"No, not exactly. The two of them were high school sweethearts. Everyone thought they'd get married right out of high school, but that was before Jeffrey Curtis came to town. He was a dashing young highway patrolman and new to town Shelly's senior year. Lombard was his first assignment. Shelly was a bit of a speed demon back then. Still is, actually." Beats chuckled. "His first day on the job he wrote Shelly a speeding ticket. It must have sparked something. They shocked everyone by getting married a couple of months after that. Mac was devastated."

"But he's still around," Jordan said. "Obviously."

"When Jeff died, Mac was there for Shelly in every way, shape or form, but for whatever reason, he's failed to win the fair lady." Beats sighed. "You may not have noticed, but Shelly has a stubborn streak a mile wide. She still won't admit she needs Mac or anyone else, but they've stayed close. They spend time together whenever he's back in town. He travels a lot, but he has an office in Butte and a private plane. My guess is he flew in as soon as he heard the news about the dogs."

While Jordan contemplated all of this, Chris Peters came out of the Silver Horseshoe carrying a small sack. She crossed the street and tapped on the truck door. It opened far enough she could reach up and hand off the sack. As she walked past Jordan stopped her. "What was in that sack?"

Chris hesitated but answered the question. "Hot coffee and two of Shelly's favorite muffins."

Jordan was incredulous. Her own stomach growled as she realized she, like Shelly, had missed breakfast. She marveled at the secure cocoon Shelly's lifelong friend had prepared for her on such short notice. She was now ensconced in the middle of the action and able to keep close track of the progress of the search. Mac had thought of everything. Jordan wondered what it would be like to have someone care about her that much. She looked around at the town in full organized chaos and wondered what it would be like to have an entire town care about her that much.

Chapter Forty

"ANY WORD ON THE dogs?" Ray said as he walked into Jordan's office.

"Nothing yet." Jordan stifled a yawn. The ongoing search for Shelly's dogs had gone well into the night, but so far had turned up nothing.

"I may have found something. While you were all out combing the hills, I was going through prison databases." He set his laptop on the desk in front of Jordan. "You were right about the Texas thing. I found an old Lombard resident who did some time in a Texas state penitentiary, and it appears that he was the cellmate of someone corresponding with our missing girl. The woman he was emailing used the name Bridget Black, but the emails match up word for word with a couple that were in Sadie's box. There's one that she didn't have saved, but I thought it might interest you anyway." Ray leaned closer, pointing out a phrase he'd highlighted.

Montana Map of Gold.

Jordan whistled. "Good work, Ray. It sounds like the one we're looking for. Have you already set up an appointment to talk to him?"

"That's the bad news. He's dead. He had a heart attack and died in prison about six months ago."

Jordan sighed. "Of course. So he can't be our guy."

"But he still might have a link to our guy. The warden said there was a box of the man's possessions just sitting in storage. I asked that they be sent here so we can take a look through them."

Jordan looked at the convict's name. "Robert Pitkin?" The name sounded immediately familiar. It took her a minute to place it, and then it came to her. "Any chance he has family around here? Whit mentioned something about running into an old friend named Tom Pitkin."

"Could be related, but the Pitkins haven't lived here for awhile."

"How soon will that package be here?" Jordan asked.

"I'm not sure. I asked him to expedite it, but there's some red tape they have to get through before they send it. The warden couldn't tell me what all was in it—he said mostly junk. It might not be anything worth our time."

"Let's hope it's more than that. Thanks, Ray."

"You want to go out to get coffee to celebrate?" Ray looked hopeful.

"Another time. I have a class to teach." Jordan stood.

"Class?"

"Yeah. I'm teaching a self-defense class at the Grange. Wish me luck."

―――――◆O◆―――――

Jordan arrived at the Grange about half an hour early. She wasn't sure how Chris had talked her into teaching this class. It meant taking time out of the investigation, but with nothing to go on and Shelly's dogs still missing, it might be the best way to offer some protection to the women of Lombard.

She was relieved to find the building unlocked and the room empty. She needed to blow off some of her built up frustration, mostly with herself. It had been ages since she'd had enough room and the luxury of time to practice. She pulled her headphones out of her bag and scrolled through her music until she found the right playlist. She bounced back and forth on her toes to the music as the bass vibrated from her ears down to her feet. She shook out her arms and rolled her shoulders. She held onto the back of a chair for balance as she stretched first one leg and then the other up above her head.

Finally warmed up, she started in on a punch and jab combo, then worked into some kicks. As she moved, Jordan thought back to what had led her to take a class like this when she was in high school. She remembered the feeling of helplessness—the man in the alley who had taken her purse and threatened to take much more. He would have too, if that car hadn't turned at the right moment and sent him running into the bushes. That self-defense class had made her feel powerful instead of vulnerable. She'd built on that feeling, coming back again and again until she could take down even the biggest man in her class. Lost in the music and memories, she didn't see the figure standing in the doorway until he stepped into the light.

She spun to face him, already crouched in a defensive stance.

"Impressive."

Whit closed the distance between them as Jordan jerked the headphones out of her ears and brushed a piece of sweaty hair out of her face. "Remind me to never tick you off."

"What are you doing here?" Jordan pulled her towel from where she'd slung it on the back of the chair and wiped her face on it.

"I was coming to unlock the door and make sure the heat was on. But it looks like you managed both on your own," Whit said.

Jordan fought to keep her breathing even. "The door was unlocked and it's plenty warm in here."

"Figures. There's a dog-napping serial killer on the loose and we can't even keep this building secure." Whit leaned against a small stage at the end of the hall. "Are you expecting to get a big turnout tonight?"

"No idea," Jordan said, still trying to catch her breath.

"I'm guessing you will. The women in town are spooked, afraid like they haven't been in years," Whit said.

"About fifteen years, I'd guess. I still don't get why a woman goes missing and people barely bat an eye, but three dogs disappear and suddenly the cavalry is called out and there's panic in the streets."

"I'd say the town was in denial. Everyone wanted to believe the Larsen woman had just moved on. When Shelly's dogs were taken, things got more real. I think they figure if something like this can happen to Shelly, it can happen to anyone."

"How is she doing, anyway?"

"Better than should be expected, considering we're on day three and there's been no sign of any of them." The voice from the doorway answered. Shelly was more composed than the last time Jordan had seen her, but she still looked shaken.

Whit crossed the room to Shelly. "Have you heard anything?"

Shelly's shoulders slumped. "Nothing."

"What are you doing here?" Jordan asked.

"Figured I'd take a refresher course, just in case my sharpshooting skills fail me." Shelly pulled her gun from the front pocket of her jacket and offered it to Whit, butt first. "Find someplace safe to stash this. I wouldn't want to accidentally shoot someone in the middle of the class."

Whit took the gun. As he headed to a back room, the first group of women arrived. By the time he came back, the Grange ballroom was fuller than it had ever been on Friday swing or Thursday bingo night. The voices weren't exactly subdued, but the tone was more serious than the usual casual gossip of Lombard's female population.

Whit walked to the front of the room to where Jordan was getting started. "I'll come by after to make sure the doors are actually locked."

Jordan stopped him as he turned to leave. "Do you have someplace to be for the next hour, Commissioner?"

"No," Whit said cautiously.

"If you don't mind staying, I could use a bad guy."

"A bad guy?" Whit looked around the circle of women, all watching him expectantly. "I don't know if—"

"I promise we won't hurt you." Jordan tried to keep a straight face, but a smile crept into her voice.

A catcall came from the corner of the room. Jordan turned her gaze toward the sound. "Sounds like we have our first volunteer. Chris?" The waitress sauntered forward with a bubble gum smile on her wide lips. Her platinum hair was pulled in a high ponytail, and she had on a pair of hot pink stretch pants and a black shirt that hugged her abundant curves. She stood in the center of the room. "Whit, approach Chris from behind. Pretend you're planning to strangle her."

Whit gave her an innocent smile that melted the rest of the room. "I don't think I can be the bad guy."

Jordan looked at him impatiently. "You're taller and stronger than I am. You're a closer approximation of what these ladies will face if they get into a bad situation."

"Okay." He sounded like a child who'd been reproved by his mother. "Where do you want me?"

As Jordan directed Whit behind a delighted Chris, Shelly's phone buzzed. She pulled it out of her pocket and glanced down once. The words on the screen sent her straight to the room where Whit had stashed her gun.

Chapter Forty-One

> MAKE NEW FRIENDS BUT KEEP THE OLD. ONE IS SILVER, BUT THE OTHER WAS GOLDEN.
>
> DEAREST DEPUTY, YOU BROKE OUR DEAL, BUT I'M WILLING TO MAKE ANOTHER ONE. IT'S NOT TOO LATE FOR SOME OLD FRIENDS. COME ALONE. NO WEAPONS. DISARMED.

SHE READ THE TEXT through one more time, but there was no mistake about who sent it. The message was similar to the ones she received in plain brown envelopes on her desk fifteen years ago. It appeared that Bonnie's killer, like the rest of the world, had upgraded his technology.

Shelly could hear Jordan and the rest of the women going over holds and throws and simple defense maneuvers. The text she just received made all of that training obsolete. Shelly picked up her gun and reached to slide it into the concealed pocket of her jacket. Her phone buzzed again.

I SAID NO WEAPONS.

Shelly startled at the text, looking around the room. There was a small window on the far side. She stepped in front of it and peered out, but she couldn't see anything beyond the streetlights outside and the hardware store beyond. She didn't know if he could actually see her, or if he'd just assumed her next step. She set the gun back in the desk drawer where Whit had left it.

ARE MY DOGS OKAY?

She sent back but wasn't surprised when there wasn't an answer.

She slipped out the door of the Grange and into the night without telling anyone where she was going. She didn't need to ask where he wanted to meet. She'd answered his messages before, back when the threat was against her family.

She knew what and where he meant by DISARMED.

The wind whistled through the rocks above her. Shelly pushed her hands into her pockets and wished for the comforting lump of metal she'd left behind.

The day had been warm, but it was too early in the year for the mountains to hold much heat. She'd be plenty warm in a few minutes anyway. It'd been years since she'd made this hike. With every step, her body reminded her that she was no longer a thirty- or even fortysomething active-duty deputy. The last time she'd answered one of his messages, her reward had been a human arm bone and a warning. It was the last bit of evidence they'd found from the Bonnie Golden case before it went cold.

This time she hoped for the return of three old friends and maybe some answers about why the person on the other end of the text had broken their deal or why he thought she had. The searchers had gone over this part of the mountain at her request at least half a dozen times. She shouldn't have been surprised they hadn't found anything. The snake had hidden his tracks for over fifteen years. He wasn't about to get sloppy now.

She paused at the opening to an old mine. Taking a chance, Shelly whistled. A whine from the back of the cavern greeted her. "Freckles?" she called. She was greeted by a chorus of weak yips. She took a quick step into the dark. Her phone rang. She glanced down at the unlisted number, took a deep breath, and answered.

"Hold there. We have some things to discuss." His voice was hoarse and gruffer than she remembered. Like before, it was familiar, but in that irritating, name-on-the-tip-of-the-tongue, can't-quite-place-it kind of way.

"What do you want?" Shelly said. She kept the phone to her ear, in case he was watching her, but opened an app on her phone that would record their conversation. She'd added it to her phone as soon as she'd found the dog collar. This was a call she'd been expecting.

"That's a funny question. Fifteen years ago, I thought the answer was that I wanted to be left alone, just like you did. But with all this searching and finding and digging up old bones, I realized I missed our little game."

"Blodgett was close, wasn't he? Close to figuring out who you are. That's why you killed him."

A hollow laugh came through the phone, but at the same time it sounded like it was coming from deep inside the mountain. "The good sheriff was a victim of his own curiosity. I can't take credit for that."

"It wasn't you." Shelly's voice went breathless with the realization.

He laughed again. "I've kept my part of our bargain. I wasn't the one who dug up the past."

"What about the other woman?" Shelly asked.

"Seems to be an epidemic of curiosity in this county. First the sheriff and then Sadie Larsen, and now you."

"I wasn't looking for anything when I dug up the collar. It wasn't until that other woman went missing that I—"

"Don't pretend you're innocent in all of this. I know you're working with that pretty, young detective. The dogs were my warning shot, Deputy. A reminder that I can get to you and get to anyone who means anything to you at any time. You might want to pass that message on to your new friend. Ask her if she's willing to bet the accuracy of her detecting skills against the speed of my knife."

The phone went dead. As if on cue, a chorus of muffled howls came from the back of the cavern. Shelly turned on the light on her phone and ventured into the dark. She followed the sound to a wall of newly stacked rocks. She shined the light through a gap in the rocks. Three shapes moved behind it.

"Hold on boys." Shelly put the phone in her pocket and started pulling the wall down one rock at a time.

Chapter Forty-Two

THE CLASS WAS OVER, the last stragglers lingering on the steps, gossiping beneath the streetlight. Jordan had just pulled herself away from another question when Chris tapped her on the shoulder.

"Can we talk for a minute?"

"Sure." Jordan leaned against the edge of the building.

"Not here. Inside."

"Okay." Jordan followed Chris back inside the entryway of the Grange.

Chris looked around. "Do you know where Whit went?"

Something twisted in Jordan's stomach. She was sure Chris was about to confess a lifelong crush on Whit and ask Jordan to stay away from him. It was a completely superfluous request; Jordan couldn't have any kind of association with Whit. Still, she braced herself for an uncomfortable conversation. "I think he's checking to make sure all the doors are locked."

Chris lowered her voice. "I didn't want to say anything before, because I knew there probably wasn't anything to it, but you asked, and I wasn't exactly forthright with my answer."

Jordan was utterly confused. "Your answer about what?"

Chris glanced around again. "Back at the Horseshoe, you asked if I'd ever seen Sadie with anyone in particular and I said no, but there was someone."

"Who was it?" Jordan asked, but she knew she wouldn't like the answer.

"A couple of times I saw her talking with someone out in the parking lot when she was on a break. Like I said, I'm sure there was nothing to it. I'm sure he was just being nice, but ..."

"But?" Jordan prodded.

"But it was Whit. I mean, Sadie was pretty, but not his type at all, so it surprised me to see them together. And when you started asking, I didn't want to get him into trouble so I—"

"Shelly?" A voice called through the doorway.

Chris walked toward the door, looking relieved at the interruption. "Hey, Mac. I think she left already."

"I was supposed to pick her up here. We were going out to a late dinner." Mac looked concerned. "Do you know when she left?"

Jordan and Chris looked at each other. Jordan tried to think of the last time she'd seen Shelly, but she couldn't remember Shelly being at the class at all. "No idea."

Mac gestured to his phone. "I can't raise her on her cell."

"Commissioner, do you know where Shelly went?" Jordan asked as Whit walked into the room.

"She's gone? Are you sure? She left her gun behind." Whit held up the revolver he'd retrieved from the back room.

Mac's face went pale. "There's no way she would have just left it here. Something is wrong."

"I agree," Whit said.

Jordan nodded, looking between the two men. "I'll call dispatch and put out a watch for Shelly's truck. Then I'll head out myself."

"I'll go check with whoever is left outside. Maybe someone saw her." Chris disappeared through the door.

"I'll start at the other end of town and work my way back," Whit said.

Mac was already heading for the door. "I can have the plane in the air in a half hour."

"It won't do much good right now. It'll be dark by then. Go up to Shelly's place. Maybe she just got distracted and forgot." Even as she said it, Jordan knew that wasn't likely to have happened. Mac nodded, relieved to have been given a job.

Shelly jumped up, grabbed the rifle she'd stashed next to the fridge, and pointed it toward the man at the door before she recognized him.

"Shelly, where have you been? The entire county is out looking for you." Mac's voice was thick with relief. He reached to pull her into his arms.

"Don't." She put the rifle down and then stashed it back beside the fridge. Her clothes were dirty and torn. One of her hands was wrapped in a rag, and blood seeped through. She'd been sitting on the floor, tending to the three equally weak and dirty dogs she'd dug out of the mountainside.

"You found them," Mac said. "Where? What happened to you?"

Shelly took a shuddering breath. Part of her wanted to let her guard down. She wanted to collapse into his arms and let him carry her away as he'd done before. But she couldn't. She couldn't risk putting him in danger. She steeled her back and stood up straight. "I got an idea of where they might be, so I left Jordan's class and went looking. Turned out they'd just wandered off after all, ended up trapped in one of the old mines."

"You scared all of us. You weren't answering your phone. You left your gun at the Grange. We thought something had happened to you."

She held up her hand, reinforcing the barrier that had always stood between them. "My phone died. I'd appreciate it if you would call the sheriff's office and have them call off the search. And I'd also appreciate it if you didn't set off a panic whenever I need some alone time."

His eyes moved over her face. "What's going on? Clearly something happened that you aren't telling me. I don't believe your dogs just ran off. Shelly, why can't you just trust me? I want to help."

She ducked her head so he wouldn't see the fear in her eyes. "I don't need your help, I—"

He reached for her hand, noticing the blood. "You're hurt. How did that ..."

"Just a little scrape. I ... fell, coming off the mountain." She turned her back on him as she moved to the sink to wash off the blood. She didn't want him to see how badly her hands were shaking. "Just please, call off the search. I don't need people worrying about me."

She kept the water running over her hand, her torn nails stinging as blood from the gash on her hand tinged the water a muddy pink color. She closed her eyes and listened as Mac called into the sheriff's office. She could hear the disbelief in Beats' response as he gave her the made-up excuse.

After he hung up, he stood in the middle of the kitchen. "Do you want me to help you load up the dogs? We could take them to Dr. Green and have them checked out."

She turned off the water, wrapped her hand in a clean towel and braced herself for what she knew had to come next. She had to cut him out of her life now, before anyone else could. She wouldn't lose him the way she lost Jeff, especially if it was in her power to keep him safe. "I can take care of the dogs myself. If I see anything that warrants Dr. Green's attention, I'll get them in first thing tomorrow."

"I could help you look them over, get them cleaned up, or I could fix you something to eat. You look like you need—"

"What I need from you right now is space." She forced the words out and clipped them into harsh bits, as if her tongue were a knife. "You don't seem to get it, Mac. I'm just fine on my own."

"Shelly, I don't ..."

"I don't need your help, I don't need your money, I don't need you to keep playing hero, and I don't need you complicating my perfectly satisfactory life."

He stared at her in disbelief as she spoke, twisting his hat in his hands. "You've been a stubborn woman your whole life, but I think you're in over your head this time. You're lying about the dogs and where you've been tonight. I know you are. What I don't know is why you won't let me help you."

She leveled her gaze to his, purposely meeting his sharp blue eyes. "I said, there's nothing to help."

"Shelly, I don't think I've kept it a secret how much you mean to me. If anything ever happened to you, I'd ..."

His words gave her the strength she needed to tell the lies that would save his life. "You've been a good friend, Mac, and I thank you for all your help, but I can't give you anything more than friendship. After all this time, I thought I'd made that clear."

She saw the moment when her words struck their mark and his hurt turned to anger. It took a few minutes for him to speak. "You're right, you've been nothing but friendly to me for the last thirty years. I guess it was my mistake for assuming I could find my way back into that stubborn heart of yours. My mistake for assuming you felt something for me that you clearly don't." He put his hat on. "Goodbye Mrs. Curtis. I guess I should be grateful that you've finally told me how it is. I won't be back. I won't disturb your personal fortress ever again."

He turned around and strode out the door. He was clearly devastated and furious, but he was too much of a gentleman to slam the door behind him.

As soon as she heard his footsteps leaving the porch, Shelly sank to the floor. She buried her face in the dusty fur of the nearest dog and allowed herself to cry.

Chapter Forty-Three

MAC WAS STANDING OUTSIDE Shelly's house when Whit arrived. Jordan had called him as soon as the dispatch went out that Shelly had been found. He went directly to her ranch to see if she was okay.

"Mac, what did you find out? How is she?" Whit said.

Mac paused with his hand on the door to his truck. He was clearly upset. "Stubborn as hell. She gave me some line about the dogs just running off. It's a lie. We both know it's a lie, but she won't tell me the truth, won't even talk to me. Except to tell me I've been wasting her time and mine." He shook his head. "Maybe she's right. Maybe it is time I moved on, quit myself of this place and that"—he jerked his head back to the ranch house—"that woman. I can't do anything with her or for her. Maybe you can figure out what's going on, Whit, but I'm done." He got into the truck, shut the door, and sped away while Whit stood there, his mouth gaping.

"Shelly!" Whit yelled as he climbed the porch. "What did you say to ..." He stopped when he saw her appearance. "What happened?"

Shelly straightened. "I found the dogs up on the ridge. They'd wandered off and gotten stuck in one of the old mines. I had to move some rocks around to get to them."

"By yourself? Why didn't you call one of us for help?"

She lifted her chin defiantly. "I didn't need any help."

Whit shook his head. It wasn't worth asking again, but he knew Shelly wasn't being any more honest with him than she'd been with Mac. "What did you say to Mac?"

Her eyes drifted to the floor. "Mac is looking for something I can't give him. It was time for me to cut him loose."

"Cut him loose?" Whit let out a frustrated huff. "Do you have any idea what that man is willing to do for you? What he's been willing to do for you all these years?"

"Whit, listen, I—" Shelly started.

"No, you listen for once. You've brushed him off, treated him like he was still the arrogant, lovesick teenager whose heart you broke. He's not that kid anymore. He's a hugely successful businessman, respected by everyone who knows him. He's the closest thing I have left to a dad. He put me through college when he knew my grandparents couldn't afford it. I know he paid the mortgage on this place for months after your husband died so you and your kids weren't put out on the street."

"And I paid him back, every red cent, with interest," Shelly snapped at him.

Whit's voice quieted. "But he never asked you to. He never asked anything from you, anything but that you give him a chance." He walked closer to Shelly. He brushed dirt off one of her shoulders like she was a little girl who'd gotten dirty playing outside. "Look, if I thought he didn't mean anything to you, if I thought you honestly had no interest in him, I could let it go. But I've seen the way you look at him. I know you feel something for him. I'd be willing to bet you love him as much as he loves you. You're just too damn independent and stubborn to admit it."

Shelly swallowed hard, then she shook her head. "You're wrong, Whit. Mac will never be anything more to me than an old friend."

Whit closed his eyes in frustration. "Keep telling yourself that, keep telling everyone you don't need any help, keep pushing away the people who love you, and you'll die a lonely old woman."

Shelly let out a harsh and bitter laugh. "You're lecturing me about dying alone? When was the last time you had anything that passed for a relationship? Your senior year of high school? The un-ropeable cowboy?" She huffed. "Try the cowboy who's too afraid to even take that first step, too afraid to risk getting his heart broken. At least I know what it is to give everything I have to someone. At least I had the courage to take the leap once."

Whit lowered his head. Shelly had hit a nerve that ran deep. "I guess if you don't need any help, I'll leave too."

He turned to go, then realized he'd left the door open when he walked in. Jordan was standing in the doorway. Her eyes met his and he read something that looked like pity in them. He wondered how much she'd heard. He straightened his hat and nodded at her as he walked toward the doorway. "Detective."

Jordan looked from Whit to Shelly. "Looks like you've had quite the night."

Whit stepped onto the porch as Shelly said to Jordan. "Come in. Close the door. There are a lot of things I need to tell you."

Chapter Forty-Four

"YOU WERE THAT CLOSE to figuring out who he was?" Jordan said after Shelly finished telling her everything about the killer she'd faced fifteen years before.

"Close enough for him to threaten my kids. He sent me pictures of them from school, when they were at sports practice, even one of my daughter sleeping. It was taken from the foot of her bed. He claimed he didn't want to hurt anyone else. He said what happened was between him and Bonnie and no one else, but if I didn't stop looking for him, he would make it personal."

"You just quit the investigation?" Jordan said.

Shelly's eyes snapped. "I did what I had to do to protect my family. You don't have kids; you wouldn't understand."

Jordan breathed in, then nodded. "What happened to your files, the evidence you'd collected?"

"I destroyed all of it. That was part of our deal."

"Why didn't you tell me what was going on from the beginning?"

"I didn't know if I could trust you then."

"And now, tonight, you went off on your own, unarmed, to confront a murderer? You should have told me as soon as you got the text."

"I had to make sure the dogs were safe first."

"Your dogs?" Jordan snorted. Shelly gave her a look that once again said she didn't understand. "So now what? Are you asking me to quit, knowing he has another victim, possibly still alive?"

"No. I'm telling you to be careful. I destroyed the evidence, but I have a good memory. I want to help you, but we need to be more discreet about it. We have to—"

"We don't have to do anything. This is my case. I can't put you at risk and quite frankly, I can't be sure I can trust you not to go off on your own and do something stupid again."

"You can't do this without me," Shelly said quietly.

"I can and I will." Jordan dug a notebook and pen out of her bag and pushed it toward Shelly. "Write down anything you remember, write down anything you think is important for me to know, then I'd suggest you and your dogs take a trip to see one of your kids, whichever one lives the farthest from Lombard. Stay there until this is resolved."

"I have a ranch to run, animals to take care of."

"Find someone to take care of them for you."

Shelly squared her shoulders. "I'm not running away from him this time."

Jordan let out a frustrated breath. "That's your call. I can't force you to leave, but I can and will prevent you from doing any more investigating. Stay away from the sheriff's office. Stay away from me."

"What are you planning to do, throw me in jail?"

"If that's what it takes. I think I have a pretty good basis for an obstruction of justice charge."

Shelly glared at Jordan and then bent over the notebook, scribbling furiously. For a few minutes the only sounds were the scratching of her pen and the dogs eating what looked like Clint's special dog food in the corner. Shelly pushed the notebook toward Jordan. "Any questions?"

Jordan looked it over. A lot of it made sense. Some of it she'd already guessed. Only the last thing Shelly had written gave her pause. "You don't believe he killed Blodgett?"

"No."

"Why not?"

"He told me he didn't."

"And you believe him?"

"Ironically, he's never lied to me before," Shelly said.

Jordan nodded. "I still think you should leave town, but—"

Shelly put her hand on top of Jordan's. "He has your number now too. He's already shown he can get to you. The break-in ..."

Jordan pulled her hand away. "I can take care of myself."

"Of course, you can." But Shelly didn't sound like she believed it.

Chapter Forty-Five

IT HAD BEEN ALMOST a week since Shelly's dogs had been found. Jordan was on her way into the sheriff's office when Beats called her on her cell phone. She took the call, curious why Beats hadn't used the radio.

"Jordan, you close?"

"Almost there. What's up?"

"Just wondering if you read the paper this morning." Beats' voice held a note that filled Jordan with dread.

"No." Jordan had briefly considered taking Whit's advice to go to the Horseshoe and read the morning paper, but with no leads in either case, she was pretty sure she didn't want to know what the local newspaper had to say.

"I thought I should warn you before you come in. You're the subject of an editorial, and it isn't good."

"For the fiasco with Shelly's dogs, wasting county resources, arresting Peyton, or overall screwing up this investigation?" Jordan asked.

"None of the above."

"What then?" Jordan's fear ran rampant. It was all she could do to stop herself from turning around.

"Let's just say, all of Lombard now knows why you left Seattle."

"Why I left ..." Jordan was silent for a long time, then she swore as the realization hit her.

"Yeah. That why. Seems like it shouldn't be anyone's business but yours, but small town ... no one gets their own business."

Jordan let out a long exhale. "Perfect."

"Sorry hon, that's only part of the bad news."

"Not sure how it can get worse," Jordan said.

"Judd is here."

Jordan swore again.

"Actually, both Judd and Heyward are waiting for you. No sign of Whit yet, but I imagine he'll be along sometime soon."

"Thanks for the heads up anyway."

Beats paused for a minute. "Is it true?"

Jordan hesitated, but there was no point in denying anything now. "I haven't seen the article, but yeah."

"And was he worth it?" Beats asked.

"Not even a little bit."

"They usually aren't. I'll have a cup of coffee waiting for you after it's over. The good stuff. Might even add a shot of something extra."

"Thanks, Beats." Jordan signed off. Her fingers went white on the steering wheel of her Expedition. She glanced toward the mountains, wondering what would happen if she turned down the road and kept driving until she ran out of gas and then lived off the land from there. She really didn't think she had the makings of a mountain man. She could just walk in and quit, but that was another thing she didn't have in her.

She slammed her hand against the steering wheel in frustration. This case and her patience had both hit a dead end. She felt further away from the answer than she'd been when she first walked into the sheriff's office. She didn't have time for a small-town smear campaign.

She pulled into the parking lot. Judd's now familiar, larger-than-life green Ford truck was parked out front. As usual, he was taking up two spots. One of them was hers. She took a breath, adjusted her jacket and prepared for the firing squad.

Chapter Forty-Six

JORDAN BARELY MADE IT through the front door before Sheriff Carlyle intercepted her. "My office. Now."

Beats glanced up and then quickly pretended to be absorbed by a pile of paperwork.

Jordan followed the sheriff to his office. Commissioner Judd and Commissioner Heyward sat in chairs opposite the sheriff's desk. Carlyle moved to the chair behind his desk and motioned for Jordan to sit.

"I'd rather stand." She didn't need another excuse for these men to look down on her.

"Suit yourself," Carlyle said as he sat.

"I assume you've heard what was in the paper this morning," Judd began.

Jordan sent up a little prayer of thanks to Beats. At least she knew what they were talking about. "Yes."

"And I don't suppose you have any explanation for it?" Judd asked.

"No, sir."

"You have no explanation, or you choose not to give one?" Commissioner Heyward asked.

"There's nothing to explain. Nothing in my actions or relationship with Commander Rexall was illegal. It was a mistake, yes, but a mistake I made well before I came here. It has no bearing on how I handle the case I've been given."

"So, you left the Seattle Police Department on your own accord?" Commissioner Heyward said.

"Yes."

"And you took the job here under the pretense that you had left the Seattle office willingly."

"Yes. And I did."

"Let's cut through the bull right now," Judd said. "You had an affair with one of your superiors who was a married man. You were pressured to leave the Seattle Police Department, so you took the job here under false pretenses."

Jordan turned to face Judd. "What pretenses? I believe I was hired to solve a murder. I believe I'm fully capable of solving that murder, given time and resources. I've made significant prog—"

Judd cut her off. "You've made no progress beyond blindly following the clues the murderer laid out for you, including one that was left in your own home, yet somehow you managed to lose that one."

Jordan glanced at the sheriff. He kept his expression unreadable, not that she expected anything like loyalty from him.

Judd continued his list of grievances. "You are constantly being distracted by things in this town that aren't part of the case you've been assigned and are frankly none of your business."

Jordan leveled her gaze at Judd. "Distractions like a significant drug stash that was being stored at the murder victim's house and was connected to your son? I can see why you wouldn't consider that my business, but there is every possibility it's connected to the sheriff's murder."

Judd's face turned from its usual red to purple. "Leave my son out of this."

Jordan opened her mouth to respond, but Commissioner Heyward cut her off. "The fact remains that you've made, at best, slow progress in the sheriff's murder case. Since you've been here, another person has gone missing and most likely has also been murdered."

"I'm working every possible angle and the rest of the department has been searching for Miss Larsen almost nonstop."

"Except for a brief break to look for three missing dogs," Judd pointed out. "Dogs that turned out to have just wandered off."

"I don't believe they just wandered off, and whether they did or they didn't, the search was initiated by community members, not by me."

"You're saying there were no sheriff's department resources involved in that search?" Heyward said. "I find that highly unlikely."

Jordan nodded across the table to the interim sheriff. "You're going to have to take that one up with Sheriff Carlyle. You've all made it pretty clear I don't get to make decisions about what the sheriff's department resources are used for."

Judd huffed out an exaggerated breath, loaded with anger, exasperation, and contempt. "And then there's the problem of our fellow commissioner."

It took Jordan a second to realize that he was talking about Whit, the one commissioner who was absent from this meeting. "Commissioner Palmer?"

"You seem to have been spending a lot of time with him lately. He was even at your house when Deputy Harding went to investigate a possible break-in. What time was it? Two, three a.m.?"

"All my interactions with Commissioner Palmer have been above board, professional, and concerning the case I was hired to investigate. But even if they were social interactions, don't I have the right to make friends while I'm here?"

"Your 'interactions' in this case point toward a repeated pattern of behavior. Although you're conducting your investigation under the direction of the attorney general, you still fall under the auspices of this department. Therefore, Mr. Palmer, along with the two of us, are the closest thing you have to a boss here in Lombard," Heyward said.

"Meaning?" Jordan asked.

"Meaning, if your pattern of behavior is to look for opportunities for advancement through 'social interactions' with your superiors, well, that's behavior we won't tolerate here," Judd said.

Enraged, Jordan retorted, "What did my 'interactions' with Commander Rexall get me besides a one-way ticket to Nowheresville, Montana?" As soon as the words were out of her mouth, she knew she'd let her tongue get away from her, again. She'd all but confirmed what they were fishing for, that she was pressured to leave Seattle. The three men exchanged a look of satisfaction. It wasn't true, not really—the choice to leave had been entirely hers, born out of frustration with herself and the humiliation of being the other woman.

"You're saying you didn't leave the Seattle Police Department of your own accord?" Commissioner Heyward said.

"I'm saying I chose to leave, just like I chose to come here. I chose to sign a contract with you gentlemen under the direction of Adam Bentley, Montana's state attorney general. If you have a problem with the way I'm doing my job or the reasons why I ended up in Lombard, I suggest you take it up with him. He can determine the legalities of dismissing me based on an incident in my past personal life and small-town gossip. Now if you'll excuse me, I have a murder investigation to conduct." She turned toward the door.

"You have not been dismissed!" Judd roared.

Jordan turned around slowly, leveling her gaze at Judd. "Let's cut through the bull, shall we? If I recall, you were sheriff when all of this went down the first time. You weren't able to solve the crime then, and the members of this community voted you out because of the way you handled it." Judd started to sputter something, but she cut him off. "I don't know why you feel like you can dictate the course of this investigation. I have more experience solving a murder than anyone in this room. Why don't you let me do my job? Is there something you're afraid of me finding out, Commissioner?"

Judd stood, towering over Jordan. "I will not tolerate being accused by some little—"

Heyward put his hand on Judd's arm. "Before this goes any further—before anyone else says something they're bound to regret, I want Detective Gibbons to understand she has options."

Jordan stepped back, catching her breath. "Options?"

Sheriff Carlyle shuffled the paperwork on his desk. "You've made it pretty clear you don't like it here. Maybe it's time to cut your losses and move on. There's a position available to you in Billings, offered up by Bentley himself. He's looking for a state investigator who would specialize in cold cases. He sent me a message about it a couple of days ago. He wanted to know if I thought you'd be a good fit for it. It's a good job, more money, more prestige. Billings isn't Seattle, but it's got more of a big-town feel. You might fit in better there. I could write you up a glowing recommendation and you could be on your way out of here in a couple of weeks."

"What about the sheriff's murder and the missing girl?" Jordan asked.

"I think we can take it from here. You have brought the investigation a ways along." Sheriff Carlyle said. Jordan didn't understand why he was suddenly complimentary to her.

"It was a mistake to bring an outsider in on the case anyway," Judd muttered.

Commissioner Heyward spread his arms as if he were making some grand peace offering. "There you have it. You have some options to think over. At any rate, we're giving you a few days off for you to think about things and to let all of this blow over."

"A few days off? In the middle of an investigation where someone's life might be on the line?" Jordan looked over each one with astonishment, ending with Sheriff Carlyle.

He met her eyes with a steely gaze. "It's not a request. Your choices are to take time off on your own or to be put on administrative leave pending an investigation into misconduct."

"Misconduct for what?"

"For the way you handled the arrest of my son," Judd said.

"I didn't—"

"Commissioner Judd has agreed to not file the misconduct charge," Heyward said.

"Yet," Judd added.

"Yet." Sheriff Carlyle repeated. "If the misconduct report is filed, you can kiss the position in Billings goodbye. If not, the position will likely be yours."

"You're much too young and too early into your career to be burning so many bridges." Heyward said it like he was appeasing an overly emotional teenage girl. "I suggest you use the time off to consider just how magnanimous we're being. Take a drive up to

Billings, see how you like it. The rimrocks up there make for beautiful country."

Jordan opened her mouth to say more but realized there was no way to win this one. The men in this room had all the power. For now.

"We look forward to hearing your decision." The commissioners filed out of the room, Judd glowering at Jordan on his way out.

Jordan stood for a minute after they left. The sheriff cleared his throat. "For what it's worth, I wasn't the one who talked to the paper. I was really hoping the thing in Seattle wouldn't come up. I was afraid it would, but I hoped."

"Sheriff, I—"

Sheriff Carlyle held up his hand. "You heard them. You have a couple days off. Looks like you could use the time."

Chapter Forty-Seven

JORDAN WENT BACK TO her office, closed the door behind her, sat at the desk, and leaned her face into her hands. She wanted to scream or throw something, but she knew that wouldn't do her any good. Nothing about this investigation had been straightforward. The entire town already thought she was incompetent, and now the very thing she had come here to escape had been thrown back in her face.

Someone knocked at the door. Expecting Beats with the promised coffee, Jordan called, "It's open."

Instead of Beats, Whit walked through the door.

"Is this true?" Jordan didn't even have to look up from her desk. She knew exactly what Whit was holding in his hand.

"Is it any of your business if it is?" she fired back.

"Since I vouched for you, since I'm one of the people who brought you here, it is my business." He slammed the paper down on the desk in front of her.

She stood, her eyes flashing fire. "The way I lived my life before I came here is my business and no one else's. I don't know why the local paper, or you for that matter, feel like you have any right to judge me for that."

"If you were having an affair with a married man who was one of your superiors, it speaks to your character, at least in this part of the country. People don't want to trust their lives to a detective who's dishonest that way."

"And if I were a man, would you feel the same way?"

"That's not what this is about," Whit said. "Stop assuming I treat you differently because you're a woman."

"Stop pretending you don't treat me differently because I'm a woman."

"Stop avoiding the question." Whit's jaw was tight.

Jordan faced him, ready to tell him where he and his backward little town could go—really, where the entire state of Montana could go. But when she caught the glint of betrayal in his eyes, it pulled the fight out of her.

"I didn't know he was married." It was a feeble excuse. She was a detective, a good detective. If anyone should have looked into the background of someone before she got involved with him, she should have. "I didn't know, and I broke it off as soon as I found out. Not that it's any of your business."

"They want you to leave the case and leave town."

"I know. I already spoke with your fellow commissioners. They have a nice position all picked out for me in Billings. As far as the sheriff's murder or Sadie's disappearance, they can 'handle that' without me," Jordan shot back. "I guess you missed the call to come meet with me."

"I didn't miss the call. I didn't come to their little gathering because I wanted to get the truth from you first," Whit said.

"Well, now you have it."

"And because I don't agree with them," he said quietly.

"What?" She stared at him, waiting for the punchline.

"I still think you're the only one who can solve this thing. You're the only one who can beat him. Sordid affair in Seattle be damned, small-town gossip and public opinion be damned. You can solve this. But you have got to let go of your pride. You need to let go of the part of you that feels like you have to constantly prove yourself. You have to be willing to let someone help you." He moved closer, so close that Jordan held her breath. "You have to be willing to let Shelly help you. Together you can stop this guy."

Jordan exhaled. Shelly. Of course. Too bad Shelly was no longer an option in this. Jordan couldn't risk the ex-deputy getting herself killed. "You don't think I should take the job in Billings?"

"I think ..." He stopped, looked down at his feet and took a couple of breaths. "I don't want to see you get hurt. I don't want to see Shelly get hurt either. But I don't think you should leave. No one wants to see a killer walk free." Whit was close enough for her to smell the coffee on his breath. He must have come straight from the Horseshoe.

She met his eyes. "I'm not giving up that easily."

A smile played across his lips. "I didn't think you would."

Chapter Forty-Eight

"YOU PACKING IT IN?" Beats walked in with a steamy cup of coffee as Jordan gathered up her things.

Jordan accepted the cup and leaned back on her chair. "I'm taking a few official days off."

"In the middle of an investigation?" Beats asked.

"Not by choice, and I said official. I'm going to use the time to do my own thing, get things straight in my head. Do some unofficial poking around."

"In other words, I shouldn't call you with any information that comes in while you're gone and I shouldn't tell you that there's a notice on Becca's desk for a certified package Ray is supposed to pick up at the post office?"

"Not officially," Jordan answered. She stood up; everything she could take with her was stowed in her briefcase.

"So where to now?"

Jordan picked up the notice. "The post office. You said there was a package for Ray."

"You're going to intercept it before he knows it's there?"

"That's the general idea. You think they'll give it to me?" Jordan felt guilty sneaking around, picking up the package Ray was expecting, but if the sheriff's department was going to tie her hands, it was going to have to take more clandestine methods to solve this.

"Just walk in like you're expecting to pick it up. No one will even raise an eyebrow. Any idea what's in the package?" Beats asked.

Jordan pocketed the notice with her cell phone. "Answers. I hope."

———◆———

The weather in Lombard was pleasant, sort of Goldilocks pleasant; not too cold, not too hot—just right. The package hadn't arrived yet, but the friendly postal employee had said it should be there any time. As Beats had predicted, no one questioned her picking up a package that was addressed to another deputy. Jordan parked her portable office down the block where she could watch for the delivery, scoop it up, and hurry home. She had no idea when the package would arrive so she adjusted her bucket seat so she could relax during what could be a long wait.

Parked as she was on what the natives called the main drag, she had a good view of most of the town's businesses. As she watched the vehicles come and go and people scurrying about, it occurred to her that things did not seem as foreign to her as they did when she first arrived from Seattle. The fact that almost everyone drove a truck and most had one dog or more in them had puzzled her. Their clothes almost repulsed her—shirts with pockets and snap closures; everyone, male and female, wearing overalls; cowboy boots as an integral part of their wardrobe; without exception all the men wearing either baseball caps or cowboy hats. She had felt she was on another planet.

Today—the same vehicles, the same obligatory dogs, the same people wearing the same clothes, and it all seemed perfectly normal to her. Had she really changed that much? They were all the same; the change had to be her. Seattle's ways were fading. Was the Montana she had hated with such intensity upon arrival starting to grow on her?

She thought back to her meetings from earlier. Despite all the threats and warnings that came from the other commissioners, the only piece that stood out was the look of betrayal in Whit's eyes. It was ridiculous for him to feel betrayed by something that had happened months before they met. Maybe it was more like he thought she was a better person, and she had disappointed him. Why did she care so much what he thought of her?

A startling thought suddenly came to her: what if it was Whit who was growing on her? God forbid if she had let that happen after her romantic fiasco in Seattle. That was exactly what the other commissioners thought was going on. The last thing she wanted to do was prove them right. Still, the argument with Whit hurt much more than the threats and accusations she'd gotten from the other commissioners.

Whit was the closest thing she had to a friend here. She wanted the other commissioners to respect her, but she didn't care what kind of person they thought she was. Whit was different. His opinion mattered to her. It seemed like he took her deception personally, but he still believed in her.

She wasn't even sure she believed in herself anymore. The bloody cloth and the message that was left in her house was hard to take, but other messages, meant for Shelly and Whit, haunted her more. Protecting herself was one thing, but she wasn't sure she could protect them too. Maybe staying was a mistake.

Jordan paused to consider what there was left for her back in Seattle. Her parents hadn't tried to contact her since she arrived in Montana. The man she thought she loved had turned out to be married with two children. Although she'd left Seattle on her own accord, the humiliation of going back after failing in little, tiny Lombard would be too much to take. Besides, Brownie wouldn't like it in Seattle. She was surprised that the dog was a suddenly a consideration. How had that become such a big deal?

Jordan was in such deep thought and so shaken by the discoveries her afternoon of quiet introspection had uncovered, she nearly missed seeing the mail truck arrive. She intercepted the package before Ray could and headed home to bury herself in work. Her time spent doing nothing had really rattled her to the core.

Chapter Forty-Nine

JORDAN LAID OUT THE contents from the box on her dining room table. Brownie had shuffled forward curiously and now sniffed at the edge of the table, like he was expecting a handout. When he didn't see anything that would qualify as food he laid his head on Jordan's leg.

The box held one set of civilian clothes including the obligatory rodeo belt buckle (the event was bareback riding this time), a pocketknife carved from some type of animal horn, and surprisingly, a sketchbook.

Jordan turned the pages. The drawings weren't very good. She wondered if Robert Pitkin had gotten any better at drawing with all the time he'd had on his hands serving a ten-year prison sentence for armed robbery. She was just about to put the book away and move onto something else when she reached the last picture in the book. There was something familiar about the drawing. She glanced out the windows and realized it was a very rough sketch of the mountains to the east. A smudged symbol was at the base of the mountains where the creek would have run through. It took her a second to pinpoint why that spot seemed familiar. It was exact location where the first piece of Bonnie Golden had been found.

She pulled out the folder she'd brought with her and compared this drawing to the one she'd found in Sadie's notebook. For the first time she realized Sadie was trying to draw the same mountains, but from more of an aerial view. The black mark was on both drawings. There was another mark next to the old mine where Shelly had found a humerus all those years ago, the place Shelly had said she'd found her dogs. She flipped back through the convict's sketchbook and found a drawing that could have been the high meadow up at Rattlesnake. There were other marks, places they'd have to search. There wasn't a mark or a drawing on the edge of the canyon by Whit's property where the skull had been found, but neither map was complete.

It looked like Ray had found the man with the promised map of gold. But if Robert Pitkin was dead, then he wasn't the man who was texting Shelly. Was he the original killer or someone carrying on a dark legacy? How was Robert Pitkin related to the other players in the case? Jordan thought back to Shelly's big board, but she didn't remember seeing his name there. Even so, she was positive Shelly would know what connections Robert Pitkin might have around town.

Jordan leaned back in her chair. She couldn't ask Shelly. She couldn't get her involved. Almost like someone was listening in on her thoughts, her phone rang. She looked down the caller ID.

It was Whit.

"There's a dance at the Grange tonight," Whit said as soon as she answered the phone. He suddenly sounded like the guy that had asked her to her eighth-grade graduation dance. She'd turned that one down too.

"Dance?" she asked, hoping in the same moment that he was, and that he wasn't asking her to come with him.

"Not really a dance. I mean there will be dancing, but..." Whit seemed to stumble around for the right words. "More of a... A fundraiser."

"A fundraiser?"

"Yeah. A Fundraiser for Angie. Sheriff Blodgett's wife. I think it would go a lot toward community relations if you went. No offense, but I think it would help improve the opinion people around here have of you." He hesitated. "Shelly will be there. It might be a good place for the two of you to—"

"What? Shake hands and make up?" Jordan suddenly felt defensive. He didn't want her to go with him. He wanted her to go because of Shelly. She was so tired of explaining to the whole town every move she made. "What I did, I did for Shelly's own good." Jordan hadn't told Whit anything Shelly had told her, only that they'd stopped working together because Shelly had gone off on her own and done something dangerous.

"I know that you need her," Whit said, like he'd read her mind and knew that right at that moment she did need Shelly. "It would be good for this town to see you interact as a normal person, instead of just a detective. I'm making my chili and I might even save a dance for you."

Jordan didn't know how to answer that. She was glad he couldn't see the flush of red that hit her cheeks or hear the uptick of her heart through the phone. Whether she wanted to go or not, the last thing she needed after Judd's smear campaign was the "un-ropeable cowboy" or anyone else in Lombard taking an interest in her.

She took a breath. "I can't. I'm on a deadline now. If I want to stay on this case, I have to show some kind of significant progress and soon. Everyone expects me to give up and take the job in Billings. I need to prove them wrong before they run me out of town."

"That's why you have to come tonight. That's why you need to talk to Shelly. She can help you. I know —"

"We've been over that, Whit. I need do this on my own. The last thing I need is Shelly or anyone else getting hurt because I dragged them into this. Thanks for the invite, but I really need to get back to work."

"Right. Have a good evening, Detective." Whit sounded frustrated or disappointed or maybe even angry. Jordan hung up feeling exactly the same way. What was his game anyway? She'd like to consider him a friend, but she wasn't sure that was quite the right word.

Jordan went back to the notebook. She set up all the files and photos from the case on the screen of her personal laptop, rearranging them in different groups, by timeline, by case, by suspect. She added Robert Pitkin. It was her version of Shelly's whiteboard. She'd slowly been crossing suspects off her list.

It was the one she couldn't eliminate bothered her the most.

Chapter Fifty

JORDAN SHUT HER LAPTOP. She needed a run to clear her head, possibly followed by a long hot bath. She changed into running clothes and tucked her headphones into her ears. Something was nagging the back of her mind, something important that she couldn't put her finger on.

She was on her way out the door when her phone rang. Sheriff Carlyle's name appeared on the caller ID. She'd given him her private number when she first got to Lombard, but until now he'd always called on the radio.

She hesitated for a few rings before deciding to answer. "Hello, Sheriff."

"Detective, you around, or did you take Heyward up on his offer to head to Billings?"

She didn't even try to keep the animosity out of her voice. "I'm home, where you told me to be. Why are you calling me?"

"Glad to hear it. I just got a tip that might blow this whole case wide open. There was a disturbance reported on 1200 East Juniper."

Jordan thought about why the address sounded familiar, then she remembered. "Commissioner Palmer's place?"

"Kind of. There's an old trailer on his property, used to belong to his parents, I think. Some kids were out on ATVs and they reported hearing shots and a woman screaming from out that direction."

"How long ago?"

"Less than half hour ago."

"Did you call the commissioner about it?" Jordan asked.

"I couldn't raise him on the phone and actually, it might be better if we went out there without him knowing."

"Doesn't that constitute an illegal search?"

Sheriff Carlyle blew out an impatient breath. "As I said, he's not answering the phone and if it sounds like someone is in imminent danger ..."

"Right. I'll meet you there as soon as I can."

Jordan strapped on her holster and added a jacket, not bothering to change out of her running clothes. Brownie whimpered at her from the corner. "I'll take you out later." He whimpered again and limped toward the door, blocking her path. She reached down and rubbed his head. "I promise, I'll be back soon." She gently pushed him out of the way. His brown eyes followed her out the door with a pitiable look.

When Jordan got into her Expedition, she automatically reached for the radio. "Detective Gibbons responding to the disturbance at 1200 East Juniper."

"Hey Jordan, thought you were off?" Beats said.

"I guess I'm back on again," Jordan answered.

"Glad to hear it. But what's this disturbance you're talking about?"

"Something out by Whit's place."

"First I've heard of it. You think you'll need back up?" Beats asked.

"No. I've got it."

"Keep us posted." Beats sounded dubious.

"Will do." Jordan hung up the radio and followed the GPS coordinates Carlyle had given her toward Whit's ranch. She looked down at her cell phone, wondering if she should try to call Whit. She shook off that idea. If she and Carlyle were going to confront a killer, she didn't want Whit to be there. If she called him, he'd come. Besides, the nagging doubt in the back of her mind involved him.

The directions took her past the main entrance to the ranch and onto a long, dirt road that turned into a little used two-track trail. A couple of miles in, she finally reached a dilapidated trailer. The siding was rusted and peeling; the windows were broken. With all of that, the skirting looked new, or at least recently repaired. Carlyle's vehicle wasn't in the yard, but there were fresh tire tracks that led farther up the road. She sat in her vehicle for a minute, debating. She reached for the radio, but then put it away. If the sheriff was trying to take someone by surprise, the radio might give him away. She wasn't going to make the mistake with the police scanner she'd made before.

She climbed out of her Expedition, her gun drawn. "Sheriff?" she called softly, but no one answered. The front door was nailed over with a sheet of plywood. She moved around to the back. The back door swung open in the wind; the board that had been covering it lying beside it. There were no stairs, only an old milk crate pushed up against the edge. Jordan walked through the broken door into a dark room. All the windows were covered with thick blankets. There were holes in the floor. The kitchen appliances were missing. Still, she could tell someone had been here recently. The remains of a loaf of bread, a crushed beer can, and a few orange peels littered the countertop. As she crept closer, something caught her eye. There was a wood frame on the dusty glass coffee table. On the back, in faded gold ink were the words "To Deputy Curtis, Map of Gold. Seek and ye shall find."

Jordan wrapped her hand with a rag from the table and turned the frame over. The edge split and the frame clunked against the table. A muffled scraping sound came from the floor below her. She moved to the kitchen, kicking aside a threadbare carpet. She listened. The noise came again, somewhere below the trailer. She got down on the floor. Where the rug had been was a seam in the linoleum. She dug her fingernails in the edges.

Footsteps behind her brought her to her feet. She spun around and leveled her gun at the figure standing in the hallway. They faced each across the darkened space.

Chapter Fifty-One

"SINCE WE'RE ALL ON the same side, you two should put away your weapons before someone gets hurt." Ray's voice from the doorway caught them both by surprise.

Carlyle stepped out from the hallway into the light of the open door. He slowly lowered his gun. As he did, a flash of silver caught Jordan's eye. Something about the gun didn't look right. He slipped it into his holster before she could get a closer look. "You almost got yourself shot."

"I could say the same for you. I told you I was coming," Jordan replied.

"What are you doing here?" Sheriff Carlyle said to Ray.

"I was near here when Jordan called in. I wasn't doing anything important, so I thought I'd come out here and provide some backup." Ray and Sheriff Carlyle exchanged a look that crackled like lightning across the small room.

Carlyle nodded to Jordan. "What'd you find?"

She indicated the frame on the table. "This was taken from the sheriff's house when he was killed."

"Looks like an aerial photograph of at least part of Keystone," Ray said.

"It is. The person who killed Bonnie Golden sent it to Shelly. Shelly gave it to Sheriff Blodgett." Jordan looked closer at the picture where the frame had slipped. The picture had been taken out before and someone had made gold marks all over the picture inside.

"That's it!" she exclaimed.

"That's what?" Carlyle asked.

"The map and the key. I'm going to bet those marks show all the places Bonnie Golden's body was buried." She looked closer. Every place where they'd found parts of Bonnie was marked, except for the one on Whit's property.

Ray whistled. "Now how did that end up here?"

"That's a good question." Jordan turned to Carlyle. "Did you find anything?"

He shook his head. "I started in the back. Checked the rooms and all the closets. Nothing."

A groan split the silence. "You checked everywhere?" Jordan asked.

"Sounds like its coming from under the trailer," Ray said.

Jordan went back to the seam in the floor, dropping to her knees. She pried at the edges, revealing a small trap door to the underside of the trailer. She pulled it open.

"Detective." Carlyle's voice had a warning note to it. It was too dark to see anything beyond the opening.

"Cover me." Jordan pulled out her flashlight and moved toward the dark opening.

"I don't think you sh—" Ray started.

"It has to be me. Neither of you will fit down there." Jordan crouched on the floor for a second, shining her light through the opening. She couldn't see anything beyond spiderwebs and tattered insulation. There was barely room to breathe in the small space, much less move. She tried to go through the trapdoor. Her holster wouldn't fit through. She climbed back out, unbuckled it, and considered her options. She couldn't carry a flashlight, her radio, and her gun.

She decided she was close enough to yell if she needed help, so she left the radio. She switched on the flashlight and put it between her teeth, then she tucked her gun into her sports bra, giving Ray a warning look when he stared. He averted his gaze and raised both hands as if in surrender. "I didn't see anything."

Jordan rolled her eyes and shimmied through the opening. Once she hit the ground she got down on all fours, moving her head from side to side to direct the light while she searched the dirty space. The ground she crawled on was cold, slightly damp, and gritty with rat droppings. Spiderwebs caught in her hair, and she tried to push back the thought of black widows and any other venomous spiders that might inhabit this wild country.

Jordan stopped as her flashlight glinted off something in the corner. It took her a second to recognize that what she was seeing was an eye. It was even longer before she realized the eye belonged to a face so streaked with blood and dirt that she could barely make out any features.

She moved closer. She was sure she was looking at a body—so sure that she reached to move a chunk of matted blonde hair to see the face more clearly.

A hand grabbed hers.

Jordan startled, dropping the flashlight.

The woman screamed.

"Jordan!" Ray yelled. He tried to scramble through the opening.

"No." Jordan collected herself and with a shaking, breathless voice called back, "Stay, stay where you are. If you get stuck, we'll never get her out."

"You're okay." She tried to soothe the woman whose hand was now cemented to Jordan's wrist. She fumbled for the flashlight with her other hand. It had gone out when she dropped it. She finally found and switched the light on.

"What's going on down there, Detective?" Brendan called.

Jordan pointed the flashlight back at the woman's face, and deep brown eyes blinked back at her. "Sadie? Sadie Larsen?"

The woman licked her swollen lips and nodded.

"How did you get down here?" Jordan asked.

"Whit." The woman said, closing her eyes with pain. "Whit Palmer."

Jordan shined the flashlight over the woman, making a quick field examination. The woman's arms and legs were slashed and crudely bandaged with strips of cloth. Her cheeks and lips were swollen and bruised. She looked at Jordan with desperation. "Water?"

"No. Sorry. But we'll get you out of here soon."

"You said Whit put you down here." Jordan tried to keep the disbelief out of her voice. "Why would he do that?"

Sadie licked her cracked lips. "He's crazy. He didn't want anyone to know what his dad did. Didn't want them to know that his dad killed her. Killed her and cut her into pieces."

"Her?" Jordan asked.

"Bonnie. Bonnie Golden." She leaned back against the side of the trailer, obviously in pain and exhausted.

"Whit's dad killed Bonnie Golden?" Jordan repeated.

Sadie nodded. "The sheriff was close to finding out the truth, so Whit shot him. He knew I was close to solving it too, so he kidnapped me. He was gonna kill me as soon as he pinned the murder on someone else, but you found me." She gripped Jordan's arm tighter, the one she hadn't let go of since Jordan had found her.

The space seemed even smaller, more claustrophobic. She gently pried Sadie's fingers from her arm, needing room to catch her breath. Carlyle had radioed for an ambulance and a fire truck to cut through the reinforced skirting on the trailer. They'd decided that would be better than trying to pull the battered woman through the small trap door. The air filled with the sounds of sawing metal and the whine of sirens. The woman cringed and huddled close to the side of the trailer.

Jordan put her hand on Sadie's shoulder. "You'll be okay."

She wasn't sure if she was talking to the woman or to herself.

Chapter Fifty-Two

"WE NEED TO MAKE the arrest tonight," Carlyle said. Jordan stood next to him and watched as Sadie was loaded into a waiting ambulance. It had taken longer than she'd expected to get both her and Sadie out. Jordan was exhausted. She looked at him without comprehending what he was saying. Everything about tonight had left her in shock. In addition to the woman, they'd dragged a gun out from under the trailer. Jordan was sure it would turn out to be the sheriff's missing revolver. A dresser in one of the bedrooms held leather stamp tools, the kind that were used to fashion the collar found in Shelly's garden. The pieces were falling into place, but Jordan wasn't sure she wanted to know what the end result of this puzzle might be.

"Whit. We have to arrest him tonight." Carlyle said, trying to draw her attention back to the present.

Jordan nodded. "Right. He'll be at the dance ... the fundraiser for the sheriff's wife at the Grange."

Carlyle raised his eyebrows but didn't ask how Jordan knew this. "I can radio someone to pick him up, or ... you can go get him yourself."

"Me?" Jordan asked.

"Unless you're not up to it. I just think it would go a long way toward showing the commissioners and everyone in town what you're made of, that you were on the right track all along."

Jordan straightened up, brushing dirt off her clothes. She took a breath. She couldn't show him that she was weak, not now. "You're right. It should be me."

The Grange had the look of a high school dance mixed with a church social from a 1940s movie. There were some cheesy streamers, a big photo of the late sheriff in the entrance, and a table full of auction items. The smell of chili and cornbread permeated the air. A band with two fiddlers performed on the stage against the back wall. There were a few older couples dancing enthusiastically in the middle of the floor, but most of the crowd just stood around eating paper bowls of chili and talking.

Everyone stared at Jordan as she pushed through the crowd, scanning the faces for Whit.

Ray followed her. "I'm here if you need back up."

Jordan nodded without looking at him. She steeled her resolve. She'd made a lot of arrests in her short life, but never someone she knew. Never someone she cared about. She'd get him outside, make it private. No matter what he'd done, she owed him that much.

Instead of seeing Whit, the first person to catch her eye was Shelly. Her expression hardened as she crossed the room to intercept Jordan. "Detective?"

Jordan heard the question in her voice, but she chose not to acknowledge it. Instead, she nodded a greeting. "Mrs. Curtis."

Shelly looked from Jordan to Ray. "What's going on, Jordan?"

Before she could think of what to say to Shelly, Whit came out from the kitchen. He raised his eyebrows at her and then nodded toward Shelly, the question sparking in his eyes, "You two made up yet?"

Jordan let out her breath. She stopped and let Whit come to her. "Glad you could make it, Detective." His expression softened and he reached like he was going to brush something out of her hair, dust or a cobweb. Jordan stepped back, quickly. "Looks like it's been a tough night."

"I need to speak to you outside, Commissioner," Jordan said.

He looked at her with a puzzled expression. "Commissioner? Is this official business?"

"Yes."

He caught the seriousness of her expression. "Of course."

"Don't." Shelly's eyes sparked.

Jordan didn't know if the warning was for her or for Whit, but she couldn't wait any longer. Commissioner Judd had stepped into the room. He looked expectant, like he was here to see the show, here to see her "results."

Jordan faced Whit, her eyes hard against his soft gray ones. She forced her voice to stay steady. "Hands where I can see them."

"What?" Whit asked, startled.

"Better do what she says, Whit," Ray said.

Looking dazed, Whit extended his hands. "I don't—"

"Whitmore Palmer, you're under arrest for the murder of Sheriff Brady Blodgett and the kidnapping of Sadie Larsen."

"No." Shelly's protestation wasn't loud. She didn't even act shocked, but her "no" struck Jordan to the core. She turned off the part of her that felt anything, reading Whit his rights with as much emotion as if he were a drunk she'd picked up on the side of the road. Ray twisted Whit's arms and handcuffed them behind his back.

At some point the music had stopped and the crowd drew into a circle around them. The room was silent; the only one speaking up was Shelly. "You're making a mistake, Detective."

Jordan turned to look at the woman she had once considered a mentor, even a friend. "I'm doing my job." Jordan put her hand on Whit's shoulder to direct him through the crowd. She felt his gaze on her but couldn't face him. She stared straight ahead, not making eye contact with anyone. Still, she couldn't miss the look of triumph and joy that shone on Commissioner Judd's face.

Chapter Fifty-Three

"DID YOU EVEN BOTHER to check his alibi before you threw Whit in jail?" Shelly stood over Jordan's desk. Jordan wasn't sure who'd let Shelly in. Carlyle had been keeping the public out of the sheriff's office ever since the crowd of concerned citizens had gathered after Whit's arrest.

"Yes," Jordan said.

"So, you know he couldn't have killed Blodgett. Whit was at a rancher's conference in Texas the weekend the sheriff was murdered. The conference ended Sunday morning. The Sheriff was killed sometime late Monday evening. Whit couldn't have made it back unless he didn't stop for sleep, or even gas. It's almost a twenty-seven-hour drive."

"If he'd flown, he'd have had plenty of time," Jordan answered.

"What makes you think he flew? Have you seen a plane ticket? Did you even ask him?" Shelly challenged.

"In case you haven't noticed, things have been kind of nuts around here." Jordan gestured to the closed blinds on her window and the crowd noises beyond it. "Whit lawyered up almost immediately, only his lawyer hasn't made it here yet. So no, I haven't had the chance to question him."

"Who's his lawyer?" Shelly asked.

"Not that I should give you that information, but we're waiting for a Mr. Sears from Butte."

"Shane Sears?"

"You know him?"

"He's an old family friend, but not much of a defense attorney."

"Whoever he is, I can't question Whit until he gets here."

"He didn't fly from Austin," Shelly said. "He wouldn't have. Whit is scared to death of planes."

The revelation startled Jordan. Whit didn't seem afraid of anything. "He never told me that."

"Well, he wouldn't have, would he? You didn't tell him you were afraid of horses," Shelly said.

Jordan sat for a second, dumbfounded. "How did you know?"

"I'm a good observer. I saw the way you were shaking when you got off Scout, and before you tell me it was because of the rough ride up, I saw the look in your eye when I mentioned you taking the mule down the hill. You thought I meant the animal. You practically climbed up the trailer to get away from Popeye. I know terror when I see it."

Jordan shook her head. "Whit told me his grandpa used to take him up in the crop duster. He said he learned some of the basics of flying."

"Enough to be scared out of his ... pardon the pun, wits. It was an old plane, known to stall at the most inconvenient times. I imagine a young and terrified Whit didn't have a very good experience going up in it. At any rate, Whit is afraid of planes, so he drove himself back from Austin to Lombard. Check the schedule for the conference, check the miles on his truck, whatever it takes. Just establish Whit's alibi and get him the hell out of that cell."

"I can't. Even if I can prove he didn't murder the sheriff, there is a battered and bled out woman who says Whit kidnapped her. Until I can prove otherwise, Whit stays in jail."

"Who is this woman anyway, and why would she lie about a thing like this? And she is lying—you know that as well as I do."

"What if Whit is the one who's lying?" Jordan said. Shelly started to say something, but Jordan cut her off. "There was no conference in Austin. I checked into it. He lied to you about that."

"Then he had a good reason to lie." Shelly spoke firmly, but Jordan could tell the revelation shook her.

"I have a bunch of people who swore they saw Whit with Sadie Larsen, just before she went missing. Her roommate said she was coming here to meet her new boyfriend, some guy with gray eyes whose name started with a W. It's looking more and more like that was Whit."

"That's not likely. Sadie Larsen isn't his type. You know Whit. He's a good man, a good person. He's not a kidnapper and he's certainly not a murderer."

"I don't have the luxury of deciding his guilt or innocence based on his good name or what kind of woman he likes. I have to go by facts, and right now the facts are not in his favor."

Shelly shook her head, frustrated. "What do we know about the woman you found under the trailer?"

"Not much. According to her, Whit found out she was going to implicate his dad in Bonnie Golden's murder, so he kidnapped her and killed the sheriff." Shelly looked away, but not before Jordan caught the shocked look she tried to hide. She narrowed her eyes at Shelly. "What do you know?"

Shelly sat silent for a few minutes. She tented her fingers beneath her chin and finally sighed. "One of the leads I was following, right at the end, just before everything went to hell, seemed to ..." She breathed again and then blurted out, "... lead me straight to Charlie."

The room was silent for a few minutes as that thought sunk in. "Charlie? You mean Whit's father?"

Shelly nodded. "When I heard Charlie was killed in an accident a couple of years later, I assumed it was over. Maybe even that justice had been served."

"That's why you said you weren't sure if Charlie was dead, because you found the dog collar and you thought he might have been the one that put it there. The belt buckle too?"

"I've had my doubts over the years about whether Charlie was really gone, but he's never surfaced, no sign of him at all."

"The man who took your dogs, the voice on the phone, was it him?"

"I couldn't tell. It's been too many years, and his voice was somewhat disguised. Disguised, but familiar."

"I don't imagine you ever told Whit any of this."

"Up to this minute, I've never told anyone what I just told you."

"Not even Blodgett?"

Shelly shook her head. "It wasn't worth dragging Whit through that, especially if Charlie was dead."

Jordan pressed her fist against her mouth, thinking. "There was a man at the rodeo, a man Whit gave money to. He said he was an old rodeo friend, Tom Pitkin. Then I find out a man named Robert Pitkin was cellmates with one of the men Sadie was writing to." She watched Shelly's expression. "Do you know who that is?"

"They're the same man—Robert Thomas Pitkin was an old rodeo buddy of Charlie's. He was still around when Whit started rodeoing and tried to be somewhat of a mentor to Whit. But he wasn't much better than Charlie. Got in trouble with the law a few years back."

"He died in prison about six months ago, so he definitely wasn't the man I saw with Whit at the rodeo. But his name was on Whit's mind for some reason, and it's another lie." Jordan sounded defeated. "Could it have been his dad?"

Shelly looked as shaken as Jordan felt. "I don't know."

"Nothing that you've told me helps Whit's case."

"I know that," Shelly said quietly. "But I also know he's innocent." She stood. "I'll keep digging, but you have to promise you will too. I know there's a lot of pressure on you to wrap this up in a neat bow, and soon, but don't let that get in the way of you finding the truth."

Jordan looked down at her hands. "I can't change the facts."

Chapter Fifty-Four

"ARE YOU HEADING IN to question the suspect?" Carlyle looked uncharacteristically concerned as Jordan straightened her paperwork and stood to move to the small room where Whit and his lawyer were waiting.

She shot him a look, waiting for the jab to come. "Yes, sir."

"You sure you're up for this?"

"Of course." The truth was she wasn't sure, but she wouldn't ever tell him that. She'd been up all night poring over everything she'd collected, making sure she had all the reasons for keeping Whit locked up, beyond the obvious one—Sadie's statement—ready to go. Whit's attorney had shown up sometime in the night. Their early morning meeting was wrapping up and then it would be Jordan's turn.

He hesitated, then finally said. "I saw the way you looked after you brought him in, and I know you've been in your office all night." He ran his hands over his face, stopping to stroke the day's growth of beard that covered his chin. He didn't look like he'd slept much either. "You can't deny this is hard on you. I know you and Commissioner Palmer have been friends. If you think that would taint anything about this interrogation, I need you to—"

"Are you asking me to excuse myself from this case?" Jordan asked, afraid that that's where he was going.

"If you don't think you can be objective."

"No. I can do this. You have to trust me to do my job."

"I do." He set a hand on her arm. This was the first time Sheriff Carlyle had displayed anything like concern or affection toward her. Maybe he meant it in a paternal way, but his touch felt unnatural, and it made Jordan's skin crawl. "You've done a great job with this case. I have no doubt you'll be able to wrap things up soon."

"Thank you," Jordan said, moving out of his reach. She had doubts, or maybe fears, that it would end soon. The evidence linking Whit to Sadie's kidnapping was damning, even if his alibi for the night Sheriff Blodgett was murdered wasn't in shambles.

She walked into what passed for an interrogation room. It was a tiny box of a space, like her office, except it lacked the small window and there was a table in the middle instead of a desk. The two chairs on the far side were occupied by Whit and a narrow-faced gray-haired man. They both stood when Jordan walked in.

She reached her hand to the lawyer. "Jordan Gibbons," she said in the way of introduction.

The man shook her hand. "Shane Sears."

They all sat, Jordan steeling herself against Whit's gaze. She didn't want to face the hurt, anger, or fear that his gray eyes might hold. She looked up, finally meeting a gaze that only seemed tired. "You're aware of your rights, correct?"

Whit nodded. "Yes."

"Let's get started."

She fired questions at Whit, one after another. He barely hesitated with his answers. If he was lying or going from a prepared statement, he was a good actor.

Finally, she asked, "How long have you known the victim?"

Whit looked genuinely confused. "The woman who was kidnapped? I told you the first time you asked, I don't know her. She served me a couple of times at the Horseshoe, but beyond that ..."

Jordan glanced at her notes. "I have statements from three different people who say they saw you with Ms. Larsen. Near her apartment, near the Silver Horseshoe, and possibly at the Montana Silver Company. Her roommate gave me a statement at the beginning of the investigation. She told me that Sadie was coming to Lombard to meet with a man who had amazing gray eyes." She made the mistake of looking into Whit's eyes when she said the last part.

"And you assumed that meant me?" Whit asked.

She kept her expression neutral but could feel the back of her neck getting hot. "Your eyes are gray."

"I guess they are."

"We'd like a list of those dates and places so we can cross-reference them against Mr. Palmer's schedule," the lawyer said.

"Of course." Jordan moved to the next set of notes. "Speaking of schedule, I'd like to go over your alibi for the night Sheriff Blodgett was killed. You told everyone here that you were at a rancher's conference in Austin, but there was no such conference in Austin that weekend. We know you went to Texas but can only verify the location of your cell phone for about half of that trip."

"The battery ran down and I'd forgotten my charger."

"That seems like a convenient excuse." Jordan said. "Couldn't you have purchased a replacement there?"

"I had a lot on my mind that trip." Whit's tone was heavy with resignation.

"The time that was missing from your cell phone records leaves it open to you leaving Austin at any point after Friday morning. If you drove straight through, you could have made it back in time to murder Sheriff Blodgett. Is there someone who can verify when you left Austin?"

Whit's lawyer turned to him, but Whit looked down at the table for a long moment. Finally, he looked at Jordan. "Before we go on, can I ask for a minute alone with—"

"You have that right," Jordan said, half-standing. "I'll give you—"

"No, not alone with Mr. Sears. Alone with you."

Jordan found herself shaking her head at the same time Whit's lawyer said, "I wouldn't advise it, Whit. Maybe you don't understand the seriousness of the charges."

"I'm not eleven anymore, Shane. I understand what's at stake," Whit said. "There's something I need to say to the detective, and for now, I'd rather say it just to her."

"This isn't a good idea, Whit." Jordan was so flustered that she didn't catch her slip, calling Whit by his first name. Her heart was pounding with fear, fear of what he wanted to say to her. If it was a confession, she wasn't sure she wanted to hear it.

"But I have the right to speak to just her? Correct?" Whit said.

The lawyer cleared his throat. "Again, I don't—"

"Do I have the right to talk to Detective Gibbons by myself or not?" The patience had drained out of Whit's voice.

"Ye-es," his lawyer said slowly.

"I can't turn the recorder off," Jordan said.

Whit looked toward the camera mounted in the corner of the room. "It's okay. I'd still like to talk to you."

Jordan exchanged a glance with the lawyer as he stood up, a glance that conveyed they both thought Whit was making a fatal mistake. "I'll be just outside the door. Don't say anything that—" The man stopped and sighed. "Let me know when you want me to come back in."

The lawyer let himself out and closed the door behind him. Jordan watched Whit as he sat in the chair, staring at his hands. He took in a breath, twisted his watch, chewed on the corner of his lip. Finally, he looked up. "I lied to you, Jordan."

Jordan's heart stopped. She didn't want to hear the rest of his statement. More than that, she didn't want it recorded for everyone to hear. She forced her voice to be calm. "What did you lie about?"

A deathly silence filled the small space for a few heartbeats. Then he said, "You asked me if there was anyone else, any heirs to my grandpa's ranch and I told you no."

It was so off from what she expected him to say, that she couldn't answer him for a few more breaths. She reached her own conclusion. "Your father is still alive?"

He shook his head. "No. He's dead. That I'm sure of."

Something about his tone made her wary. "How can you be sure?"

"My brother told me he died in a car wreck about three months after I graduated from high school." He looked up, his gaze both intense and penitent. "That was the lie. I have a brother." Whit breathed in and then continued. "From what I can tell he's my dad and Bonnie Golden's son. I didn't know he existed until he found me through some internet search. He was in some legal trouble in Texas and asked me to help him. He's an ex-con and was in danger of going back to jail. I lied to Shelly about going to the conference because I knew she'd give me hell for bailing Michael out."

Jordan stared at him for a long time, trying to take it all in. "You're sure, absolutely sure he's your brother?"

"I know he's who he says he is. He looks just like me, but about eight years younger, lighter hair, but about the same height and build, same eyes."

"Close enough that from a distance, people might mistake him for you?" Jordan said.

"Yeah," Whit said quietly.

"Have you seen him since Texas?"

Whit drummed his fingers on the table. "Just before the rodeo. That was my other lie. He was the person I was talking to there. He came looking for money. I gave him some, let him spend the night in my trailer, and offered him a job and a place to stay on the ranch. He said no to my offer but told me he was in town looking for an old girlfriend. He said she was kind of a nut job, that she was obsessed with his mother's murder. He said she wanted to be the one to solve it."

"The ex-girlfriend was Sadie," Jordan said.

"He didn't tell me her name." Whit stared down at his hands. "But I'd assumed as much."

Jordan stared at him from across the table. "Whit, do you have any idea how crazy all of this sounds? A look-alike brother? It's like something from a no-plot TV show."

He reached his hand across the table, like he was going to take hers, then pulled back like he'd thought better of it, and folded his in front of him on the table. "Do you believe me? That's the only thing that matters to me."

Jordan looked toward the camera in the corner of the room. She wished she could turn it off. The last thing she wanted was her coming across weak and spineless for everyone who would review the recording. Judd would have a field day if he saw it. She could almost hear Brock laughing at her. *Fell for the bad guy, didn't you, Gibby?* But he didn't matter to her anymore. The truth mattered, and the innocent man across from her mattered.

She took a long breath, looked directly into Whit's eyes, and said, "I believe you."

Chapter Fifty-Five

"WHAT HAVE YOU GOT?" Jordan stood beside the table where Ray had laid out everything they'd taken from the trailer. She was hoping for something that would corroborate Whit's story about his brother. She'd already found Michael Golden in a search of convicted felons in Texas. He looked a lot like Whit, but that didn't prove he was Whit's brother, that he'd ever been to Lombard, or that he'd kidnapped Sadie.

Ray passed her a stack of pictures of the inside of Whit's truck. "These show traces of blood that I'm going to guess will turn out to be Sadie Larsen's. Some of her clothing was found torn up under the seat. The gun used to shoot the dog, Blodgett's gun that was missing from evidence, was stashed under the couch in the trailer. Whit's revolver was in one of the back bedrooms."

Jordan turned over the evidence bag that had Whit's gun in it. It was the one he'd shown her in his truck. He said it had been his grandpa's gun, that he was taking it to be restored. She wondered if that had ever happened. She ran her thumb down the silver plate on the side. Something about the gun bothered her.

"Anything that ties Whit to the sheriff's murder?" Jordan asked.

"Remember the pocketknife with the unidentified print? The one that was used to pry open the sheriff's drawer?"

"Don't tell me."

"Yep. The prints matched Whit. He even said it was his knife, that he'd lost it awhile back. We didn't have his prints on file because he's never done anything wrong before." Ray sighed. "It doesn't look good."

"From a law enforcement standpoint, it looks very good," Sheriff Carlyle said from the doorway. "Like we have enough evidence for a pretty solid case." He looked between them. "I get that this is a hard one. We all thought Whit was a good man, but we can't let our feelings get in the way of doing our job."

"Right." Jordan set the gun back down. "I'm heading down to Deer Lodge to interview Ms. Larsen. I'll be back—"

"No need. I took her initial statement last night at the hospital. I already sent you the transcript of it," Sheriff Carlyle said.

"Why would you—"

"You were busy, and I wanted that taken care of as soon as possible. I went in as soon as the doctor said she was stable enough to talk." He held up his hand. "Don't look at me like that, Detective. I'm not trying to undermine you. You had a lot going on last night and you can't do everything. I'm sure you'll get your chance to talk to Ms. Larsen soon enough. For today, the doctor down there wants us to give her space to rest. She's lost a lot of blood and is obviously pretty traumatized."

He nodded to her. "You look like you could use some rest yourself. Go home. I don't want to see you back here for at least eight hours. If something comes up, we'll call you. I'm planning to take some time myself. Not much more is going to happen until we get forensics back anyway."

Jordan opened her mouth to protest, but he shut her down. "I mean it, Jordan. You're technically on leave anyway."

"Okay." Jordan nodded, but she had no intention of sleeping. Maybe not until she'd figured out what it was going to take to prove Whit was innocent.

"So Bonnie and Charlie have found a way to continue to make Whit's life hell beyond the grave," Shelly said after Jordan finished telling her everything. "Anyone know where this brother is?"

"Not yet." Jordan ran her hand over her still-damp hair, this time just tied back in a quick ponytail. She'd gone home and taken a long shower so she could think. She brought Brownie with her to Shelly's. He'd already spent almost twenty-four hours by himself, and Jordan felt guilty about leaving him again.

"What was he put away for?"

"Some con scheme. The 'almost arrest' Whit went down to help him with was for parole violations. Which he's apparently guilty of again."

"No assault or drug charges?"

"No. Nothing like what we've got going on here. The good news, ironic as it seems, is that because Whit's brother is an ex-con, we can prove he exists, even if we can't track him down. His DNA and photos are stored in the federal database."

"It might be enough for reasonable doubt," Shelly said.

"Yeah," Jordan agreed.

"But neither of us want reasonable doubt." Shelly reached down and scratched Freckles behind the ears. "We want this damn thing buttoned up and put to bed with no kind of doubt at all about Whit's innocence. What have you found out from the girl? Is she still sticking to her statement?"

"I'm going into the hospital to question her after this. I was hoping you could watch Brownie for the day." Brownie's tail thumped in response to his name.

"Of course." Shelly stood up and got a treat for each of the dogs. As she gave Brownie his treat, she said, "He looks much better. You've taken good care of him."

"He's a great dog. When I came home this morning, he was wide awake, in front of the door like he was on guard duty. He followed me around the whole time I was home, not like he needed something, more like he wanted to let me know he was there if I needed anything." Jordan knelt down beside Brownie and stroked his dark coat. "I guess I'll have to give him back to Sadie once she's out of the hospital."

"Has she asked about him at all?" Shelly said.

"There was nothing about him in the transcript of her statement I read," Jordan said.

"That seems kind of odd."

Jordan smiled. "Not everyone feels the same way you do about your dogs."

"I know that, but when I talked to Becca about Sadie coming into the sheriff's office, she said Sadie was pretty desperate to get him back, and pretty upset when he went missing." Shelly sat back on the couch. She looked like she hadn't slept much either. "How long after filing the report did Sadie herself go missing?" she asked.

"I'm not sure. No one reported her missing until we found the bone and the bloody piece of her shirt. But that was four days after she came in to report that Brownie was gone."

"And how long did Dr. Green say it had been since Brownie got shot?"

"About four days," Jordan said.

"And he was shot with a revolver that was taken from the sheriff's house?"

"No. I mean, yes," Jordan could feel her own lack of sleep catching up with her. "It was the sheriff's gun, but it was taken from the evidence locker."

"Taken from the evidence locker?" Shelly sat back in her chair. "Like someone wanted to make sure the dog getting shot was linked to the sheriff's murder."

"Or if they were actually linked," Jordan said.

"True." Shelly went back to scratching Freckles. She had a faraway look in her eye that Jordan had come to understand meant she was thinking. "The clues are almost too clear-cut." She started ticking them off on her fingers. "Whit gets called out of town suddenly by his long-lost brother the weekend that the sheriff is murdered, his phone charger disappears, so his phone dies, leaving no way to track where he's been."

"He said he forgot it," Jordan said.

"Maybe. But Whit is usually pretty on top of things like that." Shelly went back to her count. "There are enough faraway sightings of Whit's brother and Sadie to make it look like there was something going on between her and Whit. A gun goes missing from evidence and is then used to shoot the dog of a girl who later ends up missing. You said Brownie was tied up when you found him, right?"

"Yes."

"Tied up and shot from close range?"

"No, not close."

"So maybe shot by someone who was afraid to get too close to him. Someone who might have been aiming to kill but didn't have very much experience with a firearm. That's why he was just wounded."

Jordan looked at Shelly with new understanding. "You mean someone like Sadie?" Shelly nodded. "We have a room full of evidence linking Whit to the kidnapping, like someone wanted to make sure there was no doubt that he did it. You think they set him up, Sadie and Whit's brother? Why? To get Whit's land? If he was out of the way, I guess that means Michael Golden would get their grandpa's ranch."

"The land's not worth much, at least not as a big chunk. Maybe if it was subdivided, but it's pretty rough country and people aren't exactly clamoring for land in Lombard. Whit's like the rest of us around here, trying to hold onto what's ours with everything we've got."

"Maybe they don't know that."

"Maybe. Or maybe there's something else on the land they think is worth something," Shelly said, her gaze faraway again. "But how does this all tie in with Blodgett's murder?" She crossed the room to her board of names.

"Or Bonnie's murder before? Maybe a revenge thing? Maybe Whit's brother thinks Whit got what's rightfully his, or maybe he blames Whit for Bonnie's murder. Or maybe it's not even him. From what I've seen from Sadie's notes and letters, she was obsessed with murder and true crime, and Whit's brother said she was obsessed with the Bonnie Golden case."

Shelly stared at the white board, the wheels in her head spinning. Jordan glanced up at the clock. She needed to head to the hospital to interview Sadie, but she didn't want to miss whatever Shelly had to say.

Finally, Shelly's eyes cleared up and she looked at Jordan. "Do you have time tonight for a meeting of sorts?"

"What did you have in mind?" Jordan asked.

"I think it's time we got more heads together than our own. I'm going to call a few people from town together and try to shore up the details."

"Like who?" Jordan asked.

"Your neighbor, Rachel McKee, Angie Blodgett, Becca, Beats, maybe Chris from the Horseshoe."

"I've already talked to all of those people."

"You talked to them all separately. People, women especially, feed off each other. They remember things in a group that they wouldn't on their own."

"Do you think they'll be willing to talk to me? I'm pretty sure the whole town hates me since I arrested Whit," Jordan said.

"I'll tell them we're trying to exonerate him. They'll come."

"It's a bit unorthodox."

"That's the way we do things in Lombard."

Jordan laughed. "You can say that again."

Shelly's face went serious. "Don't tell anyone from the sheriff's office about the meeting tonight. I'll talk to Beats once she's off."

"You're worried about the revolver that went missing from evidence," Jordan said.

"Yeah, there's something going on in the sheriff's office that doesn't smell right."

Jordan nodded. She'd felt it too. She stood. "I need to get to the hospital. I have an appointment with Ms. Larsen." Brownie stood and took a couple of steps toward the door. Jordan looked at him, then turned to Shelly. "On second thought, I think I'll take Brownie with me."

Shelly smiled. "Good idea. Dogs are an excellent judge of character."

Chapter Fifty-Six

IT WAS A FORTY-FIVE minute drive to Deer Lodge and the nearest hospital. When Jordan had called for an update, she was told Sadie was doing well, that her wounds were mostly superficial. She'd lost less blood than they'd initially thought. She was dehydrated and scraped and bruised but should be out of the hospital in the next day or so. Jordan wondered where she would go and if Whit's brother would be the one to pick her up.

Jordan led Brownie into the hospital, through the emergency entrance. She'd stopped by the sheriff's office and borrowed one of the K9 vests to put on him. She flashed her badge at the front desk and identified herself.

The young receptionist at the desk eyed Brownie. "Is he one of those drug sniffing dogs? Are you following up on the case that Lombard deputy was asking about?" Jordan was immediately confused but tried not to show it. The woman didn't wait for Jordan to answer. "I have that report he asked for. I put it together right after I talked to him, but I've been so busy I wasn't able to call and let him know I got it. He didn't want me to email it, but I suppose I could give it to you."

Jordan didn't have any idea what the woman was talking about, but she wanted to see whatever was in the report. "Sure, I could take it to him after I'm done here."

The woman pulled from a file cabinet under the desk. "Here it is, our frequent fliers."

"Frequent fliers?" Jordan asked.

"People who come in on a regular basis asking for opiates. They fake some kind of injury or back problems or whatnot in order to get pain meds."

"Right. Thank you." Jordan was sure what the receptionist had just given her was a violation of patient rights. She was sure that whoever had asked for it also knew it was a violation of patient rights. Maybe it was Ray following up on the heroin she'd found in the barn. Maybe he was doing it quietly so Judd wouldn't find out. Or maybe there was something else. She'd have to follow up on that later. "Could you tell me what room Sadie Larsen is in?"

The receptionist consulted her computer. "204. Are you taking the dog up to sniff her room for drugs?"

Jordan thought quickly and then smiled. "No, Brownie's an emotional support K9. We use him when we question victims of violent crime. He has a calming effect on people."

"Makes sense to me. Lombard is getting to be a dangerous place—murder, drugs, and now kidnapping." The woman shook her head.

Jordan scouted the hall as she walked to the door of Sadie's room. A few doors down, she saw an open supply closet. She looked around and didn't see anyone, so she pulled Brownie inside. "Stay!" In response to his forlorn look, she patted him on the head. "Give me a few minutes." He thumped his tail and let out a soft whine but stayed while she closed the door.

Jordan turned around to face an orderly who'd been watching her. Jordan straightened up and smiled, like there was nothing weird about her leaving a K9 in a linen closet in a hospital. "I'd appreciate it if you don't open that door for a bit and tell everyone else not to. He won't be any trouble. He's very well trained."

"Okay," The man said. He appeared confused but didn't ask any questions.

"Thanks," Jordan replied. She turned and knocked on Sadie's hospital room door.

"Come in," a soft voice answered.

Sadie was perched on a pile of pillows with a phone to her ear. Now that she was cleaned up, Sadie looked a lot more like the pixie-faced blonde from the photos, with wide blue eyes and a sprinkle of freckles across her nose. The bruise below her eye and the bandage across her forehead made her look like a damsel in distress, but from reading Sadie's notes and correspondence, Jordan had learned that this woman was way smarter than she let on. If Shelly's hunch was right, she was also much more ruthless.

It took all the professionalism Jordan could muster to approach Sadie with a sympathetic smile. Sadie said a hasty goodbye to whoever she was on the phone with and reached to take her hand as Jordan introduced herself. "Hello Ms. Larsen, I'm Detective Gibbons."

"Just Sadie, please," she said with a soft Southern accent. "But you already knew that. Thank you, Detective Gibbons. I owe you my life."

Jordan withdrew her hand from Sadie's dead fish handshake. "I was at the right place at the right time."

"You say that like it was a coincidence, but I know it wasn't. I hope you don't mind I did some searching on you before you got here." She waved a hand at her phone. "You're very good at what you do."

Jordan did mind. She didn't know where Sadie had gotten the phone, but the whole thing reeked of a tainted witness. She wished she'd been able to question Sadie last night. She'd read the transcript. Sheriff Carlyle's questions seemed soft and barely skimmed the surface of what had happened. Sadie had basically repeated the story she'd given Jordan when she first found her.

"Can we get started? Do you mind if I record your statement?" Jordan asked.

"The sheriff recorded me last night. He asked a lot of questions, but he was really nice when I told him I was too tired to keep talking." She was already hinting that she might cut the interview short.

"I've read the transcripts. I just have a few follow-up questions. It won't take long." Jordan held up the recorder again. "May I?"

Sadie looked at the recorder nervously but nodded. "Of course." She adjusted herself on the pillows. Jordan got the impression that Sadie had been waiting for her big moment and it was finally here.

Jordan set the recorder on the bedside table and looked directly at Sadie. "In your statement last night, you said that Whit Palmer kidnapped you. Can you please describe your relationship with Mr. Palmer? When did you first meet him?"

Sadie didn't even pretend to think before she answered. "About five months ago. I contacted him about a case I was working on. I'm an amateur detective. Nothing like you, of course, but I like to look into cold cases. I was working on the Bonnie Golden case. I thought since Whit's father was involved with Bonnie, he might have some information for me. He agreed to meet me for drinks in Anaconda."

"How did that go? Did he have the information you needed?"

"Not really, but we kind of hit it off. We met a few times after that, started doing more than just discussing the case." Sadie said it with a coquettish smile that made Jordan's stomach twist. She fought to keep her face neutral.

"I was ready for a new start. I'd just ended a bad relationship, and Whit suggested I move to Lombard. He said it would be easier to investigate the case if I was living in Keystone County. He offered to let me stay with him at his ranch, but I wasn't ready for that yet."

"Mr. Palmer was on board with you looking into Bonnie Golden's murder?"

Sadie twisted a corner of one of the pillows nervously. "At first he was, but then things started to point toward his father being the murderer."

"You told Whit you thought his father was the one who killed Bonnie?" Jordan asked.

"Not exactly that way. I left my notes sitting out one night at my apartment. Whit found them. He went a little crazy. He said I needed to stop what I was doing, or that he would stop me."

"But you didn't stop."

"No. I was determined to find the truth. Whit kept threatening me, so I went to the sheriff. I told him everything that was going on, showed him all the evidence I'd collected, and asked him for protection. He said he believed me. He was going to bring Whit in for questioning. The next thing I knew the sheriff was dead. When I found out, I knew who had killed him."

"You believe Whit Palmer killed Sheriff Blodgett?" Jordan said.

"Yes."

"Do you have any proof of that?"

"His fingerprints were found on a knife at the crime scene," Sadie said.

Jordan stared her down. "How would you know that?"

Sadie realized her mistake. She fumbled for the words for a second and finally said, "I heard ... someone was talking about it at the Horseshoe, right after Blodgett died. There was a pocketknife left at the crime scene. I assumed Whit's fingerprints were on it."

"Good hunch," Jordan said, keeping her emotions in check. She'd caught Sadie in something. She'd probably stolen Whit's knife and planted it at the murder scene. But Jordan had no way to prove that. She needed more, but first, she needed to know if her and Shelly's hunch about who shot Brownie was right. "At what point did you acquire the dog?"

For less than a heartbeat, something flashed in Sadie's eyes, fear or maybe guilt, but she replaced it with sadness. "Brownie. Poor thing. He came to me. He was a stray. I wasn't supposed to keep him, but I thought he'd be good protection. Whit got to him too, I guess. One day Brownie just disappeared."

Jordan smiled widely. "I have good news for you. Give me a second." Sadie looked confused, but Jordan didn't give her a chance to ask any questions.

She went back to the linen closet. Brownie was poised at the door when she opened it. She rubbed the top of his head. "I need you to be a good witness, boy. Can you do that?" Brownie's tail thumped as she snapped on his leash. He followed Jordan across the hall.

"And here's my good news," Jordan said as she pushed open the door.

Sadie's eyes got huge and for a second, time stood still. A low growl started in Brownie's throat. His fur stood on end, and then he started barking furiously. He lunged for Sadie. She screamed.

Jordan held Brownie back but let him bark for a few more seconds before she told him, "Quiet!" He looked at her like she was betraying him, but he stopped barking. "Lie down, Brownie." The dog sat down at Jordan's feet, but his eyes were on Sadie.

"This is your dog, right, the one you wanted for protection? The one you said disappeared?" Jordan asked. "You don't seem very happy to see him, and he doesn't seem to like you very much."

Sadie scrunched herself on the far edge of the bed. She was frantically searching for her call light. "He was never trained, he barks at everyone, he—"

"Funny, he's been living with me for nearly a month. He's never given me any trouble."

"Get him out of here!" Sadie yelled. At her raised voice, Brownie stood and started barking again.

"Quiet!" Jordan commanded. Any minute someone in the hospital would run in to see what was going on. She spoke quickly. "I know you shot this dog. I know you faked your disappearance and I know you're trying to frame Whit Palmer. What I want to know now is why."

Sadie started shaking her head. "I didn't want to hurt the dog. I didn't want to hurt anyone. I just wanted to solve the case. I just wanted to help Michael find out who killed his mom." She took a shaky breath.

"And who is Michael?" Jordan asked, even though she already knew the answer.

"Michael Golden. My boyfriend. Ex-boyfriend."

"Michael put you up to all of this?"

"No." Sadie was crying now, black streams of mascara running down her pink cheeks. "Not

Michael. He told me to stay away from Lombard, and his brother, but I was so close to finding out what happened to his mom, I couldn't quit. But no one would listen to me. I'm not like you, Detective. I'm just an uneducated bar waitress. No one would take me seriously."

"You started leaving clues around, things that might get the investigation reopened. And when that didn't work, you faked your own disappearance."

Sadie closed her eyes and shook her head. "I want to talk to a lawyer."

Jordan looked down at Brownie. His hair was still standing on end, and he was watching her for his next move. She knew she should stop here, that she should let Sadie call a lawyer. But she was furious with what this woman had done to Whit, all in the name of trying to gain some attention. Jordan released Brownie's collar.

Brownie lunged again, knocking over the bedside table and a pitcher of water as he tried to get to Sadie. She screamed. Jordan restrained him again but let him keep barking.

Sadie cowered in the corner. "He said he'd help me. He said he'd reopen the investigation, but I had to give him something to work with. I put some clues out, but it wasn't enough. He said he needed more. He needed someone to blame."

"Who? Who are you talking about? Who was going to help you?"

Sadie's expression reached a new depth of terror. She shook her head violently. "I can't tell you that. He said if I told anyone, he'd kill me too."

Jordan pulled the dog back, feeling suddenly ashamed of herself for what she'd done. "I can protect you, but you have to tell me everything."

The door flew open. A large, red-faced doctor stalked in, followed by a smaller, elderly security guard.

"What is going on here? Who brought a dog into my hospital?" the doctor roared.

Brownie jumped to his feet, barking wildly at the two men. Jordan held onto his collar, but he wasn't going to be pacified that easily this time.

"You need to leave. Now!"

"I'm conducting an investigation," Jordan said over Brownie's barks.

"And I'm running a hospital, and this woman has been traumatized enough. Unless you want to explain to your sheriff why he has to come bail you out of our local jail on trespassing and assault charges, I suggest you and that animal leave immediately."

Jordan turned back to Sadie. "I can help you—"

"Detective," the doctor said. The security guard reached for his weapon, but his hands shook.

"I'm going." Jordan pulled Brownie toward the door, but she didn't break eye contact with Sadie. She needed the answer to at least one more question. "Why Whit?"

Sadie shook her head again, but as she walked out the door Jordan heard her say, "He has something they need."

Chapter Fifty-Seven

JORDAN REACHED THE PARKING lot and got into her Expedition. She let Brownie ride up front with her. She rested her hand on his head. "Good boy," she said, even though she knew she shouldn't be praising him for what she'd had him do. It was a bully move and she knew it. She'd thought she learned her lesson with Peyton, but here she was again, lacking information because she acted out of frustration. She was also pretty sure she'd be hearing from Carlyle as soon as the doctor had a chance to call her sheriff's department.

She stayed in the parking lot, needing to think about what Sadie just told her. She'd confirmed that Michael Golden, Whit's brother, was the man everyone had seen with Sadie. She'd confirmed that Sadie had faked the kidnapping, that she was trying to reopen the investigation into Bonnie's murder, and that someone had put her up to it. More than that, someone had asked her to frame Whit.

Someone who worked at the sheriff's department.

It had to be. The gun that Brownie was shot with had been stolen from evidence. Someone had given it to Sadie. She used it to shoot Brownie to make sure the two cases were connected. It had to be someone with enough power at the sheriff's office to reopen the investigation into the Bonnie Golden case. That pretty much narrowed it down to three people—Carlyle, Judd, and possibly Ray.

And one of them had killed Blodgett.

He'll kill me too.

Jordan's phone started to buzz, she looked down and saw the caller ID. It was Sheriff Carlyle. She wasn't ready to talk to him yet, so she reached down and canceled the call. Then she picked up the phone and made a call herself.

She'd barely identified herself to the Deer Lodge City Police Department before she was transferred to the police chief. For a good five minutes he yelled about her unprofessional behavior and her interrogation techniques. He finished by telling her that he'd put in a complaint to her sheriff. She already knew that.

When he finally stopped long enough to take in a breath, she broke in. "I'd like to request a police guard for Ms. Larsen, the kidnapping victim currently at the Powell County Medical Center."

"You are not in a position to request anything, much less that I have one of my officers sit on his ass in the hospital, guarding the woman you just traumatized with some sort of devil dog."

Jordan kept her voice calm. "I have reason to believe she's in danger. I'd send someone from Lombard, but our department is stretched to the limit with this investigation and about forty-five minutes away." And not entirely trustworthy, she added to herself.

There was silence coming from the other end. "This request should be coming from your sheriff," the chief finally said.

Jordan refused the second call from Carlyle as she said, "I'll take it up with him as soon as I can, but my request is urgent. Ms. Larsen told me that someone wants to kill her."

"I thought you had the guy locked up who kidnapped her."

"We have the wrong guy. She confirmed that," Jordan said simply.

There was another long silence on the other end. Finally, the chief let out a long sigh. "I should be throwing you in jail about now, but I'll comply with your request. I'm basing this on your record and not your actions at the hospital today. You have twelve hours of my people's time, but after that, Carlyle better send someone down to take over babysitting duty. Tell him I do not want it to be you."

I don't think that will be a problem, Jordan thought as she refused Sheriff Carlyle's third call. To the chief she said simply, "Thank you, sir."

He hung up without replying.

The next call that came in was Beats. Jordan picked up this time. "Why aren't you calling over the radio?"

"I have a message to relay that I don't think everyone with a county scanner needs to hear. Carlyle had to go to an emergency meeting with the commissioners. Before he left, he told me to politely ask that you get your county-issued vehicle, your county-issued firearms, and all other county-issued equipment currently in your possession back to the station. Except he described all those things using much more colorful language than I can. He mentioned something about calling in the state patrol and having your—again, county-issued—backside thrown into our county-issued special accommodations. He did not say whether you and Whit get to be cellmates."

"That bad?" Jordan asked.

"I have never seen a man turn so many shades of purple in such a short amount of time," Beats said. "What did you do?"

"It's a long story. Is there any way you could tell him I'm about ninety minutes out and possibly out of cell and radio range?" Jordan said. She was already pulling out the crumpled napkin that Grant Robbins had given her at the rodeo.

"Won't work. As long as you're in your county vehicle, you can be tracked."

"Right." Jordan had forgotten that little detail. She couldn't have the sheriff's department tracking her every move. She leaned against the steering wheel, thinking. "You said Carlyle was going to a meeting with the commissioners? How long will that take?"

"No telling." Beats grew serious. "Jordan, I think Brendan meant it about the state patrol thing and I'm pretty sure that meeting he's in is about throwing you off the case."

"I'm pretty sure it is too. I just need a little more time."

Beats clicked her tongue. "I don't think you have much time left."

Chapter Fifty-Eight

JORDAN SMOOTHED THE NAPKIN and dialed the number. She couldn't remember when Grant said he was going to be back from his long haul. She hoped it was now. She could hear the sound of his truck as he answered.

"Grant Robbins here."

"Mr. Robbins?" she asked.

"Just Grant. Good to finally hear from you, Detective. You must be getting pretty desperate."

Jordan had no idea how Grant recognized her voice so easily, but she didn't have time to sort it out. "You said you had information for me?"

"I do, but it's not something I'd like to disclose over the phone. You never know who might be listening. Where are you?"

Jordan didn't have time for his paranoia either. "Deer Lodge."

"Perfect. I'm on my way home and about to go through that area. I'll text you the address of an out of the way truck stop. I'll meet you there in about fifteen minutes."

"I'll be there," Jordan said.

Jordan was waiting when Grant's big rig pulled into the truck stop parking lot. Brownie was at her side, just in case. He thumped his tail as Grant climbed out of his truck. Jordan took that as a good sign. "You said the sheriff stole something."

"You have a good memory," Grant said. "Funny, because at the time I said that it was a joke and then I realized it wasn't."

"What did he steal?"

Grant looked around the parking lot, nervously, like he was expecting someone to be watching them. "I would have said something before, but I thought it was just weird, and not important. Then I saw that Whit had been arrested and I knew I had to say something and that it needed to be to you, and not anyone else at the sheriff's office."

Jordan was having a hard time following what he was trying to tell her. "You need to start at the beginning and tell the whole story, Grant."

"Right. It was almost four months ago. I was having dinner at the Silver Horseshoe. I was just getting up to pay my bill when I saw Whit's pocketknife fall out of his pocket when he pulled his wallet out to pay his bill. He didn't notice it. Sheriff Carlyle was standing behind him. He picked up the knife and put it in his pocket."

"You're sure it was the sheriff?"

"It was definitely Carlyle, only he wasn't the sheriff at that point. That was just before Blodgett was killed."

Jordan stayed silent as the pieces lined up. Carlyle had framed Whit. Carlyle had threatened Sadie. Carlyle had killed Sheriff Blodgett.

Her blood ran cold, remembering him drawing his gun on her in the trailer when they went to get Sadie. Only it wasn't his gun. She remembered the glint of silver as he put the gun away. It was Whit's gun. Carlyle had intended to kill her and blame that on Whit too.

But why? She knew who'd killed the sheriff, but she had no evidence and no motive. What did Whit have that he wanted?

The only person who might know was sitting in a hospital room. Jordan realized her mistake immediately. She should have taken Sadie with her.

"Can you take Brownie?" she said to Grant. "I need to go back for something in Deer Lodge and I can't bring him with me."

"Sure." Grant reached for Brownie and scratched his ears. Brownie looked at Jordan with uncertainty, but he didn't appear scared.

"Thank you." Jordan watched Grant pick Brownie up and put him in the cab of his truck. Brownie whined once but didn't fight the transition.

Grant tipped his hat at her. "I'll take good care of him. I used to have a dog that rode with me for my long hauls. She died a few years back. Maybe it's time I got another one."

With all that she was planning to do, Jordan wondered if Brownie might end up being Grant's dog when this was all over.

Jordan hadn't even made it out of the parking lot when her phone buzzed again. The name Deer Lodge Police Department showed up on the caller ID.

"Detective Gibbons?" the chief's voice said.

"Yes."

"As a courtesy to you, I thought I'd let you know—that woman you wanted us to protect, the one at the hospital, she's gone."

"Gone?"

"By the time we got one of our officers there, she'd disappeared."

"Did someone take her or—"

"If she went on her own accord, she didn't take much with her. If someone kidnapped her, they didn't make a big fuss about it. No one saw a thing."

"Damn it." Jordan squeezed the phone against her cheek. To the chief she said, "Keep looking, if you find anything—"

"I should also let you know, we heard from your sheriff. He said you've gone maverick on him, that he's about to put out a watch on your Expedition to every agency in the state."

"Then why did you tell me all of this?" Jordan asked.

"I told you, as a courtesy to you." The chief hung up before she could ask anything else.

Jordan held the phone as she reconsidered her options. With Sadie gone, she'd lost the only person who could prove Whit was innocent. She'd also lost her best lead as to what Sheriff Carlyle might be up to. It was also likely she was about to lose her badge and any credibility she'd had.

She reached for her radio. "Beats, this is Detective Gibbons. I'm on my way back to the station. I'm about forty minutes out. Let the sheriff know he can call off his dogs."

"Interesting choice of words." Sheriff Carlyle's voice crackled through the radio. "See you in forty. I'm glad you decided to come home."

Chapter Fifty-Nine

JUDD WAS WAITING WHEN Jordan walked back through the door to the sheriff's office. He measured her with his gaze. "You've had a busy day, Ms. Gibbons." Jordan didn't miss that he'd omitted her title.

"Where is Sheriff Carlyle?" she asked.

"Out trying to clean up your mess. He left me to deal with you." He moved closer, as if his sheer bulk would intimidate her. Jordan met his eyes and didn't back down. "You've managed to scare off our only witness. Do you think that's going to get your boyfriend out of jail?" He shook his head. "We expected so much from you." Jordan held her tongue and clenched his fists as he circled her. "Turns out you were nothing more than a love-starved female, willing to give up your entire career for a good-looking murderer. I should have followed my gut on that one. I should have never signed off on bringing in an outsider. Now look where we are."

It took all of Jordan's self-control not to answer him. "Does this mean I'm free to go?"

He looked at her incredulously. "Free? If by free you mean leave your badge and gun at the door and get the hell out of Dodge, I guess that means you're free."

Jordan removed her holster, pulled her badge out of her wallet and laid both on the table in front of her.

"So that's it? No snarky remarks, no explanations, no begging me to let you keep your job?" Judd looked genuinely disappointed.

"No, sir."

"You're just going to throw your illustrious law enforcement career on the table for some rodeo cowboy?"

"No." Jordan couldn't keep it in any longer. "I'm resigning my position because this office stinks of scandal. A good man is dead, and an innocent man is in jail because you won't acknowledge what's actually going on." She turned to go, but then added a parting shot. "I assume the state attorney general will still be interested to hear what I have to say about how things are handled here in Lombard."

Jordan walked out before Judd gathered his wits enough to say anything. Once she reached the parking lot, she realized she'd driven her Expedition to the sheriff's office and had no way to get home or anywhere else. She was just about to walk over to the Horseshoe to see if Chris would let her borrow her car when Beats came through the door.

"I heard there was a gathering at Shelly's tonight," Beats said, catching up with her. "Maybe I could give you a ride."

"I'd appreciate that, but aren't you supposed to be at dispatch?" Jordan said.

"My replacement will be here in twenty." She stopped, her hand on Jordan's shoulder. "What have you found out?"

"Whit is innocent."

"Anyone here could have told you that. Anything else?"

Jordan looked around the parking lot, but it appeared quiet and empty. "Where is Sheriff Carlyle?"

"Last I heard he was heading to Deer Lodge to follow up on our friend Sadie."

"Can you track him?" Jordan asked.

"From dispatch I can, as long as he's in his county vehicle." Beats stared at Jordan for a minute. "You think you know something?"

"Not enough, not yet," Jordan answered.

Beats whistled. "Damn. I was hoping it was Judd."

"I don't know how deep it goes yet. That's what the meeting with Shelly is about. I hope we can find something out, something concrete before—"

"Before someone else dies." Beats finished for her. "On second thought, I'm staying on for another shift. Seems like you might need me more here. Take my car, but only if you can promise you'll get it back to me, safe and sound." She gripped Jordan's arm. "Along with anyone who might be riding in it."

"I'll do my best."

Jordan was almost out of town when she saw the familiar Maverick parked at Sheriff Blodgett's house. She parked Beats's car next to it and cautiously went inside. The barn was empty except for Peyton, sitting on the stairs up to the loft. He smelled of weed again. His hands shook as he raked them through his hair.

"Peyton, are you okay?" Jordan said moving cautiously toward him.

He stood up, nearly knocking his head on the stairs above him. "I'm not supposed to talk to you."

Jordan took a few steps closer, keeping herself between him and the door. "I'm sorry for what happened before. I was wrong." Peyton didn't answer. It hit Jordan what was missing besides the stacks of straw in the center of the barn. "Where are the cats?"

Peyton looked down at the bare floor and the straggly bits of straw that were left. "Gone. They got rid of them. I came back to feed them today and they were all gone."

"Who got rid of the cats?" Jordan asked gently.

Peyton shook his head, "I can't tell you."

"The people who hid the drugs here? I believe you that they weren't yours."

"I bet it was them. They took everything else." Peyton's voice shook with anger and pain.

"Can you tell me who they were?" Jordan asked.

Peyton shook his head. "I never saw them. I was just supposed to keep people out of the barn."

"Who told you to keep people out of the barn?" Jordan asked.

She expected him to say, "My dad." Instead he said, "You wouldn't believe me if I told you."

Jordan studied his expression, things moving into place. "Sheriff Carlyle?"

Peyton's eyes got big, but he nodded. "He caught me smoking weed behind the high school. He said he'd tell my dad unless I guarded the barn for him. You won't tell my dad, will you?"

"No," she answered. "But you should go home and stay out of the barn from now on. It's not safe here."

"Yeah." Peyton nodded again and headed toward his car. Just before he climbed inside, he said. "You're a good detective, right? When you catch those guys, can you find out what they did with the cats?"

Chapter Sixty

SHELLY WAS STANDING IN front of the whiteboard when Jordan arrived. Angie Blodgett was sitting on a rocking chair in the corner. Becca stood, bouncing her pink-faced newborn daughter up and down to keep her quiet. Chris was pacing in front of the couch. The only one who seemed calm was Rachel McKee. She sat primly on the edge of a kitchen chair that had been dragged into the circle. Her dog Bunny was nestled in her lap.

Jordan brought them up to speed on what she'd found out from Sadie and Grant and now Peyton. "What we need now is hard evidence. We know Carlyle had something to do with the drugs, but Sadie said Whit had something that Carlyle wanted. We have to figure out what that is." She turned to Becca. "I saw the note you made in the ledger and the number you circled. Can you explain that?"

Becca continued bounce her baby as she spoke up. "I've had a lot of late nights up with the baby to try to figure out what I think happened. I'm positive the numbers in the ledger for the new firearms were altered."

"Do you know by who?" Jordan asked.

"I'm not sure how we could prove it, but I know the gun numbers that were switched were Carlyle's and Blodgett's." She leaned down and whispered, "Hush," to her fussy baby. "I can't say who changed it in the ledger, but I know I didn't put those numbers in the database. Carlyle insisted on doing it himself, for security reasons."

Jordan nodded. "That means the gun that was used to shoot Blodgett was originally issued to Carlyle. I'm not sure how we can prove that, but it tells me we're on the right track. Anything else?"

"Carlyle isn't the only one involved." Chris spoke up reluctantly.

"Who else?" Shelly said.

"Sheldon," Chris said.

It took Jordan a second to place the name. "The owner of the Horseshoe?"

"Yeah." Chris breathed in. "I've had an idea for a while now, but I ... I can't lose my job."

"What makes you think he's involved?" Shelly asked.

"The night I covered for Sadie, a customer came in and ordered coffee, black, to go. He wasn't someone I recognized, but I brought him coffee, just like he'd asked. He came back after a few minutes, furious with me, and asked to see Sheldon. Sheldon poured the coffee himself and told me to take it out to the man. He paid in cash, a lot more than what a cup of coffee would cost. When I asked, Sheldon just said the man owed him." Chris chewed at the pale pink at the corner of her lip. "It was in a Styrofoam cup, so I couldn't see what was inside, but it sloshed weird, like there was something solid inside of it."

Jordan's thoughts raced back to the notes in Sheldon's binder, *coffee, black*. "Something like a small block of heroine? Maybe concealed in a plastic bag?"

Chris looked around the room nervously. "Maybe. Like I said, I don't have any proof and ... and I really don't want to lose my job, but I don't want Whit taking the blame for this."

Shelly moved to the board. She erased everything on the board except the words "small-town drug lord."

Jordan looked up at the sharp intake of breath from Angie Blodgett. "Remember the story I told you before, about the plane Brady found in the field and the drug runners? He wasn't hunting alone that day. Sheldon and Carlyle were both with him."

"What the sheriff saw as an opportunity to bust a bunch of drug dealers, those two saw as an opportunity to make some money," Jordan said.

"Exactly," Shelly answered. "But what does all of this have to do with Whit?"

Bunny started barking wildly. Jordan looked at the little dog but couldn't figure out what was bothering her. "It's that damned airplane again," Rachel McKee said. "Drives Bunny crazy."

"What airplane?" Then Jordan could hear it, the drone of a small engine, heading toward the mountains.

Jordan and Shelly looked at each other. "Whit's runway."

"How often have you heard that plane?" Jordan asked Rachel.

Rachel let out an exasperated sigh. "You should know. I mentioned it on the first day we met. I've been complaining about it for nearly five months to no avail. I'm sure the complaints are all logged somewhere at the sheriff's office."

"Dammit," Jordan said. She couldn't believe she'd missed something so obvious.

Shelly nodded. "This was never about Bonnie or her murder. It was about Carlyle and Sheldon trying to keep their little side business going."

"Sheriff Blodgett must have figured it out and Carlyle—" Jordan looked at Angie; her face was ashen.

"I told him where the key was!" Angie said breathlessly. "Brendan called one day when Brady was at the station, and I was in Anaconda getting groceries. He said he needed to get something at the house that Brady forgot. I didn't think anything of it." Angie covered her face with her hands. "I told him exactly how to get into our house."

"There was no way you could have known," Shelly said, putting her arm around Angie. "We all trusted him."

"The airplane," Jordan said, turning to Shelly. "We might not get another chance."

"Right." Shelly stepped away from Angie and straightened up. "Ladies, our meeting is adjourned. I hope it goes without saying that you're going to keep this quiet." She looked meaningfully at Rachel. "Don't talk to anyone."

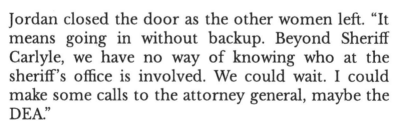

Jordan closed the door as the other women left. "It means going in without backup. Beyond Sheriff Carlyle, we have no way of knowing who at the sheriff's office is involved. We could wait. I could make some calls to the attorney general, maybe the DEA."

"Will they listen to you? I'm sure Carlyle has put in his complaint about you by now, and we really don't have any evidence," Shelly said.

"I don't know," Jordan admitted.

"We know it's happening tonight and soon. This is our best chance to get the evidence we need to implicate Sheriff Carlyle and anyone else who might be involved." Shelly didn't say it, but Jordan knew she meant Judd. "If they get spooked, we're not going to get another chance."

"Whit said it was a rough road to the airstrip. Do you think the mule will make it down?"

"It'd be better on horses," Shelly said. "But it's been a long time for me, and you—"

"I can't." Jordan ducked her head, ashamed by the fear she still felt. "I'm sorry." She misread the twist to Shelly's lips as criticism. "I know, there's nothing to fear but fear itself, right?"

Shelly huffed. "That's one of those asinine statements that people attribute to someone with brains or courage or whatever. I've been around for a while and I can tell you, there are lots of things out there that are more deadly than fear. A twelve-hundred-pound animal with a mind of its own commands a lot of respect. A horse can do a lot of damage if you don't know what you're doing. Someday you'll face that fear, but for tonight, the mule will work fine."

"You'll let me borrow it?"

"No. I'm taking you down myself."

"I can't let you do that. I can't put a civilian in danger like that."

"Civilian?" Shelly spat the word out. "Once a cop, always a cop. Anyway, I was under the impression you just turned in your badge, so you're just as much of a civilian as I am. You need backup. Someone who knows the area and the people involved. Besides, I'd bet my sharpshooting skills against the best in the county." She winked. "Maybe even the entire state."

Jordan shook her head. "You ever wonder if your arrogance is going to get you killed?"

"You sound like my oldest son. We all have to die sometime. Might as well go out in a blaze of glory, right?"

Jordan opened her mouth to protest, but Shelly stopped her by holding up her hand. "Don't worry about me. I still have a lot to live for. We'll be careful. Sneak in, take a few pictures and sneak out, right? Then let the feds hash it out while we enjoy a good breakfast back at my house."

"Okay," Jordan agreed. She knew it wasn't going to be that simple. Shelly knew it too, but there was something about this stubborn Montana cowgirl that made Jordan believe she could do anything.

Chapter Sixty-One

SHELLY AND JORDAN DESCENDED the steep canyon slowly. Shelly's rifle was strapped in the back of the mule and she had a smaller pistol in a holster at her hip. Jordan had one of Shelly's sidearms tucked in a concealed kidney holster. She wished it was one of her own, but there hadn't been time to go back to her house.

Jordan's phone buzzed and she answered immediately. Beats' voice crackled through the static. They'd called her once they'd figured out what was going on and where they were going. If something happened, at least one other person would know where they were. "You asked for Carlyle's twenty?"

"Yes," Jordan answered.

"His patrol vehicle is back at his house, but he hasn't answered any radio or cell calls for the last fifteen minutes. I could try—" The call dropped.

Jordan looked down at her phone and saw the words "searching for service."

"We're out of cell and radio range from here on down," Shelly said.

Jordan nodded. Shelly had warned her that would be the case. The path down was less than an old two-track washed out in more than one place. In some places it was so steep that Jordan felt like getting out and walking would have been safer. It was such a rough path down that she began to doubt this spot would be useful for anyone. It didn't seem like this remote airstrip was worth killing one man and framing another.

Shelly raised her arm and pointed at a thin dirt road that ascended the mountain on the other side. "There's an old logging road that comes down into the canyon from the other side. It meets up with a Forest Service road that eventually leads to the freeway."

"Is all of that Whit's land?" Jordan asked.

"No. His place ends at the edge of the flat area where the runway sits. Everything on that side is forest service or BLM land. I guess that answers the question about how they were getting the drops out without Whit knowing what was going on."

As they came around the bend, they could see the peaked roof of the hangar. It was a simple metal shed, large enough to accommodate a small plane, open on one side and badly in need of a paint job. At one point it had been painted a rust red, but now it was more rust than red. They got close enough to see that the plane had already landed. It was completely concealed except for one of the wings peeking out from the edge of the hangar.

The runway was a long strip of closely cropped weeds. It appeared to have been maintained recently. There were no other vehicles and no other activity around the airstrip.

Shelly pulled the mule off to the side and hid it behind some large boulders. "We'll have to hike the rest. If there's someone down there, we can't risk them hearing us."

Jordan nodded. Shelly unstrapped the rifle and slung it across her chest. Slowly, they made their way down to the flat piece of ground and the runway. They stopped outside the hangar and listened. There were a couple of voices coming from inside, but they were too muted to make out.

"Sounds like they're off-loading." Jordan whispered. She moved around to peer through a large split of rusty metal at the corner of the metal hanger. There were a couple of men inside, unloading boxes like the one she had discovered in Blodgett's barn. She pulled her phone out and started recording, but the men had their backs to her.

The roar of another engine cut through the quiet. Jordan turned her attention to the dirt road on the other side of the airstrip. It started with a faraway plume of dust, snaking down the mountain and then grew into a full-sized black Chevy Silverado.

"And here's our pickup guy," Shelly whispered.

As the truck got closer, Jordan could make out Sheriff Carlyle behind the wheel. She turned her camera onto him, waiting for him to get close enough for a positive ID.

"Good of him to come in person," Shelly said. "That makes this all that much easier."

"Exactly what I was thinking."

Jordan turned to face the barrel of a shotgun. On the other end was Sheldon, the owner of the Silver Horseshoe. "Nice of you ladies to show up." He nodded toward Shelly, who had already taken aim with her rifle. "I'd recommend putting that down, unless you want to see our pretty little detective's brains splattered across the side of the building." Shelly hesitated. Sheldon didn't take his eye off Jordan or his gun as he addressed Shelly again. "I know what you're thinking, and the answer is no, you're not quick enough to get a shot off before I pull my trigger." Reluctantly Shelly put her gun down.

"Pistol too." Sheldon nodded to Jordan. "And while she's doing that, why don't you go ahead and drop whatever you're packing."

Jordan unholstered the borrowed gun. Shelly exchanged a look with Jordan as she dropped their last weapon at Sheldon's feet. He glanced down. In that split second Jordan grabbed the shotgun barrel, pushing it out of her face. She hooked the stock with her other arm. The gun went off with a deafening blast as Jordan took control of it. Missing both of them, it blow a hole in the side of the hangar. Sheldon stumbled backward. A well-aimed kick brought him to his knees. The butt of the gun smashing between his eyes finished the job.

Shelly looked at Jordan for a second, stunned. "What in the Sam-hell was that?"

Jordan stepped back, deafened by the blast, and fighting back a wave of shock. "I've practiced that move a thousand times. Never had to use it. I wasn't sure if—" She looked at the man crumpled at her feet, a trickle of red sprouting from between his eyes.

"You were damn lucky." Shelly picked up the shotgun and unloaded it before she retrieved her own rifle. "They would have heard that. So much for taking pictures and sneaking off."

"Right." Jordan retrieved the revolver, not bothering to re-holster it. "Now what?"

Shelly stopped, listening. Inside the hangar, the plane's engine roared to life. "I'm going to do what I can to disable that plane before the evidence takes off."

Jordan started to protest, but Shelly waved her off. "I'll stay out of sight, shoot out a wheel or something. They won't know what hit them. Maybe you can keep the sheriff busy for a bit. I'll double back around, catch you on the other side."

Jordan nodded. "Be careful."

"You too."

Chapter Sixty-Two

FROM THE TIME JORDAN and Shelly went out of radio range, Beats' life had been a living hell. She experienced the kind of shift that dispatchers hoped would never happen to them. She'd sat in the quiet, empty sheriff's office, not knowing the fate of her officers who were also her friends. The time stretched on for what felt like hours. Beats was used to waiting, but she was also used to being the person who provided assistance. The element of surprise was imperative to Jordan and Shelly unraveling this case. Beats couldn't leave her post and she couldn't exactly call in reinforcements. Or could she?

When the feeling of helplessness got to be too much to take, Beats did something she never dreamed she'd do. Grabbing the extra set of keys, she crossed the hall to the county lockup to release the only prisoner it contained.

Whit was lying on the cot, not sleeping, just staring at the ceiling. He sat up with a start when Beats opened the cell. "Beats, what the—"

"Shelly and Jordan are in trouble."

He moved to the open cell door. "Where?"

She handed him the keys to his truck, still parked down the block at the Grange. "At the old hangar, on your ranch."

Already at a run, he burst out of the building and down the darkening street.

Shelly headed toward the opening where the wing was, keeping low. She slipped along the side of the hangar until she reached the runway. She ducked down into the grass, but it was too short to be much cover. Inside, the two men had panicked at the shotgun blast that had left a decent-sized hole in the wall of the hangar. The men were arguing about something, one in the cockpit, the other pushing a package back into the plane. Apparently, they couldn't decide whether to leave the drugs or reload what they could before they took off.

The plane looked like a single-engine modified crop duster. The sprayers had been removed. The bay door where the chemicals would have been stored was instead filled with small packages. Shelly guessed the packages contained heroin, like what Jordan had found in Blodgett's barn.

She waited. It was getting dark and the inside of the hangar was even darker. Her eyesight wasn't what it had once been, and she figured she'd only get one shot at this. She hoped Jordan was okay on her own for a little longer. She assumed she was. That city girl had surprised her a few times in the last couple of months. If they both got out of this alive, she'd have to have Jordan teach her the move she'd used to disarm Sheldon.

Eventually, the men stopped arguing. The one in the cockpit closed the door while the other one headed outside, a shotgun at his hip. Shelly tried to keep her eye on him, but he disappeared around the corner. She had to concentrate on the plane. Her aim had to be just right to disable it. The pilot was taking some time with the instruments. Finally, the props whirred to life and the plane began to move.

It taxied toward her. The noise was deafening. The props kicked up so much dust that the runway was shrouded in it, the plane nothing more than a ghostly shape. Shelly blinked and refocused on the wheels, but there was no way she was going to make the shot from her position on the ground. She stood and stepped directly in front of the plane, shouldering her rifle. Footsteps rushed toward her. The other man from the hangar swung his shotgun against his shoulder as he ran. Shelly turned and took quick aim. The man jerked back and fell as a single rifle blast struck his chest.

The roar of the engine refocused her attention on the aircraft. The plane was moving toward her, the wheels already lifting off the ground. She made eye contact with the pilot as she squeezed the trigger getting off her second shot. The plane skidded sideways, one wing dipping and jerking like a wounded bird. The pilot fought to gain control, staying low. He leveled the wings, heading straight for her. She dove for the ground, but the edge of the landing gear smashed into the rifle and then her shoulder, sending her somersaulting across the packed earth.

Chapter Sixty-Three

JORDAN MOVED AROUND THE back to where she'd seen Carlyle's truck. She kept close to the outside hangar wall, wary of being caught by surprise again.

"Sheldon? You around?" Carlyle's voice called. Jordan backed into a doorway in the hangar, concealed by the growing shadows. Carlyle reached Sheldon, bending down and sliding his fingers along the unconscious man's neck. Satisfied that he was still alive, Carlyle pulled a set of handcuffs from his belt and cuffed Sheldon to a pole on the side of the hangar.

Jordan stepped out of the shadows, her gun leveled at him. "Stop right there."

Sheriff Carlyle's face was grim as he turned to face Jordan. "I wish I could say I was surprised. You're persistent, I'll give you that."

"Drop your weapon."

Carlyle held his hands out. His gun hadn't even been drawn. "We're on the same side, Jordan. Obviously, we came to the same conclusion about this place. Sheldon has been running drugs out of here. He was working with Sadie, helped her fake her own kidnapping, and framed Whit so we'd be too distracted to figure out what he'd been up to." He stepped closer. "Was that shotgun blast your work?"

Jordan kept her gun trained on the sheriff. "It went off when I disarmed him."

"Nice." Carlyle nodded at the pistol. "That's not your sidearm, Detective. I assume that means Judd followed through with his threat and you're out of a job." He stepped closer. "Don't worry, once we get in there and arrest those bastards, we'll both be heroes. You can have that job in Billings or back in Seattle—anywhere you want to go. We might even find a nice cell to put Judd in." He put his hand on his holster. "But in order for us to make the arrest before that plane takes off, you're going to have to trust me."

Jordan adjusted her grip on the gun, suddenly unsure of everything she thought she knew about this case. "Drop your weapon and we'll talk about trust."

"Be reasonable. You're not going to be able to do this without backup."

"Who says I don't have backup?" Jordan said. The plane hadn't moved yet; she wondered how Shelly was doing.

"Okay, we'll do it your way." Carlyle reached for his holster and pulled out his gun slowly. "But you're making another mistake, acting without thinking again."

He dropped the gun on the ground and Jordan picked it up. With one eye still on him, Jordan examined the serial number of the gun. The last number was definitely a seven. She held it up. "And this is not your sidearm, Sheriff, is it? At least not the one you were originally issued. It's Blodgett's. You altered the numbers in Becca's ledger. It looked like the sheriff was shot with his own gun, but his wife was right. There's no way you could have gotten past him and broken into his locked drawer to steal his gun without him getting you first. You shot him in the back of the head, left the murder weapon on the desk, and then stole the gun out of his locked drawer to use as your sidearm."

A look of fear crossed his face before he smiled. "Detective, you're jumping to conclusions. Judd handled the issuing of the new firearms himself and Becca wrote down everyone's serial numbers in the ledger and in the computer. If she made a mistake, I'd chalk it up to her pregnancy brain. You saw how distracted she was."

A rifle blast from the other side of the runway caught Jordan's attention. She kept her eyes on Carlyle, hoping the shot meant Shelly had stopped the plane. The engine noise changed, and Jordan could tell the plane was taking off. Another shot rang out. Then the plane lifted into the sky.

"There goes our evidence!" Carlyle yelled.

Shelly screamed.

Jordan ejected the clip from Carlyle's gun. She threw the pistol as hard as she could as she ran toward the runway. She heard his footsteps behind her, but she didn't look back. Shelly was in trouble. There wasn't time to deal with him or her own uncertainty now.

Jordan reached the end of the hangar. The older woman lay in the middle of the runway. "Shelly!" she yelled, crossing the distance between them. Shelly lay face up, her eyes staring at the darkening sky. For a heartbeat, Jordan was sure she was dead. Shelly moistened her lips and spoke. "I guess my aim was off." Her eyes rolled back.

Jordan gripped Shelly's arm. "Shelly!" But Shelly lay still. Jordan felt for a pulse and found one in Shelly's neck, weak and thready.

Carlyle reached them. He leveled Shelly's rifle at her. "Don't worry, you'll be joining her soon enough."

Jordan swept his legs, sending him sprawling to the ground. He kept his grip on the rifle and Jordan dove for it. Carlyle caught her in the stomach with his cowboy boots, throwing her over his head. She landed hard on the ground, the air forced from her lungs, and lost the grip on her pistol. Carlyle stood over her. She rolled out of the way as he aimed the rifle toward her. It clicked but didn't fire. She reached for her gun, but he kicked it into the grass, and then slammed the butt of the rifle into the side of her face.

She saw stars and tasted blood, but she managed to get to her feet. The rifle jammed again. Carlyle threw it to the side. Both unarmed, they faced each other across the field.

Chapter Sixty-Four

JORDAN LICKED HER LOWER lip, the copper taste of blood bringing her back to herself. Sheriff Carlyle circled. He outweighed her by probably seventy-five pounds, but the last few minutes had taught him that she wasn't quite the easy target he thought she was. Her gun was somewhere in the grass and it was getting darker by the minute. She needed to get him talking, distract him from her search. "You were with the sheriff the night he came across the drop in Butte. What he saw as a chance to bust a bunch of drug dealers, you saw as a business opportunity."

"They were coming anyway." Carlyle said. "Better I was regulating the trade than a bunch of Mexicans."

"Your business venture required a place for a plane to land that was well hidden. Whit's place was perfect, and with Sheriff Blodgett out of the way, you could do what you wanted, and Sadie ..."

He smiled, proud of himself. "The girl came to me, almost gift-wrapped, the perfect distraction for the pretty new detective in town. Sadie was a lot like you. Always trying to prove herself. She wanted a chance to find out who killed the Golden woman. I convinced her I couldn't reopen the case unless there was a new development. She basically figured out the rest on her own."

"She gave you something to pin on Whit, a way to get him out of the way so you could have your own private airstrip."

"Like I said. She was a gift. Whit's brother helped out his fair share too, not that he was aware that's what he was doing at the time. He was good at casting suspicion on Whit though. And that Sadie." He chuckled darkly. "Quite an imagination on that girl."

"Did you kill her too?" Jordan asked.

Carlyle spit. "Just another loose end I need to tie up. I'll get to her soon enough."

"When I found the drugs in Blodgett's barn the whole thing started to unravel."

"Judd's idiot son didn't even know how to play watchdog."

"You were worried I was getting too close, so you arranged for the newspaper smear-fest and a new position for me. But I didn't leave."

"You really should have taken that job in Billings. It would have increased your life expectancy considerably."

"That night you called me to meet you at the trailer on Whit's property, you were planning to kill me with his gun. I saw it when we both drew, but I didn't recognize it until it showed up bagged as evidence against him."

"Ray, for all his bumbling stupidity, messed up my two-fer. It all should have ended that night for both you and that crazy woman. Whit, too."

Hoofbeats on the trail up the ridge echoed the pounding in her chest. Carlyle must have backup. Who else would be out riding this late?

"And yet I'm still here."

"You're stubborn, but stubborn isn't going to save you now." He raised his arm. The moon glinted off the barrel of her borrowed gun. He'd found it.

Something like a roll of thunder filled Jordan's ears. For a second, she thought it was gunfire, a crazy kind of gunfire she'd never heard before. Then she saw what looked like a looming shadow, the flash of one ghastly pale eye, and Whit, sitting astride the monster that was gaining speed with every hoofbeat.

Carlyle wheeled around as the horse bore down on him. He shot wildly. Jordan screamed as Whit fell. Popeye veered away, the horse's muscled chest clipping the sheriff's shoulder. He fell to the ground, the gun still gripped in his fist. He rose to his knees, leveling the gun at the horse. Jordan reached him before he could fire again, unleashing all the fury of her training in a furious round of punches and kicks.

The gun slipped out of his hand as Carlyle tried to face her. He turned just in time for her foot to connect with the side of his face. Her kick landed with a crunch of bone and a spray of blood. His eyes stared back at her in wide astonishment for a bloated second.

He crumpled to the ground.

Jordan hoped it was the last thing he'd ever see.

Chapter Sixty-Five

CARLYLE LAY STILL. JORDAN watched him for a few heartbeats to be sure.

Whit groaned. "Jordan?" His voice was barely a whisper.

She hurried across the field to where Whit lay. He'd managed to get into a sitting position, leaning against a tree. One arm was cradled against his side. She dropped to her knees beside him. "Are you okay?"

"I don't ..." Whit's face twisted with pain. He moved the hand that had been pressed against his side. It came back red with blood. "Didn't think Brendan was that good of a shot. I guess he got lucky."

Jordan bit her lip to keep the sob from escaping. This was exactly what she'd feared would happen. Shelly was unconscious on the airstrip and now Whit had been shot. She forced her voice to stay calm, to assess the situation like it was any other emergency. "Can you lean forward? I need to see if the bullet went through."

He slumped against her as she peeled his shirt away from a bloody exit wound. She took off her jacket, tearing the lining into strips and packing the wound as best she could. Whit gritted his teeth and dug his fingers into her shoulder but didn't cry out. Finally, she helped him lean back against the tree. There was no way of knowing how much damage the bullet had done on its way through. She tore the rest of her jacket into pieces and pressed it against Whit's side, but there was still a lot of blood seeping through. He sucked in a wheezy breath. Jordan prayed the sound didn't mean the bullet had punctured a lung.

"How is the good sheriff?" he asked.

Jordan glanced at the unmoving figure. "Out for now." Whit's eyes were closed in pain.

"How did you get out of jail?" Jordan asked.

"Beats let me go. She told me I'd better go find you and she told me where to look. I heard something crash into the mountains. Do you know what that was about?"

"Shelly's aim wasn't off," Jordan said, more to herself than in explanation.

"Where is she?" Whit asked

Jordan looked over at the figure lying on the runway. "She's hurt pretty bad. She tried to stop the plane—did, I guess—but she got hit in the process."

"And you?" Whit reached up and touched Jordan's split lip. She pulled back, not because it hurt, but because Whit's touch was like an electric shock that ran through her body.

She ducked her head so her hair hid the swelling she could feel in her cheekbone. "I'm fine."

"That doesn't look fine." Whit touched the goose egg that was forming the side of her head.

"None of us will be fine if I don't go for help." Jordan put one hand on the tree to steady herself as she rose. She retrieved her gun from where Carlyle had dropped it and handed it to Whit. "Just in case he wakes up, or our luck keeps going the way it's been going and someone else who wants to kill us shows up."

"How are you getting out of here?" Whit said.

Jordan paused. She hadn't considered that. Her head was pounding. She couldn't think her options through. "I don't know."

"How did you get down?"

"Shelly's mule. It's up the ridge."

"Won't be fast enough."

"Carlyle's truck." Jordan started to move toward the hangar.

Whit put his hand on her arm. "That road goes up into the forest before it hits anything like civilization. No cell service on that side of the mountain. It will take too long for you to get help."

She realized he meant help for him, that he knew how badly he was bleeding. "Then how ..."

"You'll have to ride out." Whit's voice already sounded weaker. "Popeye is a strong horse, and fast as hell. Ride for my house. Call as soon as you reach the rim. You'll have service there."

"I can't ... I don't know how to ..." Jordan bit her swollen lip, tasting blood. She hated her weakness and the fear the paralyzed her, even when she was out of options.

"You can do this. Popeye is trained for voice commands. He knows 'stand' and 'stop.' He'll listen to you. He knows the way home, just give him his head. Watch the trail—there are a couple of places it gets steep and narrow." He sucked in another breath and closed his eyes. Jordan could tell he was fading.

She put her hand on his cheek. "Whit, stay with me!"

His eyes fluttered open. He put his hand over hers. "Don't worry about me. I'll be right here waiting when you get back."

Jordan braced herself against the trunk of the tree that Whit was leaning against and inched her way up it until she was standing upright. She was grateful she could feel her mind clearing and her strength returning.

She turned her attention to restless Popeye, standing about thirty feet from her. Gathering the limits of her resolve, she cautiously moved toward the horse. Seeing her intent to approach him, he blew out a strong, elongated warning snort and flashed his popped eye at her. She inched closer, praying he wouldn't decide to take off. Finally, she was close enough to touch him. She fumbled for the loose reins and grasped them with a death grip, knowing if he got away from her, Whit would bleed out before she could get help.

Popeye danced from side to side, tugging at the reins as Jordan tried to mount him. A memory fixed that—"Stand!" she commanded. He froze, stiff as a heavy metal statue. She positioned the reins and clumsily climbed aboard.

Now what? He remained frozen. She went for broke. Popeye was headed the right direction, so she leaned forward a bit, touched him lightly on his mane, gathered the useless reins and grabbed the saddle horn with both hands. "Go!" she shouted. He dug down deep and blasted off with such incredible force and speed she was nearly ejected from the saddle. It didn't take long for Jordan to figure out all she had to do was hang on.

Her hair was wild, the wind tousling and tangling it behind her. Jordan looked down only once at the rapidly moving ground beneath her. It made her nauseous. She gripped tighter with her legs to keep from falling. The movement made Popeye go even faster.

The ride down in the mule had been rough and jolting and slow. Riding Popeye up felt like flying. Now Jordan knew what Whit meant when he said Popeye glided. She leaned into his neck and held on for what felt like minutes and hours all at the same time. Popeye lurched the last few steps up the edge of the canyon. As soon as they hit level ground, Jordan commanded him to "Stop!"

She slid to the ground, landing on her knees. She fumbled for her phone that was miraculously still in her pocket, praying she hadn't stopped too soon.

She almost cried when she realized she had service. She dialed the number and heard Beats' calm voice on the other end. "What's your emergency?"

"I need help Beats! Now!"

Chapter Sixty-Six

AFTER LETTING WHIT OUT of his cell, Beats had endured another hour of unnerving peace and quiet. Then all hell broke loose. Ray radioed to report that that a small plane had crashed just south of Whit's land. She had her hands full, but she knew more was to come. Beats started to summon all the agencies that were needed to handle it. She got on the radio and started waking up deputies. She was her usual calm self as she called in the rescue helicopter. She alerted the FFA, summoned the highway patrol, sent the ambulance and fire trucks. When she was radioed that there was a fatality, she called the coroner.

Then Jordan's call came in. When she heard Jordan's voice, Beats had but a moment to be relieved before she sprang into action to get the support Jordan needed at the airstrip. Such a wealth of response people required that she contact Anaconda and Deer Lodge Sheriff's Office for help.

The radio cracked with dozens of voices. Everyone expected her to respond to their needs. Helicopters were needed at both the plane crash and the hangar, so she was in communication with them also.

Beats summoned every ounce of experience she'd gained over the years to handle everything at once.

She not only had to handle them, but she had to do so calmly and carefully. She couldn't allow herself to fold from the pressure until the entire event was over.

At some point the dispatcher Beats had traded shifts with came in to relieve her. Beats waved her toward the phones and continued her conversation with the police chief from Deer Lodge. His departing words summed up how Beats felt about the whole situation.

"That new detective worth all the trouble she's caused?"

"I guess that remains to be seen," Beats answered.

With everything winding down, and everyone where they needed to be, Beats hung up the radio and handed off the dispatch office to her replacement.

That fateful night had been a night of casualties. A total of seven lives were altered forever. One died in the plane crash, one of a bullet from Shelly's gun. Sheldon Miles, the owner of the Horseshoe, was handcuffed to a pole with a whale of a headache and facing jail time, but he'd live. Shelly, Whit, and Sheriff Carlyle were hospitalized. Jordan was injured. The eighth victim was Beats.

Absent her car and desperately low on sleep, she headed toward Whit's recently vacated cell. When Ray came into the office, he was surprised to see where she was going.

"With Carlyle in the hospital I guess that means you're in charge," she said as she passed him.

Beats watched as the excitement and terror of his newfound responsibility shone in his eyes. He followed her, but she didn't have the energy to deal with him right now. She walked into the cell and lay down on the cot.

He stared through the bars at her, puzzled. "Any idea how Whit got out?"

She didn't answer. She was already asleep.

Chapter Sixty-Seven

JORDAN STARED OUT THE hospital window in Deer Lodge. The view of the mountains was spectacular. She wished she could enjoy it. She wished she'd learned to enjoy it a while ago. If she hadn't made so many mistakes along the way, maybe she wouldn't have ended up here.

The door opened, but she didn't turn, afraid of who it might be or what news they were bringing.

"Detective?" Jordan forced her expression to stay neutral as she turned to face the doctor, realizing immediately that it was the same doctor who had kicked her out of the hospital less than two days ago. Now he seemed friendly, sympathetic even. "You asked to be told when there was an update."

"Yes." Jordan held her breath.

"Mr. Palmer is out of surgery and coming out of the anesthesia."

"How did it go?" Jordan said.

"It looks like he's going to be okay. He's young and strong and the bullet didn't do as much damage as we'd initially thought." Jordan exhaled a breath she felt she'd been holding since she and Shelly first went down the canyon.

"Barring any complications—"

"Can I see him?" Jordan asked breathlessly.

"That depends. Did you bring that dog with you?" The doctor's face remained serious, but his eyes danced in the same way Whit's did when he was teasing her.

"No, sir."

"At this point in a patient's recovery we usually only allow family, but since Mr. Palmer doesn't seem to have any family, and since the first thing he asked when his mind started to clear up was 'Is she okay?' I guess we can give you a few minutes."

"Thank you." Jordan didn't correct him. She was sure Whit was asking if Shelly was okay. Jordan dreaded that part of the conversation, but she wanted to see him and see how he was in person, even if he hated her for everything that had happened.

There was a uniformed police officer sitting outside the door to Whit's room. She didn't recognize him; he must have been someone local. It hadn't occurred to Jordan that Whit was not only still considered a murder suspect, but now a fugitive.

The officer nodded as she walked up to the door, his eyes following her. Jordan was sure she looked horrible. The bruises on her face had turned a sickening yellow and her lip was still swollen. Her hair was long and wild. She had slept in the waiting room, and she hadn't changed her clothes in two days. Jordan pushed into the room that was filled with all the beeps and whooshes that occupy a hospital room.

"Jordan?"

At the familiar voice, Jordan fought back a sob. It was all she could do to suppress the urge to run to him and collapse into his arms. She worked to keep her voice even. "You're awake."

"Barely." He closed his eyes. "Not sure what they gave me, but it's pretty powerful stuff." He gestured for her to move closer. She moved to a chair by the side of the bed and leaned close, her hands gripping the rails.

"How do you feel?"

"Like a two-thousand-pound bull and a couple of good-sized ponies kicked me in the side. I imagine it'll be worse when the drugs wear off."

Jordan tried to judge Whit's tone. Did he blame her for what happened to him and to Shelly even a fraction of how much she blamed herself?

"I'm sorry." She swallowed.

He shook his head. "For which part? Throwing me in jail or for me getting shot?"

"Both. All of it. Everything." Her voice cracked on the last word.

"As far as the arrest goes, you were just doing your job. The job I brought you here to do. And the bullet?" He lifted his hand and curled his fingers around hers. "I'd take it again in a heartbeat if it meant saving you."

Jordan held onto Whit's hand like it was a lifeline. "Thank you."

"My pleasure, ma'am." He moved his hand to the bandaged cut above her eye, her bruised cheek, and finally her swollen lip. A strange mix of pity, anger, and pain shone in his gray eyes. Jordan ducked her head, so her hair covered the bruises on the side of her face. "What did he do to you?" The strength of the anger in his voice surprised her.

She raised her eyes to face him, set her expression, and forced her voice to come out strong. "Not anything I didn't give back."

"I saw that." This time his voice held something like pride. "Are you sure you shouldn't be recovering in a bed upstairs?"

"They already checked me out. Just a few bruises, a slight concussion maybe, but no real damage."

He smiled. "Sounds like you're turning into one of us hard-headed Montanans." His voice grew serious. "Speaking of which, any news on Shelly?"

"She hasn't ... hasn't woken up yet." Jordan trailed off, a lump blocking the words in her throat. "I'm sorry, Whit. I tried to protect her. I should have never let her get involved, I should have never—"

"Shelly knew what she was doing. There was no way you could have kept her out of it. And we both know there's no way you could have solved this thing without her."

Jordan dropped her eyes to the floor. "But if she doesn't—"

Whit cupped his hand around the back of her head. "She'll be okay. Shelly is the toughest person I know. She'll pull through."

Jordan leaned her head against the rail, letting Whit tangle his fingers in her hair. For a few breaths she stayed still. Finally, she looked up. "I should—" But she couldn't finish that thought. He looked at her with such intensity that she could barely breathe. He moved his fingers to her swollen bottom lip, touching it so gently that she barely felt it, but with such tenderness that sparks flowed from his fingers, into her lips, and through her entire body. Almost unconsciously she leaned closer, so close that his breath moved across her lips.

He cupped her chin in his hand. "Jordan, I—"

"She's awake."

Jordan jerked away, spinning around to face the voice so quickly that she nearly fell off the chair. She had to reach to steady herself on the bed rails.

Shelly's granddaughter, Tawny, was standing in the doorway. A flash of jealousy reached Tawny's dark eyes as she looked between Whit and Jordan.

"Grandma just woke up, and she's asking for you, Detective."

Chapter Sixty-Eight

JORDAN STOOD IN THE doorway of Shelly's hospital room. Shelly looked worse than she did. Both eyes were blackened, and her nose was bandaged. Her arm was in a sling and several ribs had been broken. She sat up painfully but smiled when she saw Jordan.

"I heard you got him."

Still reeling from what almost happened in the other hospital room, Jordan thought Shelly meant Whit and her face went red.

"Brendan. I heard you mule-kicked him in the head."

"Yeah. Yes, I did."

"You must have got him pretty good; one of the nurses said he's not quite all there, in and out of consciousness, muttering something about a ghost horse. What exactly did you do to him?"

"I used one of the most lethal Krav Maga moves. It was a rapid 360-degree turn and a kick to his temple. He went out cold."

"And Whit?"

"Whit came riding down to our rescue, got himself shot, but he'll be okay. Sheldon's in jail. The pilot crashed, and you took out the other guy. That about covers it. How do you feel?"

"Like I've been run over by a small plane, which is something I never imagined I'd say, but here we are."

"I'm sorry—"

Shelly waved her away. "It was the most excitement I've had in years. A little excitement is good for you, keeps you young. I mean, as long as it doesn't kill you."

Jordan laughed. "You really are tough as nails."

Shelly gestured to a chair by the bed. "So, Carlyle killed Blodgett and put Sadie up to fake her own kidnapping. All of this to acquire Whit's airstrip so he could continue his side business as a drug runner."

"Pretty much sums it up," Jordan said.

"Any word on where Sadie might be?"

"No. I'm not sure if she just got spooked and ran, or if ..."

Shelly's grim face grew more serious. "If our mutual friend found her."

"I haven't heard anything from him, but ..." Jordan shrugged, suddenly very tired. "The Sheriff's department is in kind of a mess right now. Ray is acting sheriff. He's in the process of hiring some new deputies."

"And what about you? Did you get your job back?"

"Sort of. I told Ray I'd stay on until he got things settled, but the job I was hired for here is done."

"What about your other job offer, the one in Billings?"

"I guess it's still mine. If I want it. It's a good position. In a lot of ways, exactly what I want, but I haven't been able to think that far ahead yet," Jordan said.

Shelly patted her hand. "That's understandable. Still, maybe you shouldn't be in such a hurry to move on." She looked out the window toward the mountains. Her expression grew wistful under the bruises. "This whole experience has helped me realize, life is too short to live in fear. If you want something, you need to go out and get it." She turned to face Jordan. "He's not going to wait forever."

Jordan studied Shelly's face. She couldn't tell if Shelly meant the attorney general, Whit, or maybe someone else.

"You haven't heard from Mac, have you?"

Shelly shook her head. "No." She was quiet for a long time. Jordan was sure this was the first time Shelly had been in trouble that Mac hadn't swooped in to help. Shelly straightened up in the bed, wincing as she adjusted her position. "As soon as I get out of here, I'm taking a bit of a vacation. I have an important lead I need to pursue."

"I think that's a good idea," Jordan said.

Shelly met Jordan's eye, her gaze boring into the younger woman with an intensity that made Jordan feel like Shelly was looking into her soul. "Maybe you shouldn't be so quick to dismiss any important leads that might come your way either."

Chapter Sixty-Nine

"IS THIS SEAT TAKEN?" Jordan asked. She'd debated so long about coming to the rodeo that the stands were mostly filled. She'd asked Chris to come along, but she'd taken over the management of the Horseshoe and was swamped. Jordan hadn't dared hope that Whit would be here. He was still recovering, and wrapping up the case and helping at the sheriff's office had taken all her time. With the exception of a couple of texts, she hadn't spoken to him much. She was both surprised and thrilled to find him sitting next to an empty seat.

Whit touched the back of the chair. "I was saving it for someone, hoping she'd show up."

"Oh," Jordan said, ducking her head in embarrassment. She started to move away.

He reached for her hand. "I'm glad she finally made it."

Jordan smiled and sat down. "This must be killing you to sit here instead of out there. I'm sorry—"

"We're done with the apologies, Detective. Besides, it's been a long time since I actually got to sit and enjoy the rodeo. Even longer since I did it with a pretty woman sitting beside me. I thought about asking you to come, but I wasn't sure how you felt about rodeos."

"They've kind of grown on me," Jordan said with a noncommittal shrug. "I guess a lot of things here have."

He grinned. "So you admit that you like the rodeo and maybe even Lombard. Funny, I'd heard a rumor that you'd taken that job in Billings."

"I did," Jordan said. "I—" She was cut off as the crowd roared. A young woman was taking the chute for the barrel racing. From the crowd's reaction, Jordan got the idea that she was at least as popular as Whit.

The horse and the woman moved as one in a clover-leaf pattern around the barrels with a speed and grace Jordan had never seen before. There was something poetic about how they moved together. As she finished the pattern, the woman barely touched the mare with her heels, and they flew across the finish line.

Jordan didn't need the crowd's reaction to guess that the woman's time was outstanding.

"She's incredible," Jordan said as the woman rode by in her victory lap.

"That she is." Whit's voice was full of admiration. The woman tipped her hat as she rode by and Whit nodded back to her.

Jordan realized who she was. "Isn't that Shelly's granddaughter?"

"Tawny, yeah. She's kind of a big deal around here, and her horse is one of the top rodeo ponies in the nation. She doesn't get back home much, but when she does, people go a little crazy."

"Oh," Jordan said. She was trying to squash the lump of jealousy that burned in her throat.

"I'm surprised Shelly isn't here to watch. She never misses one of Tawny's hometown performances. Is she still recovering?"

Jordan smiled, feeling a twinge of pride that she was finally privy to something in this small town that not everyone knew. "Shelly's out of town. She had some important business to take care of."

Chapter Seventy

MAC WAS JUST PACKING up from a busy day when his assistant, Greta, poked her head in.

"What are you still doing here?" he asked, even though Greta was as much of a workaholic as he was. Sometimes he even left before she did.

"There's a woman here to see you. She's been waiting for a couple of hours. I told her your schedule was full, but she said she'd wait."

"A woman?"

"She didn't give her name. Just said it was about the property you have for sale in Keystone County."

Mac internally cringed at the name of his home county. He'd purposely avoided any news from there for the last month. He hadn't gone back to the ranch since his argument with Shelly. He'd even gone so far as to hire a real estate agent to list his land. He'd received multiple offers, mostly from rich wannabe hobby ranchers or developers from the west coast. He hadn't sold yet. As much as he wanted to put Lombard in his rearview mirror, he wasn't sure he was ready to sell his family's four-generation ranch and watch it get cut up into little chunks or become someone's excuse to play cowboy.

Mac was tired and not in the mood to haggle with someone over the ranch, but the woman had waited a long time. "Send her in, and then you head home, Greta. You work too hard."

"You're one to talk," Greta said. She stepped out and then came back with a slim, older woman with short white hair. Even though she was wearing makeup, something Mac hadn't seen on her since she was in her twenties, he could still see the remains of the bruises on Shelly's face.

"Shelly!" Mac gasped.

Greta's eyes went wide. "This is Shelly? I'm so sorry. If I'd known, I wouldn't have made her wait."

Mac waved his hand. "Don't worry about it. Go ahead and go. I can lock up."

Greta glanced from Shelly to Mac with curiosity, then nodded and left, closing the door behind her.

Shelly stepped forward, but Mac held his ground behind his massive desk. She walked all the way across the room and set a box in front of him.

"What is this?" The spicy scent of ginger and molasses emanated from the box. "You brought me cookies?"

Shelly cleared her throat, more nervous than she'd been around Mac since the first time she presented him with cookies. "Not just cookies. Gingersnaps, your favorite. It's the same recipe I used when I brought you these before." Mac raised his eyebrows. "Maybe you don't remember. We were both fifteen. You were the only sophomore on the varsity basketball team. You were heading to the championship game, and I had a huge crush on you."

"I remember. We lost that game, but I wasn't even upset about it. All I could think of when it ended was finding you. But you ran from me."

Shelly blushed like she was still an awkward teenager. "I was embarrassed about the cookies. You were the best-looking guy in our class: football, basketball, and rodeo star, and you were from one of the richest ranching families in the county. I took a chance and then decided it was a mistake."

"I wasn't about to let you go that easily." Mac smiled at the memory. "I ran after you, caught you just as you were getting into your truck."

"My first kiss," Shelly said.

Mac set his hands on the desk, not touching the box. His face hardened. "Mine was Rita Jones, on the playground in second grade."

Shelly rolled her eyes. "If I knew we were counting grade school, I would have ..." She shook her head. She hadn't come to split hairs about the past. "There's a For Sale sign in front of your ranch."

He barely looked at her. "I know that. You interested in buying more land?"

"No." Shelly worked to meet his eye. "I'm interested in you not leaving Lombard."

He shuffled some paperwork in front of him. "I thought you'd made it abundantly clear that you had no interest in what I did or didn't do."

Shelly stared down at the dark wood of the desk in front of her. "I lied to you, Mac. I lied about the dogs, and about what had happened that night. More importantly, I lied about how I felt about you. I thought I had to, to protect you."

"To protect me?" Mac looked up, his expression still wary, but also confused.

"It's a long, convoluted story, but suffice it to say, that danger hasn't gone away."

"Us being together is dangerous? Is that why you've led me on for all these years? Because you thought you were protecting me?" His voice was incredulous.

"No. It's not the only reason, but it seemed like a valid enough reason at the time."

"You weren't going to give me a choice in this? You weren't ever going to be honest enough to let me know what was going on and what the consequences might be?" His voice got louder with each word.

"I'm sorry, Mac. I have so much to apologize for when it comes to you. I wouldn't blame you if you threw me out right now."

He sat down heavily in his desk chair. "I can't ... I can't do this anymore, Shelly. I can't keep hoping this will lead somewhere. Even I have my limits. I'm afraid you've already surpassed them."

Shelly stood for a minute, her head down. "I understand. Thank you for all you've done through the years. I couldn't have survived these past thirty years without you. It's about time I acknowledged that. It wouldn't be fair to ask for anything more." She turned, pausing for just a second to collect herself before she pushed through the door.

Mac sat at his desk, breathing in the scent of fresh gingersnaps, and staring at the space that Shelly had just vacated.

Greta appeared in the doorway. "Sir, I'm sorry. I couldn't help but hear."

Mac shook his head. He was too emotionally drained to care. "It's okay."

She stood for a minute twisting her hands like she wasn't sure if she should say anything. Finally, she spoke. "I know you haven't been following the news at all, that you've been avoiding it, but I think you should know Shelly almost died a few weeks ago. She got caught up in some drug bust, and she was hurt badly trying to stop it." Greta looked down. "I know what she's put you through. I don't know how many birthday roses or Christmas wreaths or spring tulips

I've sent to that woman's house on your behalf. I'm just saying, life doesn't offer up second chances very often, and well, you're not getting any younger. Maybe you should take them when they come."

Mac sat still for a minute more, staring at the box in front of him. Suddenly he stood, grabbed his hat as he ran past her toward the door. "Can you lock up, Greta?"

He didn't wait for her answer, instead he ran down three flights of stairs and through the front entrance. He was breathing hard by the time he reached the parking lot. He was no longer the fifteen-year-old basketball star who had sprinted across the high school parking lot after playing a hard game. He was afraid she was already gone, but he saw the dome light in her truck. She was just climbing inside. Out of breath, he stopped and yelled, "Shelly!"

She hesitated a second and then stepped out of her truck slowly. She waited, watching him as he walked toward her. In the dim streetlight, she looked just like the teenage beauty who had waited for him by her truck all those years ago.

And just like back then, he crossed the parking lot, wrapped her in his arms and kissed her.

Chapter Seventy-One

THE BARREL RACING OVER, Whit stood, his face contorted with pain. "Sitting like this is killing me. I need to take a walk." Jordan was sure he was going to congratulate Tawny. She resolved to smile and let it go. Then he reached his hand to her. "Come with me?"

She took his hand and let him help her out of her seat. He didn't let go as they maneuvered through the crowd and out of the stands. Whit still seemed unsteady, so maybe he needed the support, but Jordan caught the looks everyone was giving them as they climbed down, still holding hands.

Whit led her toward the stalls at the edge of the fair grounds. "I need to check on Popeye."

"Popeye is here?"

"Yeah. I can't ride, but I thought it would be good for him to be around the noise and the crowds."

"Oh." Jordan slowed her steps.

"If you don't want to go by the horses we can—"

"No, it's okay. I kind of owe him my life," Jordan answered. "I guess we all do."

They kept walking, passing cowboys and cowgirls preparing for or finishing their rides. There was a big corral of steers, a smaller one with the roping calves, and an area with a high fence that Jordan guessed contained the bulls. Popeye was in one of the far stalls, close enough to hear the action without being in the middle of it.

Jordan stepped toward the wild-eyed horse, testing herself. She was still afraid, but the fear was no longer paralyzing. She reached for his soft muzzle, and he blew warm breath over her hand. "Hey boy," she said softly.

Whit leaned on the fence and scratched Popeye between his ears. "Tell me about the job in Billings."

"It should be interesting. I get to choose my own cases and work whatever hours I want. No more small-town politics," Jordan said.

Whit chuckled. "You don't like small-town politics? Funny, there was a rumor that you planned to run against Ray for the job of sheriff in a couple of months. I heard he was pretty scared. After solving Blodgett's murder, you might have been a contender for the position."

"Might have been?" Jordan smiled. "You make it sound like there are people here who still don't like me."

"You know Montanans can be kind of hard-headed."

"I've seen that. People from Seattle can be kind of arrogant and close-minded."

Whit smiled, saying, "I've seen that one myself."

After another long silence, Jordan turned toward him. "Whit, I lied to you."

"Lied to me?"

"I told you I'd never ridden before, but I have. My grandpa was teaching me to ride on his old pony, Snip. Only I wasn't a very good student." Jordan tugged her T-shirt sideways, revealing a long red scar across her shoulder.

Whit reached his hand toward her the jagged scar, but at the last minute, pulled back without touching her. "That looks like it probably hurt."

"It did. I was eleven. Snip was old and slow, nothing like the pretty black mare Grandpa was boarding for his neighbor. Grandpa said she was too wild for me, but I thought I could ride her. I sneaked out of the house early one morning and tried."

"What happened?" Whit asked.

"She got spooked and ran me into a fence. I shattered my collarbone. My mom was furious with Grandpa. She took me home right after the surgery. I never saw him again. He died the next winter." Jordan readjusted her shirt. "I felt so guilty. It was my fault I'd gotten hurt. I tried to tell my mom that, but she wouldn't listen to me."

"I guess that explains why you're afraid of horses," Whit said.

"Not so much anymore." Jordan reached and stroked Popeye's powerful neck through the fence. "I might even get brave enough to try to ride again someday."

Whit smiled. "When you're ready, I'm happy to teach you."

Jordan reached up and straightened a piece of Popeye's mane. "Thanks. I might take you up on that."

Whit stood close to her, so close she could smell his cologne over the musky smells of horse sweat and leather. "When I was nine years old my grandpa took me up in his plane. He'd done it before, but this time the engine stalled out and the plane went into a free fall. I thought we were going to die. All I could think of was that I was going to abandon my mom, just like my dad did. Grandpa was able to get it under control, but that was the last time I went up with him. To this day, it's the last time I've been in a plane. It wasn't even the fear of crashing or dying—it was the fear of not being able to take care of my mom. That was the last thing my dad said to me when he left: 'Take care of your mom.' Ironic, since he didn't seem to care to, but that statement was burned into my brain so much that when she died, I was sure it was my fault."

Whit looked down, kicking at a rock. "I'm still not good at commitment. I'm afraid I'll let someone down. Specifically, I'm afraid of letting the right someone down, the way my dad did with my mom. It was easier to just not go there, until now."

"Until now?" Jordan asked, barely able to breathe.

Whit moved closer, resting his hands on her shoulders, his fingers tracing the scar through her T-shirt. "I don't know. I've never felt this way about anyone before."

Jordan looked up at him. "That's probably because no one has ever arrested you for murder before."

A wide smile moved from Whit's lips and into his soft gray eyes. "Could be."

She put her hands on his waist, one finger outlining the bandage that still covered the place where the bullet had struck him. "And I've never had anyone take a bullet for me before."

Whit met her gaze. "I'd do it again."

She shook her head. "We're quite a pair. The unropeable cowboy and the arrogant Seattle cop who swore not to make any connections here."

"I think you've made a few, anyway," Whit said.

"At least one or two that I hope last a long time."

"Me too," he replied.

At some point they'd gotten closer together, so close that their foreheads were touching. She wasn't sure who had moved.

"Brock ..." She paused, hating to even say his name in front of Whit. "He took what little trust I had in a relationship and destroyed it."

Whit moved his hands from her shoulders to her waist. "I'm all for taking things slow. Billings is a bit of a drive, but I'm sure we can work it out. I head up that way at least a couple—"

Jordan put her finger on his lips, stopping him. "Whit, I didn't take the job to get away from Lombard and make you chase after me."

He drew back, looking hurt. "Why—"

She stopped him with a kiss. His question disappeared as his lips melted against hers. After a few seconds, she moved barely a breath away, so her lips brushed his when she said, "I took the job so you wouldn't be my boss anymore."

His eyes grew wide. "Oh."

She wrapped her arms around his neck. "And I'm not leaving."

"You're ... not ..."

"I already chose my first assignment: the Bonnie Golden case. There's no better place or better team to help me figure that one out than right here."

He pulled her tight against him, so tight that she was afraid she was hurting him. That fear and everything else around her dissolved as he crushed his lips against hers.

Jordan stepped back, breathless. "I'm not sure I'd call that going slow."

Whit laughed. "It is, considering I've wanted to do that since the first time I walked into your office ... actually, probably since the first time I read your file."

The crowd from the arena roared and music blared through the speakers. Whit laced his fingers through hers. His palm was warm and rough against hers. "If we head back now, we might make the bull riding."

"I was kind of hoping for more alone time," Jordan said.

Whit stumbled over his words. "I mean I'm ... whatever you ..."

Jordan kissed him on the cheek and then pulled him toward the arena. "C'mon. It's a small town. If we're gone too long people might—"

A terrified scream from the far end of the stables cut her off.

Jordan ran toward the sound, her hand on her gun. Whit struggled to keep up, but he arrived a few seconds after her.

The stall door was wide open. Standing in the middle was Tawny, her face pale, her hands trembling.

Whit moved toward her while Jordan looked around for any sign of why the woman had screamed. The stall was empty. That, she realized, was the problem.

Tawny held up the empty halter dangling from the side of the empty stall. "Ruby." She took in a shaky breath. "She's gone."

Whit reached her just as she went limp and caught her before she hit the ground.

Epilogue

Fall in Montana
by Lea Howery

Fall in Montana is always so
exquisite.
The lilting breezes,
The majestic scenery,
Crisp air.
The combined scent of pine
and potpourri fragrance of
dying leaves and other foliage,
Overpower the senses and
make one feel almost weak in
the knees.

───◆○◆───

WHIT, JORDAN, AND MAC had gathered at Shelly's for dinner. It was one of those glorious fall days that Montana is famous for. Lombard was surrounded on all sides with spectacular high, craggy snow-capped mountains. The foliage in the valley and on the foothills was resplendent with fall color. The sun shone brightly through towering clouds. A gentle breeze was blowing, and the temperature was ideal.

The men were talking ranches and cattle while Jordan and Shelly hashed out what they'd found out about Tawny's missing horse—unfortunately not much.

As dusk was beginning to settle over the valley, an unusual, almost eerie light shone through the picture window, painting Shelly's dining room in shades of pink and orange.

Mac put his hand on Shelly's arm, stopping her mid-conversation. He nodded towards the window. "I don't think we're going to want to miss this."

As the other three stood up from their chairs, Jordan looked at them, confused. "What?"

Whit took her hand and pulled her from the chair. "You'll see." She picked up her coffee cup and followed him to the porch.

The view was spectacular. Every shade of the rainbow danced across the lofty peaks. Lower on the mountains, thick and twisted layers of every imaginable pastel hue shimmered from one side to the other. The glowing red and orange ball lazily descended and disappeared as if by magic. Jordan stood breathless at the utter grandeur of the spectacle she was witnessing.

Whit put his hand on her arm, breaking her trance. "Not bad, huh?"

Shelly wrapped her hands around her coffee mug. "I'm afraid peaceful days like this are just lull in the battle. I'm glad we solved Sheriff Blodgett's murder and brought some sense of justice to Angie. Carlyle certainly got what he deserves—not much left to his mind but the recurring thought he was run over by some kind of ghost horse. But there are still a lot of loose ends that need to be tied up. First the matter of Tawny's horse. I can't figure out why someone would steal her. If sold, the mare would net enough money for Tawny to buy a small house, but a horse that well-known on the rodeo circuit would be impossible to sell. Tawny is heartbroken. Ruby is her best friend, partner, and her main source of income, On her own accord or against her will, it appears Sadie Larsen is determined to stay missing. Our mutual friend has been silent, but won't stay that way for long." She glanced back at Mac. "It's likely all four of us will be pulled into his game."

"We still have Bonnie Golden's 15-year-old murder to solve, Commissioner Judd isn't going away or getting any easier to deal with," Jordan added, "And with the election for sheriff coming up ..."

"Troubles and challenges never cease." Shelly declared, sipping her coffee.

Mac exchanged a glance with Whit, then rested his hand on Shelly's knee. "It sounds like we should just enjoy tonight, so we're ready for whatever comes."

Shelly smiled back at him, covering his hand with hers. "I guess it would behoove us to keep calm and carry on."

Jordan looked around at the circle of friends she never planned on making, the rugged and beautiful country she'd never expected to feel like home, and the man she'd never intended to fall in love with. She reached over and laced her fingers through Whit's.

"Whatever happens, we're in this together."

The End

Like what you read? Leave a review! Reviews on Amazon help our book reach more readers. Thanks in advance for supporting our books!

We love to connect with our readers!

Please visit our website, montanamysteries.com to recieve a sample of true stories from S. C. Zipp (a former Montana deputy) and subscribe to our newsletter where you'll have exclusive access to more great stories, news about upcoming releases, and deals reserved for our friends.

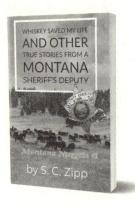

Whiskey Saved My Life and Other True Stories from a Montana Deputy

Acknowledgments

Our crazy relationship and what would become *Map of Bones* began when J. J.'s daughter, Sabrina moved onto S. C.'s Montana ranch. Within an hour of moving in, Sabrina declared, "You have to meet my mom, you two would be best friends!" Her words turned out to be prophetic. We got to know each other long distance via shared messages and swapped stories. S. C. had long been a purveyor of true stories from her colorful life as a rancher in Western Montana. J. J. had written and published young adult mysteries. Sometime in the midst of one of our late night conversations, we made the decision to write a book together with the determination that it was better to write real stories about fake people than fake stories about real people.

Making this book a reality was a nearly two year bumpy road filled with trials and triumphs including a global pandemic, births, weddings, illnesses, and the S.C.'s sudden onset of blindness and bouts of fatigue. We couldn't have done it alone. Many thanks are needed, here are but a few.

Thanks go out to Sabrina for bringing us together; to Lea Howery for being our first reader and first fan, extra set of eyes, errand runner extraordinaire, and for loving Whit as much as we do; to Susan Krieger for being yet another set of eyes, editor, reader, marketing guru, and cheerleader; to Thea Wear for her support and encouragement; to Sheriff Rick Barthule for his background information and years of experience; to Dave Ungerman for listening to S. C.'s endless book conversations and for showing interest in our project from concept to finish; to Gary for his attentiveness and for all the extra things he did so we could concentrate on the book; to J. J.'s husband David for his willingness to pick up a lot of slack; to Katie Felde for being willing to share her beautiful photos, to Stacey Shaw for his agricultural expertise, and to Kristy Amrine and Christie Carlson for beta reading. Thanks to our families for their patience and putting up with endless hours with us on the phone and/or on our computers.

Thanks to our editors: to Val Serdy for being brutally honest, Lynda Dietz for being quick and insanely thorough, and to Margot Hovely for catching a thousand little things we missed (like which direction the sun sets in Seattle!) Thanks to all those along the way who lent advice, opinions, hands, and especially eyes, even to Carissa, the bewildered, but cooperative visiting nurse who found herself in the role of typist and proofreader due to a case of mistaken identity.

From J. J.: Thanks to my Aunt Jana, for taking me to the rodeo, teaching me to ride, and encouraging my obsessive love of horses; to my Grandpa Singleton for being a real cowboy and a true gentleman; and to my parents for encouraging me to follow my dreams.

From S. C.: My fervent thanks to Helen Bucy my junior high English teacher who taught me that diagramming sentences can be fun; to Joen Painter my Arizona college English professor who inspired me to write and write and write; and to my mother, Thelma Blaine Cartwright, a school teacher, who corrected every letter I wrote to my grandmother, and taught me to love writing.

Thanks always to our Great Creator, for the life He's given us and for the beauty and inspiration that surrounds us.

We couldn't have done it alone. Many thanks are needed. APOLOGIES TO SO MANY OTHERS WE FAILED TO MENTION.

About the Authors

S. C. Zipp
S. C. Zipp once wrestled an entire stick of butter down the throat of a bloated ewe while wearing nothing but her bright red nightgown--only to discover her bemused neighbor standing in the barn door thinking what a great story this was going to be to tell his friends. But that was a minor footnote in the adventures of a lifelong Montana rancher who hobnobbed with gamblers and bartenders at the age of 4, started breaking horses and selling them at 11, was her class valedictorian, elected as a school board member at 22, and became a deputy sheriff in her forties when female deputies were non-existent in Montana.

Born with one arm, S. C. never let anything stand in her way, whether it was sharp shooting, horseback riding, or raising four rambunctious boys. She met her husband of 66 years in a kissing contest. Since his death 3 years ago, she's lived alone near one of her sons on her two-thousand-acre ranch which was once nearly twice that size, nestled near Montana's Elkhorn Mountains.

She has been actively engaged in all phases of ranching all her life and has owned and operated three businesses, one of which involved selling and installing wall coverings. In that capacity she was often referred to as the one-armed paperhanger. The other two were a tire shop and upholstery business.

Now nearly 85, S. C. still enjoys painting, crocheting, gardening, baking her own bread, and writing both fiction and real stories of the people and places that have made her life so rich.

J. J. Wolf grew up in small town Idaho where she skied, rode horses, worked in the potatoes, and took Hunter's Education as part of her sixth-grade curriculum.

She still enjoys skiing and riding horses but hopes to never have to work in the potatoes again. Despite her early training, she's never once gone hunting.

She now lives in the green forests of Western Washington. She's mom to four kids and a very spoiled dog, works in a high school library, and writes Young Adult mysteries under a different name, (but she'll tell you what it is if you ask.)

Whatever the genre she likes to surprise her readers and make them question everything they thought they knew about the characters she writes.

Made in the USA
Middletown, DE
16 September 2025

17606340R00241